Hello Stranger

ALSO BY KATHERINE CENTER

The Bodyguard

What You Wish For

Things You Save in a Fire

How to Walk Away

Happiness for Beginners

The Lost Husband

Get Lucky

Everyone Is Beautiful

The Bright Side of Disaster

Hello

Stranger

KATHERINE CENTER

ST. MARTIN'S PRESS
NEW YORK

First published in the United States by St. Martin's Press, an imprint of St. Martin's Publishing Group

HELLO STRANGER. Copyright © 2023 by Katherine Center. All rights reserved. Printed in the United States of America. For information, address St. Martin's Publishing Group, 120 Broadway, New York, NY 10271.

www.stmartins.com

Designed by Devan Norman

Library of Congress Cataloging-in-Publication Data

Names: Center, Katherine, author.
Title: Hello stranger / Katherine Center.
Description: First edition. | New York : St. Martin's Press, 2023. |
Identifiers: LCCN 2022058238 | ISBN 9781250283788 (hardcover) |
    ISBN 9781250283795 (ebook)
Subjects: LCGFT: Novels. | Romance fiction.
Classification: LCC PS3603.E67 H45 2023 | DDC 813/.6—dc23/
    eng/20221209
LC record available at https://lccn.loc.gov/2022058238

Our books may be purchased in bulk for promotional, educational, or business use. Please contact your local bookseller or the Macmillan Corporate and Premium Sales Department at 1-800-221-7945, extension 5442, or by email at MacmillanSpecialMarkets@macmillan.com.

First Edition: 2023

10 9 8 7 6 5 4 3 2 1

For my beautiful mom, Deborah Inez Detering.

Again.

It's such an honor to be your daughter.

How can I ever thank you enough?

Hello Stranger

One

THE FIRST PERSON I called after I found out I'd placed in the North American Portrait Society's huge career-making yearly contest was my dad.

Which is weird. Because I never called my dad.

Not voluntarily, anyway.

Sure, I called on birthdays or Father's Day or New Year's—hoping to get lucky and miss him so I could leave a singsongy message like "So sorry to miss you," get the credit, and be done.

But I called only out of obligation. Never for fun. Never, ever just to talk. And never—god forbid—to *share things*.

My goal was always *not* to share things with my father. How broke I was. How I was still—endlessly—failing in my chosen career. How I'd given up on yet another relationship and moved into my not-fit-for-human-habitation art studio because I couldn't afford a place of my own.

That was all need-to-know information.

And he definitely didn't need to know.

It gave me some structure, in a way—crafting ongoing fake success stories about myself for him and my evil stepmother, Lucinda. I was always "doing great." Or "crazy busy." Or "thriving *so much.*"

I didn't actively make things up. I just worked devotedly to obscure the truth.

The truth was, I'd defied all my dad's instructions eight years before, dropping out of premed and switching my college major to Fine Arts.

"Fine Arts?" my father had said, like he'd never heard the term before. "How exactly are you supposed to make a living with that?"

I gave him a little shrug. "I'm just going to . . . be an artist."

Wow, those words did not land well.

"So you're telling me," he demanded, that little vein in his forehead starting to darken, "that you want to be buried in a pauper's grave?"

I frowned. "I wouldn't say I *want* that."

It's possible my dad wanted me to be a doctor because he was a doctor. And it's possible my dad didn't want me to be an artist because my mom had been an artist. But we didn't talk about that.

He went on, "You're throwing away a good career—a good living—so that you can waste your life doing something that doesn't matter for no money?"

"When you put it that way, it sounds like a bad idea."

"It's a terrible idea!" he said, like that was all there was to it.

"But you're forgetting two things," I said.

My dad waited to be enlightened.

"I don't like medicine," I said, counting off on my fingers. "And I do like art."

Suffice it to say, he didn't think any of that was relevant. Then he went on to imply that I was spoiled and foolish and had never known true suffering.

Even though we both knew—on that last one, at least—he was lying.

Anyway, it didn't matter. He didn't get to decide what I did with my life.

I was the one who had to live it, after all.

My dad was not a big fan of losing. "Don't ask me for help when you're broke," he said. "You're on your own. If you choose this path for yourself, then you have to walk it."

I shrugged. "I haven't asked you for help since I was fourteen."

At that, my dad stood up, scooting back his café chair with a honk that announced he was done. Done with this conversation—and possibly done with fatherhood, as well.

I still remember the determination I felt as I watched him leave. It seems almost quaint now. *I'll show you,* I remember thinking, with a self-righteous fire in my eyes. *I'll make you wish you'd believed in me all along.*

Spoiler alert: I did not show him. At least not so far.

That was eight years ago.

I'd gotten that BFA in Fine Arts. I'd graduated all alone, and then I'd marched past all the families taking proud pictures, and then I'd driven triumphantly out of the university parking lot in my banged-up Toyota that my friend Sue and I had painted hot pink with flames for the Art Car Parade.

And then?

I'd embarked on many endless years of . . . *not showing him.*

I applied to contests and didn't win. I submitted my work for shows and didn't get accepted. I eked out a living selling portraits from photos (both human and pet) on Etsy at a hundred dollars a pop.

But it wasn't enough to make rent.

And whenever I talked to my dad, I pretended I was "thriving."

Because he might have been right that day. I might be headed for a pauper's grave. But I would be *under the dirt in that grave* before I'd ever admit it.

That must have been why I called him about placing in the contest.

The contest itself was a big deal—and huge prize money, if you could win it.

I guess the lure of having a genuine triumph to report kept me from thinking clearly.

Plus, don't we all, deep down, carry an inextinguishable longing for our parents to be proud of us? Even long after we've given up?

In the thrill of the moment, I forgot that he didn't care.

It was a good thing—and no surprise—that my call went straight to his voicemail. It meant I could make my next call. To somebody who did care.

"What!" my friend Sue shouted as soon as the words were out. "That's *huge!*" She stretched out the U for what felt like a full minute. *Huuuuuuuuuuuuuuuge.*

And I just let myself enjoy it.

"The grand prize is ten thousand dollars," I added when she was done.

"Oh my god," she said. "Even huger."

"And guess what else?"

"What?"

"The big show—the juried show where they pick the winner—is here. In Houston."

"I thought it was Miami this year."

"That was last year."

"So you don't even have to travel!" Sue said.

"Which is perfect! Because I can't afford to!"

"It's meant to be!"

"But is it *too* meant to be? Is it so in my favor, it'll jinx me?"

"There's no such thing as too meant to be," Sue said. Then, as if there'd been a question, she said, "Anyway, it's settled."

"What's settled?"

"We have to throw a party!" she said. Ever the extreme extrovert.

"A party?" I said, in a meek attempt at resistance.

"A party! A party!" Sue practically sang into the phone. "You've been tragically failing at life for years and years! We have to celebrate!"

Tragically failing at life seemed a bit harsh.

But *fine.* She wasn't wrong.

"When?" I said, already dreading all the cleaning I'd have to do.

"Tonight!"

It was already close to sunset. "I can't throw a—" I started, but before I even got to "party tonight," it was decided.

"We'll do it on your rooftop. You needed a housewarming party, anyway."

"It's not a house," I corrected. "It's a hovel."

"A hovelwarming, then," Sue went on, taking it in stride.

"Won't your parents get mad?" I asked. Mr. and Mrs. Kim owned the building—and technically I wasn't even supposed to be living there.

"Not if it's a party for *you*."

Sue, whose Korean given name, Soo Hyun, had been slightly Americanized by an immigration official, had also disappointed her parents by becoming an art major in college—which was how we'd bonded—although her parents were too softhearted to stay mad for long. Eventually they'd kind of adopted me, and they liked to tease Sue by calling me their favorite child.

All to say—this party was *happening*.

This was our Oscar and Felix dynamic. Sue always optimistically, energetically, and joyfully searched out ways for us to extrovert. And I always resisted. And then grudgingly gave in.

"You can't organize a party in two hours," I protested.

"Challenge accepted," Sue said. Then she added, "I've already sent the group text."

But I still kept protesting, even after I'd lost. "My place isn't fit for a party. It's not even fit for me."

Sue wasn't going to fight me on that. I was sleeping on a Murphy bed I'd found in the large trash. But she was also not brooking protests. "We'll all stay outside. It's fine. You can finally hang those bulb lights. We'll invite everybody awesome. All you have to do is get some wine."

"I can't afford wine."

But Sue wasn't liking my attitude. "How many people entered the first round?" she demanded.

"Two thousand," I said, already giving in.

"How many finalists are there?"

"Ten," I answered.

"Exactly," Sue said. "You've already annihilated one thousand nine hundred and ninety competitors." She paused for impact, then snapped her fingers as she said, "What's another nine?"

"How is that relevant?" I asked.

"You're about to win ten thousand dollars. You can afford *one* bottle of wine."

AND SO SUE set about making a last-minute party happen.

She invited all our art-major friends—with the exception of my ex-boyfriend, Ezra—and some of her art-teacher buddies, and her long-time boyfriend, Witt—not an artist: a business guy who'd been the captain of his track team in college. Sue's parents approved of him, even though he wasn't Korean, because he was sweet to her—and also because he made a good living and so, as her dad put it, she could be "a starving artist without having to starve."

Sue said—lovingly—that Witt could be our token jock.

My job was to put on the vintage pink party dress with appliquéd flowers that had once been my mother's and that I wore only on very, very special occasions . . . and then to go off in search of the most wine I could get with a twenty-dollar bill.

I lived in the old, warehouse-y part of downtown, and the only grocery store within walking distance had been there since the 1970s—a cross between a bodega and a five-and-dime. There was fresh fruit up front, and old-time R&B played on the sound system, and Marie, the ever-present owner, sat by the register. She always wore bright-patterned caftans that lit up her warm brown skin, and she called everybody *baby*.

Just as I walked in, my phone rang. It was my dad calling me back.

Now that the initial rush had passed, I debated whether to answer. Maybe I was just setting us both up for disappointment.

But in the end, I picked up.

"Sadie, what is it?" my dad said, all business. "I'm boarding a flight to Singapore."

"I was calling you with some good news," I said, ducking into the cereal aisle and hushing my voice.

"I can't hear you," my dad said.

"I just have some good news," I said a little louder. "That I wanted"— was I really doing this?—"to share."

But my dad just sounded irritated. "They've got dueling announcements going over the loudspeakers and I've got one percent battery. Can it wait? I'll be back in ten days."

"Of course it can wait," I said, already deciding that he'd forfeited his chance. Maybe I'd tell him when I had that ten-thousand-dollar check in my pocket. If he was lucky.

Or maybe not. Because right then the line went dead.

He hadn't hung up on me, exactly. He'd just moved on to other things.

We were done here. Without a goodbye. As usual.

It was fine. I had a party to go to. And wine to buy.

As I moved into the wine aisle, Smokey Robinson came over the sound system with a song that had been one of my mom's favorites—"I Second That Emotion."

Normally I would never sing along out loud to anything in public— especially *in falsetto.* But I had many happy memories of singing along to that song with my mom, and I knew it was all too easy for me to stew over my dad's toxicity, and it kind of felt, in that moment, like Smokey had showed up right then to throw me an emotional lifeline.

I glanced over at the owner. She was on the phone with somebody, laughing. And as far as I could tell, there was no one else in the store.

So I gave in and sang along—quietly at first, and then a little louder when Marie didn't notice me at all. Shifting back and forth to the beat, there in my ballet flats and my mom's pink party dress, I just gave in and let myself feel better—doing a shimmy my mom taught me and throwing in an occasional booty shake.

Just a little private, mood-lifting dance party for one.

And then something hit me, there in the aisle, singing an old favorite song while wearing my long-lost mother's dress: My mother—also a portrait artist—had placed in this contest, too.

This exact same contest. The year I turned fourteen.

I'd known it when I applied. But to be honest, I applied to so many contests so often, and I got rejected so relentlessly, I hadn't thought too much about it.

But this was the one. The one she'd been painting a portrait for—of me, by the way—when she died. She never finished the portrait, and she never made it to the show.

What had happened to that portrait? I suddenly wondered.

If I had to bet? Lucinda threw it away.

I'm not a big weeper, in general. And I'm sure it was partly all the excitement of placing in the contest, and partly the unexpected harshness of my dad's voice just then, and partly the fact that I was wearing my long-lost mother's clothes, and partly the realization that this contest was her contest . . . but as happy as I felt singing along to that old favorite song in an empty grocery store, I felt sad, too.

I felt my eyes spring with tears over and over, and I had to keep wiping them away. You wouldn't think you could do all those things at once, would you? Dancing, singing, *and* getting misty-eyed? But I'm here as proof: It's possible.

But maybe that song really was a talisman for joy, because just as the song was ending, I spotted a wine with a celebratory polka-dotted label on sale for six dollars a bottle.

By the time I made it to the register with my arms full of wine, I was feeling like Sue had the right idea. Of course we should celebrate! I'd have to put my dog Peanut—who was even more introverted than I was—in the closet with his dog bed for a few hours, but he'd forgive me. Probably.

I picked up some little taco-shaped dog treats as a preemptive apology. They'd take me over budget, but Peanut was worth it.

At the register, I eyed a little bouquet of white gerbera daisies, thinking it might be nice to have one to tuck behind my ear—something my mom used to do when I was little. It felt like she might like to see me celebrate that way. With a flower.

But then I decided it was too expensive.

Instead, I set the wine and dog treats on the counter, smiling at the store owner, and I reached around for my purse . . .

Only to realize I didn't have it.

I looked down and then felt my other hip, to see if I might have slung it on backward. Then I glanced around at the floor to see if I'd dropped it. Then I left my wine and dog treats on the counter, holding my finger up like "one second" as I dashed to check the empty aisles.

Nothing. Huh. I'd left it at home.

Not all that surprising, given the flurry of today.

Marie had already started ringing up the wine by the time I got back and so, not wanting to interrupt her conversation, I shook my hands at her, like, *Never mind*.

She looked at me like, *Don't you want this?*

I shrugged back in a way that tried to convey, *I'm so sorry! I forgot my purse.*

She dropped her shoulders in a sigh, but before she could start to cancel everything, a man's voice from behind me said, "I'll get it."

I turned around in surprise, frowning at him, like, *How did you get in here?*

But he just gave me a nod and turned back to the owner. "I can cover that."

This isn't relevant . . . but he was cute.

He was a generic white guy—you know, the kind that's practically a Ken doll. But a really, really appealing version.

Because of my job as a portrait artist, I can never look at a face for the first time without mentally assessing it for its shapes and structure and most compelling features—and I can tell you exactly why he was handsome and also why he was basic. Artistically, I mean.

Everything about him was generically, perfectly proportional. He didn't have an outsize chin, for example, or cavernous nostrils or Dumbo ears. He didn't have Steven Tyler lips or crazy teeth or a unibrow. Not that any of those things are *bad*. Distinctive features make a face unique, and that's a good thing. But it's also true that the most generic faces are consistently rated as the best-looking.

Like, the more you look like a composite of everyone, the more we all like you.

This guy was as close to a composite as I'd seen in a while. Short, neat hair. A proportional forehead, nose bridge, jaw, and chin. Perfectly placed cheekbones. A straight nose with stunningly symmetrical nostrils. And you couldn't draw better ears. Flawless. Not too flat, but not too protruding. With perfect plump little earlobes.

I am a bit of an earlobe snob. Bad earlobes could really be a deal-breaker for me.

Not kidding: I've complimented people on their earlobes before. Out loud.

Which never goes well, by the way.

There are tricks to making a face look appealing when you're drawing a portrait. Humans seem to find certain elements universally appealing, and if you emphasize those, the person looks that much better. This is a scientific thing. It's been studied. The theory is that certain features and proportions elicit feelings of "aww, that's adorable" in us, which prompts caregiving behaviors, affection, and an urge to move closer. In theory, we evolved this reaction in response to baby faces, so we'd feel compelled to take care of our young, but when those same features and patterns crop up in other places, on other faces, we like them there, too.

We can even find sea cucumbers adorable, from the right angle.

Or the man who's attempting to pay for our wine and dog treats.

Because in addition to his generic handsomeness, this guy also had elements in his features—invisible to the untrained eye—that subliminally established cuteness. His lips were smooth, and full, and a warm, friendly pink that signified youth. His skin was clear in a way that evoked good health. And the real clincher was the eyes—slightly bigger than average (always a crowd-pleaser) with a slight melancholic downturn at their corners that gave him an irresistible sweet puppy-dog look.

I guarantee this guy got every woman he ever wanted.

But that was his business.

I had a forgotten-wallet situation to deal with. And a last-minute party to host.

"It's fine," I said, waving my hands at him and rejecting his offer to pay for my stuff.

"I don't mind," he said, pulling his wallet out of his jeans.

"I don't need your help," I said, and it came out a little harsher-sounding than I meant.

He looked from me—purseless—to the counter of stuff I had yet to pay for. "I think maybe you do."

But I wasn't having it. "I can just run home for my purse," I said. "It's no problem."

"But you don't have to."

"But I want to."

What part of *I don't need your help* did this guy not understand?

"I appreciate the gesture, sir," I said then. "But I'm fine."

"Why are you calling me *sir*? We're, like, the same age."

"*Sir* is not an age thing."

"It absolutely is. *Sir* is for old men. And butlers."

"*Sir* is also for strangers."

"But we're not strangers."

"Gotta disagree with you there, sir."

"But I'm rescuing you," he said, like that made us friends.

I wrinkled my nose. "I prefer to rescue myself."

For the record, I recognized that he was trying to do something nice. I also recognized that most of humanity would've let him do it, thanked him gratefully, and called it a day. This is the kind of moment that could wind up on the internet, getting passed around with captions like *See? People aren't so terrible after all!*

But I wasn't like most of humanity. I didn't like being helped. Is that a crime?

Surely I'm not the only person on this planet who prefers to handle things on her own.

It wasn't *him* I was opposed to. He was appealing. Strongly, viscerally appealing.

But the helping—including his pushiness about it—was not.

We stared at each other for a second—at an impasse. And then, for no reason, he said, "That's a great dress, by the way."

"Thank you," I said suspiciously, like he might be using a compliment to lower my defenses. Then without really meaning to, I said, "It was my mother's."

"And you do a great Smokey Robinson, by the way."

Oh god. He'd heard me. I lowered my eyes to half-mast, displeased. "Thanks."

"I mean it," he said.

"That sounded sarcastic."

"No, it was great. It was . . . mesmerizing."

"You were watching me?"

But he shook his head. "I was just shopping for cereal. You were the one doing a cabaret show in a grocery aisle."

"I thought the store was empty."

He shrugged. "It wasn't."

"You should have stopped me."

"Why would I do that?" he asked, seeming genuinely befuddled. Then, at the memory, something like tenderness lit his expression. He gave a little shrug. "You were a joy."

I had no idea what to make of this guy.

Was he being sarcastic or serious? Was he handsome or generic? Was he kind to help or too pushy? Was he flirting with me or being a pain? Had he already won me over, or did I still have a choice?

Finally I circled back to: "Fine. Just . . . don't help me."

His expression shifted to wry. "I'm getting the sense that you don't want me to help you."

But I played it straight. "That's correct."

Then before I could lose any more ground, I turned to the owner at the counter—still chatting away with her friend—and stage-whispered, "I'll be back in five with my purse."

Then I zipped out the door.

Case closed.

I WAS WAITING at the crosswalk for the light to change when I turned back to see the grocery store guy walking out with a paper bag that looked suspiciously like it might have three very cheap wine bottles and some dog tacos in it.

I stared at him until he saw me.

Then he gave me a big unapologetic *ya got me* smile.

Fine. I had my answers: *Yes.*

When he arrived next to me to wait for the same crosswalk, I kept my gaze straight ahead, but said, like we were spies or something, "Is that bag full of what I think it's full of?"

He didn't turn my way, either. "Do you think it's full of human kindness?"

"I think it's full of unwanted help."

He looked down to examine the inside of the bag. "Or maybe I just really, really love . . . six-dollar wine."

"And dog treats," I said, glancing his way.

I could see the sides of his eyes crinkle up at that.

"Fine," I said, accepting my defeat and holding out my arms for the bag.

But he shook his head. "I got it."

"Are you going to be stubborn about this, too?"

"I think the word you're looking for is *chivalrous.*"

"Is it?" I said, tilting my head.

Then, as if the question had answered itself, I held my arms out for the bag again.

"Why should I give this to you?" he asked.

"Because you got what you wanted last time," I said, tilting my head back toward the store, "and now it's my turn."

He considered that.

So I added, "It's only fair."

He nodded at that, and then, like he'd been totally reasonable all along, he turned, stepped closer, and released the bag into my arms.

"Thank you," I said when I had possession.

The light had turned, and the crowd around us was moving into the street. As I started to move with it, I looked down to check the bag's contents, and I saw a bouquet of white gerbera daisies. I started to turn to him next to me, but he wasn't there—and when I spun back, he was still at the curb looking down at his phone like maybe he'd stopped for a text.

"Hey!" I called from the middle of the street. "You forgot your flowers!"

But he looked up and shook his head. "Those are for you."

I didn't fight him. It was his turn, after all.

If I'd known what was going to happen next, I might have handled that moment differently. I might have kept arguing just so we could keep talking. Or I might have asked him his name so I'd have some way of remembering him—so that he wouldn't just remain, in my memory after that, the Grocery Store Guy who got away.

Of course, if I'd known what would happen next, I would never have stepped into the street in the first place.

But I didn't know. The same way none of us ever know. The same way we all just move through the world on guesswork and hope.

Instead, I just shrugged, like, *Okay*, and then turned and kept walking—noting that he was the first man I'd been attracted to in all the months since my breakup, and half hoping he would jog to catch up with me in a minute or two.

But that's not what happened next.

Next, I froze right there in the crosswalk, my arms still hugging my bag of wine.

And I don't remember anything after that.

Two

I WOKE UP in the hospital with my evil stepmother Lucinda by my bed.

And you *know* it was bad if Lucinda showed up.

I opened my eyes, and I saw one of my least favorite people on the planet leaning forward, elbows on knees, peering over the bed rail, flaring her nostrils and staring at me like she'd never seen me before.

"What happened?" was all I could think of to say.

At that, Lucinda went into full gossip mode, filling me in on the details as if she were talking to a random neighbor—and I can't tell you how weird it was to be getting the story of my life from the person who had ruined it.

Anyhoo.

Apparently, I'd had what they call a nonconvulsive seizure, right there in the middle of the crosswalk in front of my building. I froze into an empty stare in the street and was almost mowed down by a Volkswagen Beetle before a mysterious Good Samaritan shoved me to the curb at the last second and saved my life.

Next, after not getting run over, I passed out on the sidewalk in front of my building.

The Good Samaritan then called 911 and handed me off to the paramedics when they arrived. According to the nurse at the hospital, I was semiconscious when they wheeled me in and was asking everyone to find my father—though that's another thing I don't remember.

I really must have been out of it to ask for my dad. Of all people. A person I would never voluntarily turn to in need.

But over and over, apparently, I asked for him, saying his name. Which the nurses recognized. Because my dad was, to be honest, a bit of a celebrity surgeon.

The staff called his office, according to that same nurse, but he was "unavailable."

Which is how Lucinda wound up here.

She was absolutely the last person I'd want at my bedside—besides perhaps her daughter. Honestly, I'd rather have woken up to Miranda Priestly. Or Mommie Dearest. Or Ursula from *The Little Mermaid*.

And from the looks of those nostrils of hers, Lucinda wasn't too thrilled to be seeing me, either.

Still, she kind of liked the drama.

Her tone was a little bit incredulous as she brought me up to speed, like how I could've chosen the crosswalk of a busy street, of all places, to have that nonconvulsive seizure was beyond her. "If that Good Samaritan hadn't saved you, you'd be flat as a pancake right now." She paused and tilted her head, like she might be picturing that. "I was at my Whining & Wine-ing group when they called, but it's okay. It's fine. Of course I dropped everything and came here right away."

Her tone made me wonder if that was true. Like maybe she'd tossed back one last glass of chardonnay.

I shook my baffled head again, like, *Wait*. "What happened?"

She leaned in a little, like I hadn't been paying attention. "You almost died in the road."

"But what caused the seizure?" I asked at last, my wits starting to come back.

"They don't know. Could even just be dehydration. But they want to do an MRI before they release you. Looks like you'll have to stay overnight."

And then, quickly, to snuff out even the possibility that I might ask her to stay—which I would absolutely never do—she added, "I'll be back first thing in the morning."

I waited for it all to sink in while Lucinda checked her texts and then gathered up her things.

She was one of those put-together ladies who always matched her shoes to her purse. She kept her hair no-nonsense and short, but she always had a full face of makeup. I'd always suspected she focused hard on her surface because there wasn't much underneath. But I really didn't know her that well. Even after all these years.

I did not anticipate, for example, that when her daughter, Parker, also known as my evil stepsister, FaceTimed her right then, Lucinda would answer the call. Or that she'd proceed to fill Parker in on everything that had just happened like she was relating the hottest of hot-off-the-press gossip. And then, when Parker said, "Let me see," that Lucinda would turn the phone around and train it on me.

I frowned at Lucinda and shook my head. But it was too late.

There was Parker's catlike face—as scary at iPhone size as it was in real life.

How long had it been since I'd seen her? Years.

I could go my whole life, and it wouldn't be too long.

"Oh my god!" Parker shrieked. "I can't believe you almost got killed by a Volkswagen Beetle! I mean, at least pick something cool, like a Tesla."

"Noted," I said.

It was strange to see her again. She'd highlighted the hell out of her hair. And she'd really taken a deep dive into the world of eye shadow. She had better style than she had in high school—in a newscaster-ish way. The sight of her kind of stung my eyes. But I couldn't deny that technically—and I say this as a professional in the industry—she had a pretty face.

Too bad she ruined it by being . . . pure evil.

"You look terrible," Parker said, squinting in faux sympathy. "Did you land on your face?"

I looked at Lucinda, like, *Seriously?*

But Lucinda just smiled and gestured for me to answer, like she thought this might be a nice conversation.

I sighed and shifted my eyes back to the screen. "I did not land on my face," I answered robotically.

"You just look so bloated," she went on.

"I'm fine."

"Did they have to pump you full of saline or something?"

"What? No."

"You just kind of look like James Gandolfini right now. That's all I'm saying."

Okay. We were done here.

"Hoo-boy," I said, checking the nonexistent watch on my wrist. "Look at the time."

Then I rolled over to face the wall.

"Is she pouting?" Parker demanded as Lucinda took the phone back.

"You'd be fussy, too, if it had happened to you."

"But it would never happen to me. If I ever get run over, it'll be by an Aston Martin."

A thousand years later, after Lucinda finally hung up and was ready to go, she paused by my bed, looking me over as if she couldn't begin to fathom my life choices.

"I hope the Betty Ford Center isn't next for you," she said then, shaking her head like I was an unsolvable mystery. "They said you showed up in the ER positively dripping in red wine."

At the words, I sucked in a breath. "Where's the dress?"

"What dress?"

"The one I was wearing. When I got here."

"Oh," Lucinda said, shaking her head with disgust. "It's in the trash."

"The trash?" I grabbed the bed rail.

"It was ruined," Lucinda said. "Wine-drenched, bloodstained—and the paramedics had to cut it off you. It's not even fit for cleaning rags now. Unsalvageable. I told the orderly to throw it away."

I don't remember starting to cry, but by the time Lucinda paused, my face was wet, my throat was thick, and my breathing was shaky. "They threw away the dress?"

"It was trash, Sadie," Lucinda said, doubling down. "It was beyond hope."

But I shook my head. "But I need it," I said.

Lucinda lifted her eyebrows, like, *This better be good.* "Why?"

"Because . . ." I started.

But there was nothing to say. Lucinda had spent her entire marriage to my dad trying to erase all traces of my mother. If she'd known that dress was my mom's, she'd have thrown it away even sooner.

And maybe set a match to it first.

". . . Because I just do," I finished.

Lucinda stepped back then and eyed me as if to say, *Just what I expected.* Like she'd called me on my insultingly obvious bluff. "It's gone," she said on her way out the door. "Just let it go."

But after she left, I pressed the button for the nurse.

When she showed up, I was crying so much, she took my hand and squeezed it. "Deep breaths. Deep breaths," she said encouragingly.

Finally, through breaths that were more like spasms, I conveyed the question. "The dress—I was wearing—when I came here—my stepmother said—to throw it away—but I need it. Is there any way to—get it back?"

Her sigh seemed to deflate her entire body. "Oh, sweetheart," she said—and by the end of those first two words alone, I knew all hope was lost. "If we threw it away, it went to the incinerator."

And so there was nothing left to do but cry myself to sleep.

LUCINDA DID NOT return "first thing in the morning." Which was fine with me. I'd already had breakfast, an MRI, and begun a consultation with a deeply serious Filipino brain surgeon named Dr. Sylvan Estrera before she showed back up, appearing in the room just as he got to the juicy stuff.

"The scan didn't reveal anything urgent," Dr. Estrera was saying. "No stroke or hemorrhage. No significant bleeds in the brain."

"That's a relief," I said.

Then he continued. "But it did reveal a neurovascular issue."

Okay, that didn't sound good. "A neurovascular issue?" The word *neurovascular* felt like a foreign language in my mouth.

"A lesion," he explained, "that should be treated."

"A *lesion*?" I asked, like he'd said something obscene.

Dr. Estrera put some images from the MRI up onto a lightboard. He pointed to an area with a tiny dark dot and said, "The scan revealed a cavernoma."

He waited for recognition, like I might know what that was.

I did not. So I just waited for him to go on.

"It's a malformed blood vessel in the brain," he explained next. "You've had it all your life. An inherited condition."

I glanced at Lucinda, like that didn't seem right.

But Lucinda lifted her hands and said, "Don't blame me. I'm just the stepmother."

I looked back at the scan—and that menacing little dot.

Could he have gotten my scan mixed up with someone else's? I mean, I just didn't *feel* like a person walking around with a malformed blood vessel in her brain.

I frowned at Dr. Estrera. "Are you sure?"

"It's plain as day right here," he said, pointing at the image.

Plain as day? More like a fuzzy blur, but okay.

"Cavernomas frequently cause seizures," he went on. "They can be neurologically silent. You could go your whole life without ever having a problem. But they can also start to leak. So your best option is to get it surgically resected."

"It's leaking?" I asked.

"It is. That's what brought on the seizure."

"The *nonconvulsive* seizure," Lucinda noted, like that made it better.

"I thought you said there was no bleed in the brain," I said.

"No *significant* bleed," he clarified.

Why was I arguing with him?

He went on, "We need to go in and resect that blood vessel."

Huh. "By *go in*," I said, "do you mean go in . . . *to my brain*?"

"Exactly," he said, pleased I was getting it now.

I was definitely getting it now. "You're telling me I need brain surgery?"

I looked at Lucinda again. There was no one else to look at.

Lucinda leaned toward the doctor like she had a juicy secret. "Her father is a very prominent cardiothoracic surgeon," she said, as if that might somehow earn me a pass. Then, with all the confidence of a woman whose biggest accomplishment was being married to a very prominent cardiothoracic surgeon, she stated: "Richard Montgomery."

Dr. Estrera took that in like a random pleasantry he was too polite to ignore. "Yes. I've met him on several occasions." He turned back to me. "It's an elective procedure, in the sense that you can schedule it at your convenience. But I'd recommend sooner rather than later."

"How can *brain surgery* be an elective procedure?" I asked. Botox was an elective procedure. Tummy tucks. Tonsillectomies.

"I'll have to refer you to scheduling," Dr. Estrera went on, "but we can probably get it done in the next few weeks."

The next few weeks! Uh, no. That wouldn't work.

I mentally scanned back through the email I had just gotten yesterday about placing in the portrait competition.

Placing in this contest—landing in the top ten of two thousand entrants—meant that I had exactly six precious weeks to plan and execute the best portrait I'd ever painted in my life. From choosing a model, a color palette, and a setting, to doing the prep work and the initial sketches, to rendering the final, full painting . . . I was going to need every minute I had.

The competition. I'd almost forgotten. I was a finalist in the most prestigious portrait competition in the country.

I couldn't blow it. After all those years of failure: just scraping by and working overlapping jobs and questioning my value as a human being, I had to win.

Sue had wanted to celebrate yesterday, but now the real work started. This was my shot. Possibly the only one I'd ever have.

So no, I wasn't going to sign up for elective brain surgery right now, thanks very much.

"Um," I said to Dr. Estrera, in a soft voice, like I didn't want to offend him, "I just don't have the time for brain surgery."

How bizarre to say those words out loud.

And then my desire *not to have brain surgery* ran into direct conflict with my desire for Lucinda *to never know anything about my life*—and I hesitated so hard to explain my situation that when it all came out, it was one rapid burst: "I'm a portrait artist, and I'm a finalist in a competition that has a deadline in six weeks, and the first-place prize is ten thousand dollars, and this really is my big break that could change everything for me, and I'm going to need every single second between now and then to create the most kick-ass portrait in the history of time because I really, really need to win this thing."

Had I just said the word *ass* in front of a brain surgeon?

"I understand," Dr. Estrera said. "But please realize, there is some urgency here. Bleeding—even seepage—in the brain is never a good thing. And while 'brain surgery'"—he made air quotes with his fingers—"sounds like a big deal, and it is, this procedure is relatively quick. You'd need only two to four days in the hospital. We can even do hair-sparing techniques to avoid shaving your head."

Was he trying to make it sound *appealing*? I hadn't even thought about anyone shaving my head.

What had started as a simple no was rapidly becoming a "hell, no." I nodded like I was thinking about it. But what was there to think about?

An old *New Yorker* cartoon of a person scheduling a meeting and say-ing, "How about never?" came to mind.

"I think," I said then, "that I'd really like to put the surgery off for as long as humanly possible."

Three

LUCINDA TRIED TO force me to ride home with her in her Navigator, but I called an Uber instead. No way was I accepting help from her.

Or letting her see my apartment, either.

Though "apartment" was too generous a term. More of an "efficiency." Or more accurately, a "shack"—built as the caretaker's quarters in the 1910s when the building was constructed as a warehouse.

Sue's dad, Mr. Kim, had renovated the building, turning it into hipster industrial condos. But the rooftop shack was last on his list—and in his words, was still "not fit for human habitation." Sue had talked him into leasing it to me as a studio space—promising him I'd use it "almost like a storage room."

That was before I left my ex, Ezra—after he fully forgot my birthday, and, while I was getting stood up in the restaurant, I wound up reading a clickbait article on my phone about narcissists . . . realizing in a sudden flourish that I was dating one. Two long years of clues I ignored, then one very enlightening article—and then suddenly I was done.

Leaving was just a relief.

Finding a place to live on the income from my Etsy shop was going to be a challenge at best, and I'd drained almost all the cash I got from selling my car—a radical choice in Houston, which is not exactly a walking city. My hovel was fine for now. For $475 a month, I didn't need a showplace.

But my living situation now was more like "a little princess banished to the servants' quarters" scenario than a "living the high life in a luxury penthouse" one.

I had promised Mr. Kim I wasn't actually living there, and he was compassionately turning a blind eye. Which is to say, one person's "not fit for human habitation" is another person's perfectly acceptable hovel.

The light alone was incredible.

Not to mention the views of downtown. And the bayou.

Sue thought my moving into my studio was a genius gaming-the-system move. Not a normal living situation, but cooler. She'd been pushing for a shack-warming party from the start. But as much as I wanted to embrace the spin that I was too fantastic to live like normal people, the truth was that I was just too broke.

Back home after that night in the hospital, nothing about my shack, or my life, or myself had ever felt less fantastic. It's a disorienting thing to know there's something wrong with you. It made everything about my life seem different. Worse. False. Like I'd been misunderstanding everything all along.

I HAD SOME portraits queued up to finish—a little girl with her cocker spaniel, a young man's graduation photo, a sweet grandmother in an eightieth birthday party hat—and I couldn't bill for them until I shipped them. They were a hundred bucks a pop, so that's what I should have been doing all day after I got back from the hospital: covering this month's rent.

But, instead, I found myself googling cavernomas.

Lots of grainy gray brain-scan images, lots of illustrations of people holding their heads like they were having the worst migraines in history, and lots of cartoon illustrations of veins with plump raspberry-shaped malformations.

Which were cuter than I would've expected.

I tried to picture the inside of my head. Had there really been a tiny little blood raspberry in there this whole time?

I also googled Dr. Sylvan Estrera. Who apparently did some amateur swing dancing as a hobby. When he wasn't, *ya know,* doing brain surgery.

When my eyes were dry from scrolling, I clamshelled my laptop and went to go sit next to my dog, soulmate, and only real family, Peanut, who was fast asleep on the sofa with his legs splayed out and his belly facing the ceiling as if nothing crazy had ever happened in the world.

I appreciated his attitude. It was nice that at least one person in my life wasn't freaked out.

He'd been a birthday present from my mom the year I turned fourteen. A rescue, but still a puppy, and he'd peed on every surface in the house until we got him trained. My dad would probably have decided not to like Peanut for that reason—if Peanut hadn't disliked my dad first. He shunned my dad from the get-go—barking and glaring at him whenever he came into the room. Later, we found out that Peanut hated all men, and we wondered if something bad had happened to him that had left some PTSD.

But my mom adored him, no matter what. He was eighteen pounds of solid cuteness—some kind of Maltese/Havanese/poodle/ shih tzu/Yorkie mix. When people stopped us to ask his breed, which they did often because he was literally the cutest dog in the world, we'd just say, "Texas fluffball." Like that was an AKC-recognized thing.

My mom had loved to put him in Fair Isle sweaters and doggie bomber jackets. When my dad grumbled about how it was "humiliating" for a dog to wear human clothes, she'd snuggle Peanut close and say, "You're just jealous."

My mom died later that same year, and I don't think my dad ever even looked at Peanut again after that. Peanut stayed in my room and came with me everywhere. I got an after-school job at a pet store and spent

much of my paycheck on toys and treats for him. We were totally insepa-
rable from then on.

Except for the two-year period when I was sent away.

But Peanut and I didn't talk about that.

Sitting next to Peanut today—as my brain spun and tried to take in
this new reality—for the first time in a while, I felt the bitter longing
that always seeped through me whenever I really missed my mom. It
stood off to the side of all other feelings, damp and cold—as if my soul
had been rained on and couldn't seem to dry out.

Most of the time, I tried to just feel grateful for the time I'd had
with her.

I knew I'd been so lucky.

Every Sunday, she bought a bouquet of flowers at the grocery store.
Then every morning, she'd snip one of the flowers out of the bouquet
and wear it behind her ear. I don't have a memory of my mom without
a flower behind her ear.

Even on the day we buried her.

Back at my hovel, sitting on my little love-seat sofa, I felt a longing
for my mom so intense, it felt like it was filling up my lungs. If she'd
been here, I would've rested my head on her shoulder and she'd have
stroked my hair. I would've pressed my ear against her chest, shushed
by the rhythm of her breathing. And then she'd have tightened her
arms around me so I'd know for sure I wasn't alone.

Because that was the most essential thing about my mom. She
couldn't always fix things for me, but she was always there.

Until the day she wasn't.

I WAS JUST wondering if this was the most alone I'd ever felt in my life
when I got a text from my father.

I *never* got texts from my father.

I didn't even know he had my contact info.

But the phone pinged, and there it was on the screen: This is Dad. I'm
at your building. Which apartment are you? I'm coming up.

Wait—at my building? *Coming up?* Wasn't he in Singapore?

You're not in Singapore? I texted.

I'm back.

Oh, no. He wasn't coming up. I'd been pretending to be success-ful in front of him for years. No way was I letting him see the truth of my life.

I'll come down, I texted.

I need to talk to you. Privately.

Wait right there.

Before he could argue, I leapt into action. He was *not* coming up here.

I was already ready for bed. It had been that kind of a day. But I swung on my favorite batik-print cotton robe—once my mom's—kicked on some fuzzy slippers, and then headed toward the top-floor hallway looking, shall we say, not exactly ready for prime time.

I slipped into the elevator just before the doors closed and only noticed when I turned around that there was someone else in there with me.

I could see nothing but his back and the back of his baseball cap, but that was enough.

He slouched against the front corner, facing away, leaning hard into that corner, like it was the only thing holding him up. He was wear-ing a vintage 1950s-style bowling jacket like hipsters love to find when they're thrifting. But he didn't seem like a hipster. And the jacket didn't seem all that vintage, either. More like a new version of an old jacket?

Who did that?

I was about to ask him to press Lobby for me when I realized that *one,* he'd already pressed it, and *two,* he was busy talking on the phone.

"Oh, my god, she's so fat," he said then to his phone, with a definite vibe like he had no idea I was there. "I thought she had to be pregnant, but no. She's just unbelievably obese."

I felt my face make an *Umm—what?* frown.

"Seriously," he went on, "her whole side of the bed was sagging. Fifty-

fifty she broke the springs. Belly fat for the Guinness book, I swear. And she does that thing where she breathes like she's choking. It's hilarious."

Hilarious? What the hell kind of conversation was this?

He went on. "Another one-night stand. Big mistake. Huge mistake. She *shredded the sheets.* Those nails. Not even kidding—I might really need stitches. But what was I supposed to do? She threw up in my entryway."

Okay. Now he really had my attention.

"I know," he went on, voice still at full volume. "But then five minutes later, she's dry-humping me again—just like in the parking garage. I think I pulled a hamstring." He tapped his head against the elevator wall. "I tried to kick her out of bed," he said next, "but she just kept coming back. And oh god, she's a moaner."

This must be the worst conversation I'd ever overheard. *Who talked like this?* I hate admitting to being this naive, but it had never even occurred to me that conversations this awful even happened.

Who *was* this guy? What a weasel.

I looked him up and down for identifying details. But there wasn't much to go on with him facing away, slumped in the corner like that. His hair was brownish. His height was tallish. The only distinctive thing about him was that bowling jacket. Red and white with cursive stitching.

He was still talking. "Yeah, I got home from work and she's still in the bed. So now it's a *two*-night stand. And last night, she did that thing where she planted her fat ass right in the middle of the mattress and then she rolled on top of my face. I almost suffocated, I swear—under a mountain of blubber."

"A mountain of blubber"???

Did I really just hear that?

I was baldly, openly staring at the back of this guy's weaselly, nondescript baseball cap now.

What the hell? Who even *thought* those things about a person they'd just spent the night with, much less said them out loud?

As we approached the first floor, just as I was thinking this conversation couldn't possibly get any more appalling, the Weasel added, "I got some pictures while she was sleeping. I'll text them to you. Oh, and there's a video. Sound up for that one. You've never heard snoring like that in your life. Go ahead and post them all."

With that, the doors slid open and he slid out, still talking, without ever noticing I was behind him.

Holy shit.

I stepped out, too, but I slowed to an astonished stop just outside the doors.

This right here was why I hadn't dated anyone since Ezra. This was why I spent Saturday nights at home with Peanut. Just the fact that *men like this existed*.

What had I just overheard? Was that unbelievable douchebag texting pictures of some poor unconscious lady to his friends? "Post them"?! What did "go ahead and post them" mean? Did he have some kind of website where he lured women back to his apartment and filmed them? Wasn't that illegal? Should I call the police and report a—A . . . ? *A morally repugnant person in the vicinity?*

Or should I go find this guy's apartment, bang on his door, rescue this woman—who had clearly just made the worst one-night-stand decision of her life—and lend her a fuzzy sweater, make her some tea, and give her a little TED Talk on Bad Men and How to Spot Them?

I was still undecided when—speaking of men who made you lose your faith in men—I felt something clamp my elbow and turned to see my dad. But not so much his face as the back of his head, because he was already dragging me off toward—where? The street, maybe?

"Hey!" I said in protest, like he'd forgotten his manners.

"We need to talk," my dad called back—not slowing or turning.

How long had it been since I'd seen him? A year? Two, maybe? Our last communication was Lucinda's three-page computer-printed holiday letter—which I hadn't read—and now not even a "Hi! How ya doing?" from this guy? He was just going to grab my elbow and steer me through my own lobby?

I tugged back to resist, like, *This is not how you do this.*

At that, my dad slowed and turned.

He took in the robe. And the slippers. Then he said, "I got the whole story from Lucinda."

"I'm sure you did," I said.

"You're going to need to get the surgery, Sadie," he said next.

I looked around to see if someone heard. That felt like an awfully private thing to just say at full volume in a public place.

I guess this was what the whole elbow-grabbing thing had been about.

"I will," I said, stepping closer and leading by example by lowering my voice. "I'm just . . . processing for a minute."

"You don't need to process," my dad said. "Just get it done."

"It's complicated," I said.

"No," my dad said. "It's simple."

My quiet voice hadn't worked. Instead, my dad went the other way and used his doctor voice—which is even louder than his usual one—on me: "Do the surgery right away. As soon as possible."

The ground floor of my building had a really great coffee shop called Bean Street that fronted to the street but also connected to our lobby. "Can I . . ." It felt so weird to say this: "Can I buy you a cup of coffee?"

My dad shoved his hand in his hair and looked evaluatively over toward the Bean Street logo—hand-painted on the glass doors by a hipster sign painter.

Then he said, "Okay," and walked over without waiting for me.

The place was almost empty. We sat facing each other in a booth, and I shifted gears, now trying to counter his doctor voice with an improvised unflappable-professional voice of my own. "I already told the surgeon that I preferred to wait," I said. "I have a project that can't be postponed."

"Lucinda told me. Your big break."

Of course she'd told him. What else did she have to talk about? "One of them," I said. "One of many. I get big breaks all the time." Then maybe one sentence too far: "My whole life is big breaks."

He flared his nostrils. "The point is, you can't wait."

I tilted my head. "This is uncharacteristically bossy of you, Richard."

"Don't call me Richard. Dad will do."

"What's the rush, exactly? The doctor said it wasn't urgent."

"You need to get it taken care of."

As I looked closer at my dad, he seemed atypically rumpled. Tie askew. Wrinkles in his Oxford cloth. He always traveled in a business suit. Formal guy. "Aren't you supposed to be in Singapore?"

"I came home early from my conference."

"For *this*?" I asked. It had to be for something else.

"This couldn't wait," he said. That sounded like a yes.

Was this all it took to get his attention? "Wow. I should have gotten a cavernoma years ago."

"You've always had it. It's congenital."

"I was joking."

But he was in no mood to joke. He actually looked . . . worried.

Huh. Worried about his daughter. Was this a first?

"It's fine," I said next. "I'll handle it."

But he shook his head. "It's done. I've already scheduled you for Wednesday."

At that, I just frowned. "*This* Wednesday?"

He nodded, like, *Affirmative.*

I tried to think if my dad had ever scheduled anything for me—even an orthodontist appointment. "Why would *you* schedule *my* surgery?"

He looked at me, like, *Duh.* "I've got some connections."

"No kidding."

"Otherwise, it was a three-week wait."

"Fine with me."

"But you need to get it done—"

"Right now," I finished for him. "Yeah. You said."

His latte sat untouched.

I stirred my own, then watched the bubbles circle around in the cup. Then I said, "Look, I'll be honest. This seems like a whole lot of interest all of a sudden for a guy who has literally not asked me one question about myself in the last decade."

"I understand."

"So what's going on?"

He nodded, like he'd been waiting for this question. "Your mom," he said then, looking down at the distressed wood tabletop.

My mom. He absolutely never brought up the topic of my mom.

He had my attention now. But then he paused so long I finally had to ask: "My mom. Okay. What about her?"

"Your mom," he said again. "She . . ."

Another pause. I tapped the table in his line of vision. "She what?"

He looked up and met my eyes. "She died of a cavernoma."

I sat back.

Heck of an adrenaline jolt there.

"I thought she died of a stroke," I said.

"She did. A stroke from a burst cavernoma."

"That seems like something I should have known sooner."

"Maybe if you'd gone to medical school you'd have learned all about it."

"Are you giving me shit about medical school right now?"

He pursed his lips together at the curse word—which seemed like the least of our problems. Next he tilted his head forward like he was forcing himself to take a calming moment. Then he said, "I'm telling you, you can't wait. You have to do this right now."

"I can't do it right now. I don't have time."

He lifted his eyes to meet mine. "That's exactly what your mother said."

Oof.

Then, before I'd absorbed that, he added, "And she might even have been wearing that very same robe when she said it."

I looked down and took a breath. Time to stop arguing. "So you're saying . . . she had this same exact thing?"

"Yes. It's inherited."

"And she knew she had it?"

"Yes."

"And she was advised to have it fixed?"

"Yes."

"But she didn't? And then she died?"

He nodded. "Precisely."

"Why didn't she have it fixed?"

My dad looked away. "I don't think we need to get into that."

"What else could there possibly be to get into?"

"I don't want to dredge up the past."

I lifted my hands, like, *What the hell?* "Too late. It's dredged."

"The point is—just get it done."

To be honest, I wasn't going to fight him. My dad might be a complicated, difficult, overly formal, pathologically reserved, not-particularly-fond-of-me person . . . but he wasn't stupid. He was, as Lucinda could verify, a "very prominent cardiothoracic surgeon." He knew his shit. He understood—if nothing else—the workings of the human body.

The point is: When Dr. Richard Montgomery, MD, FACS, FAHA, and chief of cardiothoracic surgery for UTMB, drags you down to a coffee shop in your mother's bathrobe and tells you to go have brain surgery, you don't argue.

You just go have brain surgery.

"Fine," I said. "I'll do the surgery. After you tell me why Mom didn't have hers."

"And I'll tell you about Mom," my dad shot back, "after you do the surgery."

Four

THE BEST THING—and possibly the only good thing—about the day of the surgery was meeting my new Trinidadian neuropsychologist, Dr. Nicole Thomas-Ramparsad.

When she first arrived, a nurse was beginning her third attempt at starting my IV. "The problem," the nurse was saying, "is that you're so tense." She tapped my arm some more with the pads of her fingers as if to say, *See? Nothing.* "You've shrunk your blood vessels."

I peered at my arm like I might be able to help her find one.

"You need to relax," she told me.

"I agree," I said, trying to slow my breathing down from humming-bird rate.

She added a second tourniquet. "When we get scared, our bodies pull all our blood into our core to protect the vital organs."

Relax, I commanded myself. *Relax.*

"Look at these veins," she called to another nurse, tapping around some more.

Nurse Two came over for a peek, giving a little headshake at the sight. "They're like quilting threads."

That did not sound like a compliment.

"She can't get this over with until you relax," Nurse Two said to me, a little scoldy.

"But I can't relax until it's over with," I said, aware of the Catch-22.

"Are you always a difficult stick?" Nurse One asked.

I wasn't loving that terminology. It made me sound uncooperative at best. But there was only one answer to that question. "Yes."

Nurses One and Two exchanged a look.

I tried to defend myself. "This is just how needle situations usually end for me—with tears. Or dry heaving. Or fainting." At the words *dry heaving*, I could feel my veins shrinking a little smaller.

Relax, damn it. Relax!

But that's when my future new favorite person walked in.

And let's just say she brought a totally different energy to the room.

Dr. Nicole Thomas-Ramparsad didn't just walk in, she *strode*—greeting me loudly as she did, her voice warm and rich. "Hello," she practically sang. "You're Sadie Montgomery, and I'm so delighted to be working with you today." And with that, she put a firm, comforting, totally-in-charge-of-the-moment hand on my shoulder, and said, "Please just call me Dr. Nicole"—pronouncing her name like *Ni-call*.

Let's just say her doctor voice sounded nothing like my dad's.

Which was a very good thing.

Because her voice—warm and motherly and confident—absolutely took over the room. She was such a big presence that she eclipsed everything else. It's important to note that she, in her light blue scrubs and surgical hat, looked pretty much like everybody else who worked in that hospital. She shouldn't have stood out like she had her own personal spotlight.

But she did.

Maybe it was her big fearless smile. Or the warm glow of her tawny skin. Or the laugh crinkles at her eyes. Or her tall posture, like she was the number one grown-up in the room. Or the fact that she seemed about the age my mom would be now, if she had lived.

Whatever it was, she appeared—and then positively hijacked my consciousness, leaning in close, squeezing my hand, and telling me more about herself in the first five minutes than most doctors revealed in years: She'd come to Houston from her hometown of Port of Spain, by way of McGill University in Canada—originally training to be a neurologist before getting fascinated with neuropsychology and switching tracks, much to her parents' chagrin, since psychology was not a "real" science. Her favorite types of music were calypso, soca, and steelpan, because they reminded her of home and made her feel peaceful. Her favorite flower was the bird-of-paradise, which "grows like weeds" in Trinidad. And she made the best coconut bread in the world, if she did say so herself.

"I'll bake you a loaf sometime," she told me.

"Thank you, Dr. Thomas-Ramparsad," I said.

"Dr. Nicole," she corrected, patting me on the arm.

And that's when I looked down and noticed that Nurses One and Two were gone, and the IV was already taped happily in place like there had never been anything difficult about it.

Oh god, she was a genius. Bless her.

Anyway, I adored Dr. Nicole from that moment on—instantly, the way a teenage girl might love a pop star. I would've gladly hung a poster of her on my wall.

After the IV, everything got easier—especially since there wasn't much for me to do. Also, since pretty soon I started feeling like my blood was made of maple syrup.

My dad scrubbed in for the surgery by the way—and it wasn't lost on me that this was the first thing we'd done together in years. A little father-daughter time.

At last, something about my life he could get interested in.

Hospitals have an unfortunate need to explain in advance exactly what they're going to do to you, and Dr. Estrera was no exception. When they had me good and sedated, he gave me way more information than I wanted or needed about how—and please prepare yourself for these coming words—they would *use a skull clamp to pin my head to prongs on the surgical bed,* leaning me forward and to the side so they could access the right spot, and then erecting a plastic tent around me so the surgeons could see only the area of my skull they needed and nothing else.

Hell of a to-do list. But it made sense.

A disembodied patch of skull was probably far easier to drill a hole into than, ya know, *a person.*

Next, they'd wash my hair with Betadine solution to sterilize everything, and then they'd comb it with a sterile comb, and then they'd shave just the tiniest bit, and then they'd cut and peel a flap of my scalp back . . . and then they'd *drill a four-inch hole in my head.*

Like they were going ice fishing.

No big deal at all.

I STAYED IN the hospital for the full four days after surgery, which made me feel like I was getting my money's worth.

I took a lot of naps. I slept partially sitting up on a bolster pillow to help with drainage. I ate a lot of Jell-O and wondered why I'd never appreciated it before.

The incisions in my scalp were sore for several days afterward. I had a few headaches and some shooting pains from time to time near the wound. My eyes got swollen enough that Dr. Nicole suggested I avoid the mirror for a while. All normal postsurgical stuff.

All in all, I felt back to my usual self surprisingly fast. The doctors were impressed with my resilience, and they chalked it up to my "youth and good health." I took full credit for both. I even caught myself wondering if I was doing my dad proud.

By Sunday, my last day there, I was feeling so good, I felt silly for the way I'd resisted the surgery. In fact, I felt so good so fast, I had to remind myself I was an invalid.

I was just getting discharge instructions for the next day—things like no alcohol, no driving for three weeks, no ladder climbing for three months—when a stranger came to visit me.

I mean, I'd been surrounded by strangers that whole week—nurses in bubble-gum-pink scrubs coming and going, checking stitches, vitals, surgical tape. Those pink scrubs really gave the whole staff a very uniform vibe.

But this stranger wasn't in scrubs, she was in street clothes. She came right in and pulled up a chair, and I remember wondering if she was maybe a social worker or even a reporter doing some kind of piece on cavernomas.

Maybe she'd ask me to star in a documentary. I wondered what people got paid for that.

But that's when she started talking.

And as the words accumulated, I started wondering if she really was a stranger after all.

"I came the first day," she said, "but you were so out of it. And then Witt's grandma got sick, so we had to drive to San Antonio to check on her. But don't worry, I boarded Peanut at that vet clinic around the corner from your place. Which is probably better, anyway, because Witt's pretty allergic, and he was being a great sport about it, but his eyes were, like, watering and itching the whole time. And that new clinic is awesome—though I know you like your old place. They've been sending me photos from the pup cam, and I think Peanut might have struck up a May-December romance with a Pomeranian."

She paused for a laugh, but I just said, "What?"

I mean, why was this person talking about Peanut? Or Witt, for that matter?

The stranger leaned in a little. "What about what?"

"What about all of it?"

We blinked at each other.

And that's when something impossible occurred to me.

This total stranger . . . was talking like she was my best friend, Sue.

I cannot describe the intense cognitive dissonance of suddenly knowing those two opposite things at once. But there was no other explanation. I was clearly sitting across from a person I did not know . . . and she was clearly saying things that only Sue could say.

It's fair to say *that* got my full attention.

Up until that point, all the other people who had moved through my room had been background noise. I'd taken them all for granted as I focused on postsurgical adventures like taking my meds, healing my incision, and shuffling back and forth to the bathroom.

I guess everything at the hospital had been just . . . *as expected.*

But then in came this person talking like Sue. And forced me to notice that she didn't look like Sue. Which forced me to try to figure out what she did look like.

And that's when I realized that I had no idea.

I mean, this lady in front of me had facial features. I could see them if I tried—one at a time. Eyes. A nose. Eyebrows. A mouth. They were all there.

I just couldn't snap them together into a face. Any face at all. Least of all Sue's.

"Sue?" I asked.

"What?"

"Is it you?"

"It's me," she said, like it might be a trick question.

"What did you do to your face?"

I saw her lift her hand to it. After a second, she said, "New moisturizer?"

"No. I mean—"

"Do I look weird? I switched multivitamins."

Did she look weird? I mean, the components of her face were like puzzle pieces spread out on a table. So yeah.

But I didn't exactly know how to say that.

I was just staring at her pieces, trying to Jedi-mind-trick them into clicking into their proper spots, when one of those nurses in the pink scrubs walked in.

And I realized that I couldn't see her face, either.

I mean, "couldn't see her face" is not exactly right. I could tell there was a face there. In theory. It wasn't just a blank slate. I could zoom in on eyebrows and laugh lines and lips.

It was just that the pieces didn't fit together right. They didn't make a face. It was a bit like looking at a Picasso painting.

I could *see* it, I guess. I just couldn't *understand* it.

It reminded me of that game you play as kids where you lie upside down and watch someone talking where their lips are flipped, top to bottom. Everything suddenly looked so funny. And disjointed. And cartoonish.

I felt a rising comprehension. Had I been like this all week?

As crazy as this sounds, it's true: It was only once I really started trying to look that I realized I couldn't see.

"Sue?" I said again, blinking, like maybe I could clear things up that way.

"You look fantastic," she said, leaning forward and clasping my hands in hers. "You'd never know they just popped a section of your skull out like the top of a jack-o'-lantern."

Yep. That was Sue, all right.

"I expected you to be bald, to be honest," she went on. "I was prepared to walk in here and say you looked *better* bald. I had a whole Sinéad O'Connor–themed speech prepared."

I rubbed my eyes and tried to look at her again.

But no change.

"How did they manage to keep your hair?" Sue asked.

I knew the answer to this question. Dr. Estrera had shown me in detail. But it didn't seem that important right now.

"I think I have a problem," I said then. "I can't see you."

Sue waved her hand in front of my face, like, *Hello?* "You can't see me?"

"I can see your hand," I said. "I just can't see your face."

Sue leaned forward, like that might help, just as the nurse leaned in and said, "Are you having trouble with your eyes, sweetheart?"

"I don't think it's my eyes," I said. "I think it's my brain."

WITHIN TWO HOURS, I'd done another MRI, and the entire faceless team of Estrera, Thomas-Ramparsad, Montgomery himself, and a whole posse of residents and onlookers had gathered in my room.

"The imaging shows some edema around the surgical site," Dr. Estrera said, talking more to my dad than to me.

"What's edema?" I asked.

"Swelling," Dr. Nicole explained. "Very normal. Nothing to worry about."

"It's common to have some swelling after a procedure like this," Dr. Estrera confirmed.

Then he turned to me, and as he did, I looked down at the blanket on my bed.

Looking at faces—or the modern art pieces where faces used to be—was hard. It made my brain hurt a little. Fortunately, Dr. Estrera wasn't offended. He went on. "As an artist, you know that the human face has a lot of variability."

Not sure you needed to be an artist to know that, but okay.

"Penguins, for example," he said, "don't have that same amount of facial variability. Most penguin faces look pretty much the same."

"I wonder if the penguins would disagree," I said.

He went on, "The location of your cavernoma was very close to an area in the brain called the fusiform face gyrus . . ."

He waited to see if I'd heard of it.

I hadn't.

"It's a deep temporal structure—a specialized area of the brain that allows people to recognize faces."

I nodded and kept my eyes on my blanket.

He went on. "Humans have evolved highly specialized brain systems for recognizing faces, and most of us have near-photographic memories for them. The minute you see another human face, it triggers a flood of instant information about that person: name, profession, biographical data, memories you have together . . . and the fusiform face gyrus is crucial to that process."

I nodded, like, *Interesting.* Like he was just telling me random brain facts.

Then he said, "Your cavernoma was located close to the FFG. Not in it and not touching it, but close."

"Did you nick it or something? That's why it's not working?"

Dr. Estrera turned my MRI scan on the lightboard and circled on a gray area. "We believe the normal postsurgical swelling is pressing on the fusiform face area right next to it and causing some mayhem."

"Causing some mayhem" seemed like a rather cutesy way to describe my situation, but I let it go. "What can we do about it?" I asked. "Ice it, maybe? Take some ibuprofen? Stop drinking water for a while and dehydrate myself?"

"There's not much we can do about it," Dr. Estrera said. "We just have to wait."

"Wait?!" I didn't have time to wait. "For how long?"

"People can vary quite a bit," Dr. Estrera said pleasantly, like we were just chitchatting. "I'd say it's likely to resolve in two to six weeks."

Two to six weeks? I looked up. "I'm looking at you right now, and you're like an upside-down Mr. Potato Head. Are you saying my brain could be doing that for *six weeks?*"

"I'm hoping it'll resolve before that," he said. "Assuming it does resolve."

I felt a sting of adrenaline. "Assuming it does resolve?" I echoed. "Are you saying it might not resolve?"

"I think it's very likely to resolve. Most postsurgical edema does. I can't guarantee it, of course. But I'd be surprised if it didn't."

Okay, okay. "But assuming it resolves . . . what happens then? Everything goes back to normal, right?"

"Then . . ." Dr. Estrera said, "we'll see."

Come on, man!

He must've thought he was striking a balance between being comforting and not making promises he couldn't keep. But since the possibility that *it might not resolve* hadn't even occurred to me, he was absolutely doing the freaking opposite.

"I just don't understand," I said then, my panic making me a little breathless, "how you could explain every minuscule head-clamp detail to me, and every aspect of the hair-sparing technique, but somehow fail to mention that the brain surgery I just electively signed up for might ruin my ability to see faces."

"This is a very rare outcome," Dr. Estrera said.

"I thought you said it was totally normal!"

"Edema is normal," he said. "But your cavernoma just happened to be very close to this particular very specialized area. The chances of this happening were infinitesimal."

"Do you know what I do for a living?" I demanded.

The whole room waited. They did not.

My voice was rising, but I didn't notice. "I am a portrait artist. I paint portraits! Of faces! For a living! What am I supposed to do now? What happens to my livelihood? I need my fusiform face thingy to be working!"

In the silence that followed, Dr. Estrera nodded with an apologies-for-the-inconvenience vibe.

I sighed.

I looked over at Dr. Nicole's puzzle-piece face for some help—emotional or otherwise.

"There's no reason that it shouldn't resolve," she said, taking my hand. "We'll just be patient. And I will work with you to teach you some coping skills in the meantime."

I let out a long breath. "Can I still go home tomorrow?"

"Of course," Dr. Estrera said. "Your site is healing beautifully. There's no reason for you to remain here."

My dad had been worryingly silent. I took a minute to note the unexpected high I'd been getting from being an accidental brain surgery poster child—a sudden minor celebrity in his world.

But then, when he shook Dr. Estrera's hand and left the room without a word to me, that high dropped to the ground.

Looked like it was time to be a disappointment again.

Oh well.

THE MOMENT OF truth came later, after most of the doctors, including my dad, had left.

Dr. Nicole stayed to run me through some face recognition tests. Before we got started, I needed to pee. Which meant going to the bathroom. Which, of course, had a mirror above the sink. I avoided looking as I walked in, but as I headed out, I paused.

What would happen if I looked into that mirror?

What would I see?

Don't look, I told myself.

I didn't want to know, but I also couldn't stand not knowing . . . and so I wound up standing with my eyes averted, caught between curiosity and dread, for so long Dr. Nicole finally asked if I was all right.

The knock startled me, and then I coasted off that energy and glanced up into the mirror to check my reflection . . .

And what I saw made me gasp.

My face, my very own face, the one I'd had and known and lived with all my life . . . it was nothing but puzzle pieces, too.

WHEN I OPENED the bathroom door, moving in slo-mo with the shock, I kept my eyes pointed toward the floor, which felt like the safest place. I got as far as the threshold before slowing to a stop.

"Sadie?" Dr. Nicole asked.

"I can't see my own face," I said then, a little breathless. "I just checked in the mirror, and it's not there. I'm faceless."

But Dr. Nicole wasn't giving in to my drama. "You're not faceless," she said, steering me gently by the shoulders back to bed, "you just have edema."

I wanted to be practical about it. Matter-of-fact. I wanted to fully understand that this was just a little brain glitch.

But there was nothing matter-of-fact about it.

I walked away from that mirror feeling . . . lonely.

No matter how alone you ever are in life, you always have yourself, right? You always have that goofy, imperfect face that forgets to take off its mascara before bed and wakes up with raccoon eyes. That one crooked lower tooth that the orthodontist never could manhandle into place. Those ears that stick out a little too far. Those lines on either side of your smile that always look like parentheses. That slight dimple at your chin that's just like your mom's.

Of course those aren't the only things that make you *you*.

You are also your whole life story. And your sense of humor. And your homemade doughnut recipe. And your love for ghost stories. And the way you savor ocean breezes. And the appreciation you have for how the colors pink and orange go together.

You're not just your face, is what I mean.

But man, it sure is a big part of you.

Like your shadow. So faithfully and constantly with you, you don't even notice it.

It's just always there. But then one day it's gone.

Except it's not just the shadow that's gone. It's the person making the shadow.

You. You're gone.

And the idea that anything could just disappear at any moment is something you suddenly understand in a whole new way. The way I did for a long while after my mother died.

"It's like I'm not here," I said to Dr. Nicole, my throat getting thick. "It's like I disappeared."

"You're right here," she said, taking my hands and squeezing them before holding them up to show me. "You know these hands, right?"

I nodded.

"Here you are," she said. "You haven't gone anywhere." Then she gave me a hug and said, "But let's not look in the mirror again for a while."

She wanted to get down to business. She was organizing some tests for me to take on her laptop. While I waited, a random thought occurred to me: Peanut.

"This doesn't apply to animals, right?" I asked.

"What?" Dr. Nicole asked.

"I'm suddenly worried that when I get home, I won't be able to see my dog."

"You'll definitely be able to see your dog."

"His face, I mean," I said. "I need that face. It's my primary mood-lifter."

"I understand," Dr. Nicole said, attention still mostly on her work.

"This face thingy's only for human faces, right?"

At that, she paused. "Mostly," she said, "yes."

"Mostly?" I asked. "What does *mostly* mean?"

"There's not a lot of research on animal faces. There has been some research on cars, though."

"Cars?"

"Some people with this condition have trouble recognizing their cars. They can also have trouble with direction. But it hasn't been studied enough to understand why or how."

"So . . ." Somehow this felt like the worst news of all. "You can't guarantee that I'll be able to see my dog's face?"

But she wasn't going to let me descend into self-pity. "Guarantees are overrated."

I must have been spoiling for a fight. "Guarantees are *underrated*."

But she didn't take the bait. "Let's just take one question at a time."

DR. NICOLE HAD queued up some facial recognition tests for me to take to see how bad it was. "This'll give us a baseline," she said.

The tests—the Glasgow Face Matching Test, the Cambridge Face Memory Test, along with a few others—were all online. She rotated the laptop toward me.

I folded my legs and geared up to begin. I was usually pretty good at tests. But I would not be acing these.

These tests were hard. Like if you made a kindergartner take the SAT.

Some of them asked you to look at two pictures and decide if they were the same person or a different person. Some of them asked you to study a set of faces and then find those people later in groups. Some of them showed you famous people with their hair removed. They specifically did not ask if you could name the person—because recalling names is a different brain system. They asked only if you could *recognize* them.

Could I recognize them?

I could not.

It was all—and I mean this in the fullest sense of the word—*nonsense*.

From celebrities to presidents to pop icons to Oscar winners, all the faces in all the tests looked totally indistinguishable. I couldn't tell the difference between Jennifer Aniston and Meryl Streep. I couldn't tell Sandra Bullock from Jennifer Lopez. It was like looking at pickup-stick piles of facial features. I could tell that these people had faces. I could see the pieces of the faces. I just couldn't tell what the faces looked like when you put the pieces together.

That feeling you get when you recognize somebody? That little pop of recognition? I looked at hundreds of faces that day, and I never felt it once.

By the end of the fifth test, I was in tears.

"That's enough for today, choonks," Dr. Nicole said, putting her arm around me for a side hug.

"Did you just call me *chunks*?" I asked. What on earth could that mean?

"Choonks," she corrected. "It means sweetheart in Trinidad."

That felt really good for a second. I liked being a sweetheart.

But then I started crying again.

She squeezed my shoulders tighter. "I know it's a lot."

"The thing is . . ." I said, really giving into the crying now. "The thing is . . . I just don't know what's going to happen to me."

"We're not going to worry about the future," she said. "We're going to focus on the here and now. You're healing great. You've taken care of your cerebrovascular issue. You've done the hard part."

She was patting my back now.

My thoughts were churning like a cement mixer. "What if," I said, voicing my worst fear, "I get stuck like this?"

That's when Dr. Nicole shifted her position to face me. I looked down at my blanket. "When I hear you say unproductive things," she said then, "I'm going to call your attention to them and challenge them."

"Did I say an unproductive thing?" I asked.

She nodded.

"What did I say?"

"Here's a hypothetical question," she said next. "If there's a five percent chance something bad will happen, and a ninety-five percent chance that things will be fine, which one is more likely?"

Was this a trick question? "That things will be fine?"

She nodded. "I want you to work on that."

"Work on what?"

"On which of your thoughts you're going to choose to indulge in."

"Is this about my worrying I'll get stuck like this?"

She nodded again. "Our thoughts create our emotions. So if you fixate on your worst-case scenario, you'll make things harder for yourself."

"You want me not to fixate on the worst-case scenario?"

"I want you to start practicing the art of self-encouragement."

"So when I catch myself worrying, I should try to convince myself that things are going to be fine?"

"That's one way to do it."

"But what if I don't believe it?"

"Then keep arguing."

I was supposed to argue myself into feeling optimistic? "I've never been great at optimism," I said.

"That's what the arguing is for."

"I'm not very good at arguing, either."

"Maybe this is a chance to get better."

But I'd learned long ago that arguing didn't get you very far. "Can you give me a hint?"

"Try to step back and look at the big picture," Dr. Nicole said. "That's where you can see it more clearly."

"See what?"

"That no matter what happens, you will find a way to be okay—whether your prosopagnosia is temporary or permanent."

"My proso . . ." I asked, giving up on the word halfway through. "What's that?"

"That's the condition you have right now," Dr. Nicole said, "based on these test scores." Then she handed me a diagnosis: "Acquired apperceptive prosopagnosia."

I waited for those syllables to make sense. But they didn't.

So she said it again. "Acquired apperceptive prosopagnosia." Then she added: "Also known as face blindness."

Five

AND AFTER ALL that, to add massive insult to once-in-a-lifetime injury, who should I run into in the elevator of my building on the very morning I came home?

You guessed it.

The one-night-stand guy. The Weasel.

Fresh back from the hospital, I had walked in slow motion through the lobby of my building, holding my breath as faceless people wandered blithely around me.

I kept my eyes to the carpet, stepped gingerly through the elevator doors, and pressed the button to the top floor—my hair smelling of hospital shampoo and gathered in a careful, stitches-covering ponytail. I was trying with all my might not to accidentally knock that cork in my skull loose while also holding back a tsunami of life-altering realizations about the week I'd just been through . . . just as the Weasel himself catapulted through the closing doors and tossed his arms up in victory as he cleared them at the last second.

Let's just say he wasn't matching my fragile energy.

I couldn't recognize his face now, of course. Or anything else about

his rather nondescript self. What I did recognize—other than his terrible personality—was the red-and-white *non-vintage* vintage bowling
jacket.

There couldn't be more than one of those walking around.

Oh my god! The Weasel! I'd forgotten about the woman in his bed.
I'd meant to go find his apartment that night and wake her up and get
her the hell out of there—but in all the hubbub of, ya know, *the brain
surgery,* I'd forgotten.

He wasn't still holding her captive in there, was he?

I thought about asking.

But that's when he turned to me, all friendly and breathless, and said,
"Made it!" The way a nice person might talk to another nice person.

I kept my eyes down and edged away.

*Really, pal? You think you can just wildly bad-mouth your one-
night stands and also get to be a normal member of society?*

Not on my watch, buddy.

I wasn't going to be complicit in this nice-guy gaslighting. Also:
What the hell? What adult just sprints through a building lobby willy-
nilly like that? What if he'd slammed into me? What if I'd hit my head
and the plug in my skull had popped like a champagne cork—and then
it was right back to the hospital?

I wasn't used to feeling fragile. And I definitely didn't like it. So I
glared at him, like, *Thanks a lot for reminding me.*

I could deduce that he was smiling, even despite his puzzle-piece
face. Those big teeth were pretty unmistakable.

How dare he?

It was frustrating beyond measure to look straight at a person and
have no idea what he looked like. Especially since I really might have to
pick him out of a lineup someday.

One of the tips Dr. Nicole had given me for coping with the sudden
lack of faces in the world was to notice other things about people. Most
of us used faces by default, she'd explained, but there were plenty of
other details to notice. Height. Body shape. Hair. Gait.

"Gait?" I'd said, like that was a stretch.

"Everybody's walk is a little different, once you start noticing," Dr. Nicole said, doubling down.

So I tried it on the Weasel. What did he have besides a face?

But I guess I wasn't very good at this yet. All that really stood out was the bowling jacket—which had the name Joe embroidered vintage style across the chest. The rest? Shaggy hair falling aggressively over his forehead. General tallness. Thick-framed gray hipster glasses.

And I don't know what else. Arms and legs, I guess. Shoulders? Feet? This was hard.

Normally, in elevator situations with strangers, even if you accidentally talk at the start, you settle back into standard elevator behavior pretty fast: eyes averted, quiet, as much space as possible between bodies.

But I could feel the Weasel breaking the rules. Standing too close. Trying to make eye contact.

Oh god. Had he thought I was *checking him out* just now?

I felt a sting of humiliation. That was scientific research, damn it!

I dropped my eyes straight to the floor and edged even farther away.

Unmistakable we-don't-know-each-other body language.

But maybe he didn't speak that language? I could feel him studying me as we rose to the next floor. "Great sweatpants," he said then, his voice still at maximum friendliness.

"Thank you," I replied. Nice and curt.

"Are they comfortable?"

What? Who cared? "Yes."

He paused, and I thought my one-word answers had done their job. But then he revved back up. "How are you doing today?"

How was I doing? What kind of question was that? "I'm fine."

"You look good," he said, like he was somehow qualified to state that opinion.

A memory of his saying the words *nothing but blubber* popped into my head, and it was all I could do to push out two clipped syllables. "Thank you."

"How's your health?"

My health? Um. We weren't going to talk about my health—or anything at all about me. I didn't know anybody who lived in my building well enough for a conversation like this. Except possibly Mr. and Mrs. Kim, who lived on the ground floor.

I went on the offensive. "My health is fine. How is yours?"

"Oh, good, you know. Yeah, I was up all night. But that's nothing new."

Oh my god. What a monster. How many other women had he menaced since the last time I saw him?

When we reached the top floor, we both started for the doors at the same time, and when he realized the bottleneck, he gestured for me to go ahead with a Shakespearean bow.

Really? Now he was ruining *Shakespeare*?

I went ahead. Walking a little faster than I really wanted to, trying to leave him behind.

But he followed me. "Do you rent the place on the rooftop?" he asked then as I paused to work the door code to the rooftop stairwell.

Obviously. "Uh-huh," I said.

"We're neighbors," he said, and gestured at the next closest door. "I'm right here. Just under you."

Could he hear himself?

I nodded without looking up. No eye contact.

"I'd love to get a look at your place sometime," he said then. "I've always wanted to see what it's like up there." Then he added, "Especially when you're clomping around on my ceiling."

Nope. No thanks. There was no way this wanker was ever going to "see what it's like up there."

I turned to face him, double-checking the name on his pocket.

"Look, Joe," I said, poking my finger—hard—into the embroidered name on his jacket so he'd know I knew it, "I'm not going to be inviting you up to the rooftop." Then in a tone that very unmistakably said *I know what you did to that one-night stand and you're a terrible person and we both know it*, I added, "That's not going to happen. Okay?"

That shocked him a little—which reminded me of something else Dr. Nicole had said.

During our lengthy coping-skills session before I left the hospital, as she tried to argue that face blindness was not going to be as debilitating as I feared, she told me, among many other things, that even though I couldn't *see* faces, I would still be able to read the emotions on them.

"So if someone is shocked or embarrassed or angry, you'll still be able to tell," she explained. "You won't *see* it, but you'll *know* it."

"How is that possible?" I asked.

"It's two different brain systems."

"But how can I *read* faces if I can't *see* faces?"

"You can still see faces," Dr. Nicole said. "There's nothing wrong with your eyes. Your brain just doesn't know how to put them together to show them to you right now."

Her tone of voice was so reasonable.

But nothing about this was reasonable.

"The faces aren't gone," Dr. Nicole tried again. "The faces are still there. And another part of your brain can read the emotions on them just fine. Just like always."

"I'll have to trust you on that," I'd said, not trusting her at all.

But it turned out—as it would often turn out with Dr. Nicole—she was right.

Because when I sharply rejected the Weasel's invitation for me to invite him over, I shocked him. I couldn't see it, but I could *feel* it: that unintelligible face of his was surprised. And a smidge taken aback—most likely having lived his whole life as a complete jerk without encountering nearly enough repercussions. And he was now, at last, ready to withdraw all that inappropriate warmth.

Fine. Great.

He might have fooled that poor one-night stand of his. But he wasn't fooling me.

I lowered my eyes to his jacket pocket, letting them rest on that cursive *Joe* until he looked down at the word, too.

Much too nice a name.

I might have to be his neighbor. I might have to bump into him in the elevator. I might have to carry the memory of him saying the word *blubber* for the rest of my life . . .

But I did not have to invite him up to my hovel.

Joe the Weasel nodded and stepped back. "Got it."

And it sounded like he really did.

Six

RUNNING INTO THE Weasel in the elevator was not the worst part of coming home from the hospital.

The worst part of coming home was Lucinda.

Who had decided to try to help me.

Of all things.

Starting with forcing me into accepting a ride home.

To be honest, I hadn't even noticed Lucinda when she'd first arrived that morning. That Pepto-Bismol-pink cardigan she'd chosen was almost the exact shade as the nurses' scrubs, and I just assumed she was one of them. She chatted with the nurses a good while, and I didn't catch on until she came over and said, "Ready to go?" You'd think I might have recognized the voice of *the person who ruined my life* pretty easily . . . but I didn't.

She could have been anybody.

Dr. Nicole had explained about voices, too—that my brain was used to all my senses working together in an ecosystem. Having one sense out of whack could throw the others off, too, for a while. So it might take some time to learn to recognize voices without the usual visual clues of the face. Over time, she promised, I'd get better at voices alone.

"You might even wind up better at recognizing voices than you were before. Eventually. If—" But she stopped herself.

"If I don't get the faces back?" I finished.

She nodded. "Be patient with yourself," she said. "Your brain has a lot to adjust to right now. We think of the senses like they're separate, distinct things. But they're really interconnected. It's going to be chaos in there until things settle. Even easy things will be hard for a while."

"How long?" I asked.

But I knew the answer, even as she said it. "We just don't know."

Anyway, that could turn out to be an upside, in a way.

I was in no hurry to recognize Lucinda's voice.

I'd agreed to the ride only after I made her swear up and down that she would drop me at the door—*only*—and not come up.

"But I have to get your prescriptions," she protested.

"I can get my own damn prescriptions," I insisted.

But one guess for how the drop-off went down.

That's right. She picked up my prescriptions without permission and then came up to my hovel un-frigging-invited.

I hadn't been home fifteen minutes when she showed up.

I was still standing in the entryway, trying to adjust to the unfamiliar silence. Peanut was still being boarded. There was no jangle of tags or scuttling of dog paws as he scrambled to greet me at the door, wagging his tail so hard he bapped himself on the ears. There was no— hopefully still-recognizable—loving little dog face to make me feel like everything could be okay.

It was bad.

And then, suddenly, there was Lucinda. Knocking on my hovel door. Even worse.

After a lifetime of trying to hide my extreme lack of life success from both her and my dad, her arrival was pure insult to injury.

I thought about ignoring her. But then I decided not to prolong the agony.

"This is where you live?" she asked, stepping in as I opened the door.

"I thought you went home," I said.

"I picked up your prescriptions," Lucinda said, like she'd done me a favor.

"Didn't I tell you not to do that?"

But Lucinda was looking around. "It's very . . . bohemian," she said, like that was the nicest thing she could come up with.

"How did you get up here?" I demanded.

"Mr. Kim gave me the code."

"You met Mr. Kim?"

She nodded, still looking around. "He kept calling me Martha Stewart."

At that, I stifled a smile. Mr. Kim always had everybody's number. I sighed. "That's actually a great nickname for you."

She considered that. Was she complimented or insulted?

Either way, I didn't like seeing my worlds collide. "Don't bother Mr. Kim, okay?" Mr. Kim, along with the whole Kim family, belonged to me.

But she wasn't listening. "You live here?"

I could have lied, I guess. But maybe I was tired of lying. And it was hopeless anyway. She was here. It was what it was. "It's temporary," I said.

And then, with her trademark decisiveness, she pulled out her wallet, scanned down her credit cards, and took one out. "Take it," she said.

"I don't need it," I said.

"Just take it," she insisted. "Your dad will never know."

"I'm fine," I said.

"This one gives you points," she said, waving it at me.

"So?"

"So every time you use it, we're making money."

"That is not how that works."

But she gave me a wink. "Just use it. I do all the bills, anyway. I'll never tell."

How dare she act like I needed her?

I never needed anyone. Ever. For anything.

And the reason that was true? The reason I never let myself do a very simple thing like *need other people* that the rest of humanity got to do all the time? That reason was standing right here in a hot-pink sweater.

I took hold of her shoulders and steered her toward the door. "I don't need your help. And I don't want you up here. And I'm changing the passcode. So go home, okay? And take your credit card with you."

She didn't fight me. She left without protest.

But it was only after I'd dead-bolted the door that I saw, on the table beside it, looking defiantly up at me . . . her credit card.

IT ONLY HIT me, really, after I'd gotten rid of her.

My entire life up until now had been a *before*. And now I was in the after.

I couldn't see faces. Not even my own.

I was face-blind.

Maybe I'd stay that way, and maybe I wouldn't. But one thing was certain. I would never be the same.

It was like suddenly finding myself on an alien planet. Even in the hospital, where caretaking was literally the job of every person I interacted with, people felt strange and foreign and vaguely unsafe. Either I was thinking about all the missing faces and working to avert my eyes, or I was staring at them, still disbelieving, or I was forgetting about my brain situation—and then looking up only to be startled by yet another faceless face.

To be clear, I knew intellectually that the faces were still there. If I looked carefully, I could see the individual parts. What I couldn't do was glance at a face and know in an instant exactly who that was and remember everything I'd ever learned about that person. Or in the case of strangers: know immediately that I didn't know.

This new way of being was a conscious process of deduction. There was nothing effortless about it.

Now, most of the time, rather than trying, I just let everybody be a blur.

My conscious mind understood what had happened. The FFG wasn't working. Got it. Just a little brain snafu. Not reality. Just a glitch in my system.

But my subconscious mind—the one that wasn't too used to having to rethink reality—was deeply, profoundly freaked out.

I could understand in theory that I was face-blind.

But in practice? It made no sense at all.

I learned pretty quick from obsessive research on the internet that two percent of the world's population has face blindness. So I definitely wasn't alone. Out of 8 billion people in the world—and I got out the calculator for this—there were 160 million other people who were face-blind. Besides me. That figure was larger than the population of Russia. We could start our own country and compete in the Olympics.

Except a lot of them, it turned out, didn't know they were face-blind.

I had a kind of face blindness known as acquired. The kind people procured somewhere along the way—strokes, head injuries, brain surgery. Most people with acquired face blindness know they have it. If you've always been able to recognize faces and then suddenly you can't anymore . . . you notice that.

But the much more common type was known as developmental. These folks had been face-blind all their lives—and many of them didn't even know it. Which makes sense. Because if that's how the world has always been for you, then that's how it's always been. Nothing about that would seem odd. You'd assume that everybody else was exactly the same way.

I found a couple of Facebook groups and read every comment on every post, trying to get the skinny on what it was really like to function in the world like this. Most people had tips and tricks for recognizing people without using faces as the main clue, and some people seemed very good at it.

As for how everyone felt about having the condition, I found a wide spectrum of opinions. Some people found it limiting or frustrating or depressing . . . while others thought it was *so not a big deal* that they didn't know why it merited discussion. One woman wanted to know the point of even talking about it when there were "people with actual problems" out there. Another highly likable woman described her face blindness as a "superpower," saying she treated every person she interacted with like a dear friend—just in case those people turned out to actually be dear friends. When people talked to her in the grocery store as if they knew her, she pretended she knew them right back, and asked them question after question until she could solve the mystery for herself. She learned a lot about people that way, she said—but more than that, it meant that almost every interaction she had with other people was infused with warmth and affection. In a way, there were no strangers.

She loved her face blindness. She felt like it brought her out of her shell. She wholeheartedly believed it was a gift.

Huh.

I closed my eyes and tried to see this moment in my life as a gift.

Yeah. No.

My experience of all this so far was the opposite of living in a world with no strangers. For me, right now, everyone felt like a stranger. Even me.

I mean, I just genuinely couldn't imagine walking out into a world where everyone looked like bowler-hat figures in a Magritte painting and feeling . . . awash in a gentle sea of human kindness.

Maybe it was more about the adjustment than anything. The before-and-afterness. The fact that the world—my world—was changed in ways I'd never even imagined before all this happened. The fact that a central tool for relating to the rest of humanity—one I'd relied on constantly, every day, my entire life—was suddenly just . . . *gone?*

It was scary, if I'm honest. I was never all that great with people to start with.

All to say, for the first three days I was home, I couldn't seem to make myself leave my apartment.

I mostly just did wound care. And ordered takeout. And watched old movies.

And availed myself—after much hemming and hawing—of Lucinda's credit card.

I had sworn never to need my dad or Lucinda's help. But was using that card "needing" them, really? Especially if I was buying luxury items I didn't need. That was something different from needing them. That was *punishing* them. Right?

If you thought about it the right way, it was a form of winning.

And so I went for it. I enjoyed my first bout of recreational shopping in years: a hygge-inspired tea kettle, a string of twinkle lights branded as "wishing stars," a heart-shaped velveteen pillow . . . and a totally nutty hybrid cross between a pair of footed pajamas and a fuzzy blanket called a Pajanket.

The Pajanket came same-day delivery, and after I zipped myself into it, I swore I would never take it off ever again. It was basically a rectangular human-sized pillowcase with holes at each corner for hands and feet. The foot-holes had booties and the hand-holes had mittens. And the neck had a hoodie. And the plush, buttery, nothing-can-ever-hurt-you-again fabric they'd sewn it out of? Velvety on both sides.

It was all I could do not to order a thousand.

And so I stayed home. I was on this. I *had* this. I was fine.

I was, as always, completely, utterly, astonishingly okay—putting my life back in order without too much fuss.

I shut down my Etsy shop. I put a note on the page and on my Instagram that read: "AT CAPACITY! Thanks for all your orders! This shop is taking an eight-week hiatus. Not accepting new commissions."

That sounded pretty good, right? Like I was just at capacity with work because of the unstoppable thirst the world had for my portraits?

Not like I was at capacity *emotionally*.

Or like my entire life was crumbling.

Or like I was afraid to leave the house.

Not doing any portraits would mean no money coming in. But there wasn't a choice there. Maybe I'd charge all my bills to my dad's credit card, too. Maybe it was all about attitude. If a little punishment was good, wouldn't a lot of punishment be better?

I wondered if Mr. Kim would let me charge the rent.

When I felt a rising sense of panic, I tried to see it as a positive. After all these years of nonstop hustling, it might be nice to unchain myself from my Etsy shop for a bit. Though I'd still have to check the comments every day. Most people said nice things most of the time, but occasionally a nutter slipped through with a comment like "These portraits look like circus clowns."

Anyway, that was life online. You had to keep an eye on the crazies. *Block* and *delete*.

Kinda like the rest of my life right now.

I had groceries delivered. I took careful showers.

And I tried—and failed—over and over to make myself go get Peanut at the vet clinic.

Peanut, who I missed constantly in my Peanut-less apartment.

That's how bad it was: I left my *only family* boarded at the vet for three extra days because I couldn't talk myself into leaving my building. And also, more than anything, because I was terrified that when we were finally reunited, I might not be able to see his face.

FINALLY, IN A profound act of courage, I did it. I took a shower, got dressed, and walked—as carefully as if I might slip on an icy sidewalk— two blocks filled with pixelated-faced strangers until I arrived at a vet clinic I'd never been to filled with people I'd never met.

We were in the Warehouse District, so I wasn't surprised to find that this clinic was in a warehouse. I was surprised, however, by the speaker system blasting perky oldies into the waiting area.

As I checked in, I said, "Fun music."

"What?" a faceless receptionist looked up and asked.

"The music!" I said, projecting a little louder. Then I gave a thumbs-up.

She pointed at the speakers. "We're trying to mask all the jackhammering from the construction next door."

"Ah," I said.

"It stresses the animals out," she said, clicking around on the computer to pull up my bill. "But playing Sam Cooke seems to help."

As the bill came off the printer, she read it and said, "Oh, you're Peanut's mom!"

Mom? I don't know. More like *sibling.* Or BFF. But I just said, "Yes."

"He's a big fan of the music," she said. "Did you know he's a Louis Armstrong guy?"

"I mean, it doesn't surprise me," I said. "He's a very cultured dog."

She gave me a nod, handed over the bill, and that's when I saw it had already been paid.

Lucinda.

What a menace.

That said, it was also six hundred dollars I didn't have, so I wasn't complaining.

Could Lucinda just buy my affection like that?

Today she could. I guess.

Next, I waited for the moment of truth with Peanut. When I saw him again, would I be able to see him?

What felt like a hundred years later, I had my answer.

Yes.

A tech brought him out and I saw for sure as the second the door opened: Peanut's little mug. There it was. His giant liquid-brown eyes. His yellow fur and Lorax-style mustache that got lopsided after he'd been resting his chin on something. His feathery ears that never seemed to both point up—or down—at the same time.

Question answered.

I'd know that face anywhere.

In a second, Peanut was in my arms and licking me all over. His tail was going full blast, his body was wriggling, his little heart was jumping around in his chest. If he was mad about being abandoned for eight days, he certainly wasn't holding a grudge.

Dogs were so good at forgiveness.

He alternated great-to-see-you licks with deep, soul-searching gazes—like he couldn't believe his luck that I'd returned. And he wasn't the only one feeling lucky. Because the only face I'd seen since the surgery just happened to be my very favorite one.

All to say, something about the feel of him—the softness of his fur, his salty, doggy smell, the unconditional love—made me start to cry right there in the waiting room.

Yeah. It was an emotional time.

I got started crying, and then . . . I couldn't stop. Just stood there smiling and crying and cradling my little pal while he licked the salty tears off my cheeks over and over.

"Missed you, buddy," I whispered, nuzzling his fur.

That's when I looked up to see someone watching me. A man. A vet, from the looks of it. A tall, white-coated, tie-wearing vet with an up-and-back Ivy League haircut. He had his hands in his lab-coat pockets and just stood there, staring right at Peanut and me, taking in the sight.

And once again, Dr. Nicole was right because I could tell you without even putting his face pieces together that this guy was seriously handsome.

That must be its own brain system right there.

It was the way he stood there. The way he held himself. That haircut—so professional and competent. I'd always thought handsomeness must be all about facial features and shapes and mathematical proportions. And maybe it was. But this guy also just had a way about him—like he was commanding the room without even doing anything. Just standing there generating handsomeness like a sexy, living light-up statue.

Most people nowadays made me want to avert my eyes. The intensity of those puzzle-piece faces—the impossibility of it all—was physically uncomfortable, like a buzzing in my body.

But this guy? I couldn't make myself look away. I took in the sight of him, and he did the same right back to me, for a good minute. Finally he turned and walked off down the hallway—hands in pockets and coat-tail trailing jauntily behind him like a male model on a runway—forcing me to note that Dr. Nicole was right yet again.

Because that man had one hell of a gait.

Holy shit.

It was love at first sight—and I couldn't even see him.

Okay, I take it back. It wasn't *love*.

Love requires actually having spoken to a person. At the minimum.

Maybe it was *infatuation* at first sight. Or preoccupation. Or ob-session.

Whatever it was, I wasn't complaining.

All along, I'd been classifying leaving my textbook narcissist boy-friend Ezra and then running out of money and then almost dying in a crosswalk and then getting surprise brain surgery and then having to board my dog at an unfamiliar clinic and then going face-blind . . . as *bad* things.

But now?

I was all good.

The sight of that vet—for a minute there, anyway—seemed to fix everything.

I stopped crying, at least.

I turned to the receptionist to see if her world had also been rocked by the appearance of that mystery veterinarian across the room. But nope. She was checking her Instagram.

"Was that the vet?" I asked her.

She looked down the hallway. "Oh, yeah. One of them. That's Dr. Addison." Her voice was all casual, like he was just a regular, everyday person.

"He works here?"

She nodded. "Yeah. He's the newest vet on staff."

I wanted to ask more questions—*What's his deal? What's he like? Is he as handsome as I think he is?*—but I couldn't settle on anything that didn't sound bananas.

Instead, I just said, "I think I should probably schedule Peanut for a checkup."

PEANUT, OF COURSE, had just had his checkup two months ago—with my old vet, a lady in her sixties who I'd known since I was a kid—and he was in perfect health. For a canine gentleman of his years.

But could you ever have too many checkups, really?

Preventative pet health care is so important.

Though it turned out Dr. Addison—Dr. *Oliver* Addison, I noted, when I snagged his business card off the front desk—did not have any openings for a month.

"Wow," I said. "He's really booked."

"Yeah, he books up fast."

"I'll bet."

"Plus he leaves a lot of space in his schedule for emergencies."

See that? Not just handsome, but also a thoughtful planner. Leaving space for emergencies so no one was ever turned away. Was there *anything* about this guy that wasn't perfect? More important, if I married him, would I change my name?

I pondered this on my walk home. Trying the sound out in my head as I mouthed the words: "Sadie Addison."

Sadie Addison! It was the best name ever. All those S's and D's.

I could see myself at my engagement party—tipsy with joy as I explained, "I never planned to change my last name, but Addison just felt like such an upgrade." I could see a future me, face blindness all cured, leaning confidently in to meet new people with an assertive little handshake, saying, "Good to meet you. Sadie Addison." I could picture our newlywed holiday greeting card: "Happy Holidays from Oliver and Sadie Addison." Maybe we'd wear matching Nordic sweaters.

Or should we hyphenate? "Warmest holiday wishes from the Montgomery-Addisons"?

No rush on that. So many options to consider.

I could see myself running into old beaus or former school mean girls at the grocery store while Dr. Addison and I held hands on, say, a late-night Ben & Jerry's run. We'd be so happily goofing around in the freezer aisle—him maybe tickling me or trying to pick me up as I giggled wildly like the happiest in-love person in history—that we didn't even notice whoever it was at first. Then we'd pause from our delirium for pleasant introductions. "Oh, hello. Look how well my life turned out. Please meet my so-gorgeous-he-doesn't-even-need-a-face husband, Oliver. I'm Sadie Addison now, by the way."

Yes. That worked.

Fine. Was I manufacturing a crush for myself to give my wounded brain something to focus on that wasn't deeply, hopelessly depressing?

Sure. Probably.

Was there anything wrong with that?

Not in the slightest.

If I needed a little oxytocin-filled romantic pick-me-up courtesy of Dr. Oliver Addison's *GQ*-level hairdo and Olympically handsome gait, was that really such a crime? Why not, right?

Dr. Nicole said our thoughts create our feelings.

Maybe a few good thoughts were just what the doctor ordered.

Or the veterinarian, as the case may be.

THE WALK HOME was surprisingly pleasant.

It was sunny and breezy out, and I cradled Peanut to my chest while we held our chins up and let the wind caress both of our faces. Meeting my future husband had renewed my strength and my courage, and I fearlessly enjoyed my journey back—and let all the faceless people flicker past me like butterflies.

Until I got stopped by one of them.

"Oh my god! Sadie?" It was a woman's voice, from some distance away.

I turned toward the sound.

She was tall, dressed in all gray with a pop-of-color pink scarf, and had dyed blond hair . . . and a face like a cubist painting.

She ran over and grabbed me by the shoulders, pulling me into a hug that squeezed both me and Peanut tight.

I tried to fight the rising panic. I had absolutely no idea who this was. What were the tricks I'd read about online again? *Smile a lot. Ask leading questions. Be warm and friendly. Don't say anything to give it away. Beat the clock and solve the mystery before the person figures it out.*

Before I could think of what to ask, this faceless woman said, "How long has it been?"

"Gosh," I said, stalling. "How long *has* it been?"

"You look amazing," she said next.

What else could I say? "*You* look amazing."

"What are you up to these days?"

"Oh," I said. "Same old, same old." Then, trying to turn the tables. "What are *you* up to?"

"Same," she said. "Just working and working. Trying to conquer the world. You get it."

"I sure do." I nodded big.

Then there was a pause.

I'd never realized before how much personal questions needed a little something to go on.

But I tried to encourage myself. I was doing okay! I was passing!

"Well," she said then. "It's been so great to see you."

"You too," I said with maximum warmth, like it really, really had been.

She started to walk away, but then she turned back. "Oh—and Sadie?"

"Yeah?" I asked, smiling big.

"I know you don't know who I am."

My smile dropped.

She took a step closer. "You'd never be this nice if you had any idea."

"Who are you?" I asked.

"Mom told me all about it—but, I don't know . . . it was kind of too good to be true. I had to see for myself."

"Mom"? Told her "all about it"?

And then I knew. Just as she leaned close and spoke into my ear, I knew.

It was my evil stepsister. Parker.

It wasn't until I realized who she was that I noticed her signature perfume as well. She always wears—and I swear this is true—a perfume by Dior called Poison.

So on the nose.

"Hey, Sis," she whispered, and then she patted me on the butt and strutted away.

And that, right there, settled it. Optimism canceled.

I'd find a dog-sized Pajanket for Peanut and never leave my apartment again.

Seven

WHEN I GOT back home, there was an email waiting for me from the North American Portrait Society, which reminded me I'd forgotten all about it. It had a big long to-do list of action items before the juried show, and another copy of the rules and guidelines, including:

- Portraits must be on 30 inch × 40 inch canvas.
- Portraits must feature only one subject.
- Portraits must be of a live model—no work done from photographs.
- Portraits may be either oil or acrylic, but no mixed media.
- Portraits must be new work—painted within six weeks of the deadline.

Also there was a whole attachment about a component of the evening I'd evidently missed in the original email. Not only was the show a competition that would be judged in real time, it was also a silent auction. Our portraits would be bid on over the course of the evening and sold to the highest bidder—with the proceeds going to fund classes and education.

My first thought was *That sounds nice.*

Eclipsed immediately by *Oh god. What if no one bids on my portrait?*

It was, shall we say, a pretty good reminder to get my ass in gear.

I counted back through my calendar, and I'd frittered away fourteen days since learning I was a finalist. True, I'd had a lot going on. But the North American Portrait Society wouldn't be left waiting. The portrait submissions for finalists were due three days before the actual show, and even though other people had to crate and ship theirs, and I could just Uber mine over to the gallery, I still had just over three weeks left to get this done.

Three weeks.

Not nearly enough time for my *old*, fully functioning fusiform face gyrus—not to mention that I hadn't even started painting. Or even really thought about it.

Time to pull it together. If I was well enough to marry Peanut's veterinarian, I was well enough to paint one portrait.

But . . . *how?*

The portraits I did were classic, traditional ones. One of my art teachers in college had called me "a multicultural twenty-first-century Norman Rockwell." I took all different kinds of subjects and gave them a *Saturday Evening Post* treatment—realistic, simple, easy-to-understand images with lots of warm rosy light and plenty of charm. Those were the style of portraits my mother had painted, too—and, in fact, I'd taught myself to paint by copying her portfolio. That's what I did in high school instead of drinking: stayed in the art studio twenty hours a day and copied my mother's brushstrokes.

I'd say, at this point, you could barely tell my work apart from hers, and that not only made me feel proud—it made me feel like I'd found a way to hold on to her.

But here's the truth about portraits like these: They are all about the face.

Everything in a portrait like that is directing the viewer toward the face—the lines, the angles, the framing, the colors. The face is where the emotions are, and where the story lies, and where the heart of the whole thing happens.

You can't fudge it, is what I mean. You can't put the subject in sunglasses. Or have that person facing away from you or hanging upside down or hiding under a hat. Not if you wanted to be good. Not if you wanted to win ten thousand dollars. You needed a perfectly rendered, so-detailed-it-feels-alive face—front and center.

I'd done it a thousand times. I'd *crushed it* a thousand times.

Faces were my specialty.

But now?

I had no idea what to do.

And I had only three weeks left to figure it out.

AT SOME POINT, in the wake of what Sue called my "facepocalypse," she had kindly agreed to be my live model. I had a better shot with her face, she reasoned, since I knew it so well.

And plus, as ever, she'd be willing to do crazy stuff.

I called her after getting the reminder email, and I said, "We're still on for tomorrow, right?"

"Of course," Sue said.

"Don't flake out, okay? I really need you."

"I never flake out," Sue said.

She sometimes flaked out, to be honest. But who didn't?

Sue worked as an art teacher at a primary school, and the plan was for her to come over after work every day for a week. We'd split some kind of takeout dinner, and her boyfriend Witt swore he didn't mind her "working late."

"You're not really working, though," I said. "Are you?"

"Labor of love," she said, letting us both be right.

I made Sue bring her red polka-dot dress with the ruffle sleeves. If the face was going to be weaker than usual in this portrait, then everything else had to be stronger. I'd need to render the silkiness of those ruffles in a way that made you *feel* them rustling against your own skin. Also, the red needed to be just right—rich and eye-catching without being overwhelming. I'd have Sue sit on the floor and frame the perspective from up above so I could fill as much of it as possible with that gorgeous fabric.

No question: that polka-dot dress had a lot of work to do.

Sue, I should mention, has a stunningly beautiful face. She has perfectly defined lips, an elegant nose, black hair so shiny she could sell shampoo, and monolid eyes with deep brown irises. I'd painted her twenty times, at least, and she was one of my favorite subjects.

In ordinary times, we'd already have this thing locked up.

But now, of course, things were different. Maybe I knew her face so well, I didn't have to see it to paint it? Maybe I'd painted her so many other times, my hands would know what to do by muscle memory?

I closed my eyes and tried to picture Sue's face.

But no luck.

I could see her hair. If I zoomed in, I could remember the bow shape of her mouth. The rich brown of her eyes. But all the pieces put together?

My mind's eye drew a blank.

The old me would have had this thing in the bag. But I kept pushing that thought aside. *Our thoughts create our emotions.* I wasn't going to make this harder on myself—it was hard enough. I wasn't going to freak myself out. I would practice the art of self-encouragement if it killed me.

Sue showed up dutifully every day, like a champ.

After Monday, I had the basic framing. Then Tuesday and Wednesday, I worked on the details and the drape of the fabric. Thursday, I nailed down her arms and hands.

And then suddenly it was Friday. Time to ruin it all with the face.

I dreaded it all day long, staring at the canvas's empty white face hole. By the time Sue arrived, I was ready to quit.

"I don't want to find out for sure that I can't do this, you know?" I said. "I'd rather only *suspect* that I can't do it. Doesn't that sound better?"

"No. That doesn't sound better. Because then you're not painting. And you always get really crabby when you're not painting."

She wasn't wrong.

"Even painting something bad," Sue said, "is better than not painting anything at all."

"Is it?" I asked. Guess we were about to find out.

"Maybe you'll surprise yourself," Sue said. "Maybe portrait painting is another brain system like reading emotions is. Or maybe you're so good at this, you don't even need your face area thingy. Wouldn't that be amazing?"

I nodded.

"Just jump in," she said. "I really suspect that the worst possible choice is to not even try."

I suspected that, too.

And so I tried.

I stood in front of the canvas, looking down at the dear face of my dear friend who I'd known so long, who I'd painted so many times . . . and I saw nothing but unintelligible nonsense.

But I pushed on.

My best strategy was to divide the face circle on the canvas into mathematical sections, and mark, in general, where the eyes and nose and mouth should be, and then focus on one puzzle piece at a time, plugging them in where each one ought to go.

It was a good plan.

But it didn't work.

When I finally finished the pencil sketch, I stepped back and realized that now it, too, looked like puzzle pieces.

I had *just* drawn that picture. But now I couldn't see it.

I asked Sue to check it and see if I was on the right track. She got up all eager, but then slowed way down on the approach.

I couldn't see her expression, but I could definitely read her emotion. And that emotion was "Huh."

"Tell me," I said.

"Do you want me to be honest?"

"No. Yes. I don't know."

"It's a little funky," Sue said at last.

"What does that mean?"

She paused. "It's not photorealism."

"We knew that already. What are you saying?"

"It's a little bit like a Salvador Dalí painting."

"Oh my god, is your face *melting*? Like a Dalí clock?"

"No . . . the pieces are all technically kind of in the right place. Ish. It's not surrealism, exactly. It's just . . ."

"How bad is it that you can't even find the words?"

"It's a little ghoulish."

"Ghoulish!" I had my answer. "Ghoulish is super bad. Ghoulish is a catastrophe."

But she came over and hugged me.

"It's certainly eye-catching," she said, trying to accentuate the positive. "Nobody's going to be bored looking at this thing."

But eye-catching wasn't going to cut it. *Not bored* wasn't what the judges wanted. And don't get me started on ghoulish. This was a puppies-and-kittens type of organization.

These North American Portrait Society folks were about following the rules—not breaking them.

I stared at the painting and tried to see what Sue was talking about—or any face at all. But I just couldn't. I squinted and concentrated and tried to make the pieces click for so long that frustration finally burst up out of my body like a geyser. I slammed my fist down on the paint table, accidentally hitting a book . . . that hit a glass jar of brushes . . . that went flying and shattered on the concrete floor.

"Shit," I said, deflating.

I moved to start picking up the shards, but Sue stopped me. "Go sit down. I'll get this. Take some breaths."

I did as I was told.

Sue found a broom and a pan. "What about Chuck Close?" she suggested. "He was a portrait artist with face blindness. How did he do it?"

I'd been reading up on him. He was a face-blind artist who painted enormous photorealistic faces. But I shook my head. "He superimposed a grid over a photograph. But for this competition, it has to be a live model. No photos allowed. It's in the rules."

"What do other face-blind portrait artists do?"

"Shockingly, a search of 'techniques of face-blind portrait artists' does not turn up a huge number of results."

"You've tried it?"

"Many times."

"Well, then," Sue said, frowning again at the painting. "We'll just have to get creative."

I ASKED DR. Nicole about it when we had our first meeting outside the hospital.

I'd been supposed to start twice-a-week sessions with her the day after I came home. But in my Pajanket stupor, I'd missed that first appointment. And then the next two. And I was seriously considering just never going at all when she started calling me—stalking me, really—until I finally gave in.

I Ubered to her office.

Which wasn't an office at all. It was a 1920s bungalow in the Museum District.

It's not a stretch to say that I fan-girled Dr. Nicole with the same intensity that I was now madly in love with Peanut's new veterinarian. This whole brain surgery thing seemed to have really turned up the volume on my emotions.

In the hospital, she had seemed to glow with comfort and compassion. Now, here in the real world, as she opened the door in a belted maxi dress, dangly gold earrings, and open-toed flats . . . she was even better. Her short, naturally graying hair seemed to ring her head like a halo.

"Hello, Sadie," she said, taking my hand and giving it her signature squeeze. "Come in."

What was it about her? She was so damned *together.* Her voice. Her calm. So balanced and solid and like she had it all under control.

The opposite of me, basically.

Especially now.

"I'm sorry I missed all those appointments," I said, now that I was finally here. "I didn't want to leave my apartment."

"I understand," Dr. Nicole said.

I'm not going to lie. My life lately had me questioning everything. And Dr. Nicole Thomas-Ramparsad, Ph.D., just felt like a person who had all the answers.

"Nobody has all the answers," she said when I told her that. "I'm just here to help you ask the right questions."

Exactly what someone who had all the answers would say.

Her office was bright and breezy. It had a little bit of an Old Hollywood vibe to it, with plaster walls and a wrought-iron staircase rail. Big windows. A lazily spinning ceiling fan with basket-weave blades. Potted palms and rubber trees all around—and, outside the window, positively basking in the sunlight, a cheery forest of birds-of-paradise everywhere.

Dr. Nicole made us tea and brought me a slice of coconut bread—warm with melting butter. Did neuropsychologists bake bread for their patients? Was this a thing?

No matter. Dr. Nicole clearly made her own rules.

Plus, I was so starved for comfort, I didn't care. My eyes filled with tears at my first bite.

"How is the facial perception?" she asked. "Any changes?"

I shook my head. No change at all.

"It may take some time," she said. Then, "How are you coping?"

"I don't think I'm going to win any coping trophies anytime soon," I said.

I told her about feeling like I was on an alien planet. I told her about not feeling like myself. I told her about being so terrified of not recognizing people—and then running into Parker. I told her that I wanted to be the kind of person who could think of prosopagnosia as a superpower—but I just didn't know how to get there.

"Well," she said, "getting there is the fun part."

From anyone else, that would've been insulting.

I told her about trying to paint Sue's portrait, and what a total disaster it had been, and how the thought that I'd worked so hard for so long only to finally get my big break and then *totally blow it* was keeping me up at night.

"Why do you want to win the competition so badly?" Dr. Nicole asked.

"Because it's ten thousand dollars—and I'm broke."

She nodded, like, *Fair enough.* "Any other reasons?"

"Because it could change my life," I said.

Dr. Nicole waited, like she knew there'd be more.

"Because I could use some encouragement," I said. "Because I'm ready to get something right. Because I'm just so tired of failing."

That felt like a pretty big confession, right there.

But Dr. Nicole just waited, like there was more.

"I guess I should mention," I said then, "that my mother was also a portrait artist. And she also placed in this same competition thirteen years ago. But she, um . . ." I took a sip of tea. "She died suddenly the week before the show."

Dr. Nicole sat back in her chair.

Now, at last, I'd said something real.

"We should probably talk about that."

I wrinkled my nose and shook my head.

Dr. Nicole gave a little have-it-your-way shrug. "What's your dream?" she asked then. "What do you want from your career?"

"My dream?" I asked. This felt like a trick question.

"What does the life you want look like?"

I shrugged. "I'd like to be successful." It felt weird to say that out loud, in a way. Like I was being greedy. But what on earth had I been hustling for all these years if not to be successful? Did anyone ever try like hell for years to *not* be successful? "I'd like to make a living. A good living. Maybe some job stability. And to just wake up every day and paint. I don't need to take over the world. I don't need diamonds and yachts and furs. But I'd like to get my car back. Or—okay, maybe a better car. I don't want to want too much. I think I could be satisfied with just, like, a functioning car and enough money to pay my bills."

Dr. Nicole waited, like I wasn't trying hard enough.

I went on. "But if you're asking what I *want*? Deep down, what I *long for*? I want my paintings to sell like hotcakes. I want to be admired by my peers. I want to really, truly be okay, and not just pretending. I want to be kicking ass. I want to be *thriving*. I want to prove that I was awesome all along."

"Prove that to whom?"

Whoa. This lady could use *whom* in conversation. And make it sound right. She was literally the coolest. But I didn't know how to answer that question. "I don't know. People."

"Which people?"

But I just shrugged.

Dr. Nicole changed her approach. "What would you get if you were successful?"

"What would I get?"

Dr. Nicole nodded. "Emotionally."

Ah. Emotionally. Suddenly I knew what she was asking. "You know," I said, "I don't really think that we need to do a whole lot of deep emotions in here. I'm really just here for the neuropsychology tips. You know? To snag a few coping techniques. I don't need to, like, delve into my dark past or anything."

She looked at me—and, again, I could feel this without seeing it— very kindly said, "You know it's all the same, right?"

"What is?"

"Emotions. Coping tips. Your dark past."

Ugh.

"You're very in your head," she said. "I'd like to see you dip into your heart."

"I like it in my head."

"But that's not really where we live."

"Are you trying to tell me I'm emotionally closed off?" I said. "Because I have lots of emotions. I'm great at emotions! I'm a huge fan of you, for example. I just fell madly in love with my brand-new veterinarian. I cry at *life insurance* commercials."

"Real emotions, I mean."

"Are you telling me that *love* isn't real?"

But Dr. Nicole pulled rank on me then. Pausing a good while before saying, "Is that a question designed to get us closer to the truth or to steer us away?"

God, she was good.

"The thing is," I said, "I don't talk about it. My dark past. Not even with my dog."

"We don't need to talk about it," she said. Then she added, "today."

Then she shifted topics. "What are your strategies for interacting with people?"

"I'm just going to hide in my apartment until the edema goes down."

"Why don't you want to see people?"

"It stresses me out. I'm embarrassed."

"Embarrassed that you can't recognize them?"

"Yes." Embarrassed I couldn't recognize them. Embarrassed I couldn't *see* them. Afraid of hurting their feelings or snubbing them by accident or seeming like a bitch. Humiliated to not be myself. Disappointed to no longer be a brain surgery poster child. Mortified, ultimately, to not be so *not okay* that I couldn't even hide it.

"What if you just told people?"

That question didn't even make any sense. "Told people what?"

"About what you're dealing with right now. About what you're going through."

"What? Like, wear a T-shirt that says, 'I can't see you'?"

"That's one option, I guess."

"Never," I said.

"*Never?*"

"I will never tell anyone about this face thing. Not voluntarily."

Dr. Nicole leaned forward like that was the most interesting thing I'd said all day. "Why not?"

"Because that's need-to-know information."

"It might help you feel more comfortable."

"The whole world doesn't need to know that I'm malfunctioning," I said, like that settled it. But Dr. Nicole didn't seem satisfied. So I added, "I just want to be my normal self."

"But you aren't your normal self right now." She mercifully did not add, *And might never be again.*

"I'm just going to take a fake-it-til-ya-make-it approach." That's what I'd been doing my whole life. "If I can't be okay, I'll seem okay."

"Seeming okay and being okay are not the same thing."

"Close enough."

"In fact," she said, leaning in a little, "they might cancel each other out."

"Are you saying I should just walk around wailing and weeping?"

"I'm saying," she said, "that it's better to be real than fake."

I could have argued with her. But I had a feeling I'd lose.

Dr. Nicole went on. "It might help people to know what's going on with you. It might help them help you."

"Have you *met* people?" I asked. "People don't help other people."

Dr. Nicole let that land for a second. Then she said, "I can think of a few teachers, firefighters, nurses, loving parents, and Good Samaritans who might disagree with you."

The Good Samaritan.

And just as I remembered him, Dr. Nicole said, "Didn't someone save your life recently?"

Ugh. So this was *gotcha* therapy. "Yes."

"Was that not 'helping other people'?"

"That was an emergency," I said.

"Ah," she said. But it was sarcastic.

I took a bite of coconut bread and contemplated that.

Then a thought lit up my head like sunlight breaking through clouds. "Dr. Nicole?" I asked, trying not to sound suspicious. "When you were arguing with me just now, were you . . . teaching me how to argue with myself?"

And then I could see her teeth—but also feel her big smile—as she said, "You're smarter than you look, choonks."

Eight

WHAT WERE MY coping strategies?

A full list on that was yet to be googled, but for now, I decided on the ride home from Dr. Nicole's bungalow, coping strategy number one would be art.

I mean, objectively, I had a giant deadline. So I needed to be doing art, anyway. And the truest thing I knew about myself was this: I was always happy when I was making things.

I grabbed my favorite, most bright and delightful box of watercolors . . . but then, instead of just doing something fun, I started working. On faces. Instead of just picking something, anything, colorful and pleasant to paint—a fruit basket, say, or some flowers—I bore down on myself like some kind of ruler-toting schoolmarm. Hell-bent on forcing my fusiform face gyrus into submission, I spent an entire Saturday painting face after face after face like a madwoman chasing her own puzzle-piece-shaped shadow.

How did it go?

I'm guessing not well.

But of course once they were done, I couldn't see them.

Fine. Didn't matter. Maybe if I did enough of them, things would start to shift.

Or not.

Either way, it was something to do.

So what if the grim determination of my attitude sucked the joy out of it all?

I had less than three weeks to fix my FFG.

By the end of the night, when my fingers were stained turquoise and plum and tangerine, and my eyes felt like sandpaper, I had a stack of scribbled, unintelligible faces a foot high and a whole table of others laid out to dry.

My plan was to get up the next day and do it again.

But then, the next morning, Peanut got sick.

THANK GOD THIS face-blindness thing applied only to humans.

Peanut's big, brown, perfectly round, saturated-with-affection puppy eyes had been like a balm for my weary soul. After I'd brought him home from being boarded, it was the two of us against the world. I looked at that little mug of his a hundred times a day—positively savoring his jaunty yellow mustache and that perky button nose and those ears that never could seem to both flop forward at the same time.

"*You're* not faceless, Peanut," I'd tell him, pressing my nose into his fur.

If there were a dog hall of fame, Peanut would be on all their merchandise. He was cute as hell without being full of himself. He was endlessly cheery. He was a good eater without being a glutton. He was just as happy to go on a walk as he was to spend the entire day napping. He loved a good squeaky toy, but he lost interest at exactly the same rate I did. He loved me madly—leaping in circles whenever I came back home from anywhere—but without taking it too far. Without, say, suffering from separation anxiety and eating my shoes. His self-esteem was solid. His fashion sense was legendary. His sense of humor was totally deadpan.

I preferred him to most people even in normal times, is what I'm saying.

But of course, even more so now, when "most people" were the last thing on earth I wanted to see.

And so when I woke up way too early on Sunday morning and set out his favorite breakfast dish—torn pieces of croissant from his favorite French bakery—but he sat still and stared at me . . . my heart dropped in my chest.

I just knew, you know? I sensed in an instant something was wrong.

I tried coaxing him over, holding up a piece and taking a nibble myself, hoping he'd come take it. (He didn't.) I tried picking him up and setting him in front of the dish, like that might inspire him to dive in. (It didn't.) I tried giving the dish ten seconds in the microwave, like that might make it seem fresh-baked and more appealing. (Kind of the opposite.)

But nothing.

All Peanut wanted to do was hold himself still like a statue.

I squeaked his squeaky squirrel, but he just stared at me, like, *Really?* I tossed it across the room and ran after it like we were racing, but he just blinked at me, like, *Please.* And when I finally picked up his leash and jangled it at him and watched him *fully not respond*, that's when I called the vet.

The new vet—because it was closest. They weren't even open yet, but I told the answering service it was an emergency.

They said they'd page one of the vets to meet me at the clinic.

And here's how worried about Peanut I was: I didn't even think to request Dr. Addison.

IT WAS A small clinic, not some big 24-hour place. But they did have weekend hours.

They were open only from eight to noon on Sundays, but I wrapped Peanut up in his favorite velour blanket, cradled him in my arms, power walked the entire two blocks over because I still wasn't allowed to run for skull-related reasons, and was sitting on the bench by the clinic doors at 7:45.

My heart was wheezing. I don't even think it was pumping blood at that point—just straight adrenaline and a dark feeling of dread that Peanut was dying.

Which was unacceptable. Even though he was fourteen years old.

This was no joke. I'd done a pretty impressive set of mathematical calculations involving the life spans of all the different dog breeds he was a mix of, and by every analysis, I was guaranteed at least two more years.

Some dogs in his general category made it to eighteen, even.

That's all I could think as I sat on the bench with tears positively shellacking my face. I was not letting this dog die. I was not losing the only person who loved me. Not today. Any treatment. *Anything.* I'd call Lucinda if I had to. I'd beg my dad. No bill was too high. No humiliation was too great.

A few minutes later, Dr. Oliver Addison himself showed up, and I heard his leather dress shoes tapping the pavement of the parking lot before I saw the man himself.

When I looked up, I swear he was walking in slo-mo like a superhero. That's how I remember it: backlit with a lens flare, the good doctor already wearing his white lab coat, which was unbuttoned and flapping behind him, cape-like, in the wind. This was no casual-Sunday ensemble: the man was bringing his professional A game, wearing a tie, suit slacks, and that epic, slicked-back Clark Kent hair.

And let's not forget his gait: that confident, badass, I'm-going-to-save-your-pooch stride.

How had I never noticed *gaits* before?

They were practically a love language all to themselves.

In another situation, I would have melted at the sight—dripped through the bench slats and puddled on the sidewalk.

But I stayed focused. For Peanut.

I stood up as Dr. Addison got closer, totally unaware that I was rocking the opposite of his *GQ* cover shoot vibe: I was still in the cotton calico baby-doll pajamas I'd slept in. And I should've popped on my sneakers as I headed out the door, but I somehow traveled two blocks to the vet clinic in my fuzzy slippers shaped like bunny rabbits, instead.

But the mortification of that would hit me later. Right now, there were only two things in the world: the little fuzzball dog burrito in my arms and the man who needed to save him.

Dr. Addison slowed as he got close, taking in the sight of us.

"There's something wrong," I said, my voice trembly from crying. "He won't eat. He won't move." And now, we both noticed, he was panting.

Dr. Addison nodded like an unflappable hero and said, "Let's get him inside."

He led us straight past all the exam rooms, back to the back, where the real veterinary medicine took place. All the boarded dogs in their kennels woke up as we came in and started barking and whining and rattling around.

Dr. Addison didn't even notice.

When we got to an exam table, he said, "Remind me of his age?"

"Fourteen," I said—then added, "A very youthful fourteen," like that might matter.

Dr. Addison reached for Peanut, and I handed him over like a swaddled babe. Then he unwrapped him, saying, "Hey, buddy. Let's get a look at you."

Peanut must have really been feeling bad, because even though he didn't like men in general, he tolerated Dr. Addison—holding still and crouching on the stainless-steel exam table.

Dr. Addison ran his hands all around, feeling for lumps and bumps. Palpating things. Checking his gums, which were, apparently, too white.

"That's bad?" I asked.

"They should be pinker," Dr. Addison answered, but he was already on to checking other things.

When the rest of the staff arrived, they gently led me back out to the waiting area, saying they could work faster that way. The faceless tech I'd met the first day said they'd be running blood work and chemistries, checking red and white cells and platelets and kidney and liver function. "We'll know a lot more in a few hours," she said. "You can go home. We'll call you when we get the results."

"I'll stay here, if that's all right."

The faceless tech nodded. "Sure." Then she held out a folded lab coat to me. "Dr. Addison said you might say that. And he thought you might be . . . cold."

And so I put it on and stayed. I think I was hungry, but I didn't notice. I hadn't had any coffee that morning, and I did notice the caffeine headache creeping up the back of my neck. I didn't have anything to do—hadn't even brought my phone—so I just squeezed over and over on that little spot between your thumb and forefinger that's supposed to be a pressure point for relieving tension. Pressing on one hand, then the other . . . waiting for it to work.

It didn't really work.

I kept expecting—any minute—for Dr. Addison to come striding out like a TV doctor and tell me that everything was fixed.

Instead, at noon, he came out and told me they wanted to give Peanut a blood transfusion.

That didn't sound good.

I worked my pressure points even harder.

"The labs came back," he said, "and we've diagnosed him with IMHA, which stands for immune-mediated hemolytic anemia."

Oh god. More medical terms. I shook my head. "What is that?"

"His immune system is attacking his own red blood cells. His hematocrit was at twelve when it should be closer to fifty. That's why he's panting. He can't get enough oxygen."

All I could ask was, "Why is this happening?"

It was probably more of a rhetorical, big-picture, why-is-my-whole-life-falling-apart-all-at-once question than a medical one. But Dr. Addison answered it anyway, all earnest: "We don't know what causes it," he said. "It's idiopathic. All of a sudden, the immune system just goes haywire and starts attacking itself."

"Is it curable?" I asked.

"It's life-threatening," he said, "but it can be cured. The survival rate is thirty to seventy percent."

Thirty to seventy percent? What a useless piece of information. "I really was hoping for just a flat yes."

"We're going to give him everything we've got," Dr. Addison promised. "He looks like a fighter."

At that, I felt tears flooding up in my chest. "The thing is . . ." I said then, trying to push my voice to sound normal through the tightness in my throat. "The thing is . . . I can't lose him. Do you know what I mean? I *can't*."

Dr. Addison nodded, and I could sense a new tenderness about him. "The blood transfusion should help a lot," he said next. "Give him the energy he needs to fight."

I nodded, my face wet again. "I know everybody thinks their dog is the best dog, but the thing is my dog really is actually, literally, the best." What was I saying?

"Later today," Dr. Addison went on, staying focused, "we'll want to get him eating. Can you tell me his favorite foods?"

I sat up straighter and pawed at my eyes, determined to pull it together. "Yes. He loves tortillas, doughnuts, and rigatoni Bolognese. He's a big fan of saag paneer. He goes crazy for California rolls. He also loves crepes—but only like the kind you get in Paris. If they're too pancakey, that's a no."

Dr. Addison tilted his head. "I was thinking more like . . . dog food."

"He's not really a dog food guy," I said.

"Your dog doesn't eat dog food?"

"I mean, it'll do in a pinch. But if you're asking me what he likes . . ."

"All those carbs can't be healthy for him."

I'd heard this before, and I'd defended my little guy before, too.

"He's a foodie," I said. "He has a very refined palate."

Dr. Addison took that in.

And then a little joke I'd made many times popped into my head, and I just said it now without really stopping to wonder if, in our current situation, it was still true: "You know those old guys who smoke a pack a day but live to be a hundred?"

"Yeah?"

"He's kind of like that, but with croissants."

I WANTED TO just stay in the waiting room of the vet clinic all day and all night, forever—but hunger and exhaustion forced me, not long before dinnertime, to leave Peanut in Dr. Addison's sexy but capable hands and go home.

I also wanted to take that lab coat with me, but I left it—walking home instead in my baby-doll pj's and bunny slippers, feeling extra naked and alone, and fully expecting to run into some humiliating stranger. A former boss. A premed professor. My dad.

But the person I ran into was Mr. Kim.

I knew him, of course, because he always wore dress shoes, suit pants, a button-down Oxford shirt, and suspenders. He'd been dressing like that Sue's entire life. No matter what he was doing.

And I was so glad it was him, of all people. He'd seen Sue and me— lots of times—in much crazier getups than bunny slippers.

This evening, he was tinkering with the mechanics of the elevator doors, but when he saw me, he abandoned that project. "Come see me," he said, gesturing me toward him.

"What about the elevator?" I asked.

But he waved me off. "We've got stairs."

He led me around to a quiet corner, and then he cut right to the chase. "I hear that you're not just using the rooftop as a studio—you're living there."

Mr. Kim smiled a lot. Maybe he wasn't always smiling—but he was often smiling.

But I couldn't sense him smiling now.

My heart dropped. Was I getting kicked out?

Was I really—right here, in my pj's and bunny slippers, with Peanut in the ICU, at the brokest and sickest and most disoriented I'd ever been in my life—getting kicked out of my apartment by the closest thing to a father figure I had?

His voice was pretty serious. "That won't work," he said, shaking his head with a vibe like he was truly sorry.

I nodded. *Of course.* I never should have snuck around behind the Kims' back to begin with.

"It's not an apartment," he said next. "Renting it as a studio is one thing. But it's not fit to live in. I really"—and here he shook his head—"can't rent that place as living quarters."

I nodded harder. "I get it. You're right. I'm so sorry."

Oh god, I was so screwed.

But then Mr. Kim let out a chuckle that he couldn't suppress any longer. "So I guess," he said, clapping his hand on my shoulder, "you'll just have to stay there for free."

Nine

SUE WAS SUPPOSED to come over the next day for week two of our doomed portrait sessions. But I called her when I got back from the clinic and postponed.

"I'm not in a good place," I told her after giving the lowdown on Peanut.

"But painting makes you feel better."

"Not anymore."

"I refuse to believe that."

"I painted a hundred faces the other night, and it was pure torture."

Sue took that in. "Okay. If that's how it is right now."

"That's how it is right now."

"Take some *you* time, then. Binge-watch something."

"I can't watch TV anymore," I said.

Sue was aghast. "Why not?"

"Because of the face blindness."

"I keep forgetting about that."

"I can't tell the characters apart."

"Wow," Sue said, "what a nightmare."

"It's been a nightmare this whole time!"

"But now I really get it."

"*That's* what made you get it?"

"That," Sue conceded, "and those images you texted me of upside-down faces. I, like, couldn't recognize *any* of those people. Not one. And then you sent the right-side-up version, and I was like, 'Oh! There's Michelle Obama! And Julie Andrews! And Liam Hemsworth!'"

"Are you telling me," I said, "that if Liam Hemsworth walked past you with his face upside down, you wouldn't even know?"

"I'd have no idea."

"Welcome to my life. I pass a hundred Liam Hemsworths a day."

Sue sighed like she was really getting it. Then she said, "It's his loss, though. Never forget that."

SO THAT'S HOW I spent my me time for the next few days: trying to shrink the edema in my fusiform face gyrus through sheer force of will and delivering meals of international delicacies to my beloved dog several times a day as he fought for his life in the ICU.

I confess that, after that first day, I always got a little gussied up before heading to the vet clinic. "It's for Peanut," I told Sue on the phone. "He wouldn't want to see me looking dowdy."

But, in truth, I had to redeem those baby-doll pajamas.

In general, I made it a rule to never *not be okay* in front of anyone. Especially not future husbands. All I could do was hope that Dr. Addison had been far too fixated on Peanut that first morning to really notice the falling-apart me.

I mean, he probably hadn't missed the copious sobbing. But maybe he saw that all the time anyway.

The point was, some things couldn't be helped. But from now on, I would not burst into any more tears at that clinic. I would show up looking a hundred percent "Fine, thank you, and yourself?" As a point of pride.

Which was the only saving grace on the evening of Peanut's third overnight stay there, when the pad Thai I'd ordered from his favorite spot got held up in traffic during delivery—and, desperately trying to move fast when I was still forbidden to run, I race-walked the two blocks in a ridiculous pair of heels—only to arrive just as Dr. Addison was locking up.

I knew it was him with certainty. Because all the other vets in the practice were female.

Also because of his godlike glow.

"I'm so sorry," I said, out of breath. "The delivery was late."

I held up the takeout bag.

"Is that for Peanut?"

I nodded. "Pad Thai."

Dr. Addison sighed at me then, like I was a real lunatic. But at least I was wearing my favorite sundress. And I'd taught myself how to do a crown braid around my head that perfectly hid my surgical scars. And I'd gone to the trouble of finding my raspberry lipstick after it rolled under the bed.

With a headshake like he couldn't believe he was an accomplice to the moral atrocity of feeding noodles to a sick dog, he unlocked the door.

"He needs meat," he said, stepping over the threshold.

I followed, and we were once again surrounded by pop oldies on the sound system.

"This is *chicken* pad Thai," I said, raising my voice a bit.

"Can't you get him hooked on barbecue or something? This is Texas."

"He likes barbecue," I said. "He just likes pad Thai better."

Three nights in, Peanut was doing much better. He'd had his second transfusion by now, and he'd soon be getting a third. That plus the IV fluids and the appetite stimulants had him looking much more like his usual self.

All to say, tonight Peanut greeted me with a full-body wag for the first time since this all started.

Which made me tear up. Again.

But I blinked the tears away. *No more crying at the vet clinic.*

"Looks like he's feeling better," Dr. Addison said.

"Definitely."

"Soon, I think, he'll be strong enough to start his meds."

"What are they?" I asked.

"Prednisone, cyclosporine, and azathioprine," Dr. Addison said, before realizing maybe that was overly specific and backing up a bit to explain: "Steroids and immune suppressors."

"Got it," I said.

"I'm hopeful about him," Dr. Addison said then.

"Thank you," I said, taking a second to press my face against Peanut's fur. "Thank you for being hopeful."

I was trying to move fast, but Dr. Addison, watching me, said, "Take a minute. It's okay."

"Aren't you trying to lock up? I don't want to keep you from— whatever you've got going on."

"I don't have anything going on," he said. "I'm glad to stay." Then he added, "He'll eat more if you're not rushing."

Next I got down on the floor, crisscrossed my legs, cradled Peanut in my lap, and started feeding long, floppy pinches of pad Thai noodles to him by hand.

I thought Dr. Addison would give us a minute then, maybe go back to his office and do—I don't know . . . doctorly things? What did medical professionals do when no one was looking? *Examine charts? Study textbooks? Wear glasses and look important?*

Of course, Dr. Addison didn't wear glasses.

But I'm sure he wouldn't let that hold him back.

Anyway, he didn't go off to be doctorly. He lingered there. Watching Peanut devour that entire Styrofoam box of pad Thai, slurp by slurp, like a champion.

"He really does like pad Thai."

"I'm telling you. He's a very worldly dog. Gastronomically."

"I believe you."

I wanted to think I could take the chowing-down as encouragement that Peanut must be doing better. But I couldn't discount the appetite stimulant.

"This is a good sign, right?" I asked as Peanut licked the empty container.

"It's not a bad sign," Dr. Addison said.

"I'm so glad he's doing better."

A little pause and then Dr. Addison said, "Are *you* doing better?"

I looked up. Bless that man—he'd just given me the perfect opportunity to say it: "I'm great," I said, with all the convincing, perky, don't-even-know-why-you're-asking energy I could muster. Mentally I added: *I am not falling apart. I am not standing slack-jawed and helpless at the sight of my life collapsing like a sheet of the polar ice caps. I am absolutely, undeniably, categorically okay.*

"Good," Dr. Addison said, seeming unconvinced. Then he added, "Great."

Fine. All right. Maybe my two-word statement wouldn't be enough. "We're just . . . very close," I added then. I mean, even perfectly fine people could get weepy if their dogs were on the brink of death! That wasn't evidence of emotional pathology, was it?

"You and Peanut?" Dr. Addison asked.

I nodded. "Practically litter mates. My mom gave him to me when I was a kid." Were you still a kid at fourteen? Close enough.

Dr. Addison nodded. "They really curl up in your heart, don't they?"

That seemed like a very true way of putting it.

"Do you have any pets?" I asked then.

Dr. Addison shifted. "I'm between pets at the moment."

"I guess you see enough animals at work."

"That's one way to spin it."

There was a story there, for sure.

But it was getting late. "I'm sure you need to get home," I said.

He thought about it. "I'm off to check on another patient after this, anyway. A Great Dane. She's too sick to stay overnight here unsupervised, so she's at a twenty-four-hour clinic."

"I should let you get to that," I said, giving Peanut one more squeeze.

Dr. Addison watched me clean up and then put my nose right in front of Peanut's for one last nourishing drink of the sight of his little fuzzy face. "You be good for these guys, got it?" I said to Peanut. "If they tell you to get well, you get well."

Peanut licked me on the cheek in reply with his flappy pink tongue.

I put him back in the kennel, tucked him in with his squeaky squirrel, fought back any and all not-okay feelings, and latched the latch. I was fine. I was great. I was not a person who could be toppled by a run-of-the-mill goodbye.

When I turned around, Dr. Addison was waiting to walk me back to the front.

"Thanks again so much," I said, smiling like a just-fine person.

"I have a question for you," Dr. Addison said once we were outside.

"What's that?" I asked.

He finished turning the lock and turned to face me. "Would you like to go on a date with me sometime?"

Ten

WELL, THAT WAS sudden.

In the way that something that *should've already happened* can also be sudden.

I mean, sure—I'd already decided that we were fated to wind up together. But even for fate, this was pretty fast.

"*Can* you date patients?" I asked, in lieu of shouting *Yes! Let's get married!*

"I mean, I can't date *Peanut*," he said. "But you're not a patient."

Ah. "Good point."

"What do you think?" he asked.

What did I think? Hello! I was ready to plan the honeymoon.

That said . . . I hesitated.

It was one thing to charge boldly forth toward my happily ever after with my dashing veterinarian *in theory*. It was a whole other thing to make an attempt like that in reality.

In my current reality, especially.

I mean, come on. I was a mess. I had surgical scars in my hair. I was bursting into tears at random intervals for no reason. The whole world was a faceless blur. And every single thing that mattered in my life was disintegrating around me. Would this storybook perfect man want to date—or be anywhere near—a total disaster like that?

Definitely not.

I mean, *I* didn't even want to hang out with me these days.

So how on earth could I expect this dreamy, perfect, animal-rescuing man to be any different? Was I, in this moment, in *any way* someone who would be attractive or appealing or *fun to date*?

No. No, this would never work.

Could I have just been honest with him? Could I have just told him what was going on? He was a scientist, after all. He might have found it medically fascinating. I'm sure he saw weird, crazy stuff all the time in his line of work.

But . . . he didn't *date* that weird, crazy stuff.

Dr. Addison shifted his weight.

My answer was taking too long.

So I gave the best reply I could think of: "I would *love* to go on a date with you," I told him. And then I added, "In three weeks."

I felt his frown. "In three weeks?"

I nodded like this was a totally reasonable request. "I am a portrait artist," I told him, cherry-picking selective facts about my life to not blow my cover. "And I'm a top-ten finalist in a hugely prestigious juried portrait show three weeks from now—and so I'm really directing all my time and energy into completing my submission."

How did that sound?

Dr. Addison gave me my answer. "You're a finalist in a big competition?"

I nodded, like, *Yep.* "Top ten out of two thousand entries."

"That means you beat out one thousand nine hundred and ninety other people."

Told ya he was perfect. "That's exactly what my best friend said."

"Nice," he said, and I could feel him admiring me.

"But now I have to win," I said. "So I just can't have any distractions right now."

Dr. Addison nodded like that made perfect, logical sense.

I thought I was in the clear.

But then he said, "Of course if we just happened to run into each other at the same time in a coffee shop, that wouldn't be a date. That would just be both of us self-caffeinating in close proximity."

Ah. He wasn't going to make this easy.

When I hesitated, he added, "Only if you want to, of course."

Was it a test? To gauge if I wanted to?

I wasn't waiting to find out. "I want to," I said.

I could feel a smile take over his face.

So I added, "You have to caffeinate, right?"

And there it was. If I had to go on a coffee date with the world's dreamiest veterinarian, then I guess I just had to.

ONCE I'D GIVEN in, I planned our wedding the whole way home.

We had an appointment for simultaneous coffee now. And, somehow, not calling it a date made it feel even more like a date. Did that mean we were dating?

Pretty damn close! Right?

And, of course, once you started dating someone, you inevitably got married.

So we were essentially engaged.

Where to have the wedding? Maybe on the coastal rocks of Maine, near a lighthouse? Or on the gentle sand of a Hawaiian beach? Or—hell, as long as I was fantasizing—in some quaint, timeless English village? I'd have to google timeless English villages. Maybe the Cotswolds?

This was perfect, right? This was perfect.

I'd get this face thing solved, get Peanut healthy, win this competition, disprove everybody who ever thought I was worthless—and then go on a date *with Dr. Oliver Frigging Addison.* And start living the victorious life I'd always wanted.

That worked.

I was feeling so foolishly optimistic for a minute there as I basked in that fantasy that I decided to stop by Bean Street Coffee to grab a decaf latte on my way to the elevators. Life was good today. Good enough for a celebratory latte.

Hazel One was working there tonight. This was how hip Bean Street Coffee was: it had two different baristas named Hazel.

I ordered my latte and then waited by the pickup counter, as fully afloat as if these wedding fantasies were an emotional inner tube.

But that's when I heard, "Sadie Montgomery?"

This—being recognized—had happened a few times since I'd been tricked by my evil stepsister, and I'd say, all in all, I managed okay. The big goal was always to suss out who was talking to me, but I was also happy to settle for just having a pleasant interaction and not getting caught.

"Hey there!" I answered, more confident with my strategy now. *There are no strangers.* "How are you?"

"Great! How are you?"

Clues: Blond hair in a ponytail. Tall-ish. Blue jeans. Jangly brace-let. Also: This person knew my first and last name. Her tone of voice sounded as if she was glad to see me. She was in the coffee shop of my building at this hour of night, and she was holding—get this—a hairless Sphynx cat with a rhinestone collar. I mean, could she do that? Were cats even allowed in coffee shops? Was she a neighbor? Did I know her from the elevator? The last-name thing was a confounding variable, be-cause, again, I really didn't know anybody in this building well enough to have handed out my last name.

Damn it. Who could it be?

"Love your sundress," she said then. "It reminds me of one you had in high school."

We knew each other from *high school*? I didn't keep in touch with anyone from high school.

"Wasn't it yellow?" she said then, thinking back. "You wore it to the ninth-grade picnic?"

Okay, now this was getting creepy.

"And then I'm pretty sure you stole it from me after you got kicked out and sent to boarding school."

Fuck.

It was Parker.

How, how, *how* had I not recognized her voice—again? Dr. Nicole had said not everybody was great with voices, that it might take some time to tune into them better . . . but *Parker*? I should know that voice anywhere.

It was the voice of doom.

And, yes. I *had* stolen that yellow sundress from her.

But she'd stolen my entire family from me, so we were hardly even.

"Are you kidding me right now?" I said.

"What?" Parker said, putting on a baffled, innocent voice.

"Why are you messing with me—and why are you even here?"

"I'm messing with you because it is *never not fun*, and I'm here because: Hello! I just moved in."

That didn't compute. "Moved in to what?"

"The building."

"The building? *This* building?" I demanded, pointing at the floor. Then I pointed at myself. "My building?"

"Top floor, baby!" She lifted her hand for a high five.

I ignored the hand. "You can't move in here."

"Pretty sure I just did. A cute guy helped me carry my scratching post."

"This is *my* apartment building. *I* live here."

"It's not *only* your apartment building," she said. "Lots of people live here. Including me. As of today." Then she waved her still-raised hand in my face. "You can see this, can't you? I'm high-fiving you!"

I smacked her hand out of the way. "I'm not fucking high-fiving you, Parker. Get out. You're not welcome here."

"I think the guy who carried my scratching post might disagree. I got a definite vibe."

Of all the pets I'd have picked for Parker, I wouldn't have chosen a cat. A tarantula, maybe. A tank of piranhas. A hive of wasps.

Just then, Hazel One called my name. My latte was ready.

"Did you come here on purpose?" I demanded.

Now Parker dropped her voice a little. "Do you think I'm hunting you down or something?"

"What else could possibly be happening?"

"Wait," she said then, her voice starting to ooze with delight. "Am I sensing that you still haven't moved on from high school?"

Were we talking about this? I guess we were talking about this.

"That's a hell of a question from you," I said. When she didn't stop me, I kept going. "A hell of a question from the person who framed me for stealing Madame Stein's French exam. The person who started the rumor that I slept with Kacy's boyfriend. The person who started a fire out by the field house and then put a can of lighter fluid in my locker. And let's not forget the person who bullied Augusta Ross to the brink of suicide and then pinned it all on me."

She wrinkled her nose in faux sympathy. "Not over it, then."

"Of course not," I said. "You methodically and viciously dismantled my life. Augusta Ross had been my best friend since second grade, but six months after you showed up, her parents were hauling her off to Seattle, never to return. You got me kicked out of school. You turned my own father against me. And all for what—so you could have our bedroom to yourself?"

I thought maybe holding her actions up to her in the mirror might evoke . . . something. Remorse, maybe. Regret?

Instead, Parker just said, "You forgot 'stole your boyfriend.' Which was why I needed the bedroom to myself."

Whoa. She was worse than I remembered.

Parker was loving this, though. She leaned in. "Is it all still haunting you this much? I mean, I knew I won. But I didn't know I won this epic-ally. Sweetie, in two years, we'll be thirty! Let it go."

"Don't call me sweetie" was all I could think of to say.

Remember when Dr. Nicole thought it was so perplexing that I would think that people would want to use your weaknesses against you? That there was some compelling reason to endlessly hide your vulnerabilities from the world?

Well, meet the entire reason I believed that—right here, in the flesh. Holding a cat in a coffee shop.

Hazel One called my name again.

I ignored it. Screw the latte.

"You can't live here," I said.

"I'm no landlord," Parker said, "but I don't think you can stop me."

"Why?" I asked then.

She pretended the question made no sense. "Why what?"

I tried to bend her to my will with a don't-mess-with-me tone of voice. "Why are you doing this, Parker?"

She gave a big shrug, and then she didn't fight me—and I suddenly realized she'd wanted me to ask this question all along. "I heard about you and my mom hanging out," she said, and then her voice got theatrically pouty, "and I thought, *Are they having fun without me?*"

"We were not having fun," I said. "I don't 'have fun' with Lucinda."

"She paid you a visit, though," Parker said. "At your roof-hovel."

Hey. Only I got to call my hovel a hovel.

"Now we can all have fun together," Parker went on—her voice shifting to menacingly perky.

"I don't want you here," I said, starting to feel a panic of helplessness.

"Aww, I know," she said now—lacing her voice with fake sympathy. "This is kind of your worst nightmare, isn't it?"

She waited, like I might confirm it.

I held still.

"But don't worry," Parker added then, raising her hand for another high-five attempt. "Given your whole brain-damage situation . . . you will literally never know I'm here."

Eleven

PERFECT. BETWEEN JOE the Weasel and Parker, I pretty much had to dread every single elevator ride.

Another reason to never leave the rooftop.

And yet Parker wasn't wrong. I really didn't notice she was there. Other than that our top-floor hallway suddenly started smelling like cat pee, which had to be that creepy Sphynx cat's fault. Maybe she worked all the time—what kind of terrible job would a person like Parker even have?

Or maybe she was moving around me all the time, unseen, like a ghost.

Either way, she was surprisingly forgettable.

The Weasel, however, was the opposite.

That red-and-white bowling jacket was as hard to miss as a stop sign. And he wore it all the time. Other people changed their clothes, their shoes, their hair. Sometimes they wore workout gear. Sometimes a suit for work. Sometimes jeans. It was normal human behavior to wear different clothes for different occasions and I applauded it. Of course, it made it almost impossible for me to know who was who, but at least the world was still lumbering along much as it always had.

Anyway. Not this guy.

He really must have loved that jacket.

I saw him in it almost every evening. Getting coffee at Bean Street from Hazel One or Two. Locking his Vespa at the bike rack. Crossing that same crosswalk where I'd almost been flattened by a VW Beetle. Doing normal things, mostly. But with a spotlight on him because of that jacket.

Just my luck.

Everybody looked the same except for the last guy I wanted to see.

Noticing him like that did, however, confirm my initial diagnosis: he was definitely some kind of epic player.

My first confirmation came when I saw him stumbling drunk down the hallway with the sexiest woman in our building. I was waiting to step into the elevator as they lumbered out, arms pretzeled around each other, after what had clearly been a wild night of drinking. She looked worse than he did, for sure, and as they lurched past me, I wondered if she might be in danger.

Had he roofied her? That was the first question that came to mind. Just how terrible was this guy? Was he just a douche, or was he a monster?

I wanted to ask her if she was okay, but I didn't know her name.

Sue and I always just called her Busty McGee. Which sounds terrible, now that I think about it. But I'm telling you, most of her outfits were very . . . cleavage-forward. We weren't noticing something she didn't want us to notice. Actually, she'd make a great friend for me now, because she was highly recognizable, even without a face. I'd know that chest anywhere.

And I very much admired her confidence. I, who hadn't bought new bras in so long I couldn't even tell you how long it had been.

But look, as identifiers went, those were hers. If you needed to mention her to anyone in this building, all you had to say was "the lady with the boobs," and you'd be set.

Not that you would say that. But you *could*.

Anyway, I hesitated on her name—and then I made do with "Hey."

"Hey!" I called, catching up to them. "Are you okay?"

Leaning against the Weasel, she stopped, turned in my direction, and said, "He's got me."

At that, Joe un-paused them and they continued on toward her apartment door. Should I stop them? Should I call the police? What would I even say? A fat-shaming jerk is taking a very sexy neighbor of mine back to her apartment—and he might be up to no good?

That wasn't a 911 call. People got up to no good all the time.

In the end, all I could think to do was shout after them: "Make good choices!"

They kept going—no acknowledgment.

"Be sure to respect each other's humanity!"

Not even a glance backward.

Then, "Don't make me hear about this in the elevator in the morning!" As they disappeared into her apartment and left me standing there.

After that, I started noticing Joe coming out of Ms. McGee's apartment more often. Which made me think they'd started dating. But get this: There were two other single women on our floor—not counting Parker, who I would never count, on principle—and I saw him coming out of their apartments, too, often late at night. The glasses, the floppy hair—and always that bowling jacket. Unmistakable.

What was he doing in all these women's apartments?

Something about it just bothered me.

Here I was, chastely facing all kinds of recovery and obstacles and time pressures . . . and there he was, just having his way with the entire building.

I was frantically trying to relearn how to paint. I was staying up late and getting up early and painting back over canvases. I was falling asleep at my own worktable, leaving paint and brushes out to dry and get ruined.

I was hustling like crazy all the damn time—and this guy Joe was just . . . getting lucky?

I didn't have time to obsess over what this dude was up to. And yet I was doing it anyway.

"I think he's a gigolo," I said to Sue one night, FaceTiming while we both did our dishes. "I see him going in and out of women's apartments all the time."

"Multiple women?" Sue asked.

"Multiple women," I confirmed.

"Then he's not a gigolo," Sue declared. "Gigolos are typically kept by one older woman for eye candy and sexual favors."

I paused, like, *Huh*. "Why do you know that?"

"If it's multiple women," Sue went on, proud to be helpful, "he's more likely a male prostitute."

I considered it. "Well, he must be very good. The penthouse apartments in this building aren't cheap."

"Maybe that's what the videos are for. Maybe he's extorting them so he can live in luxury."

I sighed. Maybe. "Anything's possible. People are so terrible."

"It's a shame, though. He's so cute."

"Is he cute?" I asked.

"You don't think he's cute?"

"Sue, I can't see his face."

Sue smacked her forehead. "Forgot again."

"Why can't you remember this?"

"Let me be your eyes for you. He's super handsome. That floppy hair. The hipster glasses. Plump lips. Stellar jawline. And he's very symmetrical."

She knew that would get me. I always gave extra points for symmetrical. Too many years of art classes.

"And," Sue went on, "he's got my favorite kind of teeth. Perfect but not perfect."

"Like a rabbit."

"He doesn't look like a rabbit. I'm telling you, he's attractive. And he's got a kind of bad-boy energy. You know—'cause he rides that Vespa."

"I'm not sure a Vespa creates bad-boy energy."

"Vespa . . . Harley Hog . . . whatever. The point is, he's good looking."

"I guess he'd have to be—if he's thriving as a high-class prostitute."

"He could just be a playboy, though," Sue said next, thinking about it. This was high praise from Sue. "You think he's a playboy?"

"I mean, who knows? I'm just saying he could just be handsome as a hobby."

That was true. "Joe the man-whore," I said, trying on the idea for size.

"I don't like that word," Sue said, picking up her phone to pause our FaceTime and research it. She loved looking things up midconversation. "There's got to be a better word."

"Joe the libertine?" I offered.

But she'd found a good website now. "How about seducer?"

"Not harsh enough."

"Player?"

"Too complimentary."

"If we were in England, we could call him a shag bandit."

I thought about that.

"Ooh, here's an archaic one," Sue said. "Mutton monger."

But I shook my head with a shiver. "That's the worst one so far."

"How about just keep it simple and go with a classic? Womanizer."

I nodded. Don't overthink it. "Joe the Womanizer."

"I like it," Sue said.

And with that, it was settled. Joe of the bowling jacket was sleeping with half the women in my building, mocking them in elevators the next day, and possibly extorting them for money.

What other explanation could there be?

DR. NICOLE, HOWEVER, did not agree. "Please don't call the cops on that poor man," she responded after I spent a whole session telling her all about it.

"The evidence is pretty damning," I said.

"What evidence? There's no evidence. You're talking about one overheard phone call and a few sightings in the hallway—sightings where you mostly darted into the shadows so he wouldn't see you watching him."

I shrugged. "I know what I know. A lot of things don't add up."

"Yes. But that's not him. That's you."

"I'm not the person who filmed a sleeping woman in my bed and then made fun of her."

"But you *are* the person who just had brain surgery."

"Are you saying I'm mentally defective?"

"I'm saying you're in an adjustment period."

"What does that even mean?"

"Go easy on poor Joe. And go easy on yourself. You can't entirely trust yourself right now. Your senses are out of whack. Your brain has a lot going on."

"No argument there."

"You're going to make mistakes for a while until you adjust."

"What kinds of mistakes?"

"Things like not recognizing your sister—"

"*Step*sister," I corrected.

"And not knowing familiar voices. And falling in love at first sight with your veterinarian."

"I don't think we can call meeting the love of my life a mistake, but okay."

But I wondered.

Was Dr. Nicole right? Could I not trust myself?

It was a strange thought. Who on earth could you trust if not yourself?

"Be patient with yourself," she kept saying.

What did that even mean?

Everybody kept telling me to wait, let the edema resolve, get some rest, see what happened. But I didn't have that kind of time. I had to get my portrait painted for the show. I couldn't just watch my whole life fall apart and not try to do something about it.

Then she glanced at her watch, so I glanced at my phone. We had two minutes left in the session. Time to wrap it up. "The point is," Dr. Nicole said, "you're still adjusting. You have to allow for confirmation bias."

"What's confirmation bias?"

Dr. Nicole paused for a good definition. "It means that we tend to think what we think we're going to think."

I added all those words up. "So . . . if you expect to think a thing is true, you're more likely to think it's true?"

"Exactly," she said, looking pleased. "Basically we tend to decide on what the world is and who people are and how things are—and then we look for evidence that supports what we've already decided. And we ignore everything that doesn't fit."

"That doesn't sound like me," I said.

"Everybody does it," Dr. Nicole said with a shrug. "It's a normal human foible. But you're doing it a little extra right now."

"I am?"

She nodded. "Because your senses are off. It's harder for you to collect solid information about the world around you. And because you've experienced trauma, you're on high alert for danger."

No argument there.

"So," I said. "If I think everything is terrible, then everything will be terrible?"

She nodded, like, *Bingo.*

"But I do think everything is terrible."

"In the wake of a difficult time," Dr. Nicole said then, sounding more than ever like the calm voice of reason, "as you try to readjust to a new normal—"

"I don't want a new normal!" I interrupted. "I want the *old* normal."

"The trick," Dr. Nicole continued, not letting me throw her off, "is to look for the good stuff."

"Fine," I said, thinking about it. "I'll try." Then I added, "And I won't call the cops on the Weasel. Yet."

"And maybe stop calling him the Weasel."

"But he *is* a weasel."

"You'll definitely keep thinking that if you keep thinking that."

I sighed. Another *gotcha* moment. "Confirmation bias?" I asked, already knowing the answer.

"That's my girl," she said.

Twelve

DID THE GREAT Dr. Oliver Addison, veterinarian sex god, work a miracle and restore my geriatric bestie to perfect canine health?

Kind of. Mostly.

Though he did warn me that Peanut would be "a little tired" for a week or two.

Sure enough, on the day Peanut came home from the clinic, all he wanted was to curl up under the bed and nap.

But I wanted to hang out. I'd missed him.

I'd missed him so much, apparently, that all I wanted to do was lie on my tummy, half under the bed myself, watching him sleep and reassuring myself he was okay.

Look for good things, Dr. Nicole had said.

Peanut being home is definitely a good thing, I thought as I watched him.

But there was another good thing under that bed—one I'd forgotten about until I pushed it aside to get a better view of Peanut.

A box I'd kept for years, with my mother's roller skates inside.

I hadn't seen them in ages, but I decided to pull the box out and open it up.

My mom loved to roller-skate. The two of us used to skate up and down our block, listening to Top 40 on her little portable radio, and singing along, and waving to the neighbors. My mom could skate backward, do the moonwalk, spin around on one foot, and do the grapevine. Plus a million other things. She used to pull me with a rope behind her and call it water skiing. It was our favorite thing to do on weekends.

She had her own skates—white leather with pink pom-poms on the toes. And she'd bought me a matching pair when I was little. This was the nineties, and most of the world had shifted to Rollerblades. But not my mom.

After she died, I inherited them.

By *inherited,* I mean, I took them out of her closet before Lucinda donated everything to Goodwill.

I never wore them. After I lost her, I never roller-skated again. And my kid-sized skates got lost somewhere along the way, like things do.

Wherever I went, though, I kept my mom's skates close—in that box under my bed. Not to wear. Just to have. Just because holding on to them felt like holding on to a piece of her. Just because, even though I never even looked at them, if I could save one thing in a fire—besides Peanut, of course—I wouldn't even think about it.

One hundred percent those skates.

I wondered if they would fit me now. What size had my mom's feet been? It bugged me that I didn't know.

And I didn't have anyone to ask. I could almost hear my father saying, *What the hell kind of question is that?*

And then, as soon as that thought popped into my head, I was on my way to find out.

Was roller skating on my list of approved postsurgical activities?

Hard no.

But to be fair: it wasn't on my list of forbidden ones, either.

More important: Did the skates fit?

They did.

And now I knew something new about her. We were both eight and a halfs.

I grabbed a pair of tube socks—from Sue on my birthday last year—sat on a kitchen chair, and slid my foot into the leather boot of the skate with a satisfying *shoonk* as my heel landed in place. A perfect fit. It felt like a sign. I leaned forward and tightened the laces and made double knots. And then with a stubborn optimism that I still marvel at to this day, I thought, *It's perfectly safe if I just go slow,* and then I stood and rose to my feet.

My mom loved Diana Ross and Donna Summer and Gloria Gaynor. She was in her teens in the late seventies and imprinted fully on disco music and all its perky optimism. I had a whole disco playlist I listened to when I wanted to feel close to her: KC and the Sunshine Band, the Bee Gees, ABBA. I grabbed my earbuds and turned on the playlist I'd made of her favorites. And then I made my way to the door, opened it, and felt the rooftop breeze cross my face like silk just as "I Love the Nightlife" started up.

Was I a little bit shaky at first?

For sure.

But there are things you know in your body that you just never forget.

Here's the great news: The roof of the warehouse was smooth concrete. And so other than a few seams to watch out for, it was a perfect, buttery-smooth, breezy, sunshiny space for roller skating. I swear, it felt like fate. Like this was where my entire life had been leading—to this glorious, windy rooftop moment.

Was I going to bother the tenants below? Unknown. Maybe the roof was thick enough to mask the sound. Or maybe it would just amplify it.

Either way, I got started—pushed off with one foot and rolled forward on the other.

For a while, I just pushed along jerkily, my arms out wide like a tightrope walker, feeling like I'd really left my youth somewhere back in the mists of time.

But the view from the rooftop was gorgeous—and also something I didn't stop to appreciate often enough. To the east were historic buildings and more old brick warehouses. To the west was the greenscape of Buffalo Bayou—and its walking trails and kayakers.

I was glad they couldn't see me, squeaking along like a tin man who needed oiling.

But then I could feel things start to shift as the muscle memory kicked in. The more I did it, the more I could do it.

I made big circles, sinking into the comforting rhythm of right, then left, then right, then left. Then, without overthinking it, I spun in a circle. The jerky motion faded away. I found a smooth rhythm. The rooftop was a wide open space with nothing to run into.

Minute by minute, my childhood know-how drifted back.

And then I remembered what I already knew: I could do this.

I let myself relax. Then I did a half-spin and started skating backward. Then I did a figure eight. Then I squatted down, roller derby style. Then I started grapevining and spinning and just generally grooving like a person who had just been reminded what fun felt like.

Which is about right.

How much time went by? I have no idea. I was utterly lost—in the best way. It was the exact opposite of the grueling hours I'd spent trying to paint before. That had been work, and this was just play. Who needed art when you had roller skating?

Did it make me miss my mom?

You bet.

But the delight of it—the absolute, blissful, embodied pleasure of it—made it okay somehow. I felt that familiar ache of longing, but now mixed with something new. Joy, maybe. The sunshine and the breeze and the music and the motion and the rhythm. An awareness of the glorious, impossible miracle of being alive.

Huh.

So weird to think that this feeling had been there all along—hibernating in a box under my bed, just waiting for me to wake it up.

Maybe I should have tried these skates on sooner.

I swear, at one point, I decided I could just keep skating there, round and round, lost in bliss, all day and night.

But of course that's not what happened.

In fact, not long after I had that thought, while I was skating backward in a slalom, the sound of someone shouting my name pierced my disco playlist—and I spun around to see Joe just a few feet away, calling to me.

He wasn't wearing his vintage jacket today—just a T-shirt—but by now I knew those glasses. And that floppy hair blowing in the rooftop wind. Also—process of elimination. Who else would he have been?

He wasn't Mr. Kim, and that was just about the only other option.

Recognizing him was surprising, but seeing him at all was even more surprising—especially since the door to the rooftop stairs was self-locking and nobody had the code but me.

Suddenly finding an uninvited man standing on your roof watching your roller-skating jam can add up to a heck of a surprise—and I guess I must have frozen still for a second while still gliding forward on my wheels because, next, I hit one of those seams in the roof concrete I'd been so careful to avoid, which pitched me forward—and right into Joe's arms as he tried to catch me, even though I had far too much momentum for that to work. He wound up falling back as I landed right on top of him . . . and we went skidding along the concrete.

After we came to a stop, time seemed to pause.

I should have scrambled up and skated away. But my brain took a minute to put the whole situation together. And while we waited for the moment to make sense, I was caught in suspended animation, my body fully pinning his flat to the ground, my nose almost touching his, our gazes locked together in incomprehension.

What the hell just happened?

The first head I worried about was his—because I saw it hit the concrete.

"Oh god," I said, talking loud over the disco in my ears before yanking the earbuds out by the wires. "Are you—"

"I'm okay."

And then there was a pause, as I noted that I, too, had just fallen down—and so the next head I had to worry about was my own.

I had one job these days: not to fall.

And here I was. Fallen.

Oh, shit. Did I just break my brain?

The thought pinned me there as I did a quick assessment. *Had I hit my head?* No. *Was my head bleeding?* Not that I could tell. *Did my head hurt?* No. Nothing hurt besides my scraped knees and palms. How much had Joe's body cushioned my impact? Enough?

I did a quick scan of the rooftop, half checking for a possible cork-shaped piece of skull, still skittering across the concrete on its side like a hockey puck.

Nothing. Coast was clear.

As far as I could tell, I was okay.

But that's when I realized I'd been lying on top of Joe—draped over him like a human weighted blanket—for far longer than was proper. I could feel my thighs mashed up against his. I could feel myself rising and falling on his chest as we both tried to catch our breath. I could feel my heart beating—*or was it his?*—against my rib cage.

I felt a little dizzy for a second there, but whether it was the fall or my wonky brain or just the fact that I hadn't been this close to a man in a very long time . . . I couldn't say.

Time to pull myself together.

I shifted backward, peeling myself off him, and stood up slowly.

Once I was vertical, I got a little mad. "What are you doing here? You shocked the hell out of me!" I demanded. "How did you even get up here?"

Joe didn't answer me. Still lying on the concrete, he lifted up on his elbows but paused there, looking at me in a way that felt more like he was *gazing*.

Maybe his head was injured, after all.

I crossed my arms over my chest. "Nobody ever comes up on this roof. Nobody has the passcode to that door but me!"

Joe shook his head a little, like he was trying to shift his thoughts back into place.

"This is a private space!" I said. "This rooftop is part of my—" But I didn't know how to describe it. "My *area*. You can't just come up here!"

When Joe finally climbed to his feet and started tucking his shirt in, his voice was a little hoarse. "The door downstairs was open."

"So you thought that was an invitation to just come on up here?"

"I think the lock's broken," Joe went on. "The dead bolt's frozen in the out position."

"That's a Mr. Kim problem," I said. "Unless you're a locksmith."

He put his hands in his pockets. "I was just worried about you."

He was? Huh. "Well, I was fine."

"I saw that."

Oh, god. He'd seen me skating. To headphone disco. "You clearly did."

"You can really skate," he said.

"Fine," I said, refusing to take the compliment. "So you came up here and saw I was fine. Why didn't you turn around and leave?"

"I was kind of mesmerized, to be honest."

"That's not funny."

"I'm not joking."

Mesmerized? Mesmerized by what? My skating prowess? The ridiculousness of my outfit? The comedy that always ensues when a person wearing headphones can't resist doing dance moves out loud, like a mime? I decided I didn't want to know. "I'm allowed to do what I want on my own rooftop, Joe."

"I'm not saying you're not."

"And you're not allowed to sneak up here and watch me."

"I didn't sneak up. I thought you should know."

"About what?"

"About the broken door lock."

Okay, that wasn't totally unreasonable.

"Once I de-mesmerized myself, I was trying to tell you. So you could get it fixed. But when I called your name, you didn't hear me."

"Yeah. Well. I was listening to music."

"What were you listening to?"

Not relevant! "Why do you want to know?"

Joe shrugged. "You looked happy."

"That's none of your business."

"Fair enough," he said, lifting his hands in defeat.

In case it's not already clear, I felt irrationally angry at him. I'm not sure I could even have pinned down a reason. Because he came up without asking. Because the lock was broken. Because he interrupted me. Because before I saw him, I'd been freakishly, genuinely happy, for the first time in so long and now, thanks to him, I had to be . . . whatever this was.

Annoyed.

Or maybe just plain old embarrassed. Because there is literally no way to skate-dance in silence without looking like a serious goofball.

"Anyway," Joe said, taking a couple of backward steps. "Sorry about interrupting you. Definitely call about that lock."

And then he turned and started walking back toward the spiral stairs—and that's when all that anger I'd just been full of disappeared in a puff. Because the back of his T-shirt? It was streaked with blood.

"Wait!" I called, skating after him. "Are you okay?"

He turned back. "I'm fine."

"You're bleeding," I said, skating around to get a better look.

"Am I?" he asked, trying to peek over his shoulder.

"Doesn't it hurt?"

"I mean, it stings a little," he said.

I skated back around to his front. "Take it off," I said, all business, gesturing at his shirt.

He thought for a second, and then he nodded, and then he crossed his arms, grabbed the hem of his T-shirt, and peeled it off.

Friends, Romans, countrymen—I might not have been able to see his face, but let me tell you . . . I could definitely see that shirtless torso. I mean, I had a physical reaction to beholding that thing—and it wasn't because he was chiseled or extraordinary or some airbrushed fantasy you'd see in a magazine. It was just . . . strong and solid and nice. So . . . *appealing*, somehow.

It just looked like a body that would feel good under your hands.

I pushed that thought away the second I noticed it.

But can I just add? An absolutely stellar shoulder-to-hip ratio. As a professional artist: thumbs-up.

What was that word he'd just used? Mesmerized?

Anyway, that wasn't what we were here for. I shook it off and skated back around to check out the damage on his back. "Oh, you really got scraped," I said.

"Yeah," he said. "We skidded a few feet."

"I'm so sorry," I said, the volume on "annoyed" turning itself way down as "apologetic" ramped up.

I looked down at my scratched-up palms. His back made them look paltry.

"Come on," I said, ready to remedy my guilt with stellar first aid, starting to skate back toward my door. "Let's get you cleaned up."

But when I looked back, he wasn't following.

I skated back to him. "Let's go."

"It's okay," he said. "I've got it."

"It's your back," I said. "How are you going to reach it?"

"I'll manage."

Was it his fault that he startled me and made me trip?

Absolutely. Sort of.

But was I the one who landed on him and dragged him across a roof? Also yes.

"Let me help you," I said, my voice much softer now. "You wouldn't be scraped up like this if I hadn't landed on you."

"You wouldn't have landed on me if I hadn't come up here."

"You wouldn't have come up here if the lock had been working properly."

Joe nodded. "So this is all Mr. Kim's fault."

"One hundred percent Mr. Kim," I agreed, taking Joe's hand and pulling him toward my place like a tugboat. "But I'm all you've got."

INSIDE, JOE COULDN'T stop looking around at all my paintings, and I couldn't stop looking at Joe.

He was taking in my painting supplies, and my decor, and my hovel in general—but his expression was so different from what Lucinda's had been. She'd been judging me, and he was, too—but, from his body language, he was judging me *positively*.

Like he liked it.

Which was a little bit spellbinding.

Or was it the torso? Tough call.

I mean . . . all this time I'd been disliking him, he'd been walking around with that endlessly appealing situation under his shirt? I wondered if I might have assessed him differently if I'd known.

God. Was I that shallow?

An hour ago, I'd have said no—but now I wasn't so sure.

But what choice did I have—as an artist—to let a visual situation like that go unadmired? It was practically my professional duty.

Even now, the thought of it makes me want to let out a low whistle. I mean, that chest might even have been better than a face. If I had to choose.

I made Joe lean shirtlessly over my kitchen sink while I poured hydrogen peroxide over the scrapes. He sucked in tight breaths as the cold bubbly liquid ran down his flanks.

"Ticklish?" I asked, watching his muscles contract.

He shook his head. "Only my ears."

I dried the uninjured parts of his back with a paper towel, and then I offered to wash his shirt for him.

He shook his head. "I got it. I'll just head home."

But at the words, I suddenly pictured him walking down the top-floor hallway all shirtless and someone else happening upon him—and I got the weirdest, most indescribable feeling.

If I didn't know better, I'd have called it jealousy.

"Let me put some ointment on you," I said.

"I'm really okay."

"That roof," I said, giving him a *trust me* look, "is super filthy. Birds poop on it all the time. Not to mention acid rain, nuclear waste—"

"Nuclear waste?"

"The point is, you don't want an infection."

Joe considered that, and then nodded and sat backward on one of the kitchen chairs.

I pulled up a chair behind him and used a Q-tip to dab him with ointment. The scratches weren't deep, but they covered a lot of territory.

With any luck, we'd be here a while.

He had a bright pink scar on his shoulder that looked like he'd gotten stitches. "Where'd you get the scar?" I asked. "It looks pretty recent."

"I crashed into a lamppost," Joe said, not seeming too interested.

He crashed into a lamppost? Was that the drinking-and-carousing lifestyle he lived?

So many red flags with this guy.

But I must have been much more lonesome than I realized. Here was a man who I didn't even like—but the nearness of his naked torso was putting me into some kind of a trance. What was going on with me? I was dabbing at the scrapes, but I kept losing my concentration and dabbing the wrong spots. My eyes kept wandering away from the task, traveling up his spine, out along his shoulder, down his arms. His skin was kind of buttery-tan, and he had freckles on his shoulders, like he'd worked outside a lot with that shirt off.

I pictured him raking leaves shirtless. And washing the car shirtless. Maybe tending to a vegetable garden shirtless? Then harvesting the vegetables and bringing them inside to make a shirtless meal from scratch?

Hey! I could suddenly hear my own voice saying inside my head. *Pull it together! Stop fantasizing about the Weasel!*

But the acoustics in my head weren't great. The voice sounded tinny and echoey like I was at the bottom of a well. Whereas Joe's voice—and everything else about him—was coming in loud and clear.

Honestly, Dr. Nicole would be very proud of me right now.

"You know what I love about this moment?" Joe asked then, sounding sleepy as he rested his head on his arms.

I leaned forward to take a guess. "The fact that I feel genuinely sorry about doing this to you, even though it was entirely your fault?"

"I definitely *like* that. But I'm talking about something I *love*."

By accident, right then, I caught the way his plump bottom lip pressed against his teeth when he made the V in the word *love*.

"What do you love?" I asked, now suddenly aware of my own lip doing the same thing.

He glanced back with a vibe that felt positively affectionate. Then he said, "You've still got your roller skates on."

Thirteen

THE NEXT NIGHT was Friday. The night of my synchronized caffein-ation event with Dr. Addison.

Also known as my first date with my future husband.

He wasn't calling it a date. And neither was I—*out loud*.

But that was all for the loophole.

He'd be at Bean Street Coffee—just a short walk for him from his work—at six o'clock. And I would be there, too. It was a bad idea, for sure. But more important: What should I wear? Jeans and a top? Sneak-ers? Sandals? Or god forbid—heels?

I tried many outfit options and modeled them all for Peanut. We don't need to get mathematical about it. Let's just say I was very thor-ough.

In the end, I settled on a black wrap dress with white polka dots and a ruffled hem—with the mental caveat that if it was too fancy, I could always pop back up to my place and change.

Other than the historic nature of the First Date, there was one other notable thing about today. But I wasn't sure if I was going to share it with Dr. Addison.

Today—March fourth—was my mother's birthday.

And I always celebrated my mom's birthday. Just the two of us. I'd tuck a flower behind my ear, the way she always used to, and I'd bake a cake from scratch, and I'd buy candles, and I'd sing happy birthday to her. And then I'd talk to her like she could hear me. Just out loud—alone in a room by myself. As if the birthdays of the dead were the one day of the year when they could tune in to the voices of their loved ones left behind like a radio frequency.

I'd tell her about my life—catch her up on all the nonsense and goings-on. Give her the Peanut update. Reminisce a bit about fun things we'd done together when she was alive. And then I'd always, always thank her for being my mother, and for being such a source of love and joy that I could still feel it all these years later, so long after she was gone.

That was no small feat on her part.

But it was also a choice on my part.

It was so tempting—even still—to feel bitter that I'd lost her so soon. I had to work to turn the other way: to remember to feel grateful that I'd had her at all.

I'd thank her, and then—yes—I'd cry . . . because happiness and sadness are always so tangled up. And then I'd put on a Cary Grant movie—and usually eat the birthday cake, sometimes digging straight in with a fork without even slicing it, until I conked out on the sofa.

It was quite the ritual.

I'd started out trying to feel happy. But in the end, I'd settled for grateful.

Which might be the better emotion, if I had to choose.

Anyway, the chances I'd be telling Oliver Addison, DVM, about any of this were pretty close to zero. He didn't need to do a belly flop into my sad past on our first date.

I'd be cheery and positive and funny and charming—as best I could. I'd set all my bittersweet emotions about my lost mother on a mental shelf. And then I'd shut the conversation down before I could accidentally reveal any personal imperfections . . . and go stop by the grocery store for the ingredients for the cake.

Yellow cake with chocolate icing. My mom's favorite. And mine, too.

This would work. I could have it all.

As long as I kept to the schedule.

I WENT DOWN to Bean Street at six o'clock on the dot. I found a table that faced the exterior door, couldn't resist dabbing just one more spot of a lipstick color called Passionfruit onto the poutiest part of my lower lip, gave myself a little pep talk about how doing scary things is good for you, and waited.

And waited.

And then I waited some more.

And while I waited, I could feel the confidence leaking out of me like a punctured tire. Was it cold in here? Maybe I should've brought a sweater. Should I take my hair back down? Was my lipstick too orangy? And of all the bras I owned, how had I managed to grab the one that always slid off my shoulder?

I yanked the shoulder strap up and pressed it in place sternly, like, *Stay*.

Maybe this was a bad idea. Maybe I couldn't pull this off. The entire future I'd just mapped out for myself as Mrs. Oliver Addison, DVM, was riding on not screwing up this moment.

The words *don't screw it up* kept circling around in my head like they were on an airplane banner. Great tip—but the problem was, there were so many ways to screw it up.

What if, to just take the biggest, scariest, most likely example, I didn't recognize him?

What if—and this likelihood was really only occurring to me now, as I sat there—without his lab coat on and out of the context of the clinic, I truly couldn't tell him apart from anyone else? It was more than possible.

How mortifying would that be?

I thought about the woman on Facebook who'd called her face blindness "a superpower." What would *she* be doing right now? She wouldn't be sitting here nervously ripping up a paper napkin, her stomach cold with dread as she questioned her value as a human being. Hell, no! She would put her shoulders back, embrace the uncertainty, surf that tsunami of self-doubt like a badass, and find a way to make it fun.

At the very least, she wouldn't give up on herself before she'd even tried.

You've got this, I pep-talked myself as I started mutilating a new napkin. *You know what to do.*

And with that, I did know what to do: Just smile—and positively radiate warmth and availability—at every single man who walked in through the Bean Street doors as if he were my future husband.

Not my usual strategy in life.

But not that hard to do, either.

I mean, Dr. Addison had a job to do here, too—right? He would recognize me. Sure, I looked a little different with my hair up and my passionfruit lips. But I could rely on him to know me when he saw me.

Anyway, I'd just have to put my faith in destiny.

What was meant to be was meant to be.

Except maybe it wasn't meant to be . . . because an hour—an actual hour—went by, and Dr. Addison didn't show up.

There's a very specific slow-burn heartbreak to getting stood up as the realization slowly comes into focus: No one's coming. In that one interminable hour of looking up each time the doors opened and watching every single one of them sweep on past me like we were total strangers—which we must have been—I felt myself wilting like a time-lapse version of a neglected houseplant.

It was the lethal combination of the hope with the disappointment, I decided.

I'd walked in, all fresh and bright with my green leaves lifted high toward the sun . . . and it took only an hour to render me flopped side-ways, limp and melted over the edge of my pot.

Emotionally, I mean.

The point is, untold numbers of innocent napkins gave their lives during that hour of waiting. All for nothing.

At the one-hour mark, with no text from him, I called it.

I was done here.

I stood up, feeling like the whole room of people must be watching me and shaking their heads, and started picking up all the napkin shred-dings off the table—deliberately, self-consciously. Careful not to screw this up, too.

But that's when the outside door opened again, and this time a breeze burst in with it, and that breeze sent the napkin pieces scat-tering off the table onto the floor—all my efforts destroyed, as so often happened, by some totally unrelated outside force. And despite everything, I smiled like a movie star at whoever was coming in, just in case.

It was Pavlovian at this point.

But it wasn't Dr. Addison coming in the door. It was a lady.

So I turned my attention now to the floor and the tragic heartbreak confetti now covering my section of it, squatting to start picking it all back up.

That's when a pair of shoes appeared in my field of vision.

And from the fumes of evil radiating off them and the sudden waft of Dior's Poison, I could take a pretty good guess: Parker.

I stood up.

"You look like a girl who just got stood up," she said.

It wasn't the voice I recognized. It was the viciousness.

Definitely Parker.

Nobody else on earth could make me feel that shitty that fast.

"Hello, Parker."

"How did you know it was me?" she asked, sounding overly delighted—almost sarcastically so—to be recognized.

I sighed. "By the cruelty. It has a distinct frequency."

"I saw you here an hour ago on my way out," Parker said then, enjoying a chance to savor my misery. "Now I'm back, and here you still are—wearing lipstick and everything—but still just utterly, completely alone." I could feel her gleeful pout. "It's so heartbreaking."

"What do you want, Parker?"

"I want to ask you about that super-cute guy on our floor."

"What guy on our floor?"

"The one who stares at you in the elevator."

There was a guy who stared at me in the elevator?

"The one with the bowling jacket," she said, like, *Hurry up*.

"Joe?" I asked. Joe stared at me in the elevator? Something about knowing that felt really . . . nice.

Parker had no idea she'd just made me feel nice. She snapped her fingers at me. "I need his number."

All I could think to say was "Why?"

"Because I've decided he's my future husband."

Hey. That was my thing. *I* was the person with a future husband.

"Future husband?" My body was suddenly filled with tiny firecrackers: a flash of jealousy; a flash of protectiveness; and then a final flash of *Hell, no*.

Now, I didn't know Joe all that well. And it's fair to say I'd had a lot of conflicting feelings about him since that red-and-white bowling jacket of his came onto my radar. And my jury was still out on whether he was a good guy or the full opposite.

But I would never in a million years sic Parker on him.

That was just basic human decency.

"I think he's dating someone," I said.

"So?"

"So, I think he's taken."

"So?"

"So . . ." The fact that I had to explain this was the exact reason why she was never getting his info. "It would be morally wrong of you to pursue a man who's already seeing someone else."

Parker did not take kindly to my obstructionism. "Are you the cheating police?"

"I'm just not going to help you with anything, Parker. Ever. For any reason."

I could feel more than see Parker narrowing her face in suspicion. "You like him, don't you?"

What? "No."

"The way you say no is a clear yes."

"I am protecting that guy from you the way I would protect any random stranger off the street."

"Any random stranger you had a thing for."

"No."

"Oh my god!" she said then with a thrilled gasp. "Is he the one who stood you up?"

"No one stood me up," I said.

"You're a hilariously bad liar."

Why was I even talking to her? I should have left the second I sensed who she was. "Just—fuck off, Parker. Okay? Can you do that?"

"Not until you give me his number."

And that's when we both heard a ding coming from my little purse, which had been hanging mutely from my shoulder this entire time, with the zipper unzipped and my cell phone sticking partly out. And the screen now lit up for us all to see.

There was a text on the screen: This is the front desk at Petopia Vet Clinic.

Then another quick ding: An emergency case came in just as Dr. Addison was leaving.

Then a final: He asked us to let you know.

This was the text I'd been waiting for the entire eternity of the last hour—but I didn't even have time to respond before Parker reached out to try to snatch my phone. Like it might be a message from Joe.

Just as I realized what she was doing, I spun away.

Without even skipping a beat, as if she were perhaps a person who stole other people's cell phones all the time, Parker lunged again in a one-two—this time around my other side, and with a lot more force.

It might even have worked—how hard is it to overpower someone in a coffee shop, after all?—but in the end, it didn't. Because just at that moment, a woman with very unfortunate timing was walking toward us, and when Parker lunged to my side, she slammed right into her hard enough to knock her to the ground.

I remember it in slo-mo. The *oof* the woman made as her bottom hit the floor. The *sloosh* of her cold brew spilling. The tintinnabulation of ice cubes hitting the tile. Her shocked, shallow breaths at the cold shower of it all.

In the aftermath, we both stared at the woman, her white linen outfit now saturated brown with iced coffee like a sopped-up paper towel—and then Parker did the most Parker-esque thing a person could possibly do.

"Hey!" Parker said, checking her clothes for coffee splatters, like she'd been the victim all along. "Watch it!"

And then, done with both of us, she sailed out.

Anyway, that's when the woman in the white linen dress started to cry.

I bent down beside her. "Hey. Are you okay? Bet that was cold."

"I'm okay," she said.

"I'm so sorry about that," I said then, helping her up. I glanced at the doorway Parker had just blown through. "She is the actual devil."

Once she was vertical, the woman looked down to survey the damage—and started crying harder.

"Can I run up and grab you some sweatpants or something?" I asked. "I just live upstairs."

But the woman said, "I don't have time. I have to get to the airport."

I shook my head. "You can't go like that."

We both stared at her coffee-drenched clothes. "I have to go," she said. "I'm late to pick up my boyfriend."

"You can't pick up a boyfriend like that, either," I said.

She started crying harder. "I know."

"Okay," I said. "Two minutes. Let's get this solved," and I pulled her by the hand behind me toward the bathroom.

There I toweled her off while she just stood there like a little kid. And I thought—as I often did—about how my mom would handle this situation. "Let's switch outfits," I said. "We're about the same size."

She hesitated like I was nuts.

"It's fine," I said. "I live right upstairs. I'll just pop up and change."

She wasn't sure, but there was no time to argue, and before she fully knew it, we were in our underwear in side-by-side stalls, flopping our clothes over the divider.

"Are you sure?" she asked as I watched my dress slither away and disappear on the other side.

"I'm sure," I said, wincing a bit as I slid my arm into her cold brown linen sleeve. "And, anyway, there's no time to argue."

"But . . . you looked so pretty in this."

"Ha!" I said, the way women do, like she couldn't possibly mean it, just as her compliment took its place as the best moment of my entire night. Then I went on, trying to stress how totally okay it was for her to walk out of the Bean Street bathroom in my favorite dress. "That dress was twenty dollars at Target," I said. "It was on super clearance."

"That just makes it more valuable," she protested.

Good point, in fact. She wasn't wrong.

When we stepped out, I covered how wet and cold I now felt with massive enthusiasm for the sight of her in my dress. "You look phenomenal!" I practically sang. "You were born to wear that dress!"

"I'll return it to you," she said. "I'll have it dry-cleaned and bring it back."

But now I'd been swept away by the general joy of generosity—and the specific high of channeling my mother's wisdom and kindness. "Keep it," I said. "It really does look amazing."

I mean, anybody would look amazing in my favorite dress. But still.

"Are you sure?"

"Absolutely," I said, missing it already, even as I nodded.

We both turned to give her a final once-over in the mirror.

"I look better than I did before," she said, looking herself over. Then she turned to me. "Thank you."

"You're welcome," I said.

"You weren't even the one who knocked me down," she said.

But then something occurred to me. "It's really okay," I said. "It's nice to have a reason to do something nice."

And I meant it.

Fourteen

ANYWAY, THAT'S HOW I wound up walking out of the Bean Street Coffee's ladies' room in a wet, coffee-stained, clingy-in-all-the-wrong-places outfit—and running smack into Joe.

Except for a second I wasn't sure it was Joe.

Because he wasn't wearing his bowling jacket.

So all I knew for a second was that a man—some kind of man—walked up to me and said, "What the hell happened to you?"

I smiled like I knew him and said, "Coffeetastrophe," and then I made chitchat warmly and enthusiastically while quietly deducing who he was.

It didn't take that long. Just a few seconds. The hipster glasses and the floppy hair were kind of a dead giveaway, once I got my bearings.

"Where's your bowling jacket?" I asked then as confirmation—aware of the one percent chance he'd have no idea what I was talking about.

"Gave it the night off," Joe said.

"How's your back?" I asked, for two-factor authentication.

"Magically healed."

Mystery solved. Officially Joe.

"Should we get some dinner?" Joe asked next.

I nodded. That sounded like a perfect thing to do.

Getting stood up could really make a person hungry.

"Would you like to change first?" Joe asked next.

I nodded again.

And suddenly things just felt . . . better.

If you'd asked me at the apex of my getting-stood-up misery how this day was going to end, I'd have answered with a cuss-word-laden version of "not good."

But doing something nice for a stranger made me feel better. Running into Joe—and recognizing him *sans bowling jacket*—made me feel better. The prospect of eating a nice dinner made me feel better. Even, if I'm honest, the memory of having told Parker to fuck off made me feel better.

Huh. *I could feel better.* That felt like news.

Dr. Nicole had been insisting it could happen all along. But I'd never believed her.

Had she been right?

Maybe life was full of surprises. Maybe disappointments could turn out to be blessings. Maybe tonight would end up being fun, after all.

OR MAYBE NOT.

Because when we made it up to the rooftop so I could change, Sue, whose heart was absolutely in the right place but who could not seem to comprehend even the tiniest aspect of what this face-blindness situation was like for me . . . was throwing me a surprise party.

"Surprise!" Sue shouted when she saw Joe and me cresting the spiral stairs. Then her shoulders dropped at the sight of my coffee-drenched clothes, and she asked, just like Joe had, "What the hell happened to you?"

I felt my whole body go tense. There were fifty people on my rooftop, at least. Bulb lights. Music. Beer. "What's going on?"

"It's a party," Sue said. "Duh."

"You're hosting a party? Here?"

"It's the party we never got to have. You know. When you had your brain thingy."

I glanced at Joe, who was standing attentively beside me. I hadn't told him about my brain thingy.

"We're *celebrating*," Sue said when I couldn't find any words. "You remember celebrating?"

"I mean, I *remember* it," I said. The way you remember the stone age. Or the dinosaurs. They existed. Once. "But, I mean . . ." I tried to figure out how to protest something that was clearly already happening. "A surprise party?"

"It wasn't meant to be a surprise, exactly. You just weren't here when we arrived. It never even occurred to me that you might leave the house."

"I leave the house," I said.

"Not voluntarily."

"Sue . . ." I said, astonished at the Grand Canyon–size distance between how she thought I'd feel about this forced party and how I actually felt.

"Where were you, anyway?" she asked.

"I had a date," I said, glancing over at Joe. But dancing had broken out across the roof, and he was watching one of Sue's friends do the worm.

That's when Sue whispered into my ear, "With the vet?"

I nodded.

So then she whispered, "How'd it go?"

I shook my head. And then flared my nostrils. And then gave her a thumbs-down.

"Okay," Sue said, swinging around to steer me by the shoulders toward the beer coolers. "Let's table that. You've got a rooftop full of people here to celebrate with you."

"What are we celebrating, again?" I asked.

"Hello? The North American Portrait Society? Top ten finalist? You haven't forgotten, have you?"

I hadn't forgotten. Of course. But I suddenly noticed how important timing was when it came to things like celebrating. Yes, we'd been
about to celebrate the finalist thing a thousand years ago, before my life
fell apart.

But then . . . my life fell apart.

Was it fair to say I just didn't feel much like celebrating anything
these days? I loved Sue so much, my extroverted friend. And I loved
that she was trying. But what on earth about nonconsensually bringing
fifty people into the vicinity of a person with sudden face-blindness felt
like a good idea?

Not to mention, my mom's birthday. But I hadn't told Sue about
that.

"You like parties!" Sue said.

"I like parties," I corrected, "when I know the people at them. I do
not like parties full of strangers."

"Literally no one here is a stranger," Sue said. Then she pointed
at a group of faceless guys standing around the beer coolers. "That's
Stephan," she said, running down the line. "And that's Colin. And that's
Ryan. And that's Zach and André, and oh—"

"'Oh' what?"

"Oh," Sue said. "It looks like Ezra showed up."

"You invited *Ezra*?"

Sue coughed in indignation. "Of course not. Somebody must've
brought him."

Great. One of the people here was my ex-boyfriend. But I had no
idea which one.

"At least you showed up with some eye candy on your arm."

"Eye candy?" I asked. Did Joe qualify as eye candy?

"You know," Sue said, nodding in Joe's direction. "Your male prostitute."

Guess so.

"I might have been wrong about that," I said.

Sue let her gaze linger. "Maybe he should be," she said with appreciation. "He could make a killing."

"Sue," I said. "Let's focus. This is a problem."

"What?"

"The party! The people! My ex roaming loose!"

"Why?" she said. "Everybody here loves you."

"But I can't recognize anyone."

"They won't care."

"They *will* care, Sue. They will think it's super weird when they're talking to me and I have no idea who they are."

"Then let's just tell them what's going on with you."

"NO!" I choked out.

"You don't want to tell them?"

I leaned closer. "Never. I never want to tell anyone."

"Why not?" Sue asked.

"It's humiliating."

"Why? It's not your fault."

"Trust me. Having your brain malfunction is humiliating."

"If you say so."

But Sue was realizing now that she hadn't exactly thought this through.

"Look," I said. "The only people in the entire world who know about this are you and my dad and Lucinda . . . and Parker."

"*Parker* knows?"

"Lucinda told her."

"Then it's not a secret anymore. She'll tell everyone."

"Not yet. I think she's enjoying lording it over me."

"But she will."

"Maybe it'll fix itself before then."

Sue sighed. "Okay," she said then. "Here's the plan. First, you're going to change out of those wet clothes."

"No argument there."

"And then just stick close to me. Whenever anyone talks to us, I'll say their name right away, so you've got it."

That wasn't a bad idea. "That could work," I said.

"It'll totally work."

"Just promise me," I said then, holding out my hand so we could shake on it, "that you won't leave my side."

"I promise," Sue said, pumping my hand up and down, "that I will never ever leave your side."

GUESS WHAT?

She left my side.

Not on purpose. She just got dragged away.

I went into the bathroom to change, and I never saw her again.

I was left alone, as Picasso-faced person after Picasso-faced person came up to me and forced me to Sherlock Holmes one theory after another about who I was talking to.

Looking back, I could have just left.

I could have found Joe's floppy hair and hipster glasses and steered him off to feed me that meal he'd promised. But he was lost in the faceless crowd, too—and all attempts to search for him got intercepted by faceless people hugging me, until I wound up making way-too-friendly chitchat with my ex-boyfriend for five solid minutes before realizing who he was.

All to say, the situation snowballed.

Before I even really saw it coming, I was having a panic attack out behind the utility room.

At least I think it was a panic attack.

Is it a panic attack when your entire body is utterly hijacked by . . . panic?

And you get dizzy? And you sweat and have the chills at the same time? And your heart pounds and your chest hurts and your hands go cold? And you can't catch your breath? And you feel like you're dying? And you collapse to your knees in a dark corner and press your forehead to the concrete to try to make the world stop spinning?

Is that a panic attack?

'Cause that was me.

And I sure as hell wasn't celebrating.

I have no idea how long I'd been there, trying not to pass out, when I heard a voice say, "Are you having a panic attack?"

So of course I said, "No."

"You look like you're . . . not okay."

Not okay? That was just insulting. *Okay* was my whole thing. "I am always okay," I said, to set the record straight. And then, when the person didn't accept that and leave, I said, "I'm fine." Then, my voice muffled against the concrete, I added, "I'm good."

"You don't look good."

This wasn't Parker, was it? She never missed a chance for an insult. But no—of course not. It was a man's voice. One, as usual, I couldn't recognize.

"Identify yourself, please," I said into the roof.

A rustling beside me as whoever it was sat down. "It's your pal, Joe," the voice said, closer and softer now.

"Hi, Joe." For a second, knowing it was him made me feel palpably better. But then it occurred to me to wonder if he might be filming this moment for later blackmail, and I felt worse again.

"I'm no psychiatrist," Joe said then, "but I've seen a lot of panic attacks. And this kind of looks like that."

"I'm fine," I insisted. I was always fine—whether I was fine or not.

"Okay," Joe said. "A friend of mine—who clearly had a totally different thing from you—used to find it helpful for me to pat her back in moments that were nothing at all like this."

"I'm not having a panic attack," I said.

"Great," Joe said. "Neither am I."

"So I don't need you to pat my back."

"Cool. You don't need it." A long pause while he let that settle. "But we could just do it for fun."

"Fine," I said, too busy dying to fight.

And then he really did it. I felt a hand settle between my shoulders, and then I felt it slide down my spine till it reached my lower back, then lift up a second, and appear again back up at the shoulders.

He was basically petting me like I was a dog.

But, *ugh*. Okay. It felt nice.

If I weren't feeling so nauseous, I might be struggling with all my cognitive dissonance about Joe. My first impression had been so unbelievably bad. But many of the impressions that followed had been good. Had that first impression been wrong? Or was he just hiding all the bad stuff really well to my face?

I guess I'd just have to take it one panic attack at a time.

"The fact that you don't want me to help you," Joe said, "really makes me want to help you."

"That sounds like a you problem."

"It totally is. It's the reason my wife left me." Then he corrected: "One of them."

I admit that got me. "Your wife left you because you were *helpful*?"

"Yep."

"I'm no wife, but that doesn't seem like a thing wives normally complain about."

"I am, apparently, too helpful. Problematically helpful. To sum up our many arguments: I help everybody all the time without discretion. Old ladies. Cub Scouts. Mangy cats. I have no helping filter."

"But isn't that a good thing?"

"She also thought I was a bad tipper."

"Why?"

"Because I gave everybody twenties. Hotel maids. Valets. Everybody."

"Okay, Daddy Warbucks. I'm with the wife on that one."

"She felt it was a compulsion. Being too nice."

I guess she'd never heard him say the word *blubber*.

"And it impacted her quality of life. Negatively."

"I'm trying to imagine exactly how helpful you'd have to be for a non-insane woman to divorce you over it."

"There were a few other reasons," Joe said.

"Are you *pathologically* helpful? Did you give someone your *car*? Or, like, a vital organ?"

"Not yet," Joe said.

"My last boyfriend was the opposite of helpful," I said. "Your way is better."

"That's comforting."

"I'm probably a good friend for you," I said. "Because I never need help."

"That's a relief," Joe said, continuing to stroke my back in a hypnotizing rhythm and kindly allowing me to ignore the irony.

I admit: It was relaxing.

After a while, he said, "My friend who had a completely different thing from you used to breathe while I did this, and it helped her a lot."

"I don't need to breathe, thank you," I said.

"Suit yourself," Joe said. But then he added, "Deep breaths are super healthy for you, though—even if you're totally fine. I might take a few myself. Just to improve my already stellar health."

And with that, Joe sucked in a big, loud breath, held it for about three seconds, and then blew it back out. "So refreshing," he said then. "My grandma does this every day, and she just turned a hundred."

He kept breathing like that, and what can I say? Peer pressure. I joined him.

We did about ten rounds, and then, I'm not going to lie: I did feel better.

Less dizzy. Less nauseated. Less sweaty.

"My friend's totally different thing used to pass after about twenty minutes," Joe said then.

"I don't think my thing is going to pass until this party ends," I said.

"Ah," Joe said. Then, a second later, like he'd had an idea, he said, "Are you okay here on your own for a minute?"

"I am now—and will continue to always be—one hundred percent okay," I insisted, forehead still pressed to the concrete.

"Be right back then," Joe said.

A few minutes later, I heard a *chunk* noise—just as the music cut out and it seemed like my dark corner got darker. Then I heard the ambient sound of a puzzled crowd. Then I heard Joe's voice. "Power outage, guys. Looks like the party's over."

Oh god, he was my hero.

Just knowing they were leaving drained the stress from my body.

By the time Joe came back, I was sitting up, leaning against the brick wall, breathing. Like a pro.

"Did you just flip the breaker and pretend there was a power outage?" I asked.

"Yep," Joe said.

"And everybody went home?" I asked.

"Yep."

"And then you came back to check on me?"

Joe shrugged, like, *Obviously*.

"Did you worry at all that the darkness might freak me out?"

"Nah," Joe said. "We've got the moon."

I looked up and saw it for the first time. It was brighter than I'd realized. "I guess we do."

It occurred to me then that I might have to start altering some of my opinions about Joe. Next I asked, "And once the coast is clear, are you going to take me out for that dinner you promised?"

But Joe just shook his head. "No."

I felt a flash of disappointment. "You're not?"

"Nope," Joe confirmed then, turning back to the moon. "Because I already ordered us a pizza."

Fifteen

WE ATE PIZZA on the roof, cross-legged, watching the city skyline.

I don't know if it was the breeze playing with my hair, or the receding adrenaline from the panic attack, or the layer upon layer of compassion Joe had offered to me, but I found myself bizarrely relaxed. Scarfing down that pizza with gusto, talking with my mouth full, saying things I would never—ever—normally say.

Like, for example: I told him it was my mother's birthday.

Did he need to know that information?

Absolutely not.

But I wanted to tell him. I wasn't going to be able to do my usual thing—it was far too late to go get cake-baking ingredients now, and I was much too exhausted, anyway—but I guess I just wanted to mark the moment of it, even in a tiny way.

"It's my mother's birthday today," I said.

"We should call her," Joe said, checking his phone for the time.

"Can't," I said. "She died."

Joe's shoulders fell a little at that, and his pizza slice went askew in his hand.

"It's okay," I said. "It was a long time ago."

"But you still miss her," he said, reading my expression.

"I do," I said.

Joe waited to see if I'd say more. But what was there to say, really?

Finally I went with, "Every year, on her birthday, I bake her a cake. And light candles. And watch Cary Grant movies. I tell myself that's the one day when she can hear me from heaven—and I don't even care if it's true. I talk to her, out loud, like she's there. I just let myself have that. And I try really hard to be happy that I had her in my life at all."

He was good at listening, it turned out. It prompted me to keep going.

Or maybe this was just something I really needed to say.

"She died very suddenly," I said. "And when it was all over—weeks later—I found a voicemail from her that she'd left me the day before she died. It was the most ordinary voicemail in the world. But I listened to it and relistened to it so many times that I memorized it. I memorized the words, but also the pauses and the tempo and the musical notes in her voice. I can still do it to this day. When I was really, really lonely at boarding school, I used to go on long walks and recite it over and over, like a poem."

"Recite it," Joe said then.

"What? No." I shook my head. "It's boring."

But Joe said, "It's the opposite of boring."

I hesitated.

"Just recite it for me. I'd love to hear it."

He would? Was he being sincere? I suddenly felt shy. "It's very ordinary," I said. "She's just, like, talking about what to have for dinner and stuff like that. And she calls herself Mama, even though by then I'd been calling her Mom for years."

Joe leaned a little closer, waiting.

I'd never recited it for anyone before. My dad didn't even know the recording existed. I took a deep breath. Then I fixed my eyes on a random spot in front of me.

Then I just went for it: "Hey, cutie. It's Mama. I'm at the store. I'm thinking spaghetti for dinner. Good? With garlic bread and salad? Call me if you'd rather do French toast—but I'm about to check out, so be fast. Also, they're out of that shampoo that smells like coconuts, so I'm grabbing the lemon one instead. Dad has to work late tonight. Not sure what your homework situation is, but I'm free to watch a movie if you are. Okay, that's it. Home in twenty. Love ya."

Joe was quiet after I finished. "You really know it all. Even down to the pauses."

"I've listened to it a thousand times. At least."

"It's so heartbreaking," Joe said. "But she's just talking about spaghetti."

"Because she died the next day," I said. "That's why."

"So you know the day she died."

"I don't, actually. I can't remember what day it was. It was sometime around now. Sometime in the spring. Sometime before her birthday. But as for the actual day? No idea. So funny. That day changed my life more than any other ever has. But it's just one day. You know? And it's not exactly a day you want to remember."

Joe nodded. I could feel his reaction. I'd worried the mundanity of it might be underwhelming. But he wasn't underwhelmed.

He seemed to get it.

"Anyway, that's what I do every year, but this year got a little wonky. But I guess it's okay to miss it once in a while."

"There's still time," Joe said then. He checked his watch. "It's only ten."

I wrinkled my nose. "I'm too tired to bake a cake now."

"What if we go get a cake?"

I frowned.

"There's a dessert place not too far from here. I'll take you."

IT WASN'T UNTIL we'd made it all the way downstairs that I realized he meant to take me on a Vespa. Which was probably medically ill advised.

"My dad's a doctor," I said, as Joe worked the lock.

"Yeah?" he said, like I was just making chitchat.

"He always called motorcycles 'donor-cycles,'" I said.

Joe lifted his eyebrow like he'd caught me on a technicality. "This isn't a motorcycle. It's a Vespa."

"Isn't it dangerous?" I asked.

"At ten o'clock at night when downtown is deserted?" he said. "No more than anything else."

Good news: The helmet fit in a way that didn't touch my surgical scar, which I was still tender about—emotionally, if nothing else.

With that, Joe sat on the front part of the seat and motioned for me to climb on behind him. Then he wrapped my arms tight around his torso and said, "Just lean however I lean." Then he clicked the motor on, cranked the handle, and shifted us into motion. Confidently. Easily. Like a person who knew exactly what he was doing.

And we were off.

Next thing I knew, we were motoring through the deserted night-time downtown streets, my arms snug around him. If you go exactly 20 miles per hour in downtown, you can time it so you never hit a red light. And so we just cruised along, slaloming a bit in our lane, the wind caressing us and the motor vibrating beneath, never having to stop or wait, just swept up in a current of motion.

It was highly relaxing—for such a dangerous thing.

It didn't take me long at all to melt into the moment. Joe clearly knew this scooter back and forth, and everything he did had the ease of muscle memory.

We didn't talk.

We just flowed along. Summer in Texas is deathly hot, but spring is cool and lovely. The March air felt like rippling water over my skin. We took a road that curved along the bayou, and we positively floated along it. We passed street art, the Dandelion Fountain, and the Down-town Aquarium, with its light-up Ferris wheel. It was a little like drift-ing through a dream.

How long had it been since I'd had someone to hold on to?

The dessert place was open—packed, in fact, with folks gathering for sweet treats and coffee after their evening's activities, crowded at tables both inside and out on the sidewalk. I'd passed this place a million times. I'd just never had a reason to come in.

A bright, bustling, cheery place. It felt like a party.

Now, we ordered slices of cake—mine, a yellow diner slice with chocolate icing; his, death by chocolate—and then we wedged ourselves into a small table in the middle of it all. Joe had insisted on paying, and he must have told them we were celebrating a birthday, because when the slices arrived at the table, the waiter lit two giant sparkler candles, stuck them in the slices, and shouted, "Everybody! Let's sing 'Happy Birthday' to—"

And then he looked at me.

"Nora!" I shouted—and it felt so great to just shout my mom's name.

And so the whole room began to sing. And I swear I had never thought of the "Happy Birthday" song as anything particularly special until that moment—but sitting in front of that sparkler candle as the entire room launched into a rich rendition of it, I suddenly wondered why that song didn't bring me to tears every time. Maybe it was how crowded the room was, or the acoustics, or the sound of all those people singing warm wishes to my long-lost mother: *Happy Birthday, Dear Nora . . .*

But my voice got too wobbly to sing.

I spent the second half of the song just taking it all in.

Savoring it, the way I know she would have.

It was nothing like what I usually did to celebrate my mom's birthday.

But maybe different wasn't so bad.

THERE WERE LOTS of upsides to that night.

It had felt surprisingly good to help out the girl in the coffee shop, and it had been surprisingly satisfying to tell off Parker. Sue, while woefully off target, had at least been sweetly trying to cheer me up. Joe had turned out to be great at anti-panic back rubs. And creating power outages. And I had celebrated my mom's birthday *not alone* for the first time since she died.

But what, in the end, was my takeaway?

None of the upsides. Just the one crushingly disappointing downside: *I got stood up.*

That was the sentence that ticker-taped through my head all the next day.

I got stood up. By my future husband. On our very first date.

How would we spin *that* to the grandkids?

I mean, fine. He'd had a work emergency. I got it. I wouldn't have wanted him to have left some Saint Bernard dying alone in the clinic.

He'd been busy doing something noble. It was a fair excuse.

But here was the problem. It was now the next day, and the admirable, flawless, and perfect Dr. Oliver Addison, DVM, *had not called to apologize.*

I mean, if you leave a lady sitting in a coffee shop, even for a good reason, you should call the next day and grovel a little bit. Right? Make some voice contact? Stress in real time how sorry you are? Maybe demonstrate enthusiasm by setting a new date to try again?

Nothing from this guy. Crickets.

Which forced me to wonder something horrible: Maybe this perfect man wasn't so perfect after all.

Not fair. Hadn't I already decided he was supposed to solve all my problems?

He was supposed to make things better, not worse. He was supposed to ease my worries, not create more of them. He was supposed to make me feel good—not *frigging terrible.*

Maybe he hadn't gotten the memo?

I knew of course that people weren't perfect. Life was messy. He didn't even know how much I was counting on him to be the fantasy-man mirage that kept me moving through my personal emotional desert.

I couldn't legitimately resent him.

But I resented him, anyway. Illegitimately.

He was just so disappointing.

All day long, as he continued to disappoint me, I made excuses for him—maybe he'd been up all night and fallen asleep exhausted?—while resenting the fact that I had to make excuses for him.

And while I waited, my mind drifted more and more to Joe.

Because if Dr. Oliver Addison had been disappointing . . . Joe, if I'm honest, had been the opposite.

Joe had been surprising. Surprisingly nice. Surprisingly attentive. Surprisingly not at all like what I would have expected a person I'd nicknamed the Weasel to be.

Sixteen

ON THE AFTERNOON before Sue was coming over for our second—and final—make-or-break attempt at her portrait, I took Peanut out for his first long walk since he got sick.

We'd been cleared for little walks almost from the beginning. But before Peanut could do his signature long, rambling, sniff-everything-in-sight stroll, we had to make sure his strength was back.

I didn't mind. It gave me some time to think.

I'd been hoping—so hoping—that the edema would magically resolve before I really got down to the wire and had to paint this portrait for the show. Every morning I woke up and shuffled to the bathroom mirror, squeezing my eyes closed for a silent prayer before finally peeking to see what I could see.

And every morning, of course, my own face was just a jumbled pile of disconnected features.

I missed it. I missed seeing my face.

But I'd been instructed not to give up hope, and I was nothing if not obedient.

It would come back, I kept telling myself. There was a very good chance, at least.

But now I was at the point, with just over two weeks before the portrait deadline, when I had to trudge forward—fusiform face gyrus or no. I mean, even if I magically resolved my face blindness tomorrow, I'd still need time to paint the painting.

It was a make-it-work moment.

And so I'd been researching the brain. I'd been reading up on painting techniques and neuroplasticity, and how creativity worked. I'd been hunting through different strategies for making lots of different art. My best idea was to try to bypass the fusiform face gyrus altogether, if I could. To use other senses rather than sight. To sneak around my own assumption that I had to see faces the way I'd always seen them before I could paint them.

Maybe there was another way of seeing.

Maybe if Sue described her face to me in words, the words could make a new path for me to follow. Maybe I could capture her face before my fusiform face gyrus figured out what I was up to. Another idea was to try to turn Sue's face upside down, or maybe sideways, so that my brain didn't realize it was a face. Maybe if we just thought we were doing shapes and colors and lines, the FFG would never have a reason to cause trouble. And then, if neither of those worked, I'd turn to math. My least appealing option, since I was quite math-challenged. But artist Chuck Close had mapped photographs with faces using a grid. Who's to say I couldn't do the same thing on a real face?

If worse came to worse, I might draw an actual grid on Sue's actual face.

She didn't know that yet, of course.

But these were desperate times.

AND SO THERE they were. Countless late nights of research, distilled down into my best three ideas. Or more accurately, my final three shots in the dark. I knew I couldn't paint the way I'd always done it. My only remaining chance was to try something new.

And what if none of them worked?

Well, I wasn't going to think about that.

Anyway, that's what I was planning as Peanut peed on every clover flower between my building and the bayou: all the crazy new portrait techniques I'd try tonight with Sue. I had the canvas all ready and a measuring tape and a projector with a grid. We'd start with words and go from there. Maybe it would work better than I feared. Maybe my fusiform face gyrus would surprise me.

I was giving myself that pep talk when a fat plop of rain hit my nose.

Followed by another on my arm.

And then I lost count completely as some dam broke in the sky and Peanut and I had to race-walk the half mile home through what felt like a waterfall of rain.

By the time we made it back to the building lobby, I looked like I'd just climbed out of a swimming pool in all my clothes. My hair was plastered down on my face, and my shoes were squishing like they were full of Jell-O.

Peanut and I slid through the elevator doors just as they were closing—only to look up and see two people already there. Joe in his jacket. And a faceless woman.

Standing next to each other.

"Whoa," Joe said at the sight of me.

"Yeah," I agreed.

Peanut shook himself out and sprayed them both with rainwater, which made Joe laugh and the woman beside him recoil.

And that's when I smelled Poison.

Ugh. Just my luck.

Joe took a step closer to me. "Can I help you out somehow?"

He started to unzip his jacket, like he was going to give it to me, but the zipper got stuck.

"It's fine," I said as he yanked at it. "I'm already drenched."

But Joe was determined, and when he couldn't get the zipper to give, he pulled the jacket off over his head.

It really was too little, too late—but I didn't stop him. Mostly because the sight of him wriggling was so entrancing—as his T-shirt came up, too, revealing the stripes at the waistband of his boxer briefs—that Parker and I both just stood there, enjoying ourselves.

A rare moment of unity.

When he was finally out of it, he brought the jacket over to me.

I took it—but then I wrapped it around Peanut.

"Hey," Joe said. "That was for you."

"He's wetter," I said as my clothing audibly dripped on the elevator floor.

Joe settled into place beside me. The move had had a definitive feel to it, as if we were choosing teams in gym . . . and he'd just chosen mine.

That felt good. Not gonna lie.

But not to Parker.

Acting fast, before we reached the top floor, she put her hand to her forehead and moaned a little, falling back against the elevator wall.

That got Joe's attention. "Hey—are you okay?" he asked, stepping closer.

"I just suddenly felt dizzy," Parker said.

And then, with a technique that was neither subtle nor convincing, she angled herself at Joe and then "fainted" into his arms.

He caught her, of course. Joe wasn't the kind of guy who would just let a random stranger hit the deck without helping.

Once she was caught, she lolled her head back dramatically and exposed her whole neck to him—which he might have found tempting if he were a vampire.

But Joe just looked up at me then, my unconscious evil stepsister in his arms, totally befuddled by what was going on.

Granted, he didn't know she was my evil stepsister.

The elevator door dinged and slid open.

Top floor.

I walked out and held the door for Joe as he carried Parker toward her apartment. At the door, he stopped. "Hey," he said, shaking her a little. "Wake up."

I had paused in the hallway, still dripping, to rubberneck the situation and see how it played out.

Joe turned my way. "What should we do?"

But I just shrugged, like *No idea.*

That's when Parker roused dramatically and said, "I'm so dizzy. Could you help me into my apartment?" And then she gave him the passcode.

With that, they were gone—Parker's metal door slamming so hard it left a tinny echo behind.

I looked down at Peanut, swaddled in Joe's jacket. "That was weird."

Peanut licked his wet mustache in agreement.

I was tempted to bang on Parker's door until Joe came back and then haul him out by the collar to explain that Parker Montgomery was a life-ruiner with a total of zero redeemable qualities—and the next time she fainted in front of him, he should just let her fall.

But I was too cold and too wet for that conversation. So Peanut and I made our way down the hallway toward home.

BUT THAT'S WHEN we ran into a problem.

Remember how the dead bolt had been broken the other day—stuck in the out position so the door couldn't lock?

Today, the dead bolt was stuck again, but inside the latch. So it couldn't *unlock.*

I put my passcode in over and over.

I mean yes, my fingers were cold and trembling—but not that badly.

Peanut, also cold and trembling, waited patiently while I tried again and again.

I found Mr. Kim's number and texted him.

Mr. and Mrs. Kim had done very well in Houston, developing all kinds of properties, thanks to his business sense and her eye for design. They probably could have lived anywhere, but they lived here in the building. Mostly because Mr. Kim was super hands-on.

When things went wrong, we texted Mr. Kim.

Which worked fine—unless he was busy.

I might have experienced a moment of frustration while wet, cold, worried about my dog, and desperate to go home. It's possible I tried to shake the dead-bolted door open. I might or might not have hit the handle several times with my shoe.

No luck.

Finally, there was no choice but to just wait. There were three steps up to the door to the rooftop, and so I sat down.

A wet, trembling human next to her wet, trembling dog.

Of course, in that situation, I couldn't help but notice that Joe had not yet come back out of Parker's apartment. *What was he doing in there? What could possibly be taking so long? Was she trying to seduce him? Paying him for his services? Making him unclog her shower drain?*

Anything was possible with her.

One thing was clear. I didn't like it.

For his sake.

Nothing with Parker ever, ever ended well.

I wasn't jealous, I told myself. This was the same courtesy I'd extend to any hapless human who was about to fall victim to something poisonous.

Just run-of-the-mill human kindness.

When Joe finally came out, he saw me at the end of the hall and made his way in my direction.

"What were you *doing* in there all that time?" I demanded.

"She wasn't feeling well, so I looked after her a little bit."

"She was feeling fine," I said. "She was faking."

Joe nodded. "Probably, yeah. But I did get the feeling like she just needed somebody."

"Well, she can't have you," I said.

Joe tilted his head. "She can't?"

"Trust me on this," I said. "That girl is bad news."

"Did you wait here, dripping wet, in the hallway to tell me that?" Joe asked.

"I waited here in the hallway," I answered, glad to have a legitimate no, "because the lock to this door is broken. Again."

Joe frowned, and then he took it all in—me shivering, Peanut shivering, the door handle with its new shoe-dents.

"Oh god, you're freezing," he said then, reaching out to touch my cheek.

"You're just now noticing that? My teeth have been chattering this whole time."

"Did you call Mr. Kim?"

"Three messages. And three texts."

"Okay then," Joe said, crooking his arm around my shoulders and steering me toward his door. "Come on."

JOE'S APARTMENT WAS big. And penthouse-fancy. And top of the line: Viking range. Glass fridge. It made my hovel look even more hovelly.

But also? The place was totally empty.

By *empty*, I mean there was no furniture. At all.

Except for a couple of barstools at the island and a mattress on the floor in the master bedroom . . . nothing.

I saw it when Joe steered me into the master bathroom so I could take a hot shower.

"What about Peanut?" I asked.

Joe handed me a towel. "I'll get him with the blow-dryer."

"Be careful," I said. "He doesn't like men."

"He likes me," Joe said.

"You don't have a sofa, but you have a blow-dryer?" I said. That floppy hair of Joe's definitely couldn't require much maintenance.

But Joe was already gone.

While I showered—and can I just say that his shower was far, far superior to mine, so I stayed in way too long—Joe accomplished many things. He left a T-shirt, some heather-gray sweatpants, a big plaid bathrobe, and some oversize socks that fit like Christmas stockings folded by the door for me. He blow-dried Peanut, as promised, and then talked him into eating a few pieces of cold rotisserie chicken. He left a note on the rooftop door for Mr. Kim to call me or come by Joe's place with any info on the lock. And he ordered takeout from an Italian place nearby that I just happened to love.

Pretty impressive, all in all.

When I emerged at last all layered up with my hair wrapped in a fluffy white towel, I was feeling a lot better.

The food had already arrived, and he was unpacking the bag at the island in his empty kitchen.

"Thank you for your help," I said as I approached.

Joe looked up at the sound of my voice and then stilled at the sight of me.

Whatever expression he was making that I couldn't see, I couldn't read it, either.

"Don't laugh," I said, tightening his robe around me.

"I'm not laughing."

"Don't stare, either."

"I'm not staring."

"Yes you are."

Joe dropped his head to look down.

I couldn't help but feel annoyed. I bet his last glimpse of Parker's attire had been a lace teddy. "This is the best I can do with myself right now, okay?"

"No," he said, like I was misunderstanding. "You look—"

"I look what?"

"You look . . . cozy."

I felt an unexpected ping of disappointment at that. But what had I been hoping for, exactly? "Lovely"? "Ravishing in a man's plaid bathrobe"? "So much better than your stepsister"?

The man was serving me linguine fra diavolo right now. Maybe I could cut him a break.

I took the emotional high road. "Thank you for rescuing me."

"You're not rescued yet," Joe said—and at that, I checked my texts for anything from Mr. Kim.

Nothing.

Fine. Eat first, worry later.

I glanced over to see if I should make a plate of linguine for Peanut, but he was fast asleep, a little pile of blow-dried fur.

"So," I said, settling onto a kitchen stool and gesturing around at this empty warehouse of an apartment. "What's the story here?"

"What story?"

I looked around again. "You know you don't have any furniture, right?"

"Ah," Joe said. "That's true."

No sense in pretending. "This is the saddest apartment I've ever seen," I said. "It's worse than my place, and I live in a hovel."

"A penthouse hovel," Joe pointed out.

"A *rooftop* hovel," I corrected.

"But it's surprisingly nice."

"It's much nicer than this sad . . ."—I looked around—"empty warehouse." Then I had to ask. "How long has it been like this?"

"A year."

I choked on a noodle. "*A year?*"

Joe crunched on his salad and gave me a shrug.

"Do you . . ." I tried to imagine any kind of reason at all why a grown man would live in an empty apartment for a whole year. "Are you . . . anti-furniture?"

"Not really," Joe said, like that was all he was going to say on that. Then he added, "I just gave it all to Goodwill when my wife left me."

Ah.

Okay.

He went on, "I wanted to burn it in a gasoline-fueled bonfire, but that's against city regulations. Apparently."

Wow. Joe had a past. And maybe some anger issues. Why did that suddenly make him sexier? "You checked with the city before torching your ex-wife's furniture?"

He nodded. "It's all on the municipal website." Then he tilted his head like he was noticing my point. "I'm very law-abiding."

"Fair enough."

"She must have done something really horrible to you," I said then, all casual, hoping he'd spill it all.

"Yep."

"For you to want to burn everything."

"Yep."

"And then for you to just . . . live in a mausoleum."

Joe stopped chewing and assessed me. Then he made a decision. "She cheated on me. With a guy from work. And then she left me and moved in with him. And now they're getting married."

I squeezed my whole face up like that really smarted. "Oh god."

"Yeah."

"How did you find out?" I asked.

"I surprised her on a work trip and found them together at her hotel. Naked. In her private hot tub."

"Oof."

"She got home from the trip, packed a suitcase without a word, and went to a hotel. She came back a few days later to get the rest of her stuff . . . and brought him with her. She *brought him with her.* To our apartment. She kept saying, 'I thought you'd be at work,' like that made it better. And then—long story short—I wound up beating the crap out of him."

He paused, like I might think that was a bad idea.

"Good," I said, holding up my hand for a high five.

"Yeah, well. I'm not normally violent. Just so you know."

I looked at his forkful of linguine, resting lukewarm and forgotten in his hand.

Why had I pushed to talk about this? Poor Joe. Now I'd made him lose his appetite.

"Hot tubs," I declared, like this might make him feel better, "are just crawling with bacteria."

He went on. "It's pretty cliché stuff when you think about it," he said. "Happens every day."

"But not to you."

"No . . ." he said quietly. "That was a new one for me."

But suddenly I was feeling mad for him. "What's wrong with her, anyway? What could she be thinking?"

With that, I could feel myself signing up for Team Joe. If he was the terrible person I'd originally thought, he was hiding it really, really well.

Maybe there was a good explanation.

Whatever I'd heard in the elevator, it just couldn't have been what it sounded like.

"You're very handsome and nice!" I declared then, going all in. "She should've been thanking her lucky stars!"

"You don't have to say that," Joe said.

I mean, did I know for sure he was handsome? No. But who cared? Sue said he was—and she was picky. "It's true," I insisted. "She *squandered* you."

"I'll bounce back eventually," Joe said. "I just . . . haven't found a good reason to."

I pointed at him. "Yet."

He sighed.

"Come on. Say it with me. You haven't found a good reason to—*yet*."

His shoulders sank as he resisted—like my forcing this optimism was just insulting. "Yet," he finally said. And then he stuffed that whole forkful of cold linguine in his mouth, made himself chew it, and swallowed it down.

Then, like a man who'd just accomplished something, he said, "And what's your deal?"

"My deal?"

"With that woman," Joe said, gesturing with his now-empty fork. "Across the hall."

That woman. Across the hall. Actually, Parker might come in handy as a distraction. I sat up straighter, ready to shift our focus from his misery to mine. His life might start looking better by comparison.

"She's my evil stepsister," I said.

Joe wasn't the only person here with a past.

"Wow," Joe said. "Okay. They still make those?"

I gave a little shrug. "Not just for fairy tales anymore."

Then Joe said, "Can you define *evil* here?"

I thought about it a second. Being vague was always an option in times like these. But why not just tell the truth? If she was going to keep *fainting herself into his arms,* he should know what he was dealing with.

I took a breath.

"After my mom died, my father married her mother—like, six months later, by the way—and Parker moved into my house, started attending my school, framed me for some vicious bullying that she herself was doing . . . and then got me kicked out."

Joe took that in. "Kicked out of school? Or out of the house?"

"Both."

"Wow."

I nodded. "The girl she bullied was this sweet kid named Augusta Ross. We'd been friends since we were little. She used to bake sugar cookies with me and my mom. Parker left menacing typed anonymous notes in her locker every morning. Stacks of them. She told Augusta that she was ugly—going into great detail about what was wrong with every feature on her face and every part of her body. She made up lies about how much individual people hated Augusta—and fabricated terrible things they'd supposedly said about her. She was relentless.

"And here's the clincher: She told Augusta that if she ever told anybody about the notes, she would poison her cat, Cupcake. And then she printed off pictures of cats and cut their eyes out—and started leaving those in Augusta's locker, too."

Well. We certainly had changed topics.

Joe seemed to have forgotten all about his ex-wife.

He slurped a forkful of linguine.

I went on. "Her bullying got so bad and was so relentless for so long that Augusta one night tried to swallow a whole bottle of Tylenol—which really will kill you, by the way."

Joe nodded. "Liver damage."

"Luckily, she was terrible at taking pills. When her parents walked in on her in front of a giant pile of capsules, the whole story came tumbling out. The school got involved. An investigation happened. And Parker, who had apparently been typing those notes in a hidden file on *my* laptop, went to the administration and handed it over."

"You got blamed," Joe said, astonished.

"I got kicked out," I said. "They sent me away after that. To a thing they called 'boarding school,' but it had distinct 'correctional facility' vibes."

"Nobody stood up for you? Nobody helped you?"

"Everybody sided with Parker. Including my own father."

"How could he do that?"

I shrugged. "He said the evidence was incontrovertible." I took a sip of water. "That's actually how I learned the word *incontrovertible*."

"Wow," Joe said.

"Yeah."

"She sounds like a psychopath."

I nodded. "She basically stole my life. By the end of high school, she was living in my room, wearing my clothes, hanging with my friends, and sleeping with the boyfriend who dumped me after the scandal."

Joe shook his head in protest.

"But the worst part," I said, in conclusion, "was Peanut. I couldn't take him with me. He had to spend two years living with those monsters. The day after I graduated, I made Lucinda bring him out to me on the front walk, and I never looked back."

Finally Joe said, "Holy shit."

I nodded. "Yeah."

"And now she's moved into our building?"

"Yep."

"Not by accident, I'm guessing."

"Agreed."

"But why?"

"I don't really know," I said. "But it's not because she's suddenly changed her entire personality, I can promise you that."

"Do you think she's here to mess with you?"

"I guarantee it."

"But . . ." Joe asked again, looking befuddled. "Why?"

I thought for a second. "You know those children who try to trap ground squirrels so they can torture them?"

"I guess so?"

"That's her. And I'm the ground squirrel."

Joe took that in.

"Anyway," I went on, "now she's set her sights on you, so be warned."

"What makes you think that?"

I looked into his puzzle-piece face. "She told me."

Joe paused like that was completely nuts—which, in fairness, it was. "Why would she tell you that?"

I saw this coming. I could so easily have shrugged and said I didn't know—and left it at that. But I was going to have to do a little bit of leveling with him to get him oriented. It was my civic duty to inform him what he was dealing with.

So I said, "Because she thinks I like you."

It was a hell of a thing to just . . . *put out there.*

What was I doing? What was I thinking?

Sure—I was trying to be accurate.

But I miscalculated. I thought that if I rolled my eyes a little in the delivery, he'd dismiss the underlying truth of it out of hand while still grasping the essentials: that Parker was out to get me—and he could become collateral damage.

But I far overestimated my acting skills.

An eye roll is a complex thing to manufacture. It's not just *eyes.* Eye rolls also require a slight shrug, an imperceptible tilt of the head, a microscopic retraction of the neck. Plus impeccable timing. An eye roll, when you really think about it, requires a whole ballet of delicate and precise muscular choreography timed to the millisecond. It's not for amateurs.

All to say: I flubbed it.

I came off like a kid actor in a bad sitcom.

And I realized I was overdoing it *as I overdid it*—and so then I grimaced involuntarily and gave myself one thousand percent away.

But—and I'll always be grateful to him for this—Joe didn't call me on it. He didn't put me on the spot. He didn't lean in all curious and say, *Is she right? Do you like me?*

He just graciously focused on the thing I clearly wanted us all to focus on: how incomprehensibly terrible Parker absolutely was. "Is that why she fainted in the elevator?"

"Pretended to faint," I pointed out.

"Was she—making a move?"

"She was."

"By fainting?"

"It got her into your arms, didn't it? And it got you into her apartment."

"I mean—sure. In a *medical* way."

"Baby steps," I said. "Give her time."

Joe nodded like this was all really fascinating.

"Anyway, I thought you should be warned."

"Thanks for the warning. Though I didn't need it."

How very cocky of him. "And why not?" I asked.

Joe leaned forward, swiped the garlic bread off my plate, shrugged charmingly, and then said, "Because she's not my type."

Seventeen

MR. KIM DID wind up answering my text eventually, and I did wind up standing in the hallway with him in Joe's too-big bathrobe as he got the lock working.

"Why is the handle dented?" Mr. Kim asked.

"No comment," I said.

"Where's Helpful?" Mr. Kim asked.

I frowned. "Where's—?"

"Helpful," Mr. Kim said, gesturing toward Joe's apartment with his head. "He couldn't get this fixed?"

Mr. Kim's nickname for Joe was Helpful? He had nicknames for lots of people in the building—often just their apartment numbers. But this one seemed, suddenly, especially on the nose.

"I don't think he's very mechanical," I said.

All the other locks on the penthouse floor were, of course, high-tech, digital fanciness you could operate with your phone. This lock, however, was like a 1980s punch box. Something a real estate agent in shoulder pads would operate.

"This is a terrible lock," I pointed out to Mr. Kim.

He didn't disagree. Just glanced in the direction of the roof. "Technically, nobody's even up there."

"Fair enough," I said.

Mr. Kim could fix anything, and that was a point of pride with him. He had it working again in record time—and I wasn't sure if I was glad or disappointed.

Before he left, Mr. Kim leaned in to tell me something. "When Sue calls you with her news, don't worry. He got our permission."

"Who got your permission?" I asked.

But Mr. Kim shook his head and made a little key-locking gesture at his mouth. "I've said too much already. But trust me. It's okay. They have our blessing."

"Who has what blessing?"

But he just shook his head.

Then he started down the hallway, waving goodbye, before remembering: "Mrs. Kim has some homemade kimchi for you! I'll bring it up tomorrow."

"I can come down and get it!" I offered.

But he waved the idea away, like *Pshaw*.

Just as he disappeared into the elevator, my phone rang.

It was his daughter.

"Hey, Sue," I said. "Your dad was just here."

"Don't tell him I'm on the phone!" she said.

"He's gone already," I said. "Why do you sound freaky?"

Sue regrouped. "I'm calling with news."

"Good news, I hope," I said.

Sue didn't comment on that. "I know I'm supposed to come over tonight—"

I checked the time. I'd completely forgotten about her. "Yes! And you're an hour late!"

"But I have a conflict," Sue said.

"You *cannot* have a conflict," I said.

"But I do," Sue said, in a voice that was just begging me to ask her what it was.

I sighed. "What's the conflict?"

And so she burst out, "I'm eloping!"

"You're . . . ?"

"Eloping!" Sue said again—because it was so fun to say.

"Eloping?" It didn't compute. "With *Witt*?"

"Guess what he got for us?"

Did she really want me to guess?

"Transcontinental railway tickets! Across Canada!"

Guess not. "What does that mean?" I asked.

"We're traveling from one side of Canada to the other!"

"On a train?" I asked. Did they even still have those?

"Vancouver to Halifax, baby!" she said, in a voice like we were about to high-five.

But I refused to validate this madness. "I don't understand."

"We're eloping. On a train. Witt bought the luxury package," Sue said. "He used up his savings."

"Okay, that's a red flag, right there."

"Hush. It's romantic."

"I don't know if you know this," I said, "but Canada is really big."

"Yeah!" Sue said.

"So this isn't like a weekend jaunt or anything. It'll take at least . . ." I paused to calculate.

"Fourteen days," Sue supplied.

"Fourteen days!" I repeated. Then, to confirm: "That's two weeks!" Then, just to make it sound even more ridiculous: "That's a *fortnight*!"

"It's sixteen days with travel time."

"What about work?" I demanded, grasping at straws. "Don't you guys have jobs?"

"We figured it out. Don't worry about it."

"What about your parents? Won't they be pissed?"

"He got their permission beforehand. Which made them love him even more."

She sighed like the resistance in my voice was excitement. Like we were going to swoon about this together. "It's a sleeper train," she whispered.

Why was she whispering? "Don't people get murdered on those?"

She paused. "Wait. Are you not excited for me?"

I backtracked. What kind of friend wasn't excited for her best pal when she eloped with a former college track captain? "I am *very* excited for you," I said, worrying again about my acting.

"That's a relief," Sue said.

"When do you leave?"

"That's the thing," Sue said then. "We're at the airport now. So if you have an issue, speak now or forever hold your peace."

"You're eloping—right now? As we speak?"

"It was a surprise," Sue offered meekly.

"But—" I said. Was it unsupportive of me to point out that she was abandoning me during the one week—the only week—when I needed her the most?

"I know," she jumped in, not making me say it. "We're supposed to do the portrait this week."

"I—"

"I should have called you sooner—but it was all so dramatic. He *kidnapped* me. Isn't that cute?"

I drew the line at kidnapping. "Not really."

"The point is, I had no idea."

"Wait—" I said then. "Are you calling me from the airport *in Canada*?"

"Greetings from Vancouver."

Oh god. She was already gone.

I was happy for her. I was, I was. Of course I was.

But . . . just . . . who was going to model for me now?

I was in a uniquely terrible position—because I had to do a uniquely bizarre set of things to this person. I couldn't just hire some random art model. I barely felt comfortable doing all these things to Sue. And we'd seen each other in bathing suits!

I felt an urge to cry clasping at my throat. But I swallowed it—hard.

I was not going to ruin Sue's kidnapping-elopement by bursting into tears. I just refused to be that person.

I took a deep breath instead, and I ratcheted my face into a big, bright smile. "I'm so happy for you," I said.

"You are?"

"Of course! Being kidnapped to Canada is every girl's dream."

"But what about your portrait?"

"Pah," I said, making the most dismissive noise I could think of. "Models are a dime a dozen. I'll have your replacement before you can eat a beaver tail."

"Nice Canada reference."

"You're welcome."

It dawned on me that we needed to wrap this up before my voice started trembling. "You realize, of course, I'm going to make you do a pretend second wedding later so I can be a bridesmaid."

"Done and done," Sue said.

I made her promise to text me lots of pictures. And save the bouquet. And drink a whole bottle of maple syrup. And then I blew kisses into the phone. And then I hung up . . .

And started crying.

Broken lock. Sick dog. No model. Evil stepsister. Best-friend-less, moneyless, jobless. Not to mention *suddenly face-blind at the worst possible time*. And about to fumble my first—and now probably last—big break.

What the ever-loving hell had happened to my life?

It had never been perfect before, by any means—but at least it had some potential.

I couldn't pull it together, but I couldn't make myself go back to Joe's apartment, either, so I just stood there in the hallway crying. *This is good,* I kept telling myself. *This is emotionally healthy. You've got to feel your feelings.*

I was feeling them, all right.

I felt them and felt them—until I finally looked up to see Joe coming out of his place with a box of tissues.

"I was going to let you cry it out," Joe said, holding out the box as he got to me. "But then I started worrying you'd get dehydrated. Medically."

"I'm not a big crier," I said, pulling out a tissue to blow my nose.

"If you say so."

I stuffed the tissue in my pocket and took the box from him. "Seriously."

"I eavesdropped on your conversation," Joe confessed. "Not on purpose, at first—but then I got hooked."

"It's fine." Who cared, honestly? Eavesdropping was so low on my triage list.

"Sounds like your best friend just eloped? For two weeks? Leaving you without a model for your portrait project?"

I nodded and started crying again.

Joe waited until I slowed down, and then he pulled a tissue out of the box for me. "I'll be your model."

I dabbed at my face. "What?"

Joe shrugged. "How hard can it be?"

"I can't ask you to be my model, Joe," I said.

But he shook his head. "You just have to sit there, right?"

"It's more than that," I said. "This is kind of a special project."

"Wait—" he said then. "Is it a *naked* portrait? Is this like a Burt-Reynolds-on-a-bearskin-rug deal? I'll need to grow some better chest hair."

I tolerated that. "People aren't 'naked' in art. They're 'nude.'"

But Joe was grinning at me like he had my number now. "You're going to make me take my clothes off, aren't you?"

"No!" I said. "This is a completely normal, non-naked portrait. No clothing will be removed."

"So what's the problem?"

I looked down, trying to figure out how to explain it. It didn't make a lot of sense if he didn't know about the face blindness—and I was already doubling down on never telling him about that. The more appealing he became, the more he did not need to know how messed up my life was.

But how to explain it without explaining it?

"Sue and I were going to try some unconventional techniques," I said.

"That's fine," he said.

"I've been trying to push myself as an artist," I said next. Not untrue. "And so I need to try some new strategies."

"Are *you* the one who'll be naked?"

"No one's getting naked."

"Then I don't see the problem."

"It's just . . ." I tried again. "I'd have to touch you."

"Touch me?"

"I'd have to draw a grid on your face. So there'd be a fair bit of touching. And staring. And studying. For a long time. It could be very . . . intimate."

"But you wouldn't be *punching* me, right?"

"Of course not."

"I'm still just trying to figure out which part of this is bad."

"It's not *bad,* exactly. It just might be awkward."

"I can handle awkward."

"But why would you want to?"

Joe tilted his head, like it was already obvious. "To help you out."

At the word *help,* I felt my usual knee-jerk *nope.*

I didn't want his help! I didn't *need*—

. . . But actually, I *did* need his help.

I wouldn't be standing in this hallway sobbing if I had any other options.

Would it be so terrible to just let him help me?

I thought about the very recent moment when I'd given my favorite dress to a total stranger in a public bathroom. It did feel good to help other people out sometimes.

Fine, I decided, with a long sigh. He wanted to help me? I'd let him help me.

What other choice did I have?

Maybe this was a moment of personal growth.

"Things I might do to you," I said, "include, but aren't limited to: Staring at you a lot, peering at you, and leaning in close. Studying you. Asking you to describe your face to me while I'm painting it. Projecting a grid over your face and mapping it out mathematically. Measuring your features with a tape measure. And touching your face, neck, and shoulders. Is any of that objectionable?"

"As long as you don't put me in a Burt Reynolds toupee."

"But what do you think?"

"I think I don't know why we're still talking about it."

But then I had to ask: "Would it bother your girlfriend?"

"My what?"

I tilted my head to gesture down the hall. "Aren't you dating Busty McGee?"

He looked in the direction of my gesture. "Do you mean Marie Michaux?"

"Huh. I guess she has a real name."

"You know she's a scientist, right? Dr. Marie Michaux."

"No," I said. "I just know she looks fantastic in a tank top."

Joe shook his head. "She is a trailblazing evolutionary biologist and herpetologist."

"Herpetologist? She studies herpes?"

Joe sighed. "Herpetologists study reptiles. She, in particular, studies the effects of climate change on snake coloration."

I stared down the hall at her closed apartment door. "That's not the profession I would've guessed."

"She was just featured in *Science* magazine. She's brilliant."

"So . . ." I said then, just to irritate him. "You're dating a brilliant herpesologist."

"Herpetologist," he said, making a couple of *tuh, tuh* noises afterward to emphasize the T. "And we're not dating."

That perked me up a little, though I'd never admit it.

It perked me up so much, in fact, that I did not submit any follow-up questions—on the chance that he might follow "We're not dating" with something ghastly like "We're just sleeping together."

Don't ask, don't tell. What he did or didn't do with the snake-a-tologist was his business.

"I can't pay you," I said then. "Not with money, anyway."

That got his attention. "What will you pay me with?"

"Well," I said, "I can't give you the portrait itself, because they're auctioning those off."

"That's okay," Joe said, all deadpan. "I have too many portraits of myself already."

"So," I went on, businesslike. "Let's just say you can have whatever you want."

"Whatever I want?" he asked, like it was too good to be true.

"Within reason," I said. "If you want me to paint something for you, or if you want me to buy you dinner or give you an art lesson, maybe. Whatever you can think of."

"Are you giving me a blank check?" he asked.

"No!"

"Sounds like a blank check to me."

"I'm saying you and I can find a mutually agreed-on form of payment at some point."

"So in other words," Joe said, the delight of teasing me pretty clear in his voice, "a blank check."

Eighteen

SUE'S ELOPING WAS a bummer for many reasons.

One, I'd be missing my best friend's wedding.

Two, all the stuff I was about to do to Joe was nerve-racking to say the least. He had no idea what he was in for.

And three, Sue had promised to be my date to the art show.

Which was the worst bummer of all.

Because when you have to do something genuinely scary, it's nice to have a friend.

I'd be all alone. Just standing straight and brittle with crazy eyes and a quavery smile all night while I waited for a bunch of portrait critics in tortoiseshell glasses to render judgment on my talent, my value as a human being, and my entire future.

So, yeah. Was eloping to Canada really more important than keeping me from dying of misery?

I could see both sides.

Anyway, Sue had been fully on board to help me survive it all.

Until she got kidnapped, that is.

I suppose it was possible I'd astonish us all and win this art show.

But I didn't love my odds.

That said—I had just enough hope to keep going.

That's the dark underbelly of hope that nobody ever talks about. How it can skew your perspective. How it can keep you in long past when any reasonable person would've been out. How it can land you in your own apartment on a random Tuesday night—annotating your downstairs neighbor's nose-to-lip dimensions with a tape measure.

"You don't have to hold your breath," I kept telling Joe.

"Right. Got it."

He was more nervous than he'd expected to be. I could tell from his posture. And how very scrubbed clean he was—like maybe he'd taken a shower and a half. Even from the cautious way he'd walked across the rooftop toward my door. Almost like he had half a mind to turn around.

"It's harder than it seems, huh?" I said.

"Trigonometry is hard. Climbing El Capitan is hard. Landing on the beaches of Normandy is hard. This is just . . . sitting here."

"Sitting here *while a total stranger measures every square inch of your face.*"

"You're not a total stranger."

"You're right. I'm worse. You know me just enough for this to be super awkward."

"I don't feel awkward," Joe said.

"Yeah, you do."

I'd made a graph on a canvas and I was dividing his face into one-inch sections, trying to treat each square as a different landscape. Maybe if my brain didn't know it was a face, it wouldn't cause trouble.

I worked my way from top to bottom. So far I had the hair, the hairline, the forehead, and the eyebrows. It had gone pretty well, but now we were coming to the eyes, and for some reason I didn't understand, ever since the start of the face blindness, the eyes were my hardest thing to look at.

But these weren't eyes, I told myself. These were dots and lines and color. I just had to think about it that way, and I'd be fine. Maybe that was the trick to it all. Abstract it out. Make the face *not a face*.

Easy.

But of course Joe didn't know his face wasn't a face. He kept rubbing his eyes and sneezing and looking back at me. Every time his eyes met mine, I got a jolt of something physical, like I was looking into a bright light.

"You can look down," I kept saying.

"Sorry," he'd say.

Mostly, though, he sat still.

Mostly, the problem was me.

This just wasn't how I was used to working.

I'd been painting portraits since high school. I'd patterned my techniques and methods into my brain like deep grooves.

This felt like trying to read a book upside down. In another language.

At no point did I ever just get caught up in the flow—the way I always had before when I was painting. There was no flow. There was no getting lost in the moment. The math and the struggle and the shockingly close presence of Joe's actual live human body just right there, inches away from me—breathing and generating heat and leaning in whenever I got close—kept me anchored to reality.

I blame Joe.

And that torso of his.

And don't even get me started on the imaginary judges I kept hearing in my head: "Did she use a *grid* for this? What is this, paint by numbers?"

I could feel myself losing. In advance.

I had a bad feeling. I took a picture of the portrait so far and texted it to Sue for her professional opinion.

Her reply was immediate: **Nope. Creepy.**

Salvageable? I texted back.

Not a chance.

"I don't think the grid is working," I said to Joe.

Joe shrugged. "Okay. What's next?"

I consulted my list of ideas. "Let's turn you upside down."

So that was our next attempt. Joe lay on the sofa, hanging his head backward over the arm, and I turned the canvas upside down and tried to sketch him like that.

Sue's response to this one was a simple two words: Police sketch.

So we moved down the list. I tried having him describe his face to me and painting with my back to him.

Maybe the third time would be the charm.

But no.

Sue's final response was the worst of all: Serial killer.

Okay.

We were done here.

I set my brush down and took a second to rub the kinks out of my hand. Had I ever cramped up while painting before?

Never.

Joe must have been cramping up, too, somehow. Because he watched me working on my hands for a minute, then looked up decisively and said, "I think I need a break."

We'd been at it since five o'clock, and now it was ten.

"Oh," I said. "Sure. Of course."

He started walking toward my door, and when I didn't follow, he turned back to wave me in his direction.

By *break*, I thought he meant, you know, a turn about the room or something. "Are we . . . going somewhere?"

"We need to get some air."

OUTSIDE, WE STROLLED for a bit.

Then Joe asked, "Who have you been texting all night?"

Was there any way in hell I'd be telling Joe that I had no ability to judge if my own portraits were any good?

No.

"Is it your friend who eloped?"

"I'm just getting her opinions," I said. "On the portraits."

"You're texting her pictures?"

"Yep."

"Can I see?"

"See what?"

"The portraits."

I frowned at him, like he was crazy. "Of course not." We'd already agreed.

Just then, another text came in from Sue. I glanced down to check it—just as Joe leaned over to peek.

"Hey!" I protested, hiding the phone behind my back.

But he tried to reach around me, all playful.

"Nope," I said, race-walking away. He was *not* seeing those portraits.

Now he was chasing me a little. "Your friend gets to see them, and she abandoned you for Canada."

"She didn't abandon me, she was kidnapped," I said, moving toward a patch of grass.

What was happening here? It goes without saying that Joe trying to steal my phone was much more fun than Parker trying to steal my phone.

But did he really care about seeing the portraits? Or did he just want to blow off some steam and roughhouse? He hadn't seemed to care at all earlier—but maybe he was just . . . looking for a reason to run around outside? Flirting, even?

Joe swiped at my phone again, managing to pull me into a hug-like situation as he did—and this time, he grabbed it.

I wasn't cleared for running, so I knew I couldn't chase him.

Instead, I threw my foot out and tripped him.

He hit the grass with an "oof," and then, before he could scramble off and run away, I sat on him and started tickling him.

It worked. Joe, despite his claims, was highly ticklish. He started laughing so hard, he fully dropped the phone. And it was so fun to see his reaction that even after I'd grabbed it and stuffed it deep into my pocket, I went back to the tickling.

What a strange thing to do. Had I ever tickled anyone in adult life? Definitely never. But it felt somehow like the only thing to do.

Turns out, it was fun.

"We agreed," I said, like I had to punish him with tickling now because he'd broken the rules. "You weren't going to look at the portraits until I was ready. Right?" I tickled some more. "Right?"

"Fine," Joe finally said, breathless. "Right. I give up! Peace!"

I sat back, out of breath, and then he sat up, also out of breath.

We sat companionably side by side for a minute. That whole thing had been a lot more playful than either of us had expected.

And more suggestive.

Joe was just standing to help me up when we heard a woman's voice say, "You always were ticklish."

At the sound of the voice, Joe went tight like a wire. Then he turned to stare at the woman with the intensity of a hunting dog on point.

She was standing a few feet away from us, with a man, holding his hand.

Who were they? Were they people I knew? I scanned for clues. She had a black shirtdress and sandals, and he wore khakis and a graph-check button-down.

They could have been anyone.

But not to Joe.

Joe knew exactly who they were, and his body tensed up so much, it tightened the air around him. That said, he had some grass in his hair. So I reached up to brush it out.

He didn't even notice.

"What are you doing here, Skylar?" Joe asked, his voice about as friendly as a knife.

Oh god. It was the ex-wife.

The tip-off was Joe's voice. Specifically: the fumes of loathing rising up from it.

Yeah. Definitely the ex.

Skylar turned toward the man with her, who gave Joe a little wave like they knew each other.

And this must be the man she'd left Joe for. The Hot Tub Guy.

"We were just getting coffee," Skylar answered Joe, nodding in the direction of Bean Street, and calibrating her voice to "pleasantries."

"This isn't your coffee shop anymore," Joe said.

Skylar gave a little "sorry, not sorry" shrug. "Still the best in town."

Joe didn't dignify that with a response.

So Skylar turned toward me. "And who's this?"

It's true, I couldn't make sense of her face. But everything else about her made perfect sense. She was poised. And coiffed. She could walk in heels. She seemed exactly, generically like a woman nice guys might want to marry and spend their nice lives with.

But she was also a cheater.

She had married Joe, and promised to love and cherish and be faithful to him . . . and then she'd climbed bathing-suit-less into a hotel hot tub with—I glanced over at the Hot Tub Guy beside her—*this dude.*

Gross. I could see it in my mind almost like I'd been there.

True, my first impression of Joe had been . . . pretty negative.

If that was all I had to go on, I might even be taking the ex-wife's side right now.

But every interaction I'd had with him after that first one had been positive. Very positive. I thought about Dr. Nicole saying I couldn't trust myself, and then I thought about Joe giving me his jacket when I was cold. And feeding me Italian food. And blow-drying Peanut. And offering to be my model.

Maybe the problem was me.

Maybe I should give this poor guy the benefit of the doubt.

In that second, I could just sense every miserable, conflicting, rejected, angry, hurt, abandoned emotion that Joe had to be feeling.

And in that rush of empathy, I just . . . wanted to help him.

Maybe it was the fact that he'd helped me tonight without any hesitation. Or maybe it was all the time I'd just spent measuring his face. Or the tickling we'd just done in the grass. But I felt a strong urge to help him out overtake me right then.

And I just didn't overthink it.

Right there, under the curious gazes of Joe's ex-wife and Hot Tub Guy, "Who's this?" still hanging in the air, I slid up next to Joe, hooked my arm around his waist, and tried to create the most sexually suggestive side hug in history.

I felt Skylar take it in: the way my hip rubbed against his, the way my arm tightened around his torso, the impact of my temple as it made its landing on the curve of his shoulder.

That was all she needed. "Ah."

Guess it worked.

It should have been enough. Really, it was plenty. I'd made my point, right?

Joe had rescued me so many times—and now I'd rescued him back.

But it felt better than I would've expected. Both the hug itself— touching him, slipping over close and pressing against him in so many places like that, setting off emotional sparks I didn't see coming—but also the rescue.

The brain system that reads people? It revved right up at that moment. I could feel Joe's relief at what I was doing. I could feel how grateful he was. It was palpable. His tension eased. His breath slowed. Even the feel of his arm as it came up around me in response was like a grateful caress.

Suddenly we were a team working together to pull off this moment. The two of us against the world. Or—more accurately—against Joe's ex-wife.

The point is, I didn't stop at the side hug.

While Skylar and Hot Tub Guy were still taking us in as a couple, I could just *feel* Joe's brain replaying the betrayal all over again—almost like I was feeling it with him. And I just couldn't resist the challenge of trying to take that pain away.

I didn't think it through, that's for sure.

I didn't think at all.

Joe wasn't the only person around here who could be pathologically helpful.

And at that I reached out, grabbed the collar of Joe's shirt, pulled him down toward me, and kissed him.

By the way, his lips? In that moment? As I went in for the landing? I could see them just fine. Zeroing in on the lips was easier, in fact, than trying to take in a whole face. It felt like a relief.

It was meant to be a peck, but at the moment of impact, I heard Skylar make an astonished little gasp.

And that spurred me to keep going.

To push in closer, in fact. To go bigger.

And deeper. And softer.

I shifted my hand up to the back of Joe's neck to hold him in place— not sure how he'd react to the shock of it all. The odds were fifty-fifty that he'd jump away, like *What the hell?*

But he didn't jump away.

The opposite, in fact.

In a remarkable feat of surprise improv, as soon as he realized what I was doing, he went with it. He brought his hand to my back, pulled me tighter, softened his mouth, and kissed me right back.

Just like that, it went from fake to . . . something else.

We didn't even need a hot tub.

I don't know how long that little kiss lasted. Three seconds? Five? A hundred? All I know is, when it started, we were both entirely focused on the couple standing across from us . . . and by the time it ended, that focus had shifted.

Skylar and Hot Tub Guy were forgotten.

That is, until Skylar coughed and said, "Okay. Well. Great seeing you."

It broke the kiss, but nothing else. Joe didn't even look over or loosen his arm around me or say goodbye. He just stared into my eyes until after they were gone. And I was too dazed to even mind.

Then, in unison, we snapped out of the trance. We broke eye contact and stepped back.

Next, of course, it was awkward.

Joe coughed. I tucked my hair behind my ears. Joe checked his watch. I looked down at my shoes. Finally—what choice did I have?—I smacked him on the shoulder and said, "Stop trying to peek at the portrait."

And much to my delight, that made Joe laugh. And that was something.

I looked off in the direction they'd just walked. "Your ex-wife, right?" I said, my eyes on her.

Joe nodded. "Bull's-eye."

"And Hot Tub Guy?"

Joe nodded again. "Teague Phillips."

"That's his name? Teague?"

"Yep. Valedictorian of his high school class." Then Joe added, "It's weird that I know that."

"He seems very dull," I said, maximizing my judgmentalness out of loyalty.

"Thank you," Joe said then. "My plan was to never, ever accidentally bump into them."

"How dare they come to our coffee shop?" I said. "No hot tubbers allowed."

"What you just did was . . ." Joe started.

What? What was it?

"Very kind," he finished.

Huh. Not sure about *kind*. Impulsive, maybe. Reckless. Brave.

"You really saved me," Joe said.

I held my fist up for a bump—trying to reestablish equilibrium. "You've saved me a few times."

"Not like that, I haven't."

He wasn't wrong.

"That," he went on, "was a heroic thing to do."

"Do you think it worked?"

"Oh, it worked," Joe said, like that might be true in more ways than one.

"Glad to be of service," I told him.

Later, it would occur to me to worry about Dr. Addison. I was of course aware that we weren't really engaged or even dating—yet. But we had an intention to start dating. What were the rules around kissing someone when you had a plan to start dating someone else?

I hadn't technically cheated. That much seemed clear.

But what would Dr. Addison think about that moment, if he'd known about it?

I tried to revise the memory into a simple act of altruism. Joe had been in pain, and I'd seen a way to relieve that pain. Unselfishly.

For no personally gratifying reasons of my own.

It almost made me a *better* person, in a way.

Besides. Anyway. If Dr. Oliver Addison, DVM, didn't want me offering pity kisses to hipster neighbors ambushed by their ex-wives, he should have found a way to make it to our date.

Nineteen

YOU KNOW THOSE days when it just feels like the universe is out to get you? And even though you know intellectually that the universe is way too busy to sit around planning your personal destruction, it still feels that way, anyway?

The next day was one of those days.

I hadn't been awake an hour before I'd stubbed my toe, burned my toast, and watched Peanut throw up on my seagrass rug. Which happened sometimes. It didn't necessarily mean he was sick, but I called the vet anyway. They said it was nothing to worry about, but we made an appointment for a checkup on Thursday, just to be safe. I was supposed to watch him until then and call if he seemed worse.

An appointment with Dr. Addison should have been a sunny patch upon the horizon.

But he still had never called to apologize after standing me up, so I really wasn't sure at all how he felt about me.

I wasn't entirely sure how I felt about him, either.

Because that "fake, not fake" kiss with Joe kept popping into my head in flashes: The tension of his surprise, and how fast he'd melted into the moment. The tickle of his hair as I'd cupped his neck with my hand. His arm tightening around me, pulling me closer. The velvety smoothness of the skin on his lips.

If anybody at all had asked me anything about it—including Joe himself—I'd have sworn up and down it was one hundred percent platonic.

But those flashes of memory were full-body experiences. And when they appeared in my mind, I had to suck in a quick cool breath, and then stand up and walk around for a minute.

Dr. Addison needed to pick up his pace. I could feel Joe gaining on him.

But then I remembered that I was the one who'd wanted to take things slow in the first place. What was I even doing? I shouldn't be thinking about anything at all right now except getting that portrait done—or killing myself trying. I shouldn't be going around *kissing people*! Even for humanitarian reasons.

Screw humanity! I had work to do!

But first—today—I had a long to-do list. None of it fun. Starting with a brain scan with Dr. Estrera. Which meant I had to walk along Joe's hallway and past his apartment to get to the elevator. Which was a full-body experience on its own.

This was his floor.

This was the spot where he'd handed me a box of tissues.

That was his apartment door.

And there was the man himself, in his pajamas—

—coming out—

—of Parker's apartment.

Wait—what?

I darted into the stairwell before he saw me and held my breath.

Did I just see that?

It was eight in the morning. Why on earth would Joe be coming out of Parker's apartment first thing in the morning?

Besides the obvious.

I tried to put it together. Joe. Pajamas. Parker's apartment. Eight in the morning.

It couldn't be what it looked like, right?

I mean, it was hard to ignore the probability that he had somehow, just hours after a fake kiss with me, added Parker to his charcuterie board of women. That he really was a mutton muncher, or whatever that old-timey insult was.

I so badly wanted there to be some other explanation.

But—what?

My mind paged frantically through the possibilities. Had she pretended to faint again? Had she begged him to come kill a cockroach? Maybe her toilet was clogged and he was helpfully plunging it for her, like a gentleman?

Ugh. Ridiculous.

I couldn't even convince myself.

While I waited for it to make sense, Parker's hairless cat, of all things, wandered into the stairwell, as if pets were allowed to roam the halls at will. It appraised me petulantly for a minute, and then it walked right up to me, turning as it did to back up and lift its tail. I leapt away within seconds of getting peed on.

How had it come to this?

One thing was for certain: The pleasant, Joe-infused buzz I'd been feeling all morning? It stopped buzzing.

THE DAY WAS downhill from there, if you can believe it.

I mean, by the end, this day made burned toast seem adorable.

Hiding in the stairwell made me late, so I cut it a little close with the crosswalk light. I made it across, but a guy who I inconvenienced for three seconds decided to roll down his car window, shoot the bird at me, and shout, "Fuck you!" before flooring it and tearing off.

I glared after him, like, *Really, sir? Wasn't that just a little much?*

He was clearly doomed to a life of rage and disappointment.

But it still kind of smarted, I admit.

Next, I climbed into my waiting Uber and, trying to multitask, checked the comments on my Etsy shop on the ride—only to discover the hands-down meanest review of my work I'd ever beheld.

I took a screenshot for posterity:

These portraits are an insult to the art world. Banal, trite, and cheesy to the max, this is "art" I can't unsee. Seriously. My eyes are burning. Trash like this is the reason humanity is doomed to hell.

Okay. Whoa.

You can't please everybody. I get that. But "doomed to hell"?

I mean, ArtWeenie911 clearly had some issues. The level of his or her viciousness toward pleasant, smiling, fairly photorealistic portraits of people from all walks of life was . . . a bit extreme?

I tried not to take it to heart. For all I know, ArtWeenie911 was a troll bot. Sent to sow discord in . . . *what?* The barely-making-ends-meet online portrait painting community?

Maybe not.

I was two for two with random acts of douchiness today.

Not counting the Joe-in-pajamas incident. By far the douchiest of all.

On the heels of that, after spending several cold hours in a medical gown in waiting rooms and various imaging scanners, I got a totally un-helpful report that showed no reduction in the edema—and then I was told again to "just be patient."

Which of course I would. Because what choice did I have?

But how much time and money did I waste just to be instructed to do what I was already doing? There was "no change" in my situation? I could've told you that.

I'd been hoping against hope for a last-minute disappearance of the swelling. A lifetime of movies with underdog champions had primed me to expect that I'd find a way to triumph just in the nick of time.

But that wasn't happening.

Not to mention all day long I was getting stalked by Lucinda, who insisted she needed to speak with me "urgently" about "a matter of great concern."

Texts and phone calls I ignored, of course.

Pro tip for dealing with Lucinda: If she ever says anything is urgent, just run and hide.

Add to my list of grievances: Strappy sandals that were giving me a blister. A phone with three percent battery. The moment when I forgot my purse in a waiting room and had to race back to find it. Not to mention: The art store was still out of linden-green gouache, and the grocery store was out of the only vet-recommended dog food that Peanut would eat.

By the time I limped home, the sun was setting, my Achilles tendon was stinging, and I felt like the day was positively *bullying me.* Somewhere along the way, I'd started keeping a mental tally of the insults and injuries—almost as if I could submit the list and demand a refund.

Even the prospect of seeing Joe that night felt like an attack. Either he wouldn't tell me about Parker—which would be bad. Or he *would* tell me—which would be worse.

One thing I knew: I did not want to know.

But there was no wriggling out of any of it. The only way out of this day was through. So as I geared up for the home stretch, I stopped at Bean Street for a half-caf latte—for both comfort and caffeine.

And that's when Parker descended upon me, just as Hazel One handed me my coffee.

"Lucinda's been trying to reach you all day," Parker said.

Parker. Of course. Who else would reek of Poison and know that about Lucinda?

"Yeah. Well. I've been kind of busy."

"I bet you have."

She wanted me to ask her what that was supposed to mean. So I didn't.

She went on. "Saw you smooching the Vespa guy last night. Which of course provoked me to retaliate."

Retaliate? What did that mean? Did that explain his morning walk of shame? Had she shown up at his door at midnight in a bustier and garters? I felt disloyal to myself admitting this, but Parker was, technically, a good-looking person. She had enough to work with in the looks department that she could have pulled off a stunt like that.

She wanted me to react to that. So I didn't.

And then I had a freeing thought. *I didn't have to stand here. I could just . . . leave.*

I didn't have to stay. I didn't have to let her push my buttons. I didn't want to let this escalate. I just wanted to get outside. I could see the sunshine just past the windows.

I started walking toward the exit doors. But Parker followed me. I'd just reached them when she caught up.

"You didn't let me give you my news," she said. "I'm coming to your show."

And there it was. So much for just leaving. She got me. I turned back. "My what?"

"Your little art thingy."

The portrait show? The biggest, most important moment in my entire career? She was coming to that? "You can't," I said. "You're not invited."

But she shook her head and shrugged. "Open to the public. It's on the website."

"You're *not* invited," I said again.

"Sure I am."

"You can't." Then, panicking—looking for a strong enough word: "I forbid it."

She looked at me like I was contemptibly funny. "Lucinda and Daddy and I are all going."

Had Parker just called my father *Daddy*? Nobody called my father Daddy. Not even me.

"We're going to make a night of it," she went on.

"No," I said.

She went on, "Maybe hit a Brazilian steakhouse for dinner. Too bad you can't join."

"No," I said again.

She absolutely loved how furious this was making me. "No what?" she asked, knowing perfectly well.

"No. This is my thing. And I don't want you there."

"That's so funny," she said. "Because, as usual, I don't think you can stop me." Then she waved at me all cutesy, like *Buh-bye*, before seeming to remember one last thing. "Oh! Did you get my comment?"

I shook my head. Curious, despite myself.

"The one I left at your Etsy store today." Then she gave me a mischievous shrug and turned to go.

But I guess this was when the tsunami started to reach the shore. "Why?" I called after her.

Parker turned.

"Why?" I said again—all the pressure in my body making the sound tight and sharp. "Why, why, why, why, *why* can't you just leave me the hell alone?"

And there it was. She got me in the end. As always. And now her work was done. "I don't know," she said with a cheerful shrug before turning to walk away. "It's just so fun to watch you fall apart."

I blinked after her for a second, and then I turned to push out the doors and escape into the sunshine. But as I did, all that building anger somehow shot into my arm like a bolt of lightning—and I accidentally on purpose slammed the coffee-shop door behind me.

The *glass* coffee-shop door.

Which, apparently—I was about to discover—had a broken soft-close hinge.

Because when I slammed it? It *slammed*. Hard.

It felt satisfying for a second, I'll admit. But then, as if in slo-mo, all the glass popped, shattered, and rained to the floor.

I turned back at the sound and stared at the violence of what I'd done. The gaping hole of the empty doorframe. Glass everywhere. People staring. All movement and conversation frozen. A teenager started filming with his phone.

I put my hand to my mouth. I looked up and saw Hazel One over by the coffee station. She was the first person to spring into action, and she grabbed a broom and a dustpan and came my way.

"I'm so sorry," I said as she got close. "I didn't mean to do that." Then, of course: "I'll pay for it. I'll fix it." I'd figure it out somehow.

"Don't worry," Hazel One said kindly. "The hinge is broken. Happens all the time."

It definitely did not happen all the time.

But I was too mortified to argue.

And then the craziest, trippiest, most unreal thing I've ever seen in my life happened right before my eyes. Hazel One leaned her broom against the doorjamb for a second, preparing to start sweeping up the mess, and she pulled out a ponytail holder from her apron pocket, lifted her hands behind her head to twist her hair into it, and when she dropped her hands again . . . she was Hazel Two.

What I'm saying is this: Hazel One always wore her brown hair down, and Hazel Two always wore her brown hair in a ponytail—and that's how I could tell them apart. And in that one impossible moment, I watched Hazel One become Hazel Two right before my eyes.

Like a horror movie.

I gasped out loud at the sight.

"Wait . . ." I said, taking a step back. "What just happened?"

"When?" Hazel Two asked, starting to sweep.

"Are you Hazel One or Hazel Two?"

Now she looked up. I could feel the confusion in her expression. "Huh?"

"Of the two Hazels who work here," I said, with a feeling like this question was already doomed, "which one are you?"

A pause. Then she shook her head. "I'm the only Hazel who works here."

"Always?" I asked. "Has there ever been another Hazel working here?"

"Nope," Hazel said, getting back to sweeping. "Just me."

Oh, my god. There was only one Hazel who worked here. The girl with the bob and the girl with the ponytail were *the same person.*

Twenty

I KNEW, OF course, that I couldn't trust my perceptions.

I knew that my brain was having a rough month.

But it was so strange to witness it correcting itself.

I really wasn't okay. Not yet.

The only Hazel was gesturing at me to move out of the way now so she could sweep. I started to tiptoe my way over the broken glass in my dumb strappy sandals . . . when an arm clamped around my waist to help guide me.

Joe.

I knew it before I knew it. I felt him in an instant.

Then one side glance brought confirmation: Yep. The bowling jacket.

"Let's sit you down," Joe said, starting to walk me toward a bench.

But when we got back to the safe shore of the glass-shard-free sidewalk, I sidled out of his grasp.

Joe. Pajamas. Parker. Nope.

He did not need to rescue me. Not today. Not after whatever he'd been up to with the defining bully of my lifetime. I could rescue myself, thanks very much.

Mostly, I was angry at Parker. I was angry at the man who'd shot me the bird. I was angry at the imaging tech who hadn't found any reduction of the edema. I was angry at my blister and my understocked grocery store and my dead phone battery. And at *myself* for my own inability to navigate my life—and the way I'd just brutalized that innocent glass door.

But right then, all that anger just crystallized at Joe.

How *dare* he cavort with my evil stepsister like that and then show up acting like a good person?

It wasn't just poor choices. It was a deep betrayal. And the fact that he didn't know that?

That just made it worse.

An image of Joe stepping out of Parker's door in his pajamas lit up in my head like a neon sign. Who did he think he was?

"I've got it," I said, my voice distant.

Joe hesitated. "Can I—"

"No, thanks."

"Are you—" he tried again.

"I'm good."

There was no bouncing back here. There was no redeeming this moment. Or this day.

I started walking toward our lobby doors. No way was I taking the shortcut through Bean Street. I might never get coffee there again.

As the rage receded in my consciousness, delayed humiliation took its place. I walked faster, trying to escape as soon as possible.

But that's when Joe called after me. "Are you okay?"

I just kept walking.

Joe called after me again. "Are you mad at me?"

No response there, either.

One final question from Joe. "Do we still need to finish the portrait?"

That one, I needed to answer. I stopped and turned. "The portrait," I called back, looking near him but not at him, "is canceled."

CANCELED.

The word ricocheted around in my head as I rode the elevator, climbed the rooftop stairs, served a plate of croissant morsels to Peanut, and then draped myself over my bed.

Canceled.

That felt surprisingly good.

I didn't have to do any of this.

The idea misted me with relief. I didn't have to just endlessly suffer and suffer and suffer.

I could just . . . quit.

That was a victory. Kind of. Wasn't it?

An act of self-respect: Not forcing myself to endure a contest I knew I couldn't win. Not suffering through an endless art show where I didn't belong. Not painting the portrait of a disappointing man.

I could become a family therapist. Or a scuba instructor. Or a chef. Or a handbag designer. Was there some rule somewhere that the dream you picked for yourself in college had to be the dream you kept forever?

Peanut finished his repast and joined me on the bed, and the two of us lounged there together for a while, feeling victorious.

The joy of quitting. Who knew?

I could just stop trying. I could just never paint again. I could be free.

The raw power of saying no felt so good, we just stayed like that— enjoying our perspective shift—until we both accidentally fell asleep and drifted into one of those deep, peaceful, underwater naps.

WHEN I WOKE up, I had a text from Sue.

She'd found an article about an artist who had severe face blindness whose entire body of work consisted of drawings she'd made of her own face—by feel. Thousands and thousands of portraits of her own face—done with her eyes closed as she moved her free hand around her face and took in visual information by touch.

LOOK! Sue shouted—all caps—in the text. THESE SELF-PORTRAITS ARE AWESOME!

Self-portraits are not allowed, I texted back.

Just read the article, Sue said.

I read the article. It was long. It told the story of this artist's life—of how her severe lifelong undiagnosed face blindness had led her parents, teachers, and schoolmates to think every bad thing they wanted about her. From being called stupid to uncooperative to obstinate, she'd been misunderstood and blamed her entire life, as if she suffered from an attitude problem. Or a bad personality. They blamed her and disliked her—and she blamed and disliked herself . . . until she discovered the practice of drawing by feel.

She couldn't perceive her own face, and so the process of drawing self-portraits had become a way of finding herself. She had thousands and thousands of them by now—all of them ethereal and poetic and mysterious, like she was glimpsing herself through a deep fog. I couldn't see the faces, either, when I looked at the images of the article, but I could see the smoky pencil lines, I could feel the sense of mystery, and I could read the exquisite details.

And I realized, looking at the images, that I was seeing them in a special way. Most people, I realized, saw her face itself—and her attempts to render it. But I couldn't see the face. All I could see was the emotion. The artistry. The longing.

It was like getting the inside view.

By the time I finished reading, my perspective had shifted. The artist described her self-portraits as "healing," and that was the only word I needed to hear.

I grabbed some paper and some charcoal pencils, sat straight down, and started working on a self-portrait by feel of my own.

Two seconds later, two hours had gone by.

I looked up from the finished drawing and saw the darkening sky.

Then I turned back to the self-portrait I'd just drawn—that jumble of features that I couldn't see—and I just knew, very simply, that it was good.

I texted a photo to Sue and said, This is good, isn't it?

She texted back: OMG. It's amazing!

I had barely "liked" it when another text came from her.

Do that to Joe!!! Then, Maybe this is the brain hack you've been looking for!!!

But, I texted back, I just decided to quit the competition.

Too bad, Sue said. Unquit.

NOT QUITTING MEANT I had some groveling to do. With Joe.

I went down to his apartment and knocked on the door.

"I'm sorry I was weird before," I said when he opened the door. "I had a colossally bad day—and you were just in the wrong place at the wrong time."

"Really?" Joe said.

He didn't believe me? "Really," I said. "It wasn't personal."

"It seemed kind of personal to me."

"I had just shattered a glass door," I said. "I was having a moment."

"But the way you glared at me . . ."

Had I glared at him?

"I walked away wondering what I had done."

"You didn't do anything." Not true—but I didn't want to get into it. I didn't want to hear any confessions or apologies about Parker. Because I'd never be able to be around him, or tolerate him, or put my hands all over him the way I was about to ask to do if he told me he was dating her.

Then I'd really need a new model.

The point was, I didn't want to know. I needed to keep it all professional. No confessions. No truths. Just a pleasant apology and one last portrait attempt before I gave up on all my dreams.

Joe went on, "And so I thought about it. Pretty much all day. What had I done to piss you off? And then I got it."

"You got it?"

Joe nodded. Here it was. Confession time.

"We don't have to—" I started.

But then Joe said, "The kiss."

The kiss?

"Right?" he went on. "It must be the kiss. You were just trying to help me out, and then I turned it into a whole other thing. I don't have an excuse for that. I just—I guess it was the surprise of it. And I hadn't kissed anybody in a long while. And there was definitely some sweet revenge mixed in. But mostly it was just . . . so unbelievably nice."

Really? That's what he thought I was mad about? A swoony kiss?

Who gets mad about a swoony kiss?!

In that second, my goals shifted. He wanted to have this conversation? Fine. We'd have this conversation.

It might ruin everything. But I guess that's the thing about anger. I suddenly didn't care.

"Not the kiss," I said.

"Not the kiss?"

"What else might I be mad about?"

Joe hesitated.

I was going to force him to say it now. He'd started this, and I was going to finish it. "Rack your brain," I said.

But Joe just shook his head.

And that just made me madder. "What am I mad about? What am I mad about? It wasn't the very nice accidental sweet-revenge kiss." I took a second to shake my head incredulously. "It was your walk of shame."

"My walk of what?"

"Out of Parker's apartment. This morning. At the crack of dawn."

Joe thought back. Then he remembered. Then he protested. "But that wasn't—"

"Are you saying you didn't slink guiltily out of Parker's place this morning?"

"I mean, I walked out. But I didn't *slink*."

I narrowed my eyes at him.

"Is that what you're thinking? That I got up to no good with your evil stepsister?"

"Prove me wrong."

But Joe was just shaking his head. "How could you think that? How dumb do you think I am?"

"All men are dumb when it comes to Parker."

But Joe was still indignant. "I wasn't messing around with the stepsister who ruined your life," he said. "I was feeding her cat."

Confirmation. "You were feeding Parker's evil cat? The one that keeps peeing in our hallway?"

Joe nodded. "Yep. Its name is Elvira."

I took that in. "But you were wearing your pajamas."

"Exactly!" Joe said. "People don't do walks of shame in their pajamas."

He had a point.

"Parker wasn't even there! She left at three A.M. on a flight to Amsterdam!" he said—and now it was his turn to be mad. "You think that I kissed you last night and then turned around to have some kind of illicit tryst with your worst enemy?"

I mean, yes.

Worse things happened all the time with Parker. But his outrage was humbling.

"It wasn't a real kiss," I finally said.

"It was real enough."

I shrugged, still half thinking I was right.

"How could you think that?" Joe said.

"I don't know. People are terrible."

"People may be terrible," Joe said. "But I'm not."

He really felt kind of hurt.

Maybe it was time to level with him a little. "I'm sorry," I said then, "I'm having a very weird month."

"Okay," Joe said, listening.

But how much to say, standing here in the doorway of his empty apartment? Maybe just the basics.

I took a breath and went for it. "About a month ago," I said, "I had what they call a nonconvulsive seizure in the crosswalk in front of our building. And apparently a Good Samaritan pushed me to safety just before I got mowed down by a Volkswagen Beetle. At the hospital, they did a brain scan for the cause of the seizure and found a little malformed blood vessel. They said I needed surgery to correct it, so I had surgery."

Joe shook his head, like *What?* "You had brain surgery?"

"Yeah," I said.

"A month ago?"

I nodded to confirm. Then, like a kid showing someone a boo-boo, I leaned forward and pulled my hair aside so he could see the scar behind my ear.

He peered in at it. "Wow."

I hadn't shown anybody my scar yet. Not even Sue.

"Yeah," I said. "And it's been"—here, a tremble found its way into my voice—"a weirdly hard month. Nothing's quite right. Things that used to be easy are now . . . *not*. Especially painting."

Joe nodded.

"The day of the seizure, I'd just had my first big career break. And I was all set to win it." I looked down at my hands. "But I'm having trouble painting now."

"That's why you're trying new techniques."

I nodded. I was not, not, not going to tell him about the face blindness. But maybe I could tell him about what it felt like. "My whole life, my brain was always just so . . . reliable. But now, not as much. I keep getting things wrong. I can't trust myself. The whole world looks different. And so the version of me that you're getting right now is . . . kind of a mess. Much more of a mess than usual."

If Joe had any sense of what a big deal it was for me to admit to anyone ever that I wasn't A-okay, he did not show it. "You're not that much of a mess," Joe said, his voice softer.

"I *smashed a glass door* today."

"That was a mess," Joe conceded.

"Anyway, I'm really sorry," I said. "Getting super mad at people over wrong assumptions is not normally my thing."

"It's fine. You can make it up to me."

"How?"

Joe gave a shrug. "Just un-cancel the portrait."

"Funny you should ask," I said. "That's exactly what I came here to do."

Twenty-One

BY THE TIME Joe showed at my place for the final portrait attempt, it was do or die.

Mostly die.

Because this portrait was going to lose. Big-time.

It might turn into a really compelling piece of art. It might become a fascinating character study. It might wind up beautiful or mesmerizing or powerful.

Hell, it might even be salable.

But it would not be the kind of portrait the North American Portrait Society was looking for. It would not be the kind of painting that had allowed me to beat out 1,990 other competitors. And it would not look like the work of a twenty-first-century Norman Rockwell—guaranteed.

Which was freeing, in a way.

Knowing I was going to lose?

It meant I could lose with some style.

After Joe agreed to the final attempt, Sue gave me a pep talk.

"Do you think I can do this?" I'd asked.

"What do you mean by 'do this'?"

"Win. Do you think I can win?"

"No way in hell," Sue said.

"Hey!" I said. "You're supposed to encourage me."

"I don't think you can win," Sue pushed on, "but I do think you can make something interesting. I do think you have mad artistic skills and a wildly creative brain. I do think you understand color and light like no one I've ever met. And I also think, just from the vibes I'm getting across international borders, that you might be madly in love with your subject."

So that she could get to her point, I chose not to argue.

"Maybe you need to let go of winning. Maybe there are all kinds of ways to win. Maybe it's a chance for you to make your own set of rules."

"You're saying I should give up?"

"Don't give up. Just shoot for a different kind of victory."

"You can't just not win and pretend that you did."

"Look," Sue said. "Maybe you can't do your usual thing right now. What if you do something crazy and different? What if instead of trying to make a thing you can't make, you try to do something else?"

"Like what?"

"Like try to tell the story of this moment in your life. Try to capture your world right now, cracked open, exactly the way it is. Capture the chaos and the uncertainty and the longing. And don't forget to capture whatever's going on with you and that guy—because there's some kind of fire in that."

I thought about it. "I don't usually try to tell a story about my life with portraits."

"But," Sue countered, "that's what you've been doing all along. Telling the story of a girl trying like hell to paint exactly like her lost mother. And maybe now, in the story, the girl has no choice but to paint like herself."

"But this *isn't* myself."

"Right now it is."

I thought about it.

"What if you just capture your story—right now—as it is. I'd give anything to see that."

"I'll try," I said. Because what other choice was there?

"And then text me a picture."

"Fine," I said. "But if you text back words like 'serial killer,' we're going to have a problem."

OKAY. SUE WASN'T wrong.

Before, I'd been trying to paint a portrait. A highly specific kind of portrait.

But knowing that I couldn't do that was a kind of freedom.

Now all I had to do was paint something interesting. Something compelling. Something that held your attention. Something true about my life.

I was going to paint the moment. My experience of Joe in this moment.

Whatever that might turn out to be.

What I didn't have going for me, obviously, was the face.

What I *did* have?

Joe's exquisite torso, for one. Right? I knew for a fact I could see that. Now that I thought about it, it seemed like a crime to leave a visual feast like that all covered up.

I also had going for me: form, color, mystery, composition, contrast. And attitude. I wasn't going into this painting timid. I would dive in bold—headfirst and naked.

Metaphorically naked.

Which left me feeling all the things you feel when you're about to get naked. Nervous. Awake. Churning with anticipation. Hyperaware of the fact that you're alive.

When Joe arrived, he seemed like he might be some of those things, too.

"You don't have to do this," I said as I opened my hovel door.

"Sure I do. I said I would."

"Yes, but I'm giving you an out."

"I don't need an out."

"You don't know what I'm about to do to you."

"You can do whatever you want to me."

"I'm going to touch you," I said. "Is that okay?"

"I think so?"

"What I mean is, I just read an article about an artist who does self-portraits by touch, with her eyes closed. So she's painting what she's feeling more than what she's seeing. And I'd like to do that to you."

Joe shrugged. "Fine."

Was it bravado? Or did he really not think me putting my hands all over him would be a big deal? Or maybe he wasn't yet fully aware of how *very much* I was about to put my hands all over him.

I had to warn him. "Remember when I swore there would be no nakedness?"

"Yeah?"

"I might have to ask you for a smidge of nakedness."

I could feel the grin that took over his face at that. "Are we going full Burt Reynolds?"

"No," I said firmly—like that was the full answer. Then I amended, my face crinkled with apology, "But I do need you to take off your shirt."

Joe shrugged. "Fine."

No wonder Mr. Kim called him Helpful. I couldn't get a no out of this guy.

All to say: Ready or not, we were doing this.

I led him toward my easel, where I'd placed a stool for him right up close. Everything had to be within arm's reach—the stool, the canvas, the paints. By the time I had us set up, his knees were on either side of my thigh—close enough that we kept brushing and bumping against each other, over and over . . .

In a way that I worked very hard to experience as nonsensual.

Joe waited for instructions.

But I suddenly felt shy to give them. "So now . . . if you wouldn't mind . . . I need you to take off your jacket . . . and your shirt, if that's okay. Because . . . I don't know if you know this about yourself, but your torso is really . . . compelling. And I just feel like it would be a tragic missed opportunity to leave it out."

"You think my torso is compelling?" Joe asked, shrugging out of his jacket and tossing it over my sofa. I could feel him smiling.

"Yes," I said, trying to clarify through tone of voice that my intentions were so honorable they were almost scientific. "Artistically. Visually. Mathematically, even. It's compelling. To look at. By all objective standards. And so if I can capture that in the portrait, then the portrait will be compelling, too."

Joe peeled off his T-shirt, and my eyes took in the sight without asking permission.

"You sure you're good with this?" I asked.

"You're much more nervous than I am."

"I just want to make sure I have your consent."

"I am one hundred percent consent."

I'd painted many models over the years, and it was never nerve-racking like this. But this was different. Usually the models were across the room, not right up next to me. And I never touched them—just looked. And they were not people I had kissed. Or yelled at. Or eaten linguine with. Or ridden Vespas with. Or told about my mother. Or cried in front of.

They were always strangers.

That's when I realized that Joe wasn't a stranger.

I didn't know exactly what he was to me, but he wasn't a stranger.

All the touching I was about to do to him . . . it couldn't be just an art project. It couldn't be just about shapes and textures and tones. There were emotions involved.

I didn't know how to get rid of them.

And I didn't want to get rid of them.

And I suspected, honestly, that they'd make the painting better. If I could keep it together.

I lifted my hands up for Joe to see. "So," I said, trying to make it all sound rational, "I'm going to touch everything that's going to be in the portrait with these." I shook my hands at him.

Joe nodded, like *Cool*.

"First I'm going to just kind of map you with my hands. And then once I've got a really 3-D mental picture, I'll start sketching."

Joe nodded again, like *Let's go.*

But I was still hesitating. "I'm going to frame the portrait kind of from the waistband up. So I'm really going to have to touch you everywhere."

"Got it," Joe said.

"And I want you to know," I went on, "what I'm about to do to you, I've also done to myself."

That came out unexpectedly suggestive.

I was trying so hard to pretend like this was just another day at the office. Like I did this kind of thing all the time—no big deal. But my hands were weirdly cold. And I was strangely aware of my blood traveling through my body. And then, as I reached out to touch him, just before I made contact, my hand faltered.

It just . . . stopped. Like there was an invisible force field.

But that's when Joe's hand came up, and he cupped it behind mine, and he pulled my palm to his chest. I felt the impact before I realized what he was doing: the stonelike hardness of his collarbone beneath my fingertips, the spongy firmness of his pecs beneath, the warmth of his skin.

I could feel that he was looking at me. I could feel him encouraging me. And something else, too. Something that felt like longing.

Was it his or mine?

For a second, the air in my lungs felt tight.

"Don't be shy," Joe said. "I'm fine. Just do what you need to do."

"I'm not being shy," I said. But neither of us believed me.

Anyway, that broke the ice. After that, I closed my eyes and worked my hand around his shoulders and neck and chest before making my way up past the Adam's apple and over the ridge of the jaw to his face.

Was it working? I wasn't sure.

But I'd decided I didn't have to decide.

I was just going to do it. I wasn't going to overthink it or evaluate it or judge it.

I was just going to capture the moment. For better and for worse.

This was by far the most self-conscious I'd ever been around a model. *Pull it together,* I told myself. *Doctors touch people all the time.*

But I was no doctor.

Also, I'm assuming, doctors didn't usually spend a ton of time with patients outside the office. Or have recent memories of altruistically kissing them in front of their ex-wives. Or have crushes on them they were in denial about.

The truth is, it was intense.

For one thing, we were so close to each other. You're never just inches away from people for long stretches of time like that. I was close enough to hear him breathing, and even to feel those breaths as they brushed over my arm. I could smell his aftershave, which was scented like cedar and juniper, I decided.

For another thing, I was really touching him. I was going deep— working the pads of my fingers over every inch of his face, from hairline to jaw, exploring his skin, and the muscles beneath that, and the bone structure even deeper.

I mean, I was no stranger to other people. I'd dated guys. Flirted. Kissed. Gone to bed. I'd lived with Ezra for *two years.* But even people I touched all the time . . . I didn't touch them like this.

The fact that I was exploring him *for the sake of art* didn't feel too relevant in that moment. The *what* was much stronger than the *why.*

And the *what* was skin against skin. Breath swirling around breath. Eyes closed.

To be honest, my heart was thumping so hard, I wondered if he could see it. Like my shirt fabric might actually be quivering over it like an echo.

I tried to keep it professional, I really did.

I worked my way around the landscape of his face, as I'd done before with my own. I started with the bone structure, to get oriented. The solidness of his cheekbones and the angle of his jaw.

Then the pads of my fingers went searching for details. The arc of his eyebrows. The depth and number of laugh lines at his eyes. The length of his lashes. The angles of his nose. I spent a lot of time working around the edge of his mouth, trying to get the lines and angles of his lips just right.

I felt it all. The warmth of his skin under my fingers. The feathery brush of his hair. The imperceptible hum and vibration of *being alive.*

It was artistically erotic, too. Is that a weird thing to say?

What I mean is, the whole experience was full-immersion pleasure— both physically and creatively. Shimmering with possibility. Rich and buttery with satisfaction. Igniting my attention in some very special way. Pulling me through the moment with a mounting sense of longing.

Each thing I did, each move I made, made me want more of whatever that was.

When I felt ready to start painting, I followed my instincts.

I sketched out Joe's torso—his outline leaning into the frame with that kind of friendly, Labrador retriever energy he had. I found myself so immersed in rendering his body—those shoulders, the pecs and forearms, the trim angles of his fingers, resting on his jeans—that I didn't work too hard on the face. I wasn't avoiding it, exactly. I was just following the parts that called to me. The neck, the earlobes, the flop of the hair.

Everything I'd tried to do since the surgery had been about trying to get to the *product*. But now I settled into the *process*. I just painted. I kept my eyes closed to "look" at Joe, but I opened them in front of the canvas. I wanted to see the colors. I wanted to watch the brushstrokes happen. I wanted to see the painting appear in front of my eyes.

No matter what else might happen with this painting, the process of making it was bliss.

That counted for something.

At last, when I finally worked up the courage to sketch his face, I didn't try to make it make sense.

I wasn't thinking, *What would Norman Rockwell do?*

I was thinking about what I would do. What I needed to do—with each mark and each line—to render my experience of Joe's face.

I was following my own compass. Wherever it would lead.

And it turned out, Sue was right. That was a win in itself.

I PAINTED—AND TOUCHED, and painted and touched—Joe for two solid hours that night.

He was endlessly patient. Didn't check his phone or fall asleep or even ask for a glass of water. He just stayed with me the whole time, taking it all in.

When I'd done everything I could do for the night and I had a pretty full, dynamic early painted sketch, I thanked him, like he could go.

"Anyway," I said, washing my hands at the sink. "I really appreciate you doing this for me. Congratulations. You're almost free."

"Free from what?" Joe asked.

"From me. Once the art show is over, we won't have to see each other anymore."

"Why wouldn't we see each other?"

"I'm just saying. I've taken up a lot of your time."

"I was hoping you'd give me roller-skating lessons."

"But how would Dr. Michaux feel about that?"

Joe frowned. "Why would Dr. Michaux feel anything about that?"

"Aren't you . . . *you know*?"

"What?" Joe took a swig of water. "Didn't we talk about this?"

"You said you weren't dating. But I figured you must be hooking up."

Joe coughed. "What?"

"You're always . . . coming out of her apartment," I said. *And a bunch of others.*

"Yeah? So?"

"So aren't you guys . . . together?"

"Wait—you thought we were—what?"

My fingers were still tingling from touching him. I shrugged.

Joe started laughing then, but I didn't think it was funny. He leaned his head back and let out a big sigh. "I'm not dating Dr. Michaux. I am pet-sitting her snakes."

Now it was my turn to be befuddled. "You're what-sitting her whats?"

"Her snakes," Joe confirmed. "Remember? Herpetologist? She has a whole den of snakes in there. Even an Indonesian flying snake. It's pretty complicated, keeping them healthy."

Okay. I could freak out about *a penthouse full of flying snakes* later.

First things first.

I needed to get this straight: "You're . . . a snake sitter?"

"Pet sitter," Joe corrected. "Why do you think I was feeding Parker's cat?"

"That's what you do for a living?"

I could feel Joe frowning, like that question was really odd. "It's one of the things I do for a living," he said.

"All that time . . . you were going in there to feed snakes?"

Joe nodded. "

"And so the brown bags were full of . . . ?"

"Live mice," Joe confirmed.

"Oh my god."

Joe shrugged. "Food chain."

"But," I said as I tried to snap the pieces into place, "what about that time I saw you stumbling drunkenly into Dr. Michaux's apartment?"

"Do you mean the time she had a stomach virus? And I was helping her down the hall from the elevator?"

"You weren't hooking up?"

Joe shook his head.

"You were just *helping* her? Just being a Boy Scout? Kinda like when Parker pretended to faint?"

"I'm not a Boy Scout," Joe said. "But, yes, I was helping."

I was still working to take it in. "That's what you've been doing? All this time?"

"Yep," Joe said. "Mostly cats on this floor. And one bunny. Wait. Did you think that I was *sleeping* with all those people?"

"I mean, I hoped it was something else. But I couldn't imagine what that would be."

"You have a very limited imagination."

"Well, I definitely wasn't picturing flying snakes."

"I don't know if I should be flattered that you think all those people would want to sleep with me—or offended that you think I'm a man-whore."

"Sue and I prefer the archaic term *mutton muncher.*"

Joe just stared.

"What?" I said. "You have to admit it's suspicious behavior."

"For the record, I have never slept with anybody in this building. Other than my wife. Back when she used to live here—and used to be my wife."

But that didn't track. "Wait—" I said, pointing at him. "What about the lady you fat-shamed in the elevator?"

Joe shook his head like maybe he hadn't heard me right. "What?"

"I definitely overheard you talking about a one-night stand in the elevator. A woman with a lot of belly fat who shredded your sheets and was a real breather."

I could definitely feel how Joe was staring at me. Like he could not in any universe imagine what I was talking about.

"She dry-humped you in the parking lot?" I prompted. "And threw up in your entryway?"

But Joe just waited.

"She slept in your bed," I went on, "and you almost suffocated under a 'mountain of blubber.'"

That's when Joe lifted his head. Recognition.

"Now you remember," I said.

Joe put his face in his hands. "I remember," he said. "But that wasn't a lady."

Really? We were getting into semantics now? "I definitely heard you—"

"That," Joe went on, dropping his hands to make his point, "was a bulldog."

I frowned, like he'd just said something impossible. "A *bulldog*?"

"A rescue bulldog," Joe confirmed. "Named Buttercup."

"You had a one-night stand with a bulldog?"

Joe nodded. "I did. A bulldog who was abandoned after she ate a tree branch the length of her entire body and her owners decided she was too much trouble. I fostered her for one night—actually, it turned into three—before taking her to a rescue group."

"So . . ." I said, my voice quieting as I let this one piece of information rework all my eavesdropping, "when you called her a bitch, you literally meant . . . *a bitch*?"

Now he was offended. "I can't believe you thought I was talking about a person."

Suddenly I couldn't believe it, either.

Joe kept shaking his head. "You thought I was talking about a one-night stand?" he said. "With a human woman?"

"What other kind is there?"

He shook his head in disbelief.

So I added, "You *called it* a one-night stand."

"But I was joking."

"I didn't know that."

"I wasn't talking to you."

Now all the pieces were clicking into place. "That's why you posted pictures of her online?"

Joe nodded. "Petfinder dot com."

"And that's why you felt so free to liberally mock her appearance like she had no human dignity?"

"She *has* no human dignity," Joe said. "She's a dog."

"You said some harsh things," I said. "Even for a dog."

Joe dropped his shoulders, like *Come on*.

"I see," I said.

Joe pulled in a deep breath now as the full understanding hit him. "You thought," he said, "that I had a one-night stand with a drooly, noisy, sheet-shredding actual human female and then made fun of her body the next day on the phone in a public elevator before posting sleeping photos of her online?"

I made my voice very tiny. "Kind of?"

"No wonder you were so mean to me."

"Was I?"

"Yeah! And I deserved it!"

"Right?" I said, trying to draw a tentative alliance.

Joe sighed. Then he sighed again. Then he said, "For the record. I have not slept with anyone—at all—since I walked in on my wife hot-tubbing naked with Teague Phillips, the Planet's Most Boring Wanker."

But now we had a whole new topic. "Oof," I said. "That's a long time."

"I'm aware."

"A really long time."

"Thank you."

I shook my head. "I thought . . . you were a total player."

"You thought I was a total *douchebag.*"

I hunched up my shoulders. "Sorry?"

"I'm not a player, Sadie. I'm a damned monk."

I felt a buzzing realization that this, right here, was another of Joe's problems that I had the power to do something about.

Joe sighed. "Look. Here's the truth. There's exactly one person in this entire building I have any interest in sleeping with. And I don't even think she likes me very much."

Please don't let it be Parker. Please don't let it be Parker.

My heart clamped closed. "Who is it?"

But Joe didn't answer.

In my panic, I started yammering: "Anybody but Parker, okay? I wholeheartedly endorse any and all sexual escapades with literally any resident of this building—even the snake lady—just not Parker— okay?—because she really—"

But Joe didn't want to talk about Parker.

Right then he reached for my painting smock, hooked his fingers through the apron tie, and tugged me closer to him. I stepped nearer, into the cove between his thighs, and then I felt his palms settle on my hips.

There was that cedar and juniper smell again.

"It's not your evil stepsister," Joe said.

I shook my head, like *It's not?*

He pulled me a little closer. "And it's not the snake lady, either."

I hadn't really thought it would be. But I felt a frisson of relief, anyway.

Joe leaned in a bit more. Sitting on the stool, he was just the same height as me. Our faces were just inches from each other. "Do you want me to tell you who it is?" he asked.

I nodded, watching his mouth like I was in a trance.

Finally he said, "It's you."

I'd hoped he would say that.

But just to double-check: "It's me?"

The world had been so hard to read lately. It had somehow seemed just as possible that he might say Hazel from the coffee shop.

But it was me.

And so, when he nodded, I just said, "It's you, too."

It's true, I couldn't see his face right then. Not in the traditional way. Not in the way I was used to.

But as I looked at the pieces of it—the outline of his lips, the dimple in his chin, the sandpapery stubble along his jaw—it felt almost like I could see him better than I would've otherwise. Like not seeing the big picture let me grasp the details more clearly. It wasn't like looking into a void. It was like looking with a magnifying glass. Like being closer than close.

That mouth, for example, I could definitely see. Plump and firm and practically demanding to be kissed. But for real this time.

All I had to do now was sway forward. It would be so easy to match my mouth to his. To claim him for myself like that.

Wasn't that what kisses were for, after all? To light a little spark in someone else? A spark that would burn for you?

I wanted some part of Joe to burn for me.

And I guess he wanted that back.

I edged forward.

But then I hit that force field of hesitation again. I paused right there, my mouth just an inch from his.

And then, once again, Joe helped.

His arm skimmed up my back, and his hand found its way into

my hair, and then he cupped the back of my neck with his palm and pulled me to him—shattering that force field like a glass door at a coffee shop.

As soon as my mouth touched his, he tightened his other arm around me, and I let my arms wrap themselves around his neck.

For a minute, the warm, blissful shock of it was enough.

The electric softness of his mouth. The comfort of being pressed against him. The relief of giving in to all that longing. The crazy joy of being connected like that at last. Of wanting someone so badly—and being wanted back. Of touching. Of feeling good and happy and connected, and like there was so much to look forward to.

This wasn't like the fake kiss from before. This wasn't a performance for some onlooker. This kiss was just for the two of us. Because those words he'd said just made everything real. Every feeling, every glimmer, every sparkle—the veritable weather system of emotions that had been building around me ever since Joe first pissed me off in the elevator . . . as soon as he said, *It's you*—it all became palpable.

Before I knew it, I was crawling up on the stool, perching on his thighs, grasping tighter and more madly, kissing him in a way that felt like melting into another reality.

He pulled back for a second to look at me. I forced myself to look back. No matter what I could or couldn't see, I wanted to give him the soul-deep answer we're always searching for when we look into someone's eyes.

Was this happening? Were we doing this? Should we keep going?

Yes. All yes.

But maybe we already had our answers.

He leaned in again and captured my mouth with his, and it was like a wave of bliss crashing over me and knocking me off-balance—all softness and silk and rhythm and touch.

He stood up next and carried me toward the bed, my legs wrapped around his waist, our mouths never parting, and he laid me back against the blanket, pressing himself down over me as we sank further and further into the moment, and the feeling of being tangled together, and lost with each other.

As if staying this way could make everybody else on earth disappear.

Until . . . almost like the universe just wanted to prove us wrong—in a moment of bad timing worthy of the Guinness book—there was a knock at my door.

Twenty-Two

SPOILER: IT WAS Lucinda.

A human cold shower if ever there was one.

We froze at the sound. I squeezed my eyes shut, but Joe craned around to peek at the door.

"It's a middle-aged lady," he whispered. "I can see through the glass."

"Does she look like Martha Stewart?" I whispered back.

"Yes," Joe whispered.

"With kind of a sourpuss face?"

"Yes," Joe confirmed.

"And a vibe like she maybe sucks the fun out of everything?"

"Not sure, but maybe?"

"It's my stepmother," I confirmed. "Just ignore her."

I pulled his mouth back down to mine. But at that, Lucinda started knocking again.

"That's going to be challenging," Joe said.

Lucinda talked through the glass pane in the door, her voice muffling its way into the room. "I need to talk to you," she said. "Stop ignoring me. I can tell you're in there."

She could certainly kill a mood, I'd give her that.

I sighed. Was I really about to shut down the best kissing of my life *for Lucinda?*

The knocking continued. And continued.

I guess I was.

"Promise me," I said then, looking deep into Joe's eyes, "that we are not done here."

"We are not even close to done here," Joe said. "I promise."

And so we shut it down.

Joe found his shirt and his jacket. I straightened the apron we hadn't even had time to remove. We steadied our breath. Shifted gears.

And then, with dread, I opened the door.

"How did you even get up here?" I said as Lucinda walked in.

"Mr. Kim gave me your new passcode. Because it was an emergency."

Kindhearted Mr. Kim. We'd have to have a talk about Lucinda.

"What emergency could possibly exist between me and you?" I asked.

But Lucinda was sizing up Joe. "Is this the man you stole from Parker?" she asked then.

Stole? From Parker? "I have never stolen anything from Parker," I said.

"That's not the way I heard it," Lucinda said.

"That's never the way you hear it," I said.

Joe cleared his throat. "I'm sorry, ma'am, but Sadie's right. I was not stolen."

"Look," I said to Lucinda. "We're kind of in the middle of something."

"I can see that," Lucinda said.

"Please don't come over here and peep through my windows, Lucinda," I said in a tone like we'd been over this a million times.

"I wasn't peeping. I was knocking. I couldn't see anything but feet, anyway."

"Lucinda," I said, "I'm busy."

But Lucinda remained righteous about her choices. "You left me no other options! You wouldn't answer my calls. You wouldn't respond to my texts. Do you think I wanted to trudge over to your hovel in the middle of the night? I did not. But I need to speak to you!"

"So speak," I said.

Lucinda looked Joe up and down. "Privately."

"Let's get this clear," I said, gesturing at Joe. "*He* is my guest. *You* are an interloper."

"You can't ignore me forever."

"Yes, I can. I absolutely can. Why would I do anything else?"

But now Lucinda had decided to start looking pitiful. I didn't even have to see it to know the choreography: the trembling bottom lip, the moistening of the eyes, the drooping of the brows. A signature technique for getting her way. Which worked on a surprising number of people. But not me.

Unfortunately, Joe hadn't built up an immunity to it.

He could watch for only so long before he caved. "You know what?" Joe said. "I've actually got some stuff to do."

Ugh! Damn human compassion!

"No, you don't," I said.

"Yes," he nodded at me, like, *This has to happen.* "I do."

But I was shaking my head. I could not, not, *not* be trading Joe for Lucinda. "Don't go." I followed him to the door. "It's not a real emergency. She just wants attention!"

But Joe shrugged, like he didn't know how to stay.

I couldn't blame him. Developing emotional armor for someone like Lucinda takes years. You needed, like, a *graduate degree* in emotional manipulation.

"I'll call you tomorrow," Joe said as he slipped out the door.

Tomorrow? That was an *eternity.*

As soon as he was gone, I rounded on Lucinda. "What," I demanded, "is this 'emergency'?"

Lucinda took a deep breath and crossed her arms. "Your father," she said, "has had an accident."

Okay. I admit. She got me. "*What?*"

She nodded, like my panic was legit. "And I've been trying to reach you."

"What happened? Where is he?"

And here, leaning in and just owning it, she said, "He slammed his hand in the garage door."

I paused. "He what?"

"It's very swollen and bruised. He fractured his small metacarpal."

"His pinkie?" I said. "You came all the way over here like the buzz-kill of all buzzkills to tell me that Dad fractured his *pinkie?*"

"That's a very big deal to a surgeon."

"I'm sure it is," I said. "But it's not"—and I hit the T pretty hard on *not*—"an emergency."

"It was very frightening at the time."

"Lucinda," I said, "why are you really here?"

Lucinda sighed. "The point is," she said, "because of his hand, your father won't be making his trip to Vienna next week. So I invited him to your art show."

I shook my head. "Why?"

"Because! We're family."

"Have you ever seen a family?" I demanded. "We're nothing even close."

What was this new determination to bond?

More important: Was the art show *next week?*

Wow, the time really flew after brain surgery.

After a second, I said, "He's not coming, is he?"

"Of course he's coming," Lucinda said proudly. "We're all coming. Me, your dad, and Parker."

"No," I said.

Lucinda's shoulders dropped, and her disappointment almost felt genuine.

"You're not coming," I said. "Not him. Not you. And sure as shit not Parker."

"But he had his secretary add it to his calendar."

"Make her un-add it."

"But I've already bought an outfit."

"I feel like you're not listening. You're not invited. If you show up, I will call security and have you forcibly removed."

"You wouldn't do that," Lucinda said

And then before I had a chance to say *Watch me*, she lifted up a shopping bag I hadn't noticed in her hand and held it out to me.

"What's this?"

"Open it."

I looked between Lucinda and the bag. Finally, curiosity beat out hesitation. I walked to my art table and set the bag there so I could reach inside.

And what I pulled out made me gasp.

It was pink fabric with appliquéd flowers.

I held my breath for a few minutes, was afraid to even hope . . .

"Is this . . ." I said, just holding it and staring.

Lucinda waited for me to finish the question.

But I just started over. "Is this . . . ?"

I loosened my grip so the fabric could unfurl, and then I had my answer.

It was.

"It's the dress!" I said. It was so impossible, I turned to Lucinda. "Is it the dress? From the hospital that night?"

"It is," Lucinda said.

"But how?" I said, still staring at it in disbelief. "I thought it was destroyed."

"After I left your room, I went looking for it." She paused, then said, "What's the expression? I went 'full Karen' on that hospital. I even demanded to see the manager."

"I don't think going full Karen is a good thing," I said.

"It worked, though. Didn't it?"

I marveled at the dress. "I thought it had been incinerated."

"Five more minutes, and it would've been."

I walked over to the mirror on the closet door to hold it up in front of myself.

"It's not the same," Lucinda said next. "There are a few dark spots where the wine stains wouldn't come out. We were able to reweave some of the shredded fabric, but not all of it—so the fit may be more snug."

I felt like I'd never been so astonished. "You did this?"

"Lord, no. I took it to a tailor."

"But . . ." I didn't fully understand what was happening. "You saved it."

"Yes," Lucinda said, her voice softer.

"Why?" I asked.

"Because it was your mother's."

My eyes filled with tears at those words. "I never told you that."

"You didn't have to."

She let the softness linger for a second, and then she snapped back to business. "Anyway, *that's* the emergency. We need to make sure this version fits you. Now. Tonight. Otherwise, we'll never get the alterations back in time."

"In time for what?"

But Lucinda's answer was almost as incredulous as my question. "For you to wear it to the art show."

And as I tried the dress on so she could check the fit, and as she fussed and clucked over me like real mothers sometimes do over their real daughters, one thing was pretty clear.

Lucinda would be coming to the art show.

And maybe that wasn't such a bad thing.

Twenty-Three

IT'S FAIR TO say that this was a time in my life when almost nothing made any sense.

But after that night, one thing in my life was more than clear.

I'd have to call off my engagement to Dr. Addison.

That was it. Joe was the one.

The one I would choose. The one I wanted to date. The one I could talk to and joke around with. The one I couldn't stop thinking about. The one I longed to put my hands all over. Again. And again. The one I wished were still in my bed right this very minute.

It wasn't even a contest.

Dr. Addison had only ever been a romantic daydream—and of course I'd known that from the minute I first fixated on him. He was the notion of a love match. He was the suggestion of future happiness. He was pure fantasy.

Joe, in contrast, was reality. He was scars and collarbones and the smell of juniper. He'd seen me have a panic attack, and he'd rescued me when I was locked out, and he'd brought me tissues when I was crying.

Now that the whole bulldog situation was cleared up, there was nothing left to do but give up and give in, and like him like crazy.

I liked him. This wasn't a shocking revelation. But it felt good to put it in writing in my head. He wasn't some illusion of a boyfriend I was summoning to help me through a hard time. He was a real person with an empty apartment and a wounded heart.

I didn't want to mess this up.

I didn't want there to be any confusion.

I wanted to honor my incredible luck in finding somebody like Joe by ending things cleanly and neatly with Dr. Addison.

Even though, of course, it seemed crazy to end something that had never started. We hadn't ever even had one date yet. But I just wanted to clarify with him in a nuts-and-bolts conversation. We hadn't started anything, and we were never going to.

Was it copacetic to do that at Peanut's checkup during Dr. Addison's working hours?

Probably not.

But we happened to have an appointment that day. And it felt like the sooner, the better. I couldn't imagine Dr. Addison would care too much, anyway, given the whole standing-me-up-and-then-never-calling-again situation.

I could settle things while he was palpating my dog.

How much could he possibly care?

IT WAS STRANGE to see Dr. Addison again at the appointment. I'd almost forgotten about him. It hadn't even been that long, but I guess getting infatuated with someone else made it seem longer.

As Dr. Addison strode toward me in the waiting room in his crisp white coat and tie, his hair back in that Ivy League style, I couldn't help but notice how that *GQ* look didn't do it for me anymore. How utterly eroticized floppy hair and hipster glasses had become for me now.

Validating.

Dr. Addison, my once-fantasy-fiancé obsession, had become just another random guy.

Peanut's checkup was good. The playlist that day was nonstop Louis Armstrong, and I noted that the vet tech had been right. Peanut really did like him.

Dr. Addison was being shadowed by a vet student that day, and he let her do most of the exam. By the end of the appointment, the student and Dr. Addison agreed: Peanut was just about the healthiest elderly dog either of them had ever seen.

"Must be all that pad Thai," Dr. Addison said, with a little flirty undertone that the vet student didn't notice.

"Thank you," I said, grabbing the doc's hand platonically and pumping it up and down. "You really saved him."

"It was a group effort," Dr. Addison said.

A memory of a shirtless Joe flopping me down on my bed and kissing my neck flashed through my head. Somehow I just couldn't imagine *this* guy—with his tight posture and his tie and his clicker pen in his Oxford cloth pocket—positively melting a woman in that way.

Case closed. I'd chosen well.

Time to end it.

"I'm so sorry," I said to him then. "Do you have a minute to talk privately?"

Dr. Addison checked the clock. "I have seven," he said.

Then, at my frown: "Minutes," he clarified. "Before my next appointment."

"Ah," I said. "Great."

He walked us out back to a little grassy yard for the animals.

I let Peanut off his leash, and he trotted off to sniff things. And then it was down to business.

I felt oddly nervous. I'd never dumped anyone before. I was generally the dumpee.

Although—*can* you dump someone you're not even dating?

"I so appreciate the time we've spent together," I began, busting out the monologue I'd practiced in front of the mirror, but then going off script before the end of the first sentence. "And I just wanted to clarify a little bit with you that whatever's going on or might go on between us . . ."

Wow. I was terrible at this.

Dr. Addison took a step closer.

Then he reached forward and took one of my hands—quietly, but with encouragement.

I pushed ahead. "I know we've been moving toward spending more time together lately . . ." My heart surprised me by pounding against the inside of my breastbone. "But I just want to say, in the future, from this point on . . . I think it's probably best for us to keep our relationship professional."

That surprised him.

Dr. Addison let go of my hand and took a step back.

I couldn't see his face fall, but I could definitely feel it.

"Professional?" he asked then, after a pause, sounding, really, like he had not seen that coming.

"Yeah," I said, trying to keep things light. "You know. For us to just kind of stay in the vet and client category."

Another pause. Dr. Addison reached back and palmed the back of his head. "You're saying that you just want us to have a vet-client relationship?"

I nodded. "That's right."

"Nothing more?"

I nodded again.

A long pause. Then a tense question: "Can I ask why?"

"Sure," I said, trying to keep things super friendly. "Well, it's been a bit of a crazy time for me, lately. And I actually, um, you know, not on purpose of course, but just kind of by accident . . . I guess you could say I developed a thing for somebody else."

Dr. Addison stood there a second. Then he said, "A thing? You developed 'a thing' for somebody else?"

Wasn't that what I just said? "Yeah. You know. So . . ."

"When?" he asked.

"Um," I said, my voice sliding unnaturally high. "Recently?"

"Who is it?" he asked next, sounding brittle.

"Oh, just a guy. Ya know. A guy I've had to spend some time with lately."

Dr. Addison started pacing around.

That much, I could see.

"I'm sorry," I said. "It just kind of happened. I wasn't even really sure that you were interested, anyway."

"You weren't sure I was interested?"

"I mean—were you?"

"Yes," he said, his voice sour. "I was interested."

Wow. This was not the reaction I'd been expecting from a guy who stood me up and then never called.

Dr. Addison adjusted his tie. "So . . . you're going to date this other person?"

"I think so," I said.

"And," he went on, studying the ground like he was trying to solve a problem, "if I told you that I really like you a lot, would that make a difference?"

I wasn't sure what to say.

"If I told you," he went on, "that I can't remember the last time I met someone who woke me up like you do . . . That there's something about you that I can't get out of my head . . . That I keep thinking about you and wondering if we might be . . . really right for each other . . ." He looked up. "What would you say?"

I'd say, "Don't stand me up next time?" I thought to myself.

But to Dr. Addison, I just said, "I'm so sorry. I just think it's too late."

And then—maybe out of politeness, or maybe just because it's not every day that someone saw something so valuable in me—I added, "Thank you, though. For feeling those things."

Next, the door to the clinic slammed open and a vet tech said, "I'm sorry, Dr. A. We've got a Great Dane with torsion."

Dr. Addison gave a curt *got it* nod. Then after the tech was gone, he let out a deep sigh, and said, "Do I have any chance at all of changing your mind?"

I shook my head.

"I'm sorry," I said, figuring that being honest was probably better for both of us in the long run. "I think I just . . . accidentally . . . fell madly in love."

He took that in. "Can't argue with that. I guess."

He looked up at the sky then, took a deep sigh, and walked to the clinic door.

But next, before going through, he stopped and turned back. "I wish you well, Sadie," he said. "I really do." Then, like he absolutely meant it, he added, "Be happy, okay? And take good care of yourself."

"I'll try," I said.

Then he and his tie and his white lab coat were gone.

I looked down at Peanut, who was scooting around now, scratching his bum enthusiastically on the grass.

Peanut paused to look up at my face, and I paused to look down at his, and the two of us silently agreed: I would definitely need to find a new vet.

Twenty-Four

I WENT HOME that afternoon and painted like crazy.

I had *two days* before the portrait had to be delivered to the gallery before the show.

I had never tried to complete a painting in such a short time frame before. My old method could take weeks. But I didn't have weeks. I had two days.

I'd do what I could do and let the rest go.

I'll be honest and say: I liked this painting. I couldn't entirely vouch for the face, but everything else was strong, compelling work. The curve of his shoulder. The slant of his collarbone. The shadow around his Adam's apple. Plus, the colors, which were just the right combination of bright and muted—happy and sad. The whole thing had an energy about it—a frisson of emotions—that was just . . . appealing.

It wouldn't win, of course. A faceless portrait was the last thing these judges were looking for.

But it would be something true. Something I could be proud of.

When I texted a snapshot of it to Sue—now a married woman in Edmonton, Alberta—she texted back. Wow!

Do you like it? I asked.

It's phenomenal!!! she texted back. That torso!! Then after a pause, This might be the best thing you've ever done.

That made me kiss the phone. Think it'll win? I texted back.

Not a chance, Sue replied. Then she added, But if anybody can win while losing, it's you.

I FINISHED THE painting a day early, emerging from a blissful state of flow and texting Joe: Your portrait's done.

When I didn't hear back, I decided to get more explicit. Want to come see it?

Still no response.

Maybe he was busy? Was this the busy season for pet sitters? Could some of Dr. Michaux's snakes have escaped the den? Was everything okay with Joe's hundred-year-old grandmother?

I told myself not to text Joe all these questions, but then I texted them all, anyway.

Plus a few more.

Where the heck was he?

I demanded that Sue call me from Canada, and then I said, "I think I just dumped my fantasy fiancé for a guy in my building who's now ghosting me."

"I'm sure he's not ghosting you," Sue said.

"I've sent him seven texts in the past twenty-four hours and he hasn't replied to one of them."

"For god's sake, stop texting him! Have some self-respect!"

"I just want him to text me back."

"He's clearly unavailable."

"I want to show him the portrait before I take it to the gallery."

"Can't always get what you want."

"But why isn't he replying?"

"Just give the poor man the benefit of the doubt. Maybe his grandmother's sick."

"You think they don't have cell service where his grandmother lives?"

"Maybe! You don't know! Maybe she's an ancient Sicilian lady on a remote island where there are no phones. He could be stomping grapes right now, trying to keep the family vineyard going while she fights for her life in a charming Italian ICU."

"Why does that not feel likely?"

"If you're so worried, go knock on his door."

Knock on his door?

I hadn't thought of that.

Cut to me: Sixty seconds later—knocking on his door.

No answer.

Could he be stomping grapes in Sicily?

I mean, it wasn't impossible.

But as the silence wore on, even optimistic Sue had to admit it wasn't looking good. "I'm losing hope on the Italian grandmother," she said, during yet another processing session.

"Right?" I said. "This is not a friendly miscommunication. Plus, I know he's in town because I saw him in the elevator, and he saw me heading for it—and *he did not hold the doors.*"

"Maybe he didn't see you?"

"He definitely saw me."

"Looks like it's time for interpretation B," Sue said.

"Which is?"

"He hates you."

"But why would he?"

"Maybe he overheard you saying something mean about him?"

"I haven't said anything mean about him in weeks."

"Not holding the elevator door is definitely a maximum-hostility move."

"Maybe he just got his eyes dilated at the doctor, and he couldn't tell it was me."

"That only works for close objects."

"Oh."

"There's no way of knowing if he won't talk to you," Sue said.

"My point exactly."

"But if I had to guess? He's an asshole. And he went after you for the thrill of the chase. But then he caught you and lost interest."

I didn't want that to be it.

But of all the options, this one seemed the most likely by far. Certainly more plausible than the sick grandmother. But here were the bare facts: 1. He was still in the building. 2. He was not responding to any of my attempts at contact. 3. He did not hold the elevator doors.

Plus, racking my brain did not yield anything—at all—that I might have done to him to push him away. I'd been worried that seeing his final portrait might make him run off screaming—but he hadn't even seen it yet. And other than that, I hadn't yelled at him or lied to him or—god forbid—asked him for help.

Wait—I hadn't let myself need him, had I?

I'd let myself *want* him, but that wasn't the same thing.

Unless asking him to sit for the portrait counted.

But wait—I hadn't asked him to do that! He'd *offered*!

Weren't those different things?

Should I never have accepted?

I could have asked these questions all night.

But Sue needed to get off the phone. She and Witt were headed to the dinner car for a jazz concert. "Guess what the Canadian cocktail of the day is called?"

"What?" I asked glumly.

"The Angry Canadian."

"Joke's on you," I said flatly. "There's no such thing."

"That's what I said!" Sue responded, maybe hoping we could talk about something, anything, else.

But no luck.

At last, in conclusion, Sue said, "Maybe we'll get lucky. Maybe he's got a terminal illness."

BUT I KNEW better than to hope for a terminal illness.

And I just couldn't seem to believe that he was a bad person, either.

It had to have been me.

Desperation over the art show had made me needy. I should've kept my distance. Stayed aloof. Said no when he offered to be my model. What was I thinking? Of course he'd glimpsed my life and bolted. Who'd want to get anywhere near it?

In the end, I took the portrait to the gallery without ever showing it to Joe—or seeing him at all. And then I spent the next two days being ignored and obsessing over why that was happening.

In the meantime, I rearranged my paints. Organized my canvases. Restacked the dishes in my cabinets. Painted Peanut's toenails with glitter polish. Watched a video tutorial about how to make one large T-shirt into twelve different outfits.

And stewed. Emotionally.

Oh, and I googled "Why men don't text you back."

But it wasn't very helpful.

I also had another brain scan to check my edema. And that wasn't helpful, either.

Dr. Estrera reported that, shockingly, according to the scan, the edema had now largely resolved. He compared last week's scan with this week's scan—both of which looked quite similar to me. "We're seeing an eighty-one percent reduction in swelling in the area," Dr. Estrera said proudly.

Big news, I guess—but it didn't do me much good if nothing else had changed.

And nothing else had changed.

After the scan, Dr. Nicole gave me a battery of facial recognition tests to compare to my baseline. And I was exactly the same on those as I'd been a month ago. The same identical numerical score.

I knocked my head against the table at the results.

"Please don't do that," Dr. Nicole said.

"How can I be exactly the same?" I whined.

"These results are to help you—not make you pound your head on the table."

"Well, they don't feel very helpful."

"Now that the edema is resolving, you should start to see some changes in your facial perceptions," she said, like that might cheer me up. Then she added, "No guarantees."

But I wasn't in the mood to be cheered up. I flopped down on her sofa in despair. "Nothing is going right."

"Maybe you need to broaden your definition of right."

"Don't throw that cheery nonsense at me. My life is a shit show."

This right here felt like my lowest moment so far. I thought I was supposed to be getting better, not getting worse. Learning to cope, at least. What the hell was going on?

"Tell me what has you feeling down," Dr. Nicole asked.

"Everything?" I asked. Like, did she really think she could handle that?

"Sure. Everything."

Okay. She asked for it. "I still can't see faces. I submitted a portrait to this competition that I should have won—handily—that's guaranteed to come in dead last. I'm being menaced by my evil stepsister. I'm embarrassed to go back to my favorite coffee shop. My best friend eloped to Canada and left me dateless for what's sure to be the most humiliating event of my life. My stepmother wants to build a relationship with me and she's coming to the show over my vociferous objections. My dog is a thousand years old. I broke up with my fantasy fiancé. And the very cute guy in my building who I might genuinely be in love with kissed me senseless the other night and then fully disappeared."

"Ah," Dr. Nicole said.

"That's all you've got? Ah?"

"Of all of those," she asked next, "which one is the worst?"

"All of them," I answered. Then I had an idea. "Any chance you could be my date to the art show? So I don't have to go alone?"

It was a long shot, of course.

But she didn't budge. "I find our work goes better in here," she said, "when we don't see each other out there."

BY THE SATURDAY of the art show, it had been a full four days, fourteen hours, and twenty minutes since I'd had any contact from Joe.

It seemed pretty clear at this point that he'd moved on. Though I continued to hold out hope for Sue's Sicilian grandmother scenario. Or maybe an unexpected car accident, like in *An Affair to Remember.* Or maybe some kind of head injury-induced amnesia?

There were still a few possible explanations that were forgivable.

Sort of.

Oh, well.

He was out of my life now, which was probably a good thing, I kept telling myself.

But I missed him anyway, is what I'm saying. Against my better judgment. I confess: I had moments when I felt tempted to call in sick to the art show.

I mean, how could you go to an art show that you were guaranteed to lose without any hope at all?

But on the other hand, how could I *not* go?

It's one thing for dreams to shift slowly—for you to evolve and long for different things. It's another thing to abandon your dream out of spite.

I thought about my mom. My courageous, kindhearted mom. She would have given anything to go to this exact show fourteen years ago. She would give anything to be here right now, fully alive, facing whatever life threw at her, and just cherishing it all.

Maybe the best way to hold on to her wasn't to obsess over her paintings or wear her skates or listen to her music or copy her style or worry over what would happen when I finally lost Peanut. Maybe the best way to keep her with me was to embrace her spirit. To emulate her courage. To bring the warmth and love to the world that she always—fearlessly—had.

She had loved us without reservation. She adored us wildly. And laughed. And danced. And soaked it all up—every atom of her life—every moment of her time

She felt it all. She lived it all.

That's what I loved about her. Not just that she was a great mom or a great wife or a great dog rescuer. She was a great person. She knew some divine secret about how to open up to being alive that the rest of us kept stubbornly missing.

She'd wanted me to know it, too. She'd wanted me to say yes to everything. She'd wanted me to go all in.

But when she died, I went the other way.

I'm not judging myself. I was a kid. I didn't know how to cope with losing her—or any of the hardships that followed. But I guess that's the great thing about life—it gives you chance after chance to rethink it all. Who you want to be. How you want to live. What really matters.

I did want to go to the art show. I'd earned my right to be there. I didn't, of course, want to be humiliated. But it was looking like I couldn't have one without the other. And I just wasn't going to let the things I was afraid of hold me back anymore.

I had no idea how that decision would turn out, but I knew one thing for sure:

My mom would approve.

As the time approached, I zipped myself into her pink dress—much tighter and slinkier now. Sue had gifted me a makeover from her cousin who worked at Macy's and a hair blowout from her cousin's roommate.

I did it all.

If I had to go to this art show all alone, I would do my damnedest to look good.

There was, of course, still a chance that Joe might show up in a surprise twist and whisk me off like Cinderella. But as I clanked down the metal stairs from the rooftop in a set of gorgeous but actively painful heels, he was running out of time.

I walked down our long hallway, hoping to see him.

I rode down in the elevator, hoping to see him.

I walked out to the street in front of our building to meet my Uber, still hoping to see him.

Waiting there in the late-afternoon light—my hair done, a daisy behind my ear as an ode to my mother, and with so much mascara on that I could actually see my own eyelashes—I decided to try to text him *one last time.*

This would be it. My final attempt.

And then, when he didn't reply, I'd call it: *Time of death for my thing with Joe. Saturday night, seven P.M.*

Then I'd go ahead and let myself mourn.

But after the art show.

And then, right there near the streetlamp by the crosswalk, as if the decision to give up had called forth some kind of magic from the universe, I saw him.

Joe. In his bowling jacket and his glasses. Coming out of our building. With a suitcase.

"Hey!" I shouted, my body walking toward him without my brain's permission.

My Uber pulled up as I was walking away.

"Hey!" I called again.

Joe looked up, took in the sight of me in by far the fanciest getup any of us had ever seen, and held very still.

If I had wanted him to whistle or ogle or tell me I looked great—or even longed against longing for some kind of shift in his body language at the pleasure of seeing me—I would've been sorely disappointed.

The man was a total statue.

Fortunately, I didn't want any of that. I just wanted to confront him.

I'd been having imaginary confrontations with him for days, of course. Where had he been? What was going on? Who the hell did he think he was?

But once it was really happening? I panicked.

For a second, no words came out at all. Finally, I managed: "I've been texting you."

Useless. Joe's body language stayed blank.

"And calling," I added. God, now I sounded like Lucinda.

Joe just stood there.

At last I generated an interrogative: "Have you been sick?"

And at last, a response: "No."

"Have you been . . . out of town?"

"No. But I'm leaving now."

"You're leaving town? Now?" I glanced down at his suitcase. "Right now?"

"Yes."

I regrouped. "Do you happen to remember"—I felt a hitch in my throat—"that you were going to be my date to my art show tonight?"

Joe looked away, like he couldn't stand the sight of me. The face might be unreadable, but the body language was unmistakable.

What on earth had I done to him?

Or maybe I hadn't done anything.

Sometimes when I'm watching a movie and there's a simple Big Misunderstanding between two people—he thinks she's a space alien or something—I want to shout, "Just talk to each other!"

But of course nothing in real life is ever simple like that.

Every real human interaction is made up of a million tiny moving pieces. Not a simple one-note situation: a *symphony* of cues to read and decipher and evaluate and pay attention to.

It's a wonder we ever get anything straight at all.

And of course for me, for most of my life, the number one go-to for deciphering any human interaction was facial expressions.

Which I couldn't even see.

So this conversation was destined to fail from the start.

But I still had to try.

I took a step closer, wanting to get really clear. "I guess the date's not happening now?"

Joe gazed off at some far point on the horizon.

"That's right, right? You're not coming with me to this thing? Even though you said you would?"

Nothing from Joe.

"I guess I'm just really nervous to go by myself," I went on, feeling my voice waver a little. "I don't want to go at all. But I have to go, you

know? My painting. My life goals. And even though the portrait is not
what they want, for sure—so I'm one hundred percent guaranteed to
come in dead last—I suspect it might actually really be good. In an ugly
duckling kind of way. Plus, there's a good chance my horrible family will
show up and make things a hundred times worse. And I'm going to have
to do it all genuinely, totally alone."

I held my breath for a second, trying to steady myself.

I never, ever asked for help. And if Joe's behavior the past four days
had made anything clear, he was in no mood to give it.

But I wasn't asking for him, I realized.

This wasn't about his answer. This was about my question.

And mustering the courage to ask it.

"The thing is," I said then, my voice feeling like a balloon I might
lose hold of. "The thing is . . . I'm scared to go alone. And I don't know
why, but it feels like you're the only person I can say that to. You're the
only person I *want* to say that to. I just want so badly to have somebody
with me. Anybody. And so I just have to ask if you might stay tonight.
Despite everything." I took a step closer, like that might seal the deal.
"Can you postpone your plans," I asked, "and come with me?"

If there was any hope for us at all, he'd sense my desperation—how
badly I really, truly needed him—and rescue me this one last time.

But he didn't.

He kept his face turned toward the horizon. "Are you asking me to
be your anybody?"

"I guess that's one way to put it."

Now, at last, he turned toward me. "I'm not going to be anybody for
you, Sadie. And I don't want to see the portrait. And I don't know why
you think I'd care about any of this."

But I shook my head. "I don't understand what happened."

I could feel a flash of anger in his expression like fire. "*Really?*" he
said. "I don't understand it, either, to be honest. But here we are."

I took a deep breath. "Whatever I've done, I'm sorry."

But Joe shook his head like *sorry* was the most useless word in the
world.

Worse than useless, even. Insulting.

He turned to leave. Then he stopped and turned halfway back.

"I'm moving out, by the way," he said then. "So stop coming by my place. And stop calling me. And for god's sake . . . stop texting."

Twenty-Five

THE FIRST INSULT of the art show—before all the injuries—was placement.

I arrived at the gallery to find my portrait hung in the worst con-
ceivable spot—half under a staircase, fully at the back, right near the
bathrooms, under an exposed air-conditioning vent that was literally
dripping into a bucket. There was a moldy smell to the area—not to
mention a tinge of Lysol.

You'd think that a bright, airy, recently renovated art gallery
wouldn't have a dank corner—but you'd be wrong.

And that's where they stuck me.

At the art gallery equivalent of a restaurant's sucker table.

Worst of all, the spot was hard to get to, but because of the U-shaped
layout of the gallery, it was easy to see. Everybody entering the building
could get a full view of my indefensibly tragic situation.

So any and all humiliations to come would be on full display.

And there were plenty of humiliations to come.

Starting with the fact that no one was there.

Oh, people were there—*at the show*. The show itself was packed. Just—no one came to my shadowy, mildewy, forgotten corner.

I stood courageously next to my portrait, under the cold, damp, blowing air of that drippy vent, feeling as exposed as a hermit crab out of its shell—as I watched the entire gallery milling with eager art patrons.

Everywhere—except where I was.

No one came up to me and said hello. No one talked to me at all. Only a few freakish outliers even glanced at my portrait, which was clearly, easily, the big loser of the night from minute one. I scanned people's outfits and hair and gaits for identifying clues, but I did not recognize one person.

The artist closest to me, layout-wise, was a guy named Bradley Winterbottom, who'd done a portrait of a child on the beach. He had at least twenty people gathered in his area—chatting companionably about the composition, delighting over the way he'd captured that late-afternoon sunlight, swooning over the sweetness of the child's face.

I mean, nothing against Bradley Winterbottom, but I really hated that guy right then.

He had more admirers than he deserved.

I, in contrast, had zero.

I didn't even need admirers. I would've been happy for someone to talk to. A person who needed directions, say. A lost hiker.

But no luck. It was just me. Alone.

Nothing to do but panic over life-altering decisions about where to rest my hands. They were too posed and awkward at my sides, but they felt hostile if I crossed them over my chest, and they had too much judgy-mom energy if I rested them on my hips. I just kept shifting them around. Was behind the back too goofy? Was clasped at the pelvis too meek? Was clenched into fists of misery too . . . honest?

Nothing worked. Every few seconds I tried a new pose. Like an animatronic scarecrow.

To no avail.

I had no idea where to look, either. Looking at the floor would make me seem ashamed. Looking at other people would make me seem needy. Looking at my own portrait on the wall would make me seem like I was fully, heartily giving up on my dreams in real time.

Which I was, by the way.

There is nothing—nothing—more socially awkward than standing alone in a crowd waiting for someone, anyone, to come and join you.

I cursed Sue for getting kidnapped. And for eloping. And for every Angry Canadian she'd tossed back.

Then I felt guilty and took it back.

I cursed Joe instead. For everything.

Then I felt guilty about that, too.

Then I toyed with cursing myself . . . before deciding I was cursed enough, already.

THE WHOLE EXPERIENCE was wall-to-wall agony. There were no two ways about it.

I finally set my phone's timer for eleven P.M.—the moment when the show technically ended, according to the invitation—so that I could stride out, or possibly sprint, the very second I was done.

Only two hours and forty-five minutes left to endure.

For the auction component of the show, each artist had a sleek, Jetsons-style cocktail table next to their portrait with a clipboard on it for patrons to write down their bids.

Bradley Winterbottom had to request an extra bid sheet after his filled up—front and back—but do I even need to say how many bids wound up on my clipboard during the entire time that I stood there?

Zero. That's right.

But was that the worst, most insulting part of the evening?

Wow. That's a tough call.

Let's review the options:

There were all the shocked looks people gave my portrait from across the room—hands over mouths, eyes big with pity—the way you might rubberneck past a car wreck.

There was the moment when I accidentally knocked over the bucket of A/C drippings and then apologetically mopped it up with paper towels from the bathroom, one drippy bunch at a time, while other artists and patrons glanced over with irritation like I was really bringing everyone down.

There were the endless ten minutes when another finalist, who wore a little porkpie hat, went by the single pseudonym Lysander, and apparently possessed a nervous digestive system, had to work through some brutal digestive issues in the men's room, which I could of course hear in detail from my primo spot by the bathroom doors—grunts, splashes, and all.

Oh. And there was the time when I took a pee break and overheard some judges who seized that moment to dart over and laugh at my work. Yes, that's how close my placement was to the bathrooms. I could literally hear these people talking *from the stall*.

"What is happening here?" Judge 1 asked, in a horrified whisper.

"I *know*," Judge 2 said.

"Did the artist . . . leave?"

"Wouldn't you?"

"I never would have shown up at all."

"She must have fled."

"Right? Off to *not quit her day job*."

"Or to fling herself off a bridge."

They snickered at that.

"It's just so bizarre," one went on pensively. "The body and background are so exquisite . . ."

"But then you get to the face."

"I keep thinking it's Carl Sagan."

"I keep seeing Steve Buscemi."

"It looks like a wolf face, in a way."

"Impossible. Animals are against the rules."

"Right? It's not *veterinary* portraiture."

"Whatever it is, it's like the face melted."

"Or got hit with a pie right before the sitting."

"Or landed facedown in mud."

"Or had a botched cosmetic surgery."

"I just don't understand how this piece is even here."

"Maybe they notified the wrong artist?"

"It's just insulting, more than anything."

"It kind of makes me angry."

"What a waste of a Top Ten spot."

"Too bad we can't give negative points."

"Isn't it?"

At that, I'd had enough. I pressed the toilet handle with my shoe and held it there.

Mercifully, the blast of the industrial flush was loud enough to startle them away.

In the silence that followed, I washed my hands, smoothed my hair in the mirror, smiled encouragingly at my unintelligible face, stood up straight like how I imagined a person with some remaining human dignity would, and walked back out to my post.

Just two soul-draining hours to go . . .

It was okay. It was fine. What was it Joe had said about sitting for the portrait? *"Trigonometry is hard. Climbing El Capitan is hard. Landing on the beaches of Normandy is hard."* All I had to do was stand here—and keep standing here—until my alarm went off.

And then I could go home. And brainstorm a new life's dream.

This was the big break I'd been working toward for over a decade. This was the moment I'd been waiting for—dreaming of. This was the life I'd chosen. This was a competition that if the past five weeks hadn't happened, I'd be crushing right now. This was a showcase moment for the thing I was best at in my entire life . . . Just not anymore.

Could I have used at least one person there with me in that moment? Yes.

And would I have even minded if it was Lucinda?

Not at all.

But I got fully stood up. By everyone. Even though my dad's secretary had put it on his calendar and Lucinda had interrupted my last—only—night with Joe to give me that news. Even though I'd been dreading them coming ever since I found out. Even though they were the last people I ever would've chosen.

I was out of choices.

As time wore on and the smile I'd stapled to my face quivered more and more, I found myself hoping for someone, anyone, to show up—and, if I'm honest . . . imagining how great it would be if that someone could be Joe.

It wasn't impossible, was it?

Crazier things had happened, right?

If nothing else, imagining it gave me a nice distraction. Joe: Having an epiphany in line at the airport, abandoning his suitcase, hailing a cab, but then hitting too much traffic, sprinting the final blocks here only to burst through the doors and shove past elderly art critics to my dark corner like it was the only place he'd ever wanted to be . . . and then breathlessly begging my forgiveness while declaring his undying love—thereby validating my entire existence for everyone here, including me.

Maybe I should pop out for some air freshener.

Thanks a lot, Lysander.

Anyway. I knew it was impossible. Joe had already refused to be my anybody.

But be careful what you hope for.

I did get an anybody—at last, two hours in . . .

But it was Parker.

Confirmed: Hope is the worst.

YOU KNOW THAT saying that people look like their pets? Parker slinked over to me like a human Sphynx cat, and I swear her pupils were vertical slits. "Aw," she said, with delighted faux sympathy. "Did Daddy and Lucinda stand you up?"

"They weren't invited," I said. "And neither were you."

Parker looked at my dress and said, "Are you headed to the prom?"

That was her best insult? It was almost disappointing. "Maybe," I said.

Then she stage-whispered, "Are you totally alone over here?"

"No," I said. I clearly was.

Then she looked around theatrically. "Looks like they put you at the sucker table."

"It's mood lighting," I said.

"Why does it smell like diarrhea?" Parker asked next.

I glanced over at Lysander, now back at his station. But I said to Parker, "Must be your perfume."

At that, Parker turned her attention to the portrait and studied it a good while.

"Who's it supposed to be?" she asked at last. "The guy from *The Hobbit*?" She shifted her stance. "Wait—is it John Denver?" Then she took a step back. Then like she'd nailed it at last: "Hold up! *Danny DeVito.*"

"Don't you have anything *at all* better to do?" I asked.

"There's nothing better than this."

"Know what your being here right now tells me?"

"That I'll always win?"

I gave it a beat. "That you still don't have any friends."

"I don't need friends. I stole yours."

"Yes, you did. But you didn't get what you wanted."

"Neither did you."

She wasn't wrong.

Parker looked around the room. "This is so brutal," she said then. "Your painting sucks, your dress is awful, I'm pretty sure you're being shunned by the art world, and your nemesis is right here, gloating."

"Parker?" I said. "Get out."

"No."

"Get out before I call security."

But Parker just smiled. "You won't do that. You're already at maximum humiliation."

"Joke's on you. I don't *have* maximum humiliation."

But did the universe hear me right then and think, *Challenge accepted?* Because we were about to redefine maximum humiliation.

"Parker," I said, "just go."

"No way. I want to savor every minute."

"Why are you the worst person in the world?" I asked, like she might try to answer.

"Oh my god. You're always the victim, aren't you?"

"Well, whose fault is that?"

"You just have to blame me for everything."

"I don't blame you for everything. You actually *do* everything."

But she leaned in. "Your persecution complex is unreal."

"I don't have a persecution complex!" I said. "I am literally being persecuted."

"It's not my fault your mother died," Parker said then. "It's not my fault your dad married my mom. It's not my fault we sold our house, and I gave up my room, and we got thrown together every minute of every day. I didn't ask for that, and I certainly didn't ask for you. I was not consulted—about any of it! And yes, I did all those terrible things! I framed you and lied about you and coaxed them both into pushing you away. But your dad not loving you? That's not my fault, either. He stopped loving you well before we met. You lost him all on your own. And you want to know how you did that? Because you"—and here she seemed to rise up on her dragon haunches—"are the reason that your mother died."

I guess our voices had accidentally gotten loud.

When she stopped talking, there was not a sound in the gallery.

I could hear the A/C dripping into my bucket.

I could hear a toilet flush.

And I could hear all those people who'd been ignoring me earlier suddenly taking a new kind of interest.

I lowered my voice, in a comical shot at privacy. "What are you talking about right now?"

"I overheard them talking one night—Dad and Lucinda. He told her what happened. That your mom had a messed-up blood vessel in her brain. That he'd begged her to get surgery to fix it. But she refused. She put it off till summer. The two of you had planned a spring break trip, to go visit some artist's museum, and she wasn't going to disappoint you. Your dad told her to cancel the trip. He *begged* her. But she wouldn't listen. She went anyway. And then one week later, she collapsed."

What was she saying?

I felt a weird pain in my chest, like the shell of my heart was cracking.

"That's what he said that night," Parker went on. "That it was your fault. That try as he might, he couldn't help but blame you. I heard him say those words out loud. So you can stop thinking I ruined your relationship with your father. It's not my fault he doesn't love you. It's not my fault you lost your family. You did all that to yourself."

Was something going on with the floor? It felt like the room was shaking.

So much for staying until the end.

I looked up for an escape route, and that's when I saw my father. I knew it was him at a glance from that navy polka-dot bowtie he'd been wearing to fancy events ever since I was little. And I'd know his stance—not to mention his outline—anywhere. And there he stood, a forgotten bouquet of grocery store flowers in his non-bandaged hand— watching us, his sheer motionlessness telegraphing that he'd just witnessed the whole thing.

And that it was true.

I didn't even bother to walk closer. There were no secrets with this crowd now.

"Is she lying?" I said to my father. "Or is it true?"

My dad took a half step forward, then paused.

I stood up straighter. "Tell me she's lying," I said. Then, yelling: "*Tell me she's lying!*"

Where the hell was Joe when I needed him to flip the breaker and save me?

Oh, well.

I guess I'd have to save myself.

Twenty-Six

THAT MOMENT MUST have been so fun for Parker.

She broke me. She really did.

All that effort I'd made to be there and withstand it all and stay until the end?

Annihilated.

I charged past my still-motionless dad, through the still-gaping crowd, and pushed my way toward the exit, feeling weirdly like I was underwater and hoping desperately that there might be more air outside than in.

But nope.

Outside was just as airless.

I felt woozy. I stopped just past the entrance and pressed my palms and forehead against the brick wall, trying to pull it together.

Easier imagined than done.

Before I'd stabilized, I heard a voice. And sure, I wasn't great at voices, but it didn't take me long to figure out who it was.

"There you are! It's not over is it? I was just parking, but your dad should already be in there. Did he find you? I'm so glad I double-checked after we got Parker's email," she was saying. "We almost missed this entire thing!"

I lifted my head away from the brick wall and turned around.

I looked straight at Lucinda's scrambled face, still breathing hard. "What," I asked, "did you double-check?"

Lucinda took a step closer. "The show tonight," she said. "Parker thought it was canceled."

In that moment, my dad showed up behind Lucinda. And Parker behind him.

I took in the scene. Lucinda, very slow on the uptake about what was going down; my dad, looking crushed, upside-down bouquet still forgotten in his good hand; and Parker, standing behind them both, her face the very definition of smug.

"Parker emailed you," I said then, "to say that the art show was canceled?"

Lucinda nodded. "We almost didn't come. Good thing I—"

"The show was never canceled," I said.

"We know that now," Lucinda said. "Thank goodness I thought to call the gallery."

But she was missing my point. "Parker lied to you."

"No, no," Lucinda said. "I'm sure she—"

"She lied to you," I said, "because she wanted you to stand me up."

Lucinda's utter incomprehension at this idea made me want to light myself on fire. She shook her head. "I think she just—"

But I couldn't bear to listen to her try to explain.

I cut her off. "She lied to you because she always lies to you. She lied to you because she wants us to hate each other. She lied to you because it's fun for her! Because she delights in messing with people! Because *you let her!* You never question her. You never challenge her. You never use any kind of critical thinking. Even when her facts don't add up! Even when nothing makes any sense! She's making up a story of this family—and it's not even a good one! But you just believe it—every damn time."

"I know you're upset," Lucinda said. "But let's not slander Parker.

She really thought it was canceled. If I hadn't texted her to set her straight, she'd have missed it, too."

"You always believe her—no questions asked! And you never, ever believe me. Even when—as *always*—I'm telling you the truth."

Lucinda and my dad looked at each other, like, *Here we go again.*

Sure. Had I said this to them a thousand times? Yes.

I had yelled it to them as an angry teenager. I had sobbed it to them in a school parking lot. I had written it to them in countless careful, logical, please-believe-me letters.

Had it ever worked?

Never. Not once.

Talk about confirmation bias! They had decided decades ago who Parker and I both were—and those decisions had hardened into stone by now. But I didn't care.

Here we went again. "If Parker said I stole your grandmother's ruby hat pin out of your jewelry box, you believed her. Even though it was Parker who stole it and took it to a pawnshop downtown and used the money to buy tickets to a concert she wasn't even allowed to go to! She had to sneak out! But she told you it was me, so it was me. I got grounded for stealing, and she took my boyfriend to a concert!"

Lucinda tried to make her voice soothing, like you would with a dog. "Sweetheart, that was all so long ago—"

"Was it? Is it? It's still going on! Right now! This, right here, is Parker telling you I crashed your car—and you believing her. This is Parker telling you the stolen math exam answers in our room were mine—and you believing her. This is Parker—bullying the hell out of poor, kind-hearted Augusta Ross so viciously and so toxically that the girl *ate a whole bottle of Tylenol* and then telling the school administrators that it was me—and you, all of you, believing her!"

I could hear my voice go off the rails. Starting to sound like Janis Joplin. Louder and screechier—as if volume or desperation or hysteria could get through to them.

Though it certainly never had before.

A new crowd of people was starting to gather around us. Lucinda glanced around at them uncomfortably. She lowered her voice. "Sadie, let's all just try to move on."

Which made me want to bang my head against that brick wall.

What did any of them think I was trying to do?

"When did you text her?" I demanded of Lucinda then.

"What?"

"When did you text Parker to let her know that the show was happening after all?"

Lucinda looked over at Parker, like Parker might hint at how to answer.

"When!" I shouted.

"About ten minutes ago," Lucinda said.

I nodded. "Guess when Parker got here? An hour ago. She's been taunting me at my own art exhibition for *over an hour.* And guess what she said right as she walked in? She said, 'Guess they stood you up.'"

Lucinda stared at me, taking that in.

"She *engineered* this. She created it. She saw you trying to be nice to me, and she torpedoed us all. Again."

But Lucinda was shaking her head. "Sweetheart, I—"

"You never believe me," I said. "But it's the truth."

Just as I said it, a woman stepped out of the crowd and walked up to us all, standing there. "Hello," she said, in a chipper voice.

It was so odd that she would approach us right then, mid-fight. I mean, *Come on, lady. Read the room.*

But she clearly wasn't put off by the family squabble.

She just plowed right on ahead.

She stuck out her hand to shake Lucinda's and then did the same thing to my dad, and then she said, "Mr. and Mrs. Montgomery, you probably don't remember me . . ."

My dad and Lucinda shook their heads to confirm.

"But my name," the lady went on, "is Augusta Ross."

Okay, we may not have remembered the person—but absolutely no one in our family could *ever* have forgotten that name.

Lucinda dropped her purse at the sound of it, and Augusta politely picked it up for her.

"Augusta Ross?" Lucinda confirmed.

"It's so lucky I ran into you," Augusta went on with determined brightness. "I've been wanting to reach out."

"Why," Lucinda asked, "would you want to do that?"

"And it's so lucky that I arrived just when I did, don't you think? Here I was, coming to see the art show of my dear old friend Sadie, and what should I hear as I walk up to the building but Sadie herself, shouting my name."

Nobody knew what to say to that. Not even me.

I was still wrapping my head around it. Augusta Ross was here? *The* Augusta Ross?

"Just to bring you up to speed," Augusta said, her voice still aggressively bright. "After my suicide attempt all those years ago, my parents moved us across the country. As you can imagine, they cut off all contact with people we'd known back here. Life was hard enough for a while, and I just did my best to put it all behind me. Blah-blah-blah—I grew up, went to Stanford for art history, got offered a fantastic job with Rice University, and wound up moving back here last summer. Over my parents' objections, of course."

Safe to say, nobody in my sad little family had any idea where all this was heading.

"Anyway," Augusta went on, all chatty, "after I moved back, I started bumping into old classmates and hearing the craziest stories about that whole me-getting-bullied-to-the-brink-of-suicide thing. The craziest of all was—and I just keep feeling like this can't be true—that Sadie was the one who got blamed for the bullying. That's not right, is it?"

I glanced at Parker. The smugness had most definitely faded from her vibe.

"Well . . ." Lucinda said, glancing at my dad. "The school takes a zero-tolerance stance on bullying . . ."

"As they should," Augusta said. "But *Sadie,* as I believe she was just telling you, is not the person who bullied me."

We all just stared at Augusta in mute astonishment.

"The person who bullied me," Augusta went on, "was Parker."

"Parker!" Lucinda said, as if Augusta had just said "Taylor Swift."

"Oh, yeah," Augusta went on. "That whole year. She left notes in my locker. She picked on my clothes. She told me I was ugly, and no one would ever love me, and I should just give up. Daily. Hourly, sometimes. *Hooooo-boy*—she was vicious."

Lucinda took a stunned step back.

"Sadie was always super nice," Augusta said, nodding at me approvingly. "In fact, she's still nice."

Then Augusta walked closer to me and handed over a little bundle. "Here's your dress back," she said.

I looked down. "My dress?"

"Your ruffle dress," she said, just as I saw the polka-dot fabric.

I put it together. "You're the coffee girl? That was you?"

"You didn't recognize me that day," Augusta said. "I've changed a lot."

Hadn't we all?

"But *I* recognized *you*," she went on. "I was just coming over to say hi when Parker knocked me down. And then you were helping me up and giving me your dress. Sweet as ever. I thought about saying something then, but I was so late. I googled you later to find a way to bring your dress back, and I saw the notice about the art show."

"Did you make it to the airport?" I asked.

Augusta nodded and held up a sparkly engagement ring. "I did." Then she turned back to my dad and Lucinda. "I was going to write you a letter to set things straight. And I really just came here tonight to say hi to Sadie and support her show. But then I wound up eavesdropping . . . and I couldn't resist jumping in."

Augusta turned back to me. "Parker framed you for it, huh?"

I nodded. "They kicked me out of school."

"I'm so sorry," Augusta said. "I had no idea. After we left, my parents shielded me from every single thing related to this place."

"Understandably," I said.

"Anyway," Augusta said, turning back with false brightness to the slack-jawed pair of my father and Lucinda. "I couldn't help but overhear Sadie saying that you never believe her. But here's a little pro tip from somebody who knows both of your daughters pretty well. If you have a choice between Parker and Sadie? Pick Sadie—every time."

Twenty-Seven

WAS IT A big cathartic moment when my family realized they'd been wrong all along only to burst into tears of regret and beg me for forgiveness?

Uh, no.

We never even got to see Parker's reaction because when we looked over, she had taken off—slipped her disgraced and guilty self off into the night before ever having to own up to anything.

And then Lucinda promptly got the vapors and asked my dad to take her home. I wound up stuck outside my own art show holding up the near-to-fainting Lucinda as we waited for my dad to bring the car around.

There were no apologies. There was no Greek chorus of remorse.

But did it feel nice to have my name cleared at last?

It did. Too little and way too late—but nice, all the same.

Plus, I got my favorite polka-dot wrap dress back.

And in fact, Augusta had barely left to go into the show when Mr. and Mrs. Kim showed up with the most enormous, elegant, fuchsia-colored potted orchid I'd ever seen. Mrs. Kim wanted to hand it to me, but my arms were busy holding up my evil stepmother, so she wound up setting it lovingly at my feet.

"What's wrong with Martha Stewart?" Mr. Kim asked.

"It's a long story."

"Shouldn't you be inside?" Mrs. Kim asked.

"That's an even longer story."

"You've worked hard," Mrs. Kim said.

"We are very proud of you," Mr. Kim said.

"You don't have to go in," I said to them. "Just coming by is more than enough."

But Mr. Kim shook his head. "We want you to win."

"I have no hope of winning," I said.

"We'll see about that," Mr. Kim said, and they went in anyway.

My father showed up with the car then, and I thought that would be it: car doors slamming, red taillights in the sudden distance, me left standing on the sidewalk alone. But to my dad's credit, after he helped Lucinda get settled in the passenger seat, he turned back to me and lingered for a minute—offering a little moment of closure.

"Is it true? About you blaming me?" I asked. "Or was Parker lying?"

My dad looked down at the sidewalk as he said, "I don't think she was lying."

"You don't *think* she was?"

"I did say all that stuff once," he said. "To Lucinda. Late at night. I was horrified to hear the words coming out of my mouth. I think I hoped that saying them might get rid of them. But I guess it just gave them a different life."

"I guess it did," I said.

"I remember worrying afterward that you might have overheard us," my dad said. "So I went to check your room. But you were fast asleep. I didn't think to check on Parker."

"Why didn't you tell me about Mom?"

"I didn't want you to blame yourself."

"But you blamed me."

"That was my problem. I knew it was wrong. I knew it wasn't fair. That's why I married Lucinda so fast. I knew I was letting you down. I hated how quiet the house was. I wanted, honestly, as strange as it must sound . . . to find you another mother. I thought, *Let's hurry up and heal and get back on our feet.*"

"You can't replace mothers like appliances."

"I wasn't thinking too clearly."

"And now you're stuck with Lucinda."

"I actually like Lucinda."

"I kind of do, too. Occasionally."

Then I forced myself to ask: "Do you *still* blame me?"

My dad rested his hands on my shoulders. "Sweetheart . . . of course not."

His voice sounded dismayed that I could even ask. But how could I *not* ask? "You did once."

"I did once," he confirmed, "yes—but I was . . ."—he searched for words to describe it and finally settled on—"crazed with grief."

I looked down.

"I couldn't even see straight," he said. "I blamed everyone. You, yes. But your mom, too, for being so damned stubborn. And the doctor, for explaining her situation so casually that she could think putting the surgery off was even an option. I even blamed the Norman Rockwell museum. I had fantasies of driving to Massachusetts and burning the place down. I blamed her friends, her travel agent, and most of all— more than all of the rest of you put together—I blamed myself. How had I not insisted? How had I let her just ignore it? Knowing what I knew? Doing what I do for a living? I could have stopped her. She could still be here right now. Our lives could have been so different. Everything could so easily have been okay."

I nodded. "She wasn't really one to be bossed around, though."

My dad laughed a little.

I went on. "You make it sound easy when you say you should have stopped her. But how would you have done that?"

He shook his head. "Stolen her keys? Tied her to the newel post? Kidnapped her for the surgery?"

"She wouldn't have taken too kindly to any of that," I said.

"And then we lost her," he said, his voice going gravelly. "And I didn't know how to go on." He took my hand. "This isn't an excuse," he said then, "but it's true. I couldn't look at you without seeing her, too—getting flashes of the two of you dancing to oldies, or spraying me with the hose while you washed the car, or disco skating. I don't know how to describe it, but my chest would seize up so bad I thought I might suffocate. It hurt so much, it scared me—and I was afraid to feel that pain. So I turned away."

"I remember that," I said. "You averting your eyes whenever you had to talk to me."

My father nodded. "I was ashamed."

Then I added, "You still do it. To this day."

We'd been talking like this was all the distant past. But so much of it was still going on.

"I want to apologize to you," my dad said then.

"For what?"

"For lots of things. But right now—for the way I disappeared after your mom died."

Ah. That.

"I wasn't . . . okay."

"Neither was I."

"I was drinking a lot. Every night in my room."

"I remember," I said. "You'd lock the door."

"And you'd sit outside in the hallway."

I nodded. "And cry."

My dad squeezed my hands, but he kept his head down. "I can still hear the sound of you crying. In my head. I can hear you calling for me, begging me to come out."

"But you never did."

My dad shook his head. "A doctor friend gave me some sleeping pills. I'd take them and pass out. It was the best I could do. It's not an excuse. I don't expect you to forgive me. I left you alone when you needed me. If I could go back in time, I would. I'd rip open that door and gather you up in my arms and say everything you needed to hear: *You're not alone. We'll be okay. I love you.*"

Then my dad pulled me into a hug, and I could feel that he was crying.

"I'm sorry, Sadie," he said. "Your mom would hate me so much for how I failed you."

My knee-jerk impulse was to say, *You didn't fail me.*

But of course he had. Not just then, but after—over and over.

So instead I said, "But you're here now. And you brought her favorite flowers."

His voice was almost a whisper. "Of course."

And then, with his bandaged hand, he broke one of the yellow marigolds out of my bouquet and tucked it behind my ear with the daisy.

Did this one moment magically make everything better?

No.

But it didn't make things worse, either.

I'll give it that.

And now whenever I see a marigold, I think of my mom, of course, as ever—but I think of my dad, too. Apologizing.

AFTER HE DROVE away with Lucinda, I picked up my orchid from Mrs. Kim and then eyed the gallery entrance.

There were still forty-five minutes left.

A courageous person would return and stay till the end. But I wasn't sure how courageous I was. It was one thing to not leave my post—it was another thing to be out and then force myself back in.

I might be a few guts short of the guts I needed to do that.

But I'd barely had time to consider that before, in rapid succession, I got that primal feeling of someone watching me, turned to see who it was, and caught a fraction of a glimpse of Parker, edging around the corner, out of sight.

She was still here.

Lingering at the scene of one of her many crimes.

I took a few steps in that direction, thinking she was running away and I might chase after her. But then I saw her shadow on the sidewalk. She hadn't run away. She was just hiding.

Hiding.

I would've expected her to be out here, gloating. Cackling. Savoring the misery she'd wrought.

Hiding made me wonder. Was she ashamed of herself? Could she even feel shame? Did she feel guilty? Remorseful? Even—and I shook my head, even as I thought it—*sorry*?

I'd overheard a few things about Parker's life, too, during the years when we all lived in one house together. I once heard Lucinda on the phone telling a friend the whole story about how Parker's dad walked out very dramatically one night—with his mistress waiting in the car. Parker had tried to hold on to his leg to keep him from going, but he shook her off the way you might shake off a terrier—and he had kicked so hard, Parker slammed her head against the metal doorstop and had to go to the ER.

In my more generous moments, I'd sometimes wonder if her father's leaving like that haunted her. If she was still reckoning with that moment somehow. If she'd rather do bad things and make herself into a bad person than have to face the idea that she might've been unlovable just as she was.

Or maybe she was just a psychopath.

Or even a sociopath.

And yes—I'd done enough armchair research on Parker over the years to know the difference between the two. I'd once even printed out a flowchart. I guess I'd known her too long and too well to hold out hope that she might change.

That said, this moment felt like an opportunity. All our normal stories about ourselves and our family had kind of gone through a paper shredder tonight. Right now, with everything in shambles, it felt like I could say something true. And whether or not she would hear me or understand me or use it against me, I decided right then to go ahead and say it.

For my sake, if not for hers.

"Parker," I said, watching her shadow to see if she'd run off at the sound. "I know you're there."

The shadow didn't move.

I went on, "I don't know what drives you to go after me like you do. I once read that people who hurt others think there are only two choices in the world—to hurt or to be hurt. And so they hurt others so they can feel safe. Like, if they're the bully, they can't be bullied. If they're the victimizer, they can't be the victim. As if anything in life could ever be that simple. But maybe that's what it is for you. Maybe it's faulty logic. Maybe it's something that you'll rethink in the future and regret. Or maybe there's—I don't know—something wrong with your brain, and this is how it'll always be. Me, always cast as the squirrel, and you always cast as the neighborhood pyromaniac who douses the squirrel with lighter fluid . . ."

I paused then, in case she might have something to say.

She didn't.

So I went on. "The irony of it is . . . I always wanted a sister."

This moment was almost over—I could feel it. And the shadow was still listening.

Then something became very clear to me: As terrible as Parker made my life, she made her own even worse. Nothing she could do to me was as soul-crushing as what she did to herself. In turning away from kindness, she'd chosen a life of torment.

Maybe I didn't have to punish her.

Maybe she was already punishing herself.

Spoiler: I would find out the next day that my portrait came in dead last in the contest. I would get a total of zero votes from the judges. But I really would come away with a whole new understanding of what it meant to win. And standing in that dark street alone, talking to Parker's shadow, I was already getting a glimmer of what that would feel like.

"I just want you to know," I said then, "that it doesn't have to be this way. We don't have to be enemies. I believe you can change, and I know I'm not vindictive. If you ever decide that you want to stop acting this way . . . I will genuinely try to forgive you."

Twenty-Eight

THAT NIGHT, ON top of it all, I left the most bananas voicemail of my entire life.

Because that apology I'd gotten from my dad? It didn't magically fix everything about my childhood—of course. We can't go back in time.

But it did leave me thinking a little differently.

Like, hearing his side of the story changed my understanding of the story.

Hearing him apologize for the way he'd left me out in the hallway all those nights? It had never once occurred to me that what happened then had been anything other than my fault.

I'd always figured that my desperate neediness all those nights had driven him away.

My fourteen-year-old interpretation had been to assume that I'd caused that moment to unfold that way. That I'd driven my father away with my neediness. And I'd emerged from that time in our lives with a wrong lesson about how the world works, thinking that if I wanted to be loved—and who doesn't?—I needed to make sure to never need anybody. Ever.

Oh, the comedy.

All this time, I'd been doubling down on the wrong thing.

I thought that the only way to be close was to stay far away.

Except for with Joe, of course. Who wouldn't take "far away" for an answer.

A montage of memories kicked off in my head. Joe coming up to the roof to tell me my lock was broken. Joe offering to be my model. Joe taking me for a Vespa ride. Joe guiding me through a panic attack and then ordering us a pizza. Joe so patient while I ran my hands all over him.

And on and on.

If there was anyone on this earth who was not put off by neediness, it was Joe. He had a superpower for seeing me at my worst—and not turning away.

No wonder I'd fallen in love with him.

He'd bypassed all my usual rules.

Of course . . . then he'd disappeared. Full ghosting—with a dash of hostility.

Why had he done that again?

I still wasn't totally clear on it.

But I thought about Dr. Nicole saying that my brain was an unstable ecosystem these days. And I thought about how desperately I'd tried to hide that from everybody who knew me for fear that it might make me seem pathetic. Or ridiculous. Or—god forbid—needy.

The more I'd liked Joe, the less I'd wanted him to know what was going on with me.

But if that mental montage had just made anything clear, it was that Joe didn't turn away when I needed him. He came closer.

Before I knew it, I was picking up my phone to call him and leave the longest voicemail in the history of voicemails.

I SAT OUTSIDE on the roof, and looked up at the stars, and decided to be honest about my life at last.

Here's the full, unedited transcript:

"Hey, Joe. This is Sadie. I'm leaving you one last message. Don't hang up! It's a nice message. You told me not to contact you anymore—and I won't after this, I swear. But I just really need to say one last thing, and it's: *Thank you*. I'm calling to thank you. Sincerely. I don't know . . . what exactly happened with us. But I do know this. The show happened tonight, and our portrait did not win. Which is no surprise. It got zero votes from the judges . . . but they didn't light it on fire, either, so that's something. I like it, personally. I think you will, too, if you ever see it."

I sighed.

"Why am I calling you? Why am I really calling you? Some crazy shenanigans went down tonight at the show, and now I'm up here on the roof thinking about what really matters in life, and who I want to be, and how I want to live. And I've decided to share the fascinating news with you . . . about me . . . that part of the reason I've been falling apart so much lately—part of the reason you keep finding me weeping in corners and hallways—is that . . ." I coughed a little, then went on: "Wow, it's so strange to say out loud . . . but the, little, uh, brain surgery I had not too long ago . . . it left me with a condition called acquired appercep-tive prosopagnosia. A lot of syllables there, huh? It basically means face blindness. It means that I can't see faces anymore. I can see other things. All other things, in fact—just not faces. Ever since that surgery. Which was six weeks ago now. The doctors really hoped it would resolve at some point, but it hasn't yet, and it might never resolve, they tell me. Or it might. I maybe should've told you about this sooner. But I . . . didn't want to, you know? I didn't want to say it out loud. I didn't want it to be true. I didn't want people to feel sorry for me—or to be broken or changed or different. I didn't want to not be okay. I thought, if I just pretended to be fine and not need anyone or anything, that would be enough. That's how I've always managed. I've been pretending to be okay pretty much since the day my mom died. But I'm not okay, Joe. That's the truth. I'm absolutely, astonishingly . . . not okay right now. And I don't even know sometimes what okay even is. But my neuropsychologist says you can either pretend to be okay or you can actually be okay, but you can't do both. So this is my first step, I think. To stop pretending. To start being honest about my life in the bravest, boldest way possible: on a voicemail that no one will ever listen to."

I paused a second. Then I went on. "I'm sorry I've been such a mess. These last weeks have been so strange and so hard . . . but I want you to know that, for me, you were the best thing about them. All the times you rescued me, all the times you looked after me. You were a genuine force for good in my life. I'm grateful. I'll always be grateful—no matter what happened or where you are or how it ended. So. Thank you. Thank you for being a friend to me when I really, really needed one. And thank you for the most phenomenal kiss in the history of all time. And I think I'm in love with you, by the way—or at least I was. Before you ghosted me. But don't worry. I'll get over it."

Wait—

Did I just say "in love with you"? Out loud?

I started trying to hit End, but my finger was so panicked it just kept uselessly slapping the phone. "Shit! Shit! Shit!" I said, still recording, as I failed to hang up.

Finally, mid-flail, I added, "Okay, then. Best wishes!"

And with that—on attempt number four thousand—I finally landed the pad of my finger on End. And we were done.

The silence that followed was brutal, as those final seconds of that message echoed around in my head: "I think I'm in love with you, by the way." Then a gasp—and "Shit! Shit! Shit!" Then, of all things: "Best wishes!"

Best wishes? *Best wishes?*

That's how I ended the most humiliating voicemail in human history? *Best frigging wishes?*

But then I had a comforting thought:

It was fine. It really was.

He'd never listen to it, anyway.

Twenty-Nine

I WENT TO bed that night feeling at peace with my choices.

But I woke up the next day feeling nice and angry.

Had I really just called the guy who ghosted me—*and thanked him*? Thanked him?

Where exactly was my self-respect?

You don't thank people who put your heart in a meat grinder. You don't thank people who abandon you. You don't thank people who stare at you cold as ice and then turn away when you beg them for help.

That was my plan? To absolve him of all responsibility and then pleasantly move on?

He had dumped me and left town for no apparent reason without even an explanation—and he'd acted like I was the problem.

Not cool.

And I thought it was a good idea to *leave him a grateful voicemail* for that?

Yes. Apparently I did.

Which made me even angrier. At both of us.

Because how was I supposed to get over it if I was consumed with rage?

Or maybe getting consumed with rage was part of getting over it . . .

Fine then. No more moping, no more weeping, no more pining for the future I'd lost hold of.

It was time to be okay. For real.

The anger was very healing—burning through me with a purifying fire.

Sue approved.

When she returned from her kidnapping elopement a few days later, we gave the Joe debacle one last, long hearty evening of processing, decided it was a lucky near miss for me, made a list of guys Witt could set me up with, and spent the rest of the night brainstorming what the hell, now, I should do with my career.

Sue voted for "textile designer" because she thought I had a way with color. But we also considered interior designer, knitting-store owner, and boutique hotelier in the Swiss Alps.

The other big news was that Sue's parents were throwing her an elopement party.

"They're not mad that you got married without them?"

"Nope," Sue said, like that question had been bananas. "They love him. My mom knitted him a sweater with a heart on it."

Apparently, Sue's mom thought the kidnapping elopement was very romantic. And she thought Witt was a sweet boy and a good provider. And she was a huge fan of Canada.

Turned out, Mrs. Kim and Sue had been planning a little welcome-home wedding celebration during Sue's entire cross-Canada train ride—texting pictures of flower arrangements and table settings back and forth—and her mom already had everything worked out for the Friday night after the newlyweds returned.

"Wow," I said. "Between me and your mom, you barely had time to enjoy your kidnapping."

"I managed," Sue said.

"Witt's just lucky to get any time with you at all," I said.

Sue agreed.

"By the way," she said. "My mom wants to know if we can borrow your rooftop."

"It's not my rooftop," I said. "It's her rooftop."

"So it's okay?"

"Of course it's okay."

"Good," Sue said. "Because it's all already arranged."

ON THE FRIDAY of the Kims' party, three astonishing things happened all at once.

One: I got a letter from the North American Portrait Society letting me know that even though my portrait had not won the competition on the night of the show, it had drawn the highest bid of the night in the auction—raising over a thousand dollars for their scholarship program.

The email listed the winning bidder as one Mr. Young Kim.

Who just happened to be out on my rooftop as I was reading the email, helping his wife arrange banquet tables for the party.

I walked out to confront him, Peanut trailing after me.

"Mr. Kim," I called out, my voice full of both scolding and affection. "What were you thinking, bidding on my portrait?"

He and Mrs. Kim were unfolding a tablecloth together, and it fluttered in the breeze before they smoothed it down and turned to me.

They made their faces very innocent. "We like it," Mr. Kim said.

Apparently, Mr. and Mrs. Kim had each taken an auction paddle as they walked in for a premeditated plan of bidding each other up all night. But then another lady came in and started bidding them up. And then another. "It got bloodthirsty," Mr. Kim said. "But we won in the end."

(Later, in a fit of curiosity, I called the gallery to ask for the names of the other bidders. The receptionist looked it up disinterestedly and reported back: "Looks like it was one patron by the name of Thomas-

Ramparsad, and another by the name of Ross." Ultimately, it sold for twice as much as any other portrait in the room.)

"What were you thinking?" I demanded.

Mr. Kim shrugged. "We love it. We're going to hang it in the lobby."

"The lobby?" I asked. "Of this building?"

Mr. Kim nodded. "Mrs. Kim says it looks a little like Korean top star Gong Yoo."

Did it? Huh. Man, I wished I could see this painting.

Mr. Kim shrugged. "And you know how she loves Gong Yoo."

"But, Mr. Kim," I said, still struggling, my head just shaking itself. "All that money . . ."

"Don't worry about it," he said.

"I'll try really hard to get famous someday so that painting will be worth something in the end."

Mr. Kim waved me off. "It's already worth enough." Then he gave me a big triumphant smile. "Besides. It was for charity."

"I'm so sorry," I said. "But the North American Portrait Society is not really a charity."

But Mr. Kim smiled tolerantly and shook his head, like I was missing his point. "Not them," he said. Then he pointed at me. "You."

"Me?" I asked.

Then he gave me a wink. "We just really, really wanted you to win."

With that, Mr. Kim started to walk off—but then he remembered something and turned back around.

"Sue tells us that 515 is bothering you?"

I felt my shoulders tighten. That was Parker. "Yes," I said. "A lot."

"Good news," he said to that. "Her lease has been canceled."

"Canceled? Why?"

He gave a little shrug. "She violated the terms."

I couldn't resist asking. "What terms did she violate?"

Mr. Kim looked straight at Peanut. Then he smiled at me. Then he shrugged. "No pets," he said.

"No pets?" I asked. Was that a rule? I held very still in a caught-red-handed kind of way.

"It's right there in the contract," Mr. Kim said, shaking his head, like, *Oh, well.* "Contraband pets are grounds for termination."

I decided to just pretend Peanut didn't exist and to nod conversationally, like, *Interesting.*

Then Mr. Kim said, "Good thing I've never seen any other pets in this building. Have you?"

Mr. and Mr. Kim had a Havanese named Cosmo. "Never," I said.

"That's right," Mr. Kim said, nodding. "And let's keep it that way."

THE SECOND CRAZY thing that happened was that a mysterious package arrived for me. It was a large cylindrical tube with a letter inside that fell out when I opened one end.

I knew the handwriting in half a second.

It was from my dad, on his hospital's stationery:

Dear Sadie,

I brought this with me on the night of your show to give to you— but in all the hubbub, I forgot. I know you'll know what it is the minute you see it, but if you have any questions or just want to talk, I'm here.

I feel like our visit the other night was a good one, and I hope you do, too.

Proud of you, sweetheart.

Love,
Dad

Well, that was intriguing.

It took me a minute to pull the contents—a rolled-up canvas—out of the tube. But once I spread it out on a table, I saw he was right.

This canvas needed no introduction.

It was the portrait my mother had been painting—of me—when she died. The portrait she'd been planning to submit to her own art show.

I'd never seen it before.

I held my breath at the sight.

It was me. At fourteen. Looking straight ahead, leaning forward over a picnic table, chin resting on my hands. The whole portrait seemed to be lit from within. The dappled sunlight. The shine of the eyes. The glow of the skin. I had been so awkward at fourteen—and my mom didn't shy away from that, or paint my braces away or try to make me something different. She just painted me exactly as I was. But glowing. As I really looked—but bathed in sunlight and warmth and a lovable mischievousness.

So lovable, this kid on the canvas.

It was like getting a glimpse of the past through her eyes.

Was this how she'd seen me? I wondered. *Just like the real me—but better?*

I looked at my fourteen-year-old face, so clear-eyed and bright. I remembered sitting for that portrait—how I didn't want to stay still. How we'd gone morning after morning to the park near our house. And this was the result: she'd somehow captured all the sunlight, all the spring breezes, all my exuberance and naughtiness, and all her warm and tolerant love for me right here on this one canvas.

Looking at it, I lost all track of time. There was so much life in that portrait—so much of my mom in it—that it felt for just a minute like she must be here with me. And I heard myself talk to her, as I was lost in the sight: "You shouldn't have waited. You shouldn't have put things off. What were you thinking? I didn't need a vacation. I just needed you. And I so, so, so wish I could see you again."

There were tears all over my face long before I came to.

And just as I noticed the tears, I noticed something else.

The third crazy thing.

I'd just spent some undetermined amount of time staring at a portrait of my face.

And *I could see that face.*

I could see it all. The mouth, the braces, the irises of the eyes. All the pieces were there and in the right order—all snapped together, exactly where they should be.

And then, before I could talk myself out of it, I snuck to the bathroom mirror to take a peek . . . but I closed my eyes at the last moment and then found myself standing in front of the mirror, afraid to open them.

Dr. Nicole had warned me that when—if—the faces came back, I wouldn't necessarily get them all back—or not all at once. On the spectrum of prosopagnosia, more familiar faces were easier to see. The theory was that the more visual impressions the brain had of a face, the more likely it was to be able to put the pieces together.

"It's okay," I told myself.

No future was ever certain. None of us ever knew what might happen next. I didn't need to know how many other faces I could see—or calculate where, exactly, my fusiform face gyrus would settle on the spectrum of face-blind to super-recognizer.

It was going to be what it was.

I'd just take it one grateful step at a time.

I covered my face with my hands and then opened my eyes to peek through my fingers. Slowly I pulled my hands away.

And there I was.

My face. Straight ahead in the mirror. Not as separate pieces, but as a whole. Not as unconnected eyes and lips and nostrils, but as *me*. "Hello, stranger," I said out loud.

And there I was. Me. Peering curiously at the mirror.

All put back together as if I'd never been apart.

Thirty

THE ELOPEMENT PARTY was quite a shift from the last—and only other—party I'd attended on this roof.

In the space of a single day, Mrs. Kim oversaw a total rooftop transformation. She'd brought in a band, set up a dance floor, hung a thousand bulb lights, and placed elegant dinner tables along the west side of the roof, overlooking the bayou, so we could eat dinner while watching the sunset.

When I say *elegant dinner tables,* I mean linen tablecloths, crystal stemware, hotel silver, candles in faded brass hurricanes, copious arrangements of magnolia flowers and eucalyptus . . .

Think of the most gorgeous outdoor table spread you've ever seen in a decor magazine—and then triple it.

Mrs. Kim had *style*. And Sue was her only daughter.

She took my hovel's rooftop and turned it into the most elegant place on earth.

So . . . quite different from the last party I'd been to up here. Where people were doing the worm.

Also different: I knew it was happening in advance.

I did not arrive wearing someone else's coffee-spilled clothes.

In fact, Sue had even lent me one of my favorite dresses of hers to wear. A pale blue bias cut maxi dress with layers of ruffles at the hem. Blue because that was Sue's favorite color. Ruffles because they looked like they were just longing for a reason to go up to a rooftop and give themselves to the wind.

Miracle of miracles: It fit. Like, something about the way it hugged me around the ribs and then cupped under my butt just made me feel slinky. In the very best way.

No Pajanket tonight.

It was all for Sue, of course—to celebrate the beginning of her married life with Witt. But I decided I could also quietly celebrate a new beginning for myself as well.

I mean, it had been a hell of a spring.

I'd faced some tough truths about life and myself and my family. I'd failed miserably at the only career I'd ever wanted to succeed in. I'd fallen madly in love with two people and then lost them both. I'd lost everything, in a way.

But then found other things. In other ways.

The point is, I was ready.

Ready to face the party. And the rest of my life. And all the impossible faces.

Though I wasn't sure exactly how many of them I'd be able to see.

AS THE GUESTS clanked their way up the spiral stairs and filled up the roof, I'd guess my facial-recognition rate was fifty percent. I can't say for sure, but the pattern seemed to be related to familiarity—to, maybe, the number of impressions my brain had already stored.

If I knew the person joining us on the rooftop, the features snapped right into place—fast and easy, like normal. When I saw Sue and Mrs. Kim—looking positively ethereal in their traditional hanbok dresses—I saw their lovely faces right away. I could see Witt and Mr. Kim just fine in their suits as well—their faces just sensibly resting on their heads as if they'd never been gone.

If I didn't know the person at all, though—Witt's grandmother, for example—the faces stayed disjointed. If I knew the person a little bit—an acquaintance, say . . . the face might start out unreadable but then slide into place a little later, like it resisted for a minute and then finally gave in.

It was unbelievably trippy.

But it was also progress.

I confess, I'd been hoping to put on that dress, walk out on that roof, and see every face with total ease in a blaze of triumph—just exactly like old times.

But it wasn't exactly like old times.

In some ways, it was better. Because seeing familiar faces again was a joy. And not seeing unfamiliar faces?

It was fine.

It was manageable.

The last time I'd been on this roof at a party, I was positively nauseated with fear.

But tonight? I was okay.

If I recognized a person, great. If I didn't, that was okay, too.

That was triumphant in its own quiet way.

Before the party, I'd come up with a throwdown phrase in case I started to panic, and it went like this: "Help me out here. I have a facial recognition problem. Have we met before?"

Want to know what the hardest part of that phrase was? The word *help.*"

Which, as we know, had never been my thing.

But I wasn't asking anyone for anything hard, I told myself. I wasn't asking for help with trigonometry, or climbing El Capitan, or storming the beaches of Normandy. All anyone had to do was answer one easy little question.

This, I reminded myself, like all hard things in life, was an opportunity.

A chance for me to practice asking for help.

And: *Have we met before?* You couldn't buy a better starter phrase for that. A person could fulfill that request with *one syllable.*

That's what I told myself. No big deal.

I practiced it over and over while I was getting dressed, and then I'd walked across the roof—as ready as I'd ever be—while arguing with the nervousness in my chest in a way that would make Dr. Nicole very proud. This was doable. No dry heaving out behind the mechanical room necessary.

I could just . . . breathe.

And admire Mrs. Kim's magazine-worthy tables. And feel the rays of the setting sun warming my skin. And enjoy my skirt's ruffles swishing around my calves. And sway a little bit to the music of the band.

If that's not a triumph, I don't know what is.

ON A SCIENTIFIC level, it was totally fascinating to watch the fusiform face gyrus somewhere in between functioning and not functioning— seeing it do its thing in real time. It kept prompting me to think about everything my miraculous body did all the time without ever needing help or acknowledgment.

Which made me feel grateful. Scientifically and otherwise.

There was one confounding variable, though, in my data-gathering. One totally unfamiliar face that should have—by all established patterns—been unintelligible . . . showed up on the rooftop fully intact.

I could see it loud and clear.

A guy in a dark blue suit arrived maybe half an hour in . . . and I recognized him right away—even though I'd never seen him before.

I sidled my way over to Sue and elbowed her until I had her attention. "What?" she said.

"Tell me who that is," I said, tilting my head in the blue suit guy's direction.

Sue peeked over. "Oh god, I'm sorry!" she said. "My dad invited him."

"Tell me it's not—"

"It's Joe," Sue confirmed, with a no-sense-fighting-it nod.

"No, no, no," I said. Had I *just* been boasting about how okay I was?

"My dad loves him, apparently," Sue said. "He's helped him move furniture so many times, my dad nicknamed him Helpful. Did you know that?"

"I did," I said.

"My dad invited him as a setup! For you! I cleared it all up and explained that being willing to help move furniture does not definitively make anyone a good person and that a setup was useless because he'd already dumped you and broken your heart. But by then it was too late."

He'd already dumped me and broken my heart.

Wow. He sure had.

While Joe greeted the Kims, up here in the breeze, against a brilliant pink sunset, I let myself watch him.

Seeing my mom's portrait had been bittersweet bliss. Seeing my own real face in the mirror had been a relief. Seeing Sue and the Kims and various friends from art school had been all varying levels of fun.

This was something different.

First of all, I wasn't seeing Joe *again*.

I can't even capture how mind-bending it is to see someone for the very first time—and recognize him.

I mean, I had *kissed* this guy! Twice!

But I'd never seen him before.

A memory of Joe's naked torso as he threw me down on my bed rumbled through my memory like thunder.

I shook it off. Fine, fine—I'd seen him but hadn't seen him. It was a brain glitch. Not news. We got it.

But here's what *was* shocking: how dreadfully good-looking he was.

He didn't just have a face. He had a really, really good one.

Strong, straight features. Angles and edges. A chin! An Adam's apple! Plus a nose, two eyes, and—here, a close-up memory flashed through my mind—that mouth.

Astonishing.

And dreamy. And heartbreaking.

And . . . the opposite of fun. Given that *he'd already dumped me and broken my heart.*

My awareness of his attractiveness—and the fireworks of longing it was setting off in my body—came into focus and permeated everything I saw before I'd had time to tell my fusiform face gyrus *no*. I mean, the man had a silk pocket square! And he could tie a double Windsor knot! And that blue suit! It looked so good, it made me angry. No one should ever be allowed to look that good in a suit. *Who tailored that thing?*

Agony.

Mr. Kim must have said something funny then, because Joe smiled and looked down. I stared, mesmerized, at the scruff of his neck as he leaned forward and nodded. He shook hands one more time and then turned to join the party, walking a few steps before I looked away.

But seeing a few of Joe's steps were enough.

Confirmed: Definitely Joe. With that heartbreaking gait.

No wonder I'd fallen for him so hard.

"Just ignore him," Sue said—watching me watch him—like, *You got this.* "And stay close to me."

Ignore him. Ignore him.

Sue took my hand then and walked me over to her very dashing cousin, Daniel. She gestured back and forth between us. "Daniel? Sadie. Sadie? Daniel."

Daniel was faceless, but he had great hair.

Sue went on. "Sadie is my best friend, and she has a situation tonight, so I'm putting you in charge of flirting with her for the rest of the party."

And Daniel, bless him, gave a no-problem nod and said, "You got it."

Sue was, of course, the star of the evening—so staying close to her was easier said than done. Fortunately, Daniel was happy to adopt me, and he took me all around, introducing me to his cousins and friends. So I spent the hors d'oeuvres portion of the evening nursing a glass of champagne and heartily doing that thing where you never, ever look at the only person you want to look at.

That thing where you pretend to not even be aware of the only person you're aware of.

That thing where you give an Oscar-level performance of being totally, utterly, blissfully fine because the person watching you from across the party never kissed you senseless and then broke your heart.

Did that even happen? Because you sure as hell don't remember it.

You're too fabulous to remember it. You and your ruffly dress and your flirty new rooftop companion are far, far too awesome for a thing like being dumped—and then ghosted and then treated with contempt—to even matter.

Daniel turned out to be highly accomplished at flirting—and then it didn't take that long before his face delighted me by coming into focus.

"Oh, hello," I said, with a frisson of delight when it happened. "There you are."

"Here I am," Daniel agreed gamely, with no clue what I meant.

"You are cuter than Sue said," I said.

At that, Daniel laughed and gave me a side squeeze, and that's when I looked up to see Joe watching us.

"Say something funny," I said to Daniel real quick.

"Like what?" Daniel asked.

And then I burst out laughing like that was it.

Then Daniel laughed because I was laughing.

When we settled, Daniel said, "So. That guy who's been watching you this entire time? Are you trying to make him jealous?"

Joe had been watching me this entire time? That felt like a sad little victory.

"Yes, please," I said.

"Let's go dance, then," Daniel said, nodding at the empty floor.

"I don't think it's time for that yet," I said, glancing over at Mrs. Kim, not wanting to mess up her schedule.

"Oh, it's definitely not," Daniel said. Then he gave me a nod. "Even better."

And that's how I wound up slow-dancing with Sue's cute cousin, adding another kind of triumph to the evening, until the caterers started serving dinner. I then made my way toward the tables to find my place card and discovered that Mrs. Kim did not get the Joe memo—and she had seated us right next to each other.

The place cards were in Korean and English. The English on mine read *Sadie*. And the one in front of the empty chair next to me read *Helpful*.

Mr. Kim, you adorable troublemaker.

Joe walked up next to me, read his own place card, and realized the same thing.

We turned and met eyes.

Did I say he was heartbreaking from across the roof?

Up close, he was worse.

Those lips. That jaw. Those eyes. I'd seen them all before—in pieces. And here they were, miraculously together and adding up to far more than the sum of their parts.

"Sadie," Joe said, acknowledging me with a nod.

"Joe," I acknowledged back—noting how odd it was to know that for sure.

And so here he was. The man who had charmed me relentlessly with his sweetness and his thoughtfulness and his uncanny ability to rescue me. The man who'd shown up when I was at the most lost I'd ever been in my life—and cajoled me into crushing on him in a way I hadn't crushed on anybody in years. Or ever.

And then he'd changed his mind.

Faced with an entire dinner seated next to him, I wanted to slump down into my chair.

But I didn't.

I stood *taller*, damn it.

I stood straighter.

I summoned all the dignity I could access, took my seat, turned to Witt's grandmother on my opposite side, and then made the best, most scintillating, most *relentless* octogenarian-themed chitchat of my entire life.

IT TURNS OUT, I am really good at ignoring people.

Who knew? Another unmarketable skill.

I ignored Joe through the salad course with gusto. And then through the main course with determination. And then all through dessert with a miserable kind of glee. If I had to pass him a bread basket, I didn't even rotate my torso. If he dared to ask me for the sugar, I edged it toward him with the side of my hand and then leaned back in toward Grandma Kellner and demanded, "Tell me all about your garden."

"Everything?"

"*Everything.*"

I hope Grandma Kellner enjoyed the attention.

I treated her like a movie star on Oscar night.

Was I dying inside?

One hundred percent.

Seeing Joe was like being struck by emotional lightning.

But can we also appreciate how I was *racking up* the triumphs? I wasn't weeping. Or hyperventilating. Or vomiting.

I was handling myself. Poised. Gracious. And ignoring my hemorrhaging heart like a legend.

All I had to do was make it to the end of dinner—when, with any luck, Joe would suddenly realize that even though he'd been invited, he wasn't really welcome.

With any luck, he'd be just as eager to leave as I was to see him go.

Then I could relax.

Then I could dance the night away with Daniel and his adorable friends.

Then I could let this whole weird chapter of my life go at last—and move the hell on.

Thirty-One

BUT JOE DIDN'T leave. He stayed.

He lurked around the party long after dinner and well into the dancing—watching me with such purpose as I boogied defiantly with Sue and Daniel and all their cousins that he felt like a predator stalking his prey.

I didn't care that he was here.

I didn't care that he was here, damn it.

He couldn't just *stare me down* into giving up all my joy.

I had moved on. And bounced back. And if he didn't understand what he'd lost, then I was better off on my own.

I was fine, I was fine, I was fine.

But you can dance your ass off with bold, hysterical, can't-touch-this energy for only so long.

Eventually, you have to take a breather.

As soon as I stepped off the dance floor, Joe moved in for the kill.

I didn't want to talk to him. That should have been perfectly clear. What other message could ignoring him all night possibly convey? And yet there he was, as soon as I'd separated from the herd, moving toward me—with purpose.

But I didn't have to just stand frozen there like a gazelle and let him pounce. I wasn't some prey animal. As soon as I saw him making his way toward me, I started making my way toward . . . *what?* We were on a roof. It wasn't like I could catch a city bus and disappear into the night.

But I had to try, anyway.

I headed off toward the far corner, like maybe if I could dart around behind the mechanical room and break his line of sight, he might lose me.

As I sped up, he sped up.

I'd gotten pretty good at speed-walking in these postsurgery weeks, so for a minute there, I was actually starting to lose him . . . until he broke into a run.

"Sadie!" he called, like that might slow me down.

Wrong. It sped me up.

"Sadie! Wait!" he called again as I rounded the corner.

Rounding the corner did help—for about one second.

Until, as soon as I got there, I realized it was a dead end. A dark dead end with—actually—a fabulous view of the downtown skyline.

I didn't come to this side very often.

I slowed down, defeated, and then walked to the far edge of the roof, leaning against the railing as if gazing at the view had been my urgent purpose all along.

No escape now, I thought as I heard Joe's running footsteps approaching behind me.

I took a long-overdue deep breath, felt it swirl in my lungs, and willed it to give me peace.

And then . . . Joe showed up next to me at the railing.

I felt him land before I turned.

"Hey," he said, a little breathless.

I pretended I didn't hear him. Like that glittering skyline had so enraptured me that commonplace things like human interaction didn't even register.

But he wasn't deterred. "Could I talk to you for a minute?" he asked, standing so close and looking at me so hard, I had no choice but to respond.

He wanted to *talk to me*? Hadn't this night been agonizing enough? "Do you have to?" I asked.

He frowned like he wasn't sure how to answer.

"Why are you even here?" I asked. "Sue's not your friend."

"Mr. Kim invited me."

"That was an accident."

"Okay," Joe said, not too interested in Mr. Kim. "But I'm also here because I got your voicemail."

I held still. My *best wishes* voicemail.

Joe waited for a response while I kept my eyes on the city.

"Did you listen to it?" I finally asked.

"Yep."

"All of it?" I asked.

"Yep."

Why was he bringing this up? "And?"

"And . . . I didn't realize you were going through such a hard time. I'm sorry."

Wow. So little and so late. I made my voice flat. "It's fine."

"Thank you for telling me."

"I thought for sure you'd ignore it. Like you ignored all my other voicemails."

Joe let that dig go as he edged closer to me.

So I turned toward him. He wanted to do this? Fine. We could do this. But once we were facing each other, I realized there was a lot more to that verb than I'd ever noticed before.

"So . . ." he said. "Can you not see me right now?"

"I can *see* you," I said, maybe a tad more irritated than I needed to be. "You're standing right there."

"My face, I mean, though."

I sighed. "I can actually see your face tonight. For the first time ever."

Joe frowned. "For the first time ever?"

I thought maybe he was having a hard time with the idea that I'd been looking straight at him all these weeks—had touched him, talked with him, even kissed him—and had never seen his face. It was a tricky thing to comprehend, to be fair. I was just about to launch into a whole neurological explanation of how acquired face blindness worked when he jumped in.

"You never saw me before your surgery?" he asked.

I thought back. "There was that one time. In the elevator. When I overheard you talking about your one-night stand with the bulldog."

Joe shook his head. "But I've lived in this building for two years."

Okay. "But I only moved in not long before the surgery. So I was new."

"But you've been using that space on the roof as a studio for a year."

I frowned. "It's weird that you know that."

"I know that," Joe explained, "because I helped you carry up your art supplies when you first moved in."

I thought back. "You did?"

"All this time, you didn't know that was me?"

I shook my head. "*Was* that you?"

"Are you sure you weren't face-blind all along?"

I gave him a look, like, *Very funny.* But then I thought about it. "I remember the guy from that day. But he had a huge crazy beard."

"Yeah. That was me."

"Hell of a beard, bro. You could park your Vespa in that thing."

"My wife had just left me. I'd abandoned all grooming."

"Hence the baseball cap."

"Exactly."

But I was calling it: "I don't think you get to mock me for not recognizing you from that day. You were basically ninety-eight percent beard." I reminded myself to stay bitter. We were not friends.

"I'm just amazed that you didn't know who I was," he said. "That whole time."

I conceded. "I did not know you were Art Supply Guy."

"I said hi to you sometimes, even—but nothing."

"Did you?"

"I'm just thinking about how it wasn't until after you got face blindness that you started to recognize me."

"I recognized the bowling jacket," I corrected. "Not you."

"How are you doing now?" he asked. Like he really wanted to know.

How *was* I doing now? "Better, maybe?" I said. "I had swelling in my brain right near the area that recognizes faces. They kept telling me I might get the ability to see them back once the swelling went down . . . but it kept not going down. Until recently."

"And did you get the ability back?"

"Sort of?" I said. "Partly. I can see some faces, but not others."

"But you can see mine."

"Weirdly, yes. Even though I've never seen you before."

"But as we've just established, you've seen me a lot."

"Apparently so."

"I guess your brain remembers me, even if you don't."

"I guess it must."

"Well," Joe said then, like maybe he was winding it down, "I really am sorry. I would have been nicer to you if I'd known." And then, like an afterthought, he added the most wrong thing I'd ever heard anyone say. "Even after you dumped me."

Even after I—*what*? What was he saying? "I didn't dump you, dude. *You* dumped *me*."

Joe looked at me like I was nuts. "I didn't dump you."

"You fully did," I said. "You ghosted me."

"I ghosted you," Joe admitted, "but only after *you* dumped *me*."

Wait.

Hold on.

"Joe," I said. "I did not dump you. I'm madly in love with you. So, A, I would never do that. And B, I would definitely remember."

But Joe stepped closer, looking into my eyes in wonder. "You're madly in love with me?"

I looked away. "*Was,*" I corrected. "Past tense. Was."

"Why did you break up with me if you were madly in love with me?"

"I didn't break up with you!"

"You told me you liked someone else."

Someone else? Fine. Okay. Full confession time: "I did like someone else—briefly. And by 'like,' I mean I briefly decided I had a desperate, obsessive crush on my veterinarian. And okay, *whatever,* I may have spent some time googling Nordic locations for our destination wedding and fantasizing about taking his last name. But I really think it was more about trying to manufacture something to look forward to during the craziest low point of some very crazy weeks. It was never real, you know? It was just a fantasy."

But Joe was shaking his head. "Your veterinarian?"

"Yes, okay? My dashing veterinarian."

"Who?"

"*Who?* Are you, like, going to give him trouble or something? It doesn't matter—"

"*Who?*" Joe demanded.

I blinked for a second. "He saved Peanut for me, okay? He brought him back from death's door. His name is Dr.—"

And then, in unison, we both said, "Oliver Addison."

I frowned. "You know him?"

But Joe had already slapped his forehead and spun around to start pacing the roof. "Oliver Addison?" he said, almost more to himself than to me. "You dumped me for your veterinarian, *Oliver Addison?*"

My voice got quieter. "Sounds like you do know him."

I mean, obviously he did. What exactly had I done? Was this Joe's ex-bully from high school? Or his best friend from college? Or maybe his secret twin brother?

He was clearly somebody important. Joe was still pacing around.

"What's going on?" I asked.

Joe was taking deep breaths now. Then he came over to me and put his hands on my shoulder. "You broke up with Oliver Addison . . ."

I nodded.

"At his vet clinic . . . during a workday . . . out in the side yard . . ."

I nodded again. How did he know this? Were they friends?

"And you told him that you liked somebody else."

Another nod from me.

"Was the somebody else that you liked"—even as he was saying it, he was shaking his head—"*me*?"

I sighed. Was he really going to make me say it? I met Joe's eyes. "Yes. Obviously. Of course it was you."

Joe let go of my shoulders and dropped his head, in a gesture like, *Unbelievable.*

Then he reached behind his neck and rubbed it absentmindedly as he looked around the roof like nothing made any sense.

A gesture that looked oddly familiar.

I felt compelled to explain. "*Broke up* is too strong!" I said. "I wasn't even dating Dr. Addison! Honestly! We just had *a plan* to go on a date. We never really went. He stood me up, actually. It was that day we bumped into each other at Bean Street and I was covered in spilled coffee—remember? And he never called after that or apologized, so I couldn't technically have dumped him because we weren't even dating. But after—you know—after that epic, life-changing kiss with you . . . I just wanted to make things really clear with him—that nothing was going to happen—because I really, really liked you, and I wanted to keep all the boundaries totally clear." I could feel my chest welling up, but I kept going. "I felt like . . ." I took a breath. "I felt like, with you, I'd found something genuinely special . . . and I just wanted to protect that. You know?"

I was done with the speech before I realized how much I'd accidentally confessed.

Damn it.

Joe took a step closer. "Sadie," he said, meeting my eyes, "the person you dumped . . . was me."

Hadn't we been over this? "I'm telling you, I didn't dump you!"

"Sadie," Joe said again, waiting this time until he had my full attention. "I *am* Dr. Oliver Addison."

But that didn't make any sense.

"Um," I said, like I was awkwardly correcting him. "You're *Joe*."

"I'm not Joe," Joe said. "You've been calling me Joe for weeks, but that's not really my name. My name," he said again for posterity, "is Dr. Oliver Addison."

He was going to have to give me a minute for my brain to explode.

"I'm sorry. Wait. Are you Joe—or Dr. Addison?"

"I am both," Joe said. "Those two people are the same guy."

Now it was my turn to pace around like nothing made any sense.

"Hold on," I said. "You're saying . . . you're saying the guy who lives downstairs—the guy who fed me dinner at his place when I got locked out, and talked me through a panic attack during a party, and kissed me senseless not that long ago . . . that guy is the same person as the guy at the vet clinic who rescued Peanut?"

Joe nodded. "The same guy."

"You," I said, pointing, "are both Joe *and* Dr. Addison?"

Joe nodded again.

"How is that possible that you're only one person?"

"How is it possible that you thought I was two people?"

I frowned. Good question.

Joe gave me a minute to try to puzzle it out.

"This isn't the first time this has happened," I said, thinking of Hazels One and Two. "Apparently, the brain is an ecosystem. If one part isn't doing its job, it can throw other things off, too."

But this much? Really?

We tried to take in the impossibility of it all.

"But . . . Joe has glasses and floppy hair." I mimed with my hand the way Joe's hair flopped over his forehead, even while suddenly noticing that the Joe I was talking to was not wearing glasses and did not have floppy hair. In fact, he had . . . Dr. Addison's hair. "And Dr. Addison has"—I reached up to touch it—"this hair."

Very gently, at my touch, Joe nodded some more. "No glasses at work. Just contacts. But they make my eyes tired, so I take them out before I go home."

I was trying so hard to make it make sense. "And you slick your hair back for work, but you don't bother with it at home?"

"It doesn't stay neat very long," Joe said.

I was vacillating between struggle and acceptance. "But aren't you"—and I felt how goofy the words were, even as I said them—"a freelance snake sitter?"

"You think that I'm a snake sitter, and that's all I do?"

I tried to picture Joe in a white vet coat. "So you're a veterinarian who . . . does snake-sitting as a side hustle and also . . . rescues homeless bulldogs?"

"Broadly speaking, sure—that works."

"But you don't look like a veterinarian."

"I get that a lot. Hence the lab coat."

I shook my head, like, *What does that mean?*

"Most vets just wear scrubs. But when I started, nobody ever thought I was the vet. So I decided to cultivate a more professional look. I committed to the coat. And the contacts. And the hair."

"You sure did."

"There's a psychological component to health care. People need to feel like you're qualified before they'll do what you tell them to. People need a lot more bossing around than you'd think."

"So . . ." I said. "I only ever saw Dr. Addison in his lab coat, and I only ever saw Joe in his bowling jacket."

"I wore other jackets sometimes," Joe said.

But I shook my head. "Almost never. It's how I recognized you."

"That's why you called me Joe?" Joe asked.

"Why else would I call you Joe?"

"I thought you were kidding. I thought you were making fun of the jacket."

"I *was* making fun of the jacket. But I also thought you were a guy named Joe. Who really, really liked bowling. Enough to buy a reproduction vintage bowling jacket and have his name embroidered on it."

"Okay," Joe said, like now we'd gone too far, "that's a lot of mental leaps."

There wasn't much to say to that.

Joe and I took a minute to stare at each other in disbelief.

How was this happening?

"You never dumped me," Joe said in amazement as it sank in. Then, correcting: "I mean, you did dump me. But you dumped me . . . *for me.*"

"And you never ghosted me. Or—you *did,* but only after I had broken up with you . . . without realizing it was you."

Joe nodded. "It's like an M.C. Escher drawing."

I nodded, too. "It's like a Rubik's Cube." Then after a pause, I added, "You must have thought I was nuts to keep calling and texting you like that."

"I really, really wanted to respond," Joe said, his voice more tender now. "I had to lock my phone out on the balcony."

"I guess I should call you Oliver now," I said, looking up into his face and trying out his name for real.

"I'll be Joe for you, if you want."

And then I couldn't resist. I reached up to touch that face that had caused all this trouble, and my palm cupped his jaw. Then I ran the pads of my fingers up to touch all the pieces of it—cheekbones, nose bridge, brow—so neatly put together now, satisfying like a finished jigsaw puzzle.

He held his breath at the touch.

I could feel his stubble against my palm like sandpaper. I traced down his neck and let my hand rest on his collarbone. "So . . . I thought you were breaking my heart, but I was also breaking yours."

He closed the distance between us as he nodded. "And the guy you liked . . . the one you dumped me for. The one I was so bitterly jealous of that I couldn't sleep . . ."

"That was you."

"That was me."

"I liked you both a lot," I said, "if it's any consolation."

"It's *all* consolation," he said, his eyes running all over my face like he still couldn't take everything in.

Then his eyes came back to look into mine—and stayed there. And it didn't feel uncomfortable to look into them. It felt good. And so we gazed at each other as we waited for it all to make sense.

It was crazy. It was impossible.

And yet here we were. Standing at the rim of this realization like it was the Grand Canyon—astonished and breathless and awestruck. I could see him breathing deep, and then I realized I was, too. We'd had the story all wrong. And it might take some time to put it right.

One thing was clear: He was here right now, and so was I.

And we were both so glad to be wrong.

Was he leaning closer to me or was I leaning closer to him? Somehow our faces were just inches away from each other. My hand slid down to rest against his chest.

"Sadie," Joe said then, "I noticed you from the start. Since that day I carried all those canvases up to the rooftop for you."

"Thank you for that, by the way."

"But it really got real," Joe went on, his mouth so close to mine it was just a swoon away, "when I saw your Smokey Robinson impression in the grocery store."

That broke the trance. *Hold on.* "What?"

Joe nodded.

"That was you? You bought me that cheap wine?"

"You owe me eighteen bucks. Plus tax."

"Why didn't you tell me?"

"Why would it occur to me to tell you?"

"But the night I told you about the Good Samaritan. You must have realized I didn't remember you. But you didn't say anything."

"It was awkward at that point. Besides, you were having a moment."

"Were you"—it was all clicking into place now—"the one who pushed me out of the crosswalk?"

Joe nodded. "Of course."

All I could do was repeat. "Of course?"

"You were walking away as it happened."

"And what were you doing?"

"Me? I was checking you out."

It had been Joe? In the crosswalk that night? "You saw me freeze—and then you ran into the street to save me?"

"Well, yeah. You were about to get killed."

"But *you* could have been killed!"

"I didn't really weigh the pros and cons."

"You saved me?"

"Nick of time. We were moving so fast, we tripped on a hunk of asphalt at the curb. But I cushioned your fall."

"Is that how you hit the lamppost?" I tapped my own shoulder. "Your scar?"

Joe reached around to rub the scar on his shoulder like he'd forgotten. "Yeah. Scraped it on a bolt. Ten stitches."

"So you went to the hospital, too?"

Joe nodded. "Later that night. And then I wandered around the halls to find you and make sure you were okay."

Joe hadn't just rescued me. He'd saved my life.

For a minute, all I could do was shake my head.

Then I finally said, "You were the Good Samaritan, too." No wonder he didn't look like a stranger.

Joe nodded.

"How is it possible," I said, gazing at the sight of him in wonder, "that you were everywhere? All along?"

Joe shrugged. "You can't see when you're not looking, I guess." Then he tightened his hold on my gaze. "Anyway. You're the one who was everywhere."

It was nonsense, but I knew exactly what he meant.

At that, I grabbed hold of his tie, pulled him down close to me, and pressed my mouth to his.

The second we touched, his arms came around my rib cage and clamped tight, and mine rose up around his neck and did the same thing. I cradled the back of his head with my hands as he ran his over me—back, shoulders, neck, hair. All arms and hands and exploring and holding on.

Both of us just drunk on the bliss of being in each other's arms at last.

After a few minutes, he paused, breathless, to meet my eyes. "I really need to thank you for leaving that voicemail."

I met his right back. "I really need to thank you for saving my life."

WHEN WE FINALLY walked back to the party, it was winding down.

Daniel was still there, and when he caught sight of us, rumpled, wind-blown, clearly together, secretly holding hands . . . he gave me a nod of appreciation, like, *Mission accomplished.*

Mr. and Mrs. Kim waved good night at us from their table, as if they already understood everything that had happened and were sending me their full approval.

But Sue wanted details. She walked up to us and put her hands on her hips. "Where've you two been?"

"Oh," I said, waving absently toward our personal corner, "just over there."

She narrowed her eyes. "You look suspiciously happy."

Joe coughed. I smiled and looked down.

"What's going on there?" she asked, pointing at our clasped hands.

We broke them apart, like we'd been caught.

"What just happened?" Sue asked. "Did you two—? Are you two—? Hey, I know it's very pretty and romantic up here, but—"

"Funny story," I jumped in before she got too outraged at the notion of me just *giving in* to a man who had cruelly ghosted me. "And this is going to sound so crazy . . ."

"Nothing could be crazier than what's going through my head right now," Sue said.

"Wanna bet?" Joe said.

"Remember," I said, "how I was totally crushing on my veterinarian, but then he stood me up for our first date and then I wound up—how to put it—transferring my affections to Joe from the building?"

"Yes," Sue said, like, *Hurry up and get to the point.*

"Turns out," I said, "as impossible as it sounds . . ."

Sue put a hand on her hip, like, *Move it along.*

"They're the same guy."

Sue froze. Then she shook her head.

So I nodded mine, trying to help her get there. "The dashing vet-erinarian, whose face I couldn't see . . . and the douchey guy in the building—"

"Hey!" Joe protested.

"Whose face I also couldn't see . . ."

I let Sue catch up. "Were the same guy?" she finished for me.

Joe and I nodded at her. Then he grabbed the moment to take my hand again.

"How is that possible?" Sue asked, still shaking her head.

"My brain's been a little wonky lately," I said with a shrug.

"This isn't *wonky*," Sue said. "This is . . ." But then she didn't know what it was.

"Dr. Nicole kept warning me about stuff like this," I said. "About how the five senses really work together, and if one of them is suddenly altered, it can throw your whole perceptual game off for a while, espe-cially if you throw in our human love affair with confirmation bias."

I was gearing up to do a whole TED Talk, but Sue was pulling out her phone. "What's the vet's name?" she demanded as she started googling.

"Dr. Oliver Addison," Dr. Oliver Addison supplied.

"Are you *googling* him?" I asked.

"What's more likely?" Sue said, scrolling. "That you thought one person was two fully different people—or that this guy . . ."—she ges-tured with her phone—"is some kind of scammer trying to lure you into his sex dungeon?"

"Likely?" I started.

But then before I could refer her back to the intricate workings of the ecosystem of the brain, Sue said, "Oh," and held up her phone for us to see.

And there was Dr. Oliver Addison. In a photo on the vet clinic's *Meet the Staff* page on their website. In that white vet coat and tie, with his hair back in that Ivy League do. Looking utterly dashing, legiti-mately crush-worthy, and exactly like the guy standing next to me.

It was hitting Sue now. "You are Joe from the building?" she asked him.

Joe nodded.

"And you are also this guy?"

Joe nodded.

Sue turned to me. "You thought this *one guy* was two different people?"

I nodded. "I also did it to a barista in the coffee shop."

Sue was turning it all around in her head. "So the night the veterinarian stood you up . . ."

I looked over at Joe.

"I didn't stand you up," he said. "I was just late."

"So," I said, "when I came out of the bathroom and bumped into you, we weren't just bumping into each other? You were there for our date?"

Joe nodded.

"And that's why you never texted or called to apologize for standing me up?"

"Right," Joe said. "Because I didn't stand you up. We had an epic first date, if you remember. Panic attack and all."

I thought of Joe stroking me on the back, and then I said, "Wait a second. When you were helping me through that panic attack, were you petting me like a dog?"

No hesitation. "Yes."

"So does that mean your 'friend' with panic attacks is—"

Joe nodded. "An Irish setter. With an irrational fear of fireworks."

I put my head in my hands.

Sue was loving this. "So the whole time you were on a date together, you thought he was standing you up?"

"Yes. And I was super mad," I said. I looked at Joe. "Even that day that I dumped him—I mean *you*—and he—*you*—seemed so weirdly upset, and I was like, *I don't know why this dude who stood me up and didn't even apologize even cares.*"

"But how did you not put it together?" Sue wanted to know. "There weren't any hints along the way?"

Everything that Dr. Nicole had explained about confirmation bias came back—about how we think what we think we're going to think.

"There were tons of hints," I said. "I just didn't notice them."

Joe was looking at me like he was curious about this, too.

"There was a vet at the clinic, and there was a guy in my building. Why would they be the same? They had different clothes and different hair, and one wore glasses, while the other didn't. I saw them in different places for different reasons. I didn't have that one big thing we all rely on—the face—to put them in the category of 'same person,' and the factors I was relying on were all different. So I assumed they were different. And then once I made that assumption . . . once I had decided they were different people . . . any evidence to the contrary just . . . didn't register."

"But what about his voice?" Sue said, still struggling. "You didn't recognize that it was the same?"

"I'm bad at voices," I said.

"But also," Joe offered helpfully, "when you saw me in the clinic, I would've been using more of a professional voice."

I thought about my dad's doctor voice—how he made it a little deeper and a little louder when he talked to patients so he could assume the role of wise purveyor of knowledge. Maybe that was part of the professional medical persona—sounding like you were in charge.

"You change your voice when you're at work?" Sue asked, like maybe he was a pervy scammer after all.

"I don't change it, exactly," Joe said. "I just . . ." He paused like he'd never really tried to articulate this before. "I just lean on the parts of it that sound the most competent and in charge. So it's maybe a shade deeper—or louder. I'm sure as hell not cursing in front of patients. Or acting silly and giggling. You know. I'm being a professional."

"Plus," I added helpfully, "your clinic plays oldies on the speaker system twenty-four seven."

"That's true," Joe said. "I would've had to project a bit over Sinatra."

"Even when she dumped you at work?" Sue challenged. "Were you using a professional voice then?"

"No," Joe said, his shoulders sinking a bit at the memory. "That was definitely my real voice."

"But none of that mattered," I said. "That's the point. I had already decided who he was. You would never just be hanging out with someone and think to yourself, *Hey, maybe this person is also the same person as someone else.* That thought would never occur to you. And of course not! Because it's impossible! Unless your brain is a little haywire."

Sue nodded, like she was giving up the fight. "So when you dumped the vet for Joe . . ."

I nodded. "I was dumping him *for him.*"

"But I didn't know that," Joe said to Sue.

"Of course not," I said in support.

"So after she broke up with me, I wanted to stay as far away from her as possible—go off and lick my wounds. But she kept showing up at my place and texting me and wanting to hang out."

"That's terrible breakup etiquette," Sue agreed.

"Right?" Joe said. "The dumper is supposed to give the dumpee a little space."

I winced. "But instead, I demanded that you come as my date to my art show."

Joe looked at me with affection. "I thought you were so mean."

"It was mean!" I agreed. "By any normal standard, it was objectively super mean!"

Joe shrugged. "Except that we left normal standards behind a long time ago."

"Exactly."

Sue looked at us gazing at each other. "So, okay. You've cleared this all up. What now?"

Joe and I turned to look at each other. And I suddenly felt so awash with gratitude for this moment—for everything we'd been through. For the fact that I'd called Joe and left that voicemail. And that Mr. Kim had decided to matchmake us. And that Joe had chased me across the rooftop to try to get the story straight. We could have let it all go long before now. We could have tried less hard. We could have given up in the face of all our misunderstandings.

But we didn't.

It takes a certain kind of courage to be brave in love. A courage you can only get better at through practice.

Standing here on this rooftop, with the wind rustling my skirt and the sky floating above us, I was so grateful to Joe for giving me a reason to try.

"It's like that, is it?" Sue said, taking it all in.

"Yeah," I said, my eyes still locked on Joe's. "It's like that."

"Guess you guys don't want to stay and help clean up, then?"

"Not especially," I said. "No."

"Fine then," Sue said. "You're excused."

Epilogue

ONE YEAR AFTER that party, Mr. and Mrs. Kim kicked me out of my hovel. They were making a rooftop garden and needed it for a potting shed.

"You're kicking me out?" I said.

But Mr. Kim wasn't having it. "Go marry Helpful. You're practically married, anyway."

"Maybe I will," I said, and then I held up the engagement ring on my finger.

I wasn't spending much time at my place by then, anyway—now that I'd helped Joe refurnish his apartment.

I mean, that Viking stove of his was a significant draw.

And so, of course, was Joe himself.

Oh, and you heard that right. I'm still calling Oliver "Joe."

He just looks like a Joe to me.

And we really are getting married.

I admit: the idea of Joe's wanting *to be a family with me* has taken the pressure off Peanut to defy all laws of nature and live for another twenty years.

It's also taken the pressure off Lucinda to be anything other than her limited self. She still defends Parker. But sometimes I can see her side. What mother could possibly go against her own child?

Parker got transferred to Amsterdam for two years, anyway. So for now I have my father and Lucinda to myself, and we have dinner together from time to time.

Turns out it's easier to be less mad at people when other parts of your life are happy.

Sometimes Joe and I try to place bets on Parker's destiny. Will she always be evil, or will she grow out of it? He's a bit more optimistic than I am, but he defers to my expertise.

She might grow out of it, though. Who knows?

People can definitely change. I sure did.

And if Parker does, I'll cheer for her.

I'll also lose a hundred dollars on that bet. But happily.

IT'S SO STRANGE to me now, looking back on that upside-down time in my life, how many good things came out of it. If you'd asked me at the time, I'd have told you everything was ruined forever.

But of course the fact it was all so hard is part of what made things better.

It forced me into therapy for a while, for one.

It forced me to rethink what making art meant in my life.

It forced me to reevaluate some ideas that I'd never questioned about who we all are and what it all means. Because things were so overwhelming, I had no choice but to accept some help. And then I found out that letting people help you isn't so bad.

It's definitely the kind of thing you can get used to.

I mean, a woman who didn't believe in help somehow wound up madly in love with a compulsive helper.

Isn't it lucky when we're drawn to people who can teach us things we need to learn?

Like how to let other people make us tea, for example. Or run to the store when it's late. Or walk the dog on a rainy night.

Sometimes, now, I'll lie on Joe's sofa and say, "Could you kindly help me out and bring me those cookies? And the fuzzy blanket? And a big cup of milk? And my book?"

And he'll flare his nostrils at me like I'm annoying but adorable, and I'll be like, "Hey. This is win-win."

Peanut is also learning things from Joe. Because Joe's trying to break his Parisian crepe addiction so he can keep Peanut in top geriatric shape. And he's willing to hand-feed Peanut slivers of rib eye to do it.

It's working, too. Peanut takes three walks a day and has the downy fur of a teenager. He'll outlive us all.

It's so funny to me now that I met Joe so many times before I ever actually saw him. Sometimes I study that face of his while he's sleeping and wonder why every single encounter I ever had with it didn't set off buzzers and flashing lights and confetti showers.

How could I ever have walked right past him?

Dr. Nicole was so right, of course. We see what we're looking for.

Knowing how much I used to be missing has taught me to pay better attention. To pause from the hustle more often and just take it all in.

Of course, I'm not hustling quite as much now as I used to be because I'm no longer quite as broke.

That night of the contest? When my painting got zero votes from the judges? It really was an ugly duckling. A scout from a fine art gallery named Ellery Smith was there that night, and she loved my painting. In fact, the very thing that the judges and the other artists and the patrons all disliked about it—namely, the face—was the thing that she liked the most.

She liked the mystery of it. How hard it was to read. How full of emotion it all was. She said it left her fascinated. She could never get tired of looking at it. It raised more questions than it answered.

She got in touch a week or so later to see if she could represent me, and six months after that I was doing a show in her gallery of ten similar portraits. All of which sold for three thousand dollars a pop.

Seriously. Mr. and Mrs. Kim got a bargain.

They did hang the painting in the lobby, by the way. And when I saw it hanging there for the first time, I decided it didn't look like Gong Yoo or John Denver or Danny DeVito.

It didn't look exactly like Joe, either, to be honest.

But it *felt* like him. It felt like my experience of trying to see him. It looked like all the mysteries and emotions that surrounded the man I fell in love with—before I had any idea who he was.

Artistically, it was good.

And it made me wonder if maybe these were the kinds of paintings I should have been doing all along. If I'd been trying so hard to be exactly like my mother that I hadn't left room to explore or to play or to be a little more like me.

The experience of painting the portraits is different now, of course. Because it doesn't take that long before the faces of strangers come into view. I've got only about three impressions before I see them like everyone else does.

I draw the face first and try to capture all that mystery. And I view that early time 'as a chance to see the world like no other artist I know does.

The superpower lady? From Facebook?

Now I know exactly what she means.

Seeing the world differently helps you see things not just that other people can't—but that you yourself never could if you weren't so lucky. It lets you make your own rules. Color outside your own lines. Allow yourself another way of seeing.

Most of the time now, if I see someone I know, the face comes together pretty fast. But not always. If it's been a while since I've seen that person. Or if I'm tired or preoccupied. I've walked up to Joe in Maria's grocery store more than once and put my arms around him—only to realize I've just freaked out a total stranger.

It happens.

But I find the antidote to that is just keeping a sense of humor. And staying humble. And laughing a lot. And doubling down on smiling. We're all just muddling through, after all. We're all just doing the best we can. We're all struggling with our struggles. Nobody has the answers. And everybody, deep down, is a little bit lost.

Knowing I don't have it all figured out—facing that somehow in some way every day—forces me to be compassionate with myself. Which has made me so good at compassion that I can hand it out to other people like I'm handing out champagne at a party. When someone gives me the wrong change. Or messes up my order. Or flips me off in traffic.

I see you, humanity, I think.

We're all so limited and disappointing and so, so wrong. Much of the time. Maybe even most of the time. We're all so steeped in our own confirmation bias. We're all so busy seeing what we expect to see.

But we have our moments, too.

Moments when we see that tire blowout and stop to help. Moments when we pay for the person behind us in the drive-through. Or offer up our seat to a stranger. Or compliment someone's earrings. Or realize we were wrong. Or apologize.

Sometimes we really are the best versions of ourselves. I see that about us. And I'm determined to keep seeing that about us. Because that really might be the truest thing I'll ever know:

The more good things you look for, the more you find.

A Note About Prosopagnosia

There are two different types of face blindness, or prosopagnosia.

The type that Sadie has in this story is called acquired. It results from some sort of damage to the fusiform face gyrus—from surgery, for example, or a lesion, or a traumatic brain injury—and it results in a change in the ability to perceive faces.

The other type of prosopagnosia is developmental, and it's typically a condition people have had all their lives. It's more commonly associated with memory than with perception. People with developmental prosopagnosia can generally see faces in the moment—they just have trouble remembering them later. This type is by far the most common—up to one in fifty people have it—but many people don't realize they have it. Because there's no noticeable shift from before to after, many people who have this type assume that's just how everyone is.

If you're interested in learning more about face blindness, a good place to start is FaceBlind.org, a joint website of the Prosopagnosia Research Center of Dartmouth, Harvard, and the University of London. There you can read more about it, access online tests to measure your own ability to perceive and remember faces, and even volunteer to participate in research.

Author's Note

One year, for my birthday, I got a historical romance novel as a gift.

After years of studying creative writing and Serious Fiction in school, I had never really read romance before. But I pushed past the decidedly nonliterary cover and opened it up to the first chapter to "take a look" at it.

Three hours later, I was in the car—driving to the bookstore to get another one.

I felt like a person who'd spent her entire life eating boneless, skinless chicken breast . . . and I had just discovered chocolate cake.

That book was *delicious*. It was *blissful*. It was *life changing*.

It redefined reading for me. And fun.

It was the biggest writing epiphany of my life.

I mean, I knew I loved love stories. I'd been raised on Nora Ephron, after all. But those were *movies*. Movies were entertainment. Books, in my head at least, were work—not play.

After that first gateway romance novel, I spent the next several years reading historical romances in a blissful haze.

Did I say "reading" them? Sorry—I meant "devouring" them.

I put duct tape over the chesty man-candy on the covers—but I kept reading. In the bubble bath. At stoplights. While stirring spaghetti sauce on the stove.

There you have it: *I fell in love with romance novels.*

For a long time, if you'd asked me why that was, I'd have shrugged and said, "Because they're fun?" But now, after much overthinking it, I've figured out—at least in part—*why* they're fun.

It's because love stories really are unlike any other kind of story.

All stories have an emotional engine that drives them. Mysteries run on curiosity. Thrillers run on heart-thumping adrenaline. Horror stories run on fear.

And the fuel for those emotional engines is anticipation. We piece the clues together and predict what's going to happen, and we feel emotions—sometimes very strong ones—about what we're predicting.

Stories use different scenarios in different ways to create that anticipation, but most novels use a fair bit of what's called negatively valenced anticipation. A sense of worry. A concern that things might get worse. You know: You're reading along, picking up the breadcrumbs of foreshadowing the writer's dropped for you, and you're like, "Oh god. That kid's going to get arrested." Or, "Ugh. That man's going to have a heart attack." Or, "Bet you a thousand dollars he's cheating on his wife."

But guess what kind of anticipation romance novels use?

Positively valenced.

Romance novels, rom-coms, nontragic love stories—they all run on a blissful sense that we're moving toward something better. Percentage-wise, the majority of clues writers drop in romance novels don't give you things to dread. They give you things to look forward to.

This, right here—more than anything else—is why people love them. The banter, the kissing, the tropes, even the spice . . . that's all just extra.

It's the structure—that "predictable" structure—that does it. Anticipating that you're heading toward a happy ending lets you relax and look forward to better things ahead. And there's a name for what you're feeling when you do that.

Hope.

Sometimes I see people grasping for a better word than *predictable* to describe a romance. They'll say, "It was predictable—but in a good way."

I see what they're going for. But I'm not sure it needs pointing out that over the course of a love story . . . people fell in love. I mean: Of course they did! I don't think it's possible to write a love story where the leads getting together at the end is a surprise. And even if it were, why would you want to? The anticipation—the blissful, delicious, oxytocin-laden, yearning-infused, building sense of anticipation—is the point. It's the cocktail of emotions we all came there to feel.

I propose we stop using the hopelessly negative word *predictable* to talk about love stories and start using *anticipation*.

As in: "This love story really created a fantastic feeling of anticipation."

Structurally, thematically, psychologically—love stories create hope and then use it as fuel. Two people meet—and then, over the course of three hundred pages, they move from alone to together. From closed to open. From judgy to understanding. From cruel to compassionate. From needy to fulfilled. From ignored to seen. From misunderstood to appreciated. From lost to found. Predictably.

That's not a mistake. That's a guarantee of the genre: Things will get better. And you, the reader, get to be there for it.

It's a gift the love story gives you.

But no type of story gets more eye rolls than love stories. "They're so unrealistic," people say, as they start another zombie apocalypse movie.

What *is* that? Is it self-protection? Self-loathing? Fear of vulnerability? Is it pretending we don't care so we aren't disappointed? Is it some sad, unexamined misogyny that we as a culture really, really need to work on?

I think love stories are deeply misunderstood—in part, at least, because they don't work like other stories.

Love stories don't have happy endings because their authors didn't know any better. They have happy endings because those endings let readers access a rare and precious kind of emotional bliss that you can only get from having something that matters to look forward to.

Yes, misery is important.

But joy is just as important. The ways we take care of each other matter just as much as the ways we let each other down. Light matters just as much as darkness. Play matters as much as work, and kindness matters as much as cruelty, and hope matters as much as despair.

More so, even.

Because tragedy is a given, but joy is a choice.

Romantic fiction thrived during the pandemic, and there were lots of theories about why. People thought we were lonely. We needed escape. We wanted some laughs.

All true.

But I think, more than that, it's because *love is a form of hope*.

We all sense it deep down, I suspect—past the snark and the tough-guy exteriors. Love is healing. It's nourishing. It's unapologetically optimistic. It's the thing that leads us back to the light.

So I write stories about how love does that—about people healing from hard things, and trying to connect, and working like hell to become the best versions of themselves, despite it all. About the genuine emotional courage it takes to love other people, and about the joy that courage can offer us. I hope this story made you laugh. And swoon. I hope it kept you up way too late reading and gave you that blissed-out, longing-laden, tipsy feeling that all the best love stories create. I hope it gave you something to think about, and maybe a new perspective. But what I know for sure is that reading love stories is good for you. That believing in love is believing in hope. And doing that—choosing in this cynical world to be a person who does that—really is doing something that matters.

Acknowledgments

I always panic when it's time to write acknowledgments because I'm terrified of leaving someone out. Let me not forget to thank my friend Dale Andrews—founding member of our legendary Romantic Book Club of Two—for reading (and loving) early drafts of both *The Bodyguard* and *Hello Stranger*.

Many grateful thanks also to my friend of many years Karen Walrond, who so joyfully took the time to teach me about the culture of her home country of Trinidad—even helping me think through Dr. Nicole's wardrobe and baking me some homemade coconut bread. So much gratitude, also, to my dear friend Sue Sim, for consulting with me on the Korean American character of Sue Kim (who I wound up naming after her). The real-life Sue is one of my all-time favorite people, and she graciously met me for coffee many times—even though we kept getting distracted and talking about our kids. Many grateful thanks as well to Sue's dad, Mr. Young Kim, for letting me borrow his name.

I must also thank my friend (and vet!) Dr. Alice Anne Dodge, DVM, for letting me spend a day observing behind-the-scenes life in her clinic. My friends Vicky and Tony Estrera kindly let me borrow their last name. Artist Gayle Kabaker let me interview her about portraiture and life as a working painter, and I also found much inspiration in the work of Sargy Mann, an artist who kept painting even after entirely losing his sight. The work of face-blind artist Chuck Close was also fascinating to learn about, and I owe much to the BBC article "Prosopagnosia: The Artist in Search of Her Face."

Science is not exactly my area of expertise. Huge thanks to Lauren Billings (half of the Christina Lauren writing duo), who saw a post about my researching science-y stuff for this story and DM'ed me to say: "You know I have a Ph.D. in neurobiology, right?" Thanks also to Paula Angus and Elise Bateman for sharing resources about neurology and memory. I also learned much about the brain from neuroscientist Jill Bolte Taylor's book *My Stroke of Insight*. Deep gratitude to Dr. Erin Furr Stimming, professor of neurology at UT Health Houston McGovern Medical School, for letting me interview her—and also referring me to Dr. Mark Dannenbaum of the Department of Neurosurgery of McGovern Medical School so I could ask some very unscientific questions (like "Is it kind of like ice fishing?") about brain surgery. Both were so generous with their time and so delightful to talk to.

My most extensive research, of course, was on prosopagnosia. I knew very little about the condition when I started, and I had a lot to learn. For that, I owe much to neurologist Dr. Oliver Sacks's writings about prosopagnosia, a condition that he himself had. I also listened to every episode of Jeff Waters's podcast *FaceBlind*—some many times—and found it profoundly helpful.

I could not be more thankful to two people I reached out to cold after hearing them interviewed together on a podcast about face blindness. Dr. Joe DeGutis, assistant professor of medicine at Harvard Medical School who also co-runs the Boston Attention and Learning Lab, made time to talk with me and patiently answered many questions. The charming and delightful science writer Sadie Dingfelder, who met Joe while learning about her own prosopagnosia in his lab, also talked with me at length about face blindness. Sadie's *Washington Post* article "My Life with Face Blindness" was a massively helpful resource, and I'm so happy that when

I described my idea for the plot of this book to her and asked, "Could that happen?" she replied with so much enthusiasm, "That could totally happen!" I'm also beyond grateful to her for taking time to read an early draft of this book.

No discussion of prosopagnosia would be complete without mentioning the very helpful website FaceBlind.org, run jointly by Dartmouth, Harvard, and the University of London—where you can learn much more, and even participate in online research studies.

So many adoring thanks to the good people of St. Martin's Press—in particular, my brilliant editor, Jen Enderlin; cover designer Olga Grlic; unstoppable publicist Katie Bassel; genius marketers Brant Janeway, Erica Martirano, and Kejana Ayala; and the lovely Christina Lopez. Huge thanks also to my fantastic agent, Helen Breitwieser of Cornerstone Literary, who has stuck with me from the very start.

Many hugs to my family. My astonishingly enthusiastic and supportive husband, Gordon, and my endlessly helpful and encouraging mom, Deborah Detering, are always tied for Most Helpful Superstars when it comes to getting my books written and out there. Thanks to my fun kids, Anna and Thomas, for just being such delightful humans. Much gratitude to my two sisters, Shelley Stein and Lizzie Fletcher, for their support, and to my dad, Bill Pannill, for memorizing "The Walrus and the Carpenter" with me when I was a kid.

And last—but never least: Thank *you*.

If you're reading this, *thank you!* This is my tenth novel, and I'm willing to bet there's no writer on earth more grateful than me for every tiny butterfly-wing flap of help, word spreading, and recommendation that readers—and bookstores and other writers—do. My career has been the definition of a long, slow burn and there's nothing about it that I take for granted.

Writers can only write stories if there are people out there who want to read them—and I'm so grateful to you for being one of those people. And for helping find more of them. And for allowing me to spend my life obsessing over stories and practicing their soul-nourishing, page-turning, life-changing magic.